GW00598925

THREE NOVELLAS

George Gissing

George Gissing 1895

THREE NOVELLAS

George Gissing

EDITED AND INTRODUCED BY
PIERRE COUSTILLAS

Grayswood Press

The three novellas were first published separately
in London in 1895 and 1896.

This edition published in 2011
by Grayswood Press
Rockfield, Ash Tree Close
Grayswood, Surrey GU27 2DS
Great Britain

Introduction and notes copyright © Pierre Coustillas

ISBN 978-0-9546247-7-4

British Library cataloguing-in-publication data
A catalogue record of this book is available from the British Library

Printed in Great Britain by CPI Antony Rowe,
Chippenham, Wiltshire

Contents

List of Illustrations

Front Cover: *Hampstead Hill, Looking Down Heath Street* by John Atkinson Grimshaw, 1881, oil on card.

Frontispiece: George Gissing, 1895.

Page 15: Illustration by Walter Paget from *Illustrated London News*, 12 January 1895, p. 41.

Page 47: Illustration by Walter Paget from *Illustrated London News*, 26 January 1895, p. 106.

Acknowledgements

The publication of this book has been facilitated by a grant from the Stanhill Foundation. We would like to express our warm thanks to Mr Ilyas Khan, founder of the Stanhill Foundation, for making this publication possible.

We also express our gratitude to the Bridgeman Art Library for supply of the picture by John Atkinson Grimshaw reproduced on the front cover.

Preface

A novelty in Gissing studies as well as a partial reorganisation of the author's artistic corpus, this volume offers in a new edition the three short novels that he published with as many publishers from April 1895 to January 1896. In *Eve's Ransom*, which is set partly in Birmingham, partly in London and Paris, we follow the fortunes of a young disgruntled industrial draughtsman who tries to win the favours of an equally dissatisfied though emancipated young woman. In *Sleeping Fires* Gissing takes us to Greece, where his leading character encounters a young man who indirectly alters the course of a humdrum yet comfortable existence, while *The Paying Guest*, a satirical comedy of suburban life, provides a survey of some middle-class pretensions at the turn of the century.

The three novellas have been edited and reset, annotated where necessary, and editorially placed in both their biographical and historical contexts. There is also a selection of the most important reviews which provide interesting contemporary comments on Gissing's work.

~ *Introduction* ~

by Pierre Coustillas

THE year 1895 was a memorable one in Gissing's literary career. Generally rather slow on the uptake, professional critics, led by Henry Norman whose faith in the vitality of his works was then at its apex, no longer hesitated to look upon him as one of England's three leading novelists, bowing only to George Meredith and Thomas Hardy in point of merit. Gissing's earnings for the year reached a peak, largely because he had recently decided to embark on a second career, yielding to the attraction of fairer payment for short stories than for novels of regulation length, hitherto his main source of income. But the improvement of his material conditions did not entirely depend on choices at his command. The artistic world, after decades of stagnation, was changing quite suddenly. Since the days of Walter Scott, English novels had as a rule been published in three volumes, far less frequently two and still more rarely one, a system which had been called by people whose look extended beyond the Channel at once an abomination and an absurdity. The cause of this peculiarity was the coalition of economic interests which had come into existence with the rapid development of Mudie's Circulating Library, a network of lending libraries which all publishers were eager to please. A publisher whose first edition of a book had not been commercially profitable, as Gissing had seen with a few of his early novels, might not be tempted to publish a new edition, all the less as a new one-volume edition presupposed a costly resetting of the text. Because for complex reasons the interests of libraries, which needed some decent time to make their lending of books profitable, and those of publishers did not invariably coincide, and because public taste, with the growing prominence of new generations of readers, evolved more quickly than it had ever done, the business of bookselling went through a revolution which Charles Edward Mudie, the founder of the tentacular Circulating Library, had not foreseen in 1842, when he had begun to lend books.

Like his fellow writers Gissing watched the metamorphosis of the English novel at this crucial moment of its history, but he had no difficult decision to make. Circumstances somehow played into his hands. His last long novel, *In the Year of Jubilee*, had been very positively received at the turn of the fourth year of the last decade of the century, and he knew that the serial which C. K. Shorter had asked him in mid-January 1894 to write for the *Illustrated London News* would start to appear only in the next year. The story, to be entitled *Eve's Ransom*, had been written at Clevedon under difficult material circumstances which were to look like nothing compared with those under which the illustrations were produced by Wal Paget after Fred Barnard, who had become by then a hopeless drunkard, had failed to honour his commitment to Shorter. So Gissing's break with the three-volume style of publication quite naturally took the form of a reissue in one volume after the serial had run out. Several publishers offered to bring out the novel but Gissing was determined to remain faithful to Lawrence and Bullen, and after the thirteenth and last instalment of Eve's vagaries had appeared from 5 January to 30 March in the *Illustrated London News*, the story of her adventures was published in volume form. Immediately Shorter, a blunder-prone editor if any, sent Gissing an angry protest against Bullen's apparently precipitate procedure. But once he had received the novelist's polite but resolute reply, in which Gissing retorted that he could not see how the publisher had infringed the editor's rights, Shorter beat a prompt, if not craven, retreat. Still a flat fee of £150 for the serialization and an advance of 50 guineas on royalties from Lawrence and Bullen clearly showed to the struggling author that the days of starvation belonged to the past, that is to the days of Remington, Bentley and Chapman, who had all proved to be unreliable, irresolute or stingy.

Fresh evidence that the bulky publication style, which Kipling had brilliantly satirized in his famous poem "The Old Three-Decker," was doomed became obvious in the autumn of 1894 and by the time *Eve's Ransom* began to appear in Shorter's illustrated weekly Gissing found additional signs in his mail that the tide had turned. He who early in the decade had found it so difficult to place, even with the assistance of A. P. Watt, the supposedly best literary agent, his powerful novel *Born in Exile*, was now receiving apparently tempting offers for one-volume stories. In quick succession he was approached by six firms – Henry & Co., Smith & Elder, Methuen, Unwin, Ward & Lock and Cassell – and felt able to close with two of them, which unsurprisingly were firms of good repute with which, unlike Smith & Elder for instance, he had never had frustrating dealings. The £150 offered by Unwin for all rights was indeed a flattering transaction and, it would seem, a profitable one for both author and publisher, as Unwin kept asking for further titles in subsequent years and eventually published a Colonial edition of *By the Ionian Sea*. Thus it was that in early December 1895 *Sleeping Fires* appeared in Unwin's Autonym Library at 2 shillings in cloth and 1 shilling sixpence in paper, the second volume to materialize the author's emancipation from the dominant publication format. Gissing having sold the copyright, he never received any information about the print run or the sales of the attractive, slender volume, but he cannot have failed to read in the book that volumes in this copyright collection "may be introduced into all European countries and British Colonies."

As hinted in *George Gissing: The Definitive Bibliography* (Rivendale Press, 2005), *Sleeping Fires* must have been the source, in the spring of 1895, of some (at least tacit) disagreement between T. Fisher Unwin and one of his two readers. If one of them, W. H. Chesson, submitted to his employer a markedly positive estimate of Gissing's manuscript (actually a typescript of it done at his request and expense as he realised that his ever smaller handwriting might be pronounced troublesome by the printers), the second report, by the still largely unknown Edward Garnett, was aggressively hostile. The young man, who was not discovering Gissing's highly personal work, disliked *Sleeping Fires* and suggested that its author should be argued into producing something better. Furthermore, he declared himself convinced that the novelist could do so. It is only known that his strongly worded advice was not followed. Proof-reading and publication passed without a hitch, and Gissing most likely never heard of Garnett's rather brash objections. Evidence that his work was valued by T F U, as the publisher signed himself, reached him when contributions by him were solicited for the prestigious trilingual quarterly *Cosmopolis*, a noted Unwin publication, in 1896 and 1898. He was fully aware that being published in an international journal of this standing was an enviable honour. "A Yorkshire Lass" and "The Ring Finger" give the full measure of his talent in a too little prized artistic medium.

The commitment to Cassell, a publisher who lived as much in the past as in the present and from whom genuine innovation could hardly be expected, blossomed into the publication of *The Paying Guest*. The firm obviously followed in Unwin's footsteps, but even though its catalogue tried to give Gissing's work a colour which reviewers had rarely given it, its pocket library was short-lived. The first two weeks of July 1895 sufficed Gissing for the composition of this 25,000-word story which he had promised Max Pemberton for the end of September. Pemberton's apologetic note to his fellow writer when he had requested a contribution from him to the timidly launched Pocket Library was hardly promising and all the "puff" (which Gissing disliked) in the publisher's catalogue failed to alter the commercial prospects of the book. It was clear that Cassell did not push the sale of their wares properly. Gissing enjoyed writing this social comedy which is one of his brightest efforts at short fiction, but he did not exaggerate its artistic value – "tolerably facetious" and "a frothy trifle" are his own phrases about it. As Pemberton had managed to sell the book to Dodd, Mead for the American market, we are confident that the story did not bring in its author less than £75. Dated 1895 on the title page, but not present on the writer's shelves until 8 January, *The Paying Guest* completed Gissing's fictional triplet between his last three-volume novel *In the Year of Jubilee* and his resumption of long, thoughtful fiction of the kind associated with his name for fifteen years.

~ *I* ~

Eve's Ransom was not the first one-volume novel that Gissing offered to the reading public. In 1891 A. H. Bullen, then a new name on the publishing scene, had asked him to write such a story, known to biographers as "The Radical Candidate," retitled *Denzil Quarrier* after Bullen, making a concession to booksellers afraid of the political epithet, had asked his new author to choose a tamer title. And nobody was then aware that Gissing's prompt submission of a manuscript had been facilitated by his reshuffling of an earlier unpublished text, "All for Love," dating back to the days of *Workers in the Dawn*, which, had it caught the fancy of a low-brow publisher, would barely have covered a hundred pages. So writing fiction on a shorter scale than the length favoured by the circulating libraries was by no means a novel experience for Gissing. Nor did the choice of a subject greatly tax his inventiveness. On receiving Shorter's request for a serial story, he spontaneously contemplated turning to account his unfinished manuscript of "The Iron Gods," which he had put aside on 22 April 1893 when he was within twenty pages of the end. "Would prefer to rewrite and re-construct the whole thing," he had confided to his diary; a statement which links up satisfactorily with his earliest diary notes on *Eve's Ransom* prior to composition on 19 April 1894. "I am using as much as possible of my old Birmingham story." All that is known of it can be found in the diary and correspondence of the period concerned – the fruit of a three weeks' stay in a suburb of Birmingham.

In this novel as in others Gissing shows a strong sense of topography. *Eve's Ransom* incorporates both his knowledge and his aesthetic vision of the horrors of industrialization. His exploration of Birmingham and its environs, to use a favourite word of obsolete guide books, parallels his evocation of working-class London in the early novels. The descriptions have the ring of historic authenticity attested by notes traceable in his private papers. Most certainly only a spare use was made of the long non-narrative parts scattered in "The Iron Gods," but the socio-economic philosophy which attended them functions as an intermittent background to the story. When Hilliard, a product of his time and social milieu, crosses the Channel with his two women friends, the social climbing Eve and her semi-faithful companion Patty, they are seen in a *fin-de-siècle* Paris, visited by Gissing in 1886 when he had chosen to watch the publication of *Demos* from afar, and again two years later, when he had set foot again in the French capital as a stepping-stone towards classical lands. His mentions of Paris streets and boulevards are those of a foreigner who knows his way as a native might do. Neither here nor elsewhere in foreign parts can Gissing be faulted. His sense of orientation, his knowledge of Continental realities are those of an authority. Eve and Patty, and later Narramore and Birching, are guided in Paris by the author's experience, which is conferred upon Hilliard. When a character happens to be in London, again autobiographical knowledge transpires. One *genus* on which Gissing was an expert was that of landladies, of whom a full list from *Workers in the Dawn* to *The Private Papers of Henry Ryecroft* would baffle the basic principles of humanity and decency, let alone sound arithmetic. They are often led to play the role of go-between, honest or dishonest, and get involved in cat and mouse games. The sociological interest of *Eve's Ransom* probably transcends the novel's value as a psychological study of an apparently random sample of highly plausible characters might suggest.

With the passing of time the novel has come to assume the aspect of a period piece. Because Gissing could not forecast developments of public urban life in future decades, the movements of his characters are more difficult to reconstruct mentally by later generations than they were in his time. Consultation of old maps of public transport in London shows to what extent the network of railway and underground have been altered in a hundred years. At a time when public exhibitions in large towns were relatively new things, young women in quest of adventure could crowd to them without being pursued successfully by jealous husbands of the

Widdowson kind. Bankruptcies being events of almost daily occurrence in the 1890s, Gissing, who found them reported in his paper and drew conclusions from articles about economic affairs, introduced the phenomenon in his story, and again later in *The Whirlpool*. On the personal plane, as he himself had experienced early in his career, a man's fate could be seriously affected by a legacy from some wealthy relative. If Narramore is to be made a happy man, money at the end of the story is more likely to be the cause of it than the self-seeking Eve, whose humdrum future domestic life is all too easy to imagine. A safe guess as well as a safeguard is offered by Gissing himself in one of his letters to Edward Clodd written during the last year of his life. Commenting on Carlyle's stormy matrimonial life, which critics liked to discuss at length whenever a volume on the subject gave them an opportunity, he added: "Sufficient to know that his marriage was, like most marriages, half a blessing and half a burden."

Perhaps the most original part of the book, without any equivalent in any other text from his pen, is his picture of the Midlands, still fresh after his stay there a couple of years earlier. It had remained engraved in his memory. He knew Birmingham and its history, which he could not fail to parallel with that of Manchester, another town he recoiled from. Nowhere else in his works, except perhaps in *Demos*, did he let fly with such force at the horrors of that industrialization which made of England the "workshop of the world." Detestation made him eloquent. "This," Hilliard (his spokesman) explains to Patty Ringrose as they go round the town, "is the Acropolis of Birmingham. Here are our great buildings of which we boast to the world. They signify the triumph of Democracy – and of money. In front of you stands the Town Hall. Here, to the left, is the Midland Institute, where a great deal of lecturing goes on, and the big free library, where you can either read or go to sleep. I have done both in my time. Behind yonder you catch a glimpse of the fountain that plays to the glory of Joseph Chamberlain – did you ever hear of him? And farther back still is Mason College, where young men are taught a variety of things, including discontent with a small income. To the right there, that's the Council Hall – splendid, isn't it? We bring our little boys to look at it, and tell them if they make money enough they may some day go in and out as if it were their own house. Behind it you see the Art Gallery. We don't really care for pictures; a great big machine is our genuine delight; but it wouldn't be nice to tell everybody that." This devastating account of the guided tour harmonizes with the message conveyed by the descriptive pages of the opening chapter, which plunges the reader in *medias res*.

Just as the setting of the story strikes one as an innovation at this stage of his career, the narrative technique reveals Gissing's capacity to adapt his art to the demands of serial publication, a capacity which is still largely unrecognized. There is no record of a discussion between editor and author of the problems involved, and the only novel by Gissing that had first been printed in instalments before the mid-nineties was *A Life's Morning*, which James Payn had not originally planned to publish piecemeal in the *Cornhill Magazine*. No codification of the demands to be fulfilled by a good serial had ever been written down, but any narrator who was not an absolute tyro was familiar with the practice of serialization, of which the magazines and journals, not to speak of the Sunday newspapers, had been giving countless examples since the early decades of the century. Dickens, as Gissing had known since childhood, short of giving the recipe, had proved a major practitioner. The problems inherent in serial publication were common knowledge among novelists but they had to be dealt with in connection with narrative suspense, the reader's curiosity having constantly to be piqued and the process of unveiling to be carefully handled. The focal point of this curiosity had to be kept mobile, so as to follow logically the evolution of the major characters and to accord with the promise or promises contained in the title – a title which in the present case gave a good deal of trouble to journalists who mentioned the book in their articles and to translators despite, or perhaps because of the heroine's partly truthful confession in the ultimate chapter of the novel. In this story, whose events are almost exclusively propelled by dialogue, the narrator had to juggle constantly with his characters' degree of knowledge of the supposed intentions of their familiars and with their changing purposes. As early as his American short stories in the 1870s Gissing had been faced with such difficulties, but here in mature work like this serial story, plausibility must not be transgressed. And Gissing never swerves from what the more exacting of Gissing's readers have a right to expect.

As always George Orwell was right when he entitled his first article on Gissing "Not Enough Money." Right from chapter I when Hilliard calls the dishonest braggart Dengate a rascal to the last page or two, when Eve thanks her former lover and benefactor with words that can only be used by people with fat wallets in moments of self-conscious mellowness, money or lack of it lies at the root of the main characters' behaviour, Gissing being fully aware of its capacity to corrupt love. The two protagonists – floating, unattached elements in the indifferent world of Victorian society – Hilliard and his socially ill-defined potential companion have much in common: they are ill at ease in an unattractive world; they hate poverty, as Hilliard loudly admits on his first appearance on the ugly social scene, and as Eve eventually also acknowledges once safely at anchor in untroubled matrimonial waters. She defends herself against Hilliard's and the reader's accusation of scheming. She has no philosophy of life beyond the desirability of material comfort. In her unsophisticated eyes, a wealthy man, whether he makes an honest living of brass bedsteads or a less crassly material occupation being a side issue, is by definition a marriageable one. Narramore does not feel or think that he has bought Eve's affection and company; she denies that she has been manoeuvring though it is abundantly clear, once Hilliard the *voyeur* has tracked her successfully, that she has been. With an apparent temperamental generosity which costs her little if anything, she tells Hilliard that he has ransomed her, but Hilliard is content to smile at her appeasing assertion. One closes the novel with the impression, shared by most analysts, that she has ransomed herself. As for Hilliard, whose eyes have apparently been unsealed, he is narratively left away from the clangour of men's hammers, at peace with the "slow decay of mellow autumn," "a free man," Gissing writes ambiguously, "in his own conceit." But will he ever be genuinely free?

~ *II* ~

The idea of writing another short novel for publication in 1895 must have occurred to him in early January of the new year. T. Fisher Unwin, who was planning two series of novels which would celebrate the long-lost freedom for authors to write stories of a length suggested by artistic requirements instead of narratives that aimed at pleasing Mudie and his network of private libraries, had noticed that a new Gissing novel was being serialized by C. K. Shorter in his weekly, the *Illustrated London News*. His contact with Shorter proved fruitless since Gissing, for the publication in volume form, was determined to remain faithful to Lawrence and Bullen. But as Gissing observed in a letter of 17 January 1895 to his friend Clara Collet, the situation concerning his reputation and the sale of his books was changing suddenly and he was prepared to swim with the tide. His letter of 12 January to Unwin meant as much. He pounced on the opportunity he was given. "Your mention of the autonym series brought at once to my mind a story I have for some time been wishing to write, one which would fit well, I think, with volumes of that size. It will be rather out of my wonted track – neither "squalid" nor "depressing," – the familiar charges against me. Much of the narrative would pass at Athens, – the world of ruin making a background to figures peculiarly modern." He would set to work very soon and hoped to make something fairly good of it.

He must have had a vision of the abundant notes he had taken in his diary during his stay in Athens in November and December 1889, and which, with the exception of a glorious sunset over Athens described by Reardon in *New Grub Street*, he had never turned to any account and might conveniently use with artistic impunity. Readers of the novel who are familiar with the Greek portions of the diary and his correspondence with his relatives and friends like Eduard Bertz and W. H. Hudson can easily spot resemblances between picturesque factual details in the relation of Langley, Louis Reed and Worboys's adventures and some passages in the non-fictional writings. Langley, much like Gissing, is found on several occasions reading Aristophanes, one of many intellectual interests they have in common. It is in winter, like his creator, that we must imagine him visiting a land whose history, language and culture have meant so much in the remote past of western countries. At the hotels where Gissing and Langley put up the waiters have no English, only a smattering of French and Italian. Both men go from their hotels to the market on foot and no women are to be seen there. Louis Reed, while going round the Athens cemetery, is struck by a marble life-sized medallion of a man in whose shirt-front the studs are gilded like those he wore in actual life, a singularity that Gissing had noted in his diary. Lastly but not exhaustively, both author and character report having read in the same place a public notice painted on a board in continuous lettering without intervals between words.

That Gissing took great pleasure in writing this novel is particularly evident in the chapters set in Greece, where his classical culture shines on every page without becoming in the least obtrusive. From his table at breakfast time Langley sees the Parthenon "honey-coloured against a violet sky, and at the opposite limit of his view the peak of Lycabettus," and between and beyond Hymettus "basking in the light of spring." We are taken by both Gissing and his protagonist to picturesque places immortalized by our heritage from ancient historians and dramatists. The attitudes to the past of late nineteenth-century tourists and visitors have the double function of defining the narrator's contemporaries and of sending them back mentally to that dead world which to Worboys, the hyper-pedantic tutor, matters more than his flesh-and-blood fellow creatures. Archaeological connotations suggest themselves through the names of ancient ruins and those of modern streets. With contained passion Gissing is constantly invited to confront his vivid bookish knowledge garnered in his school and college days – first at Wakefield in Harrison's school, then in Manchester, where his professors with little if any concrete knowledge of the subject filled his intellect with facts, dates and names – with tangible realities observed *in situ*.

Inclined though he often is to cast an admiring glance upon the relics of Periclean civilization, he wisely brushes aside the temptation to seek a model for modern times in the best aspects of the ancient world in its palmy days with its noble ideal of vigour. The crux of the matter is summed up in the imaginary conversation that Langley, who denies to be a scholar even if he likes the old Greeks, has with the fragile young man whom the story reveals to be his son: "What do you suppose it amounts to, all we know of Greek life! What's the use of it to us?" What the cultured Greeks of old regarded as their gospel – vigour, sanity and joy – remains what we should aim at, but like so many desirable things, it will never be reached, or even approached. The capacities of the average man forbid humanity at large to entertain such a dream. With his inborn sagacity Langley replies to Louis, who considered human recollection of the short-lived flowering of art and thought as of interest to all but a fraction of mankind: "Lots of us, who might make it a reality, mourn through life." And not only was this Gissing's deep-seated conviction in the mid-nineties; he lent it to his alter ego in a thoughtful section of his meditations: "It is idle to talk to us of 'the Greeks.' The people we mean when so naming them were a few little communities, living under very peculiar conditions, and endowed by Nature with most exceptional characteristics. The sporadic civilization which we are too much in the habit of regarding as if it had been no less stable than brilliant, was a succession of the briefest splendours, gleaming here and there from the coasts of the Aegean to those of the western Mediterranean. Our heritage of Greek literature and art is priceless; the example of Greek life possesses for us not the slightest value. The Greeks had nothing alien to study – not even a foreign or a dead language. They read hardly at all, preferring to listen. They were a slave-holding people, much given to social amusement, and hardly knowing what we call industry. Their ignorance was vast, their wisdom a grace of the gods" (*The Private Papers of Henry Ryecroft*, Autumn XVI).

The deflationary note is almost audible. Gissing flatly refuses to

idealise the Greek citizen of yore. Ryecroft disagrees with neither Langley
nor Louis Reed: "Leave him in that old world, which is precious to the
imagination of a few, but to the business and bosoms of the modern
multitude irrelevant as Memphis or Babylon." What the author of *Sleeping
Fires* is prepared to admire unreservedly is the landscapes of Greece,
which he had learnt to know so well from afar. When the narrative waxes
descriptive, as at the beginning of chapter IV, one feels the novelist's
aesthetic delight. He imagines himself enjoying the splendid view from the
window of Langley's bedroom: "Over the straggling outskirts of Athens he
looked upon the plain, or broad valley, where Cephisus, with scant and
precious flow, draws seaward through grey-green olive gardens, down
from Acharnæ of the poet, past the bare hillock which is called Colonus,
to the blue Phaleric bay. His eye loved to follow a far-winding track, mile
after mile, away to the slope of Aigaleos, where the white road vanished in
a ravine; for this was the Sacred Way, pursued of old by the procession of
the Mysteries from Athens to Eleusis." The sublime beauty of the
landscape prompts him to imagine for himself a life which would fruitfully
contrast with the humdrum solitary one he had been leading since he had
to renounce the prospect of happiness with Agnes Forrest.

But he cannot overlook the seamy side of Greek life as it was in ancient
times with its degrading practice of slavery, its wars between city-states,
its institutional inequalities, the prevalent state of ignorance in its
population. And the beauty of the landscape he sees around him cannot
blind him to the horrors of the present, witness again a passage of chapter
IV, where the magnificence of a panorama is spoilt for Louis by the sight
of girls and women breaking stones with primitive tools in a quarry. The
present, to Gissing as to Louis, is still fraught with matter for social and
philosophical indignation which, at the purely narrative level, jars with the
relics of the golden age of Hellas showing the appeasing representation of
approaching death on some sculptures in the Central Museum. How
touching, compared with the view of death that has stemmed from
Christianity, was the pagan ethos of mortality and the inscriptions on the
simple tablets bearing "the noblest thought of man confronting death." His
admiration for the reasonable attitude to the natural, if distressing,
conclusion of human life is instinct with peaceful acceptance of the
inevitable: "No horror, no gloom, no unavailing lamentation; a tenderness
of memory clinging to the homely life of those who live no more; a clasp
of hands, the humane symbolism of drooping eyes or face averted; all
touched with that supreme yet simplest pathos of mortality resigned to

fate." Herein appears in its quietest form one of the most engaging expressions of Gissing's rationality, which was never to desert him.

The theme of the guilty secret, as critics have called it, is once more exhumed from the writer's conscience, and the narrator "plays" with it in a way which is markedly different from that of earlier and later examples. The treatment of the lapse from standard behaviour has undergone many variations since the first identifiable introduction of it in the earliest American short story, "The Sins of the Fathers," a phrase which Gissing could never banish from his mind and which indeed turns up in chapter IX of *Sleeping Fires*. In *Demos* Hubert Eldon had been removed off stage as a consequence of a shady affair with an actress; in *Born in Exile*, Godwin Peak had left Whitelaw College after his vulgar, thick-skinned uncle had aired his intention of opening dining-rooms for students just outside the college; and Denzil Quarrier, in the eponymous novel, by living with a young woman without benefit of clergy had supplied his hypocritical rival Eustace Glazzard with an argument likely to mar his political career and to jeopardize the mental balance of his fragile common-law wife. Nor was Gissing, after *Sleeping Fires*, to give up introducing into his fiction "irregular" situations which in his artist's mind were, however obliquely, condemnatory evocations of the puritanical moral climate prevailing among the middle and upper classes. His last return to the subject that the welcome liberalization of manners eventually sapped, then exploded, was in his courageous anti-imperialist novel *The Crown of Life*, published some four years after *Sleeping Fires*, which, as regards the main emotional theme, reads like a major step towards it. No such thematic *rapprochement* seems ever to have been made, doubtless because from *The Whirlpool* to *The Town Traveller* Gissing was looking in other directions, and the moral rigidities of English society had ceased to foster his artistic meditations. The important fact, however, must be stressed, that *Sleeping Fires* in some major respects anticipates *The Crown of Life*.

Above all, *Sleeping Fires*, which was published in the mid-nineties, that is at a time when the Victorian certainties were gasping their last, strikes us as a plea against asceticism, as an apology for sanity and clarity. Light in this figurative sense of the term, Gissing the classicist was culturally convinced, could come from an extinct Mediterranean civilization. Without undue optimism he offers us a resolute instance of revolt against respectability of the sternest kind, which he had so often found cluttering his way, notably in his own family after his father's death, and in the publishing world, where the invisible but ever present Mrs. Grundy remained a sneaking agency. Agnes Forrest, afterwards Lady Revill, is shown for whole chapters as a slave to the Victorian ethical code which paradoxically coexisted in English universities with the love of Greek culture, the latter being supposed to increase men's moral excellence and invigorate their nature. The Greeks, unlike the English, had no sense of sin, and were exempt from those prejudices, which in Lady Revill amount, when her thoughts are concerned with human behaviour, to a form of mental paralysis that her ward Louis Reed, though still a very young man, comes to feel as particularly detestable. In a way classical culture, among the educated, acted as a counterpoison. It is no wonder that, in the eyes of free-thinking Victorians who could ignore Christianity and all its shaky dogmas and mind-boggling traditions, ancient Greek thought offered a more advanced stage of civilization than their own spiritual systems based on secular beliefs resting on untenable creeds. In a limited sense they considered Greece as nearer to perfection than England was. The confrontation of Langley's and Lady Revill's ideal, is one between intelligence and obscurantism. But Gissing's satire of Worboys shows that unconditional admiration of what ancient worlds had achieved would lead modern generations into blind alleys.

An additional element which is part and parcel of any evaluation of Gissing's political and ethical stance in this all too neglected novel consists in the role played in the whole novel by Mrs. Tresilian, who appears simultaneously with Louis Reed, and whose influence on him counteracts the ideologically opposite influence that Lady Revill desperately attempts to exercise upon him. A casual reader might at first mistake her for an extraneous and almost superfluous presence in the narrative, but the more we know her the more we like her to the detriment of her opposite, Lady Revill, whose opinion of her is ultimately corrected by the omniscient narrator. Far from being, as her enemies depict her, a shallow social agitator who meddles in the life of Lady Revill and her ward, she in the final analysis proves herself to be a discreet and disinterested friend of the young man whom fate wrenches from the social stage. When she is made to feel *de trop*, she turns out to be a woman whose philanthropic zeal, if coloured by the do-goodism of the period, is rather estimable than otherwise. Langley soon realizes that she is an enlightened social worker – as does Lady Revill after discovering in her chastening conversation with Langley that Lord Henry Strands is an ill-behaved booby: "I have done her injustice," she piteously admits. "Probably I have been misled by public opinion." Personal contact with her brings him to revise his view of life. "Among the little group of people assembled for dinner at his friend's house," the narrator's account of Langley's "odd experience" reads, he "found at least three whose names had long been held by him in contempt or abomination. There was a political woman, from whose presence, a short time ago, he would have incontinently fled; this evening he saw her in a human light, discovered ability in her talk, and was amused by her genial comments on things of the day. A man known for his fierce oratory in connection with 'strikes,' turned out a thoroughly good fellow, vigorous without venom, and more than tinctured with sober reading. The third personage, an eccentric offshoot of a noble house, showed quite another man at close quarters than as seen through the medium of report."

Thus Mrs. Tresilian proves a conciliator and peace-bringer. By smoothing down the rough edges of Lady Revill's ascetic arrogance, she paves the way to a happy ending of the novel which, beginning somewhat exotically among the ruins of ancient Greece, ends with a defeat of rigid moral rectitude and an apology for broad-mindedness in a country that still had to shake off all the archaic bonds of Puritanism. Wisely perhaps Gissing closes his narrative with the prospect – only the prospect – of the long-delayed marriage between Edmund Langley, a man of forty-two with warm blood in his veins and an intellect which earns him the reader's esteem, and a widow of thirty-seven whose brain and heart bade fair to become petrified in sterile conventionality. We close the book with moderate hopes for what Blifil, a young man with little enough experience of life in *Tom Jones*, naively calls "connubial bliss."

~ III ~

Hardly had Gissing received Unwin's handsome fee for *Sleeping Fires* in late March 1895 when a fresh offer to contribute to one more series of one-volume novels reached him. It came from the respectable but not very active firm of Cassell through Max Pemberton, the editor of what was to be Cassell's Pocket Library. An offer of £50 for a 25,000-word story was not irresistibly tempting, as Pemberton admitted, but it was more advantageous than short stories and the invitation was immediately accepted. The manuscript would be ready for the autumn. His immediate response, besides the fact that Cassell was not in his black list of publishers to whose catalogues he could not contemplate adding his name, probably meant that he had, as in the case of *Sleeping Fires*, some clear idea of the light subject he could easily turn to account. His Memorandum Book, which contains entries covering the years 1895-1902, offers several on p. 7 of Bouwe Postmus's edition of it, which have an unquestionable rapport with the topography of some descriptive passages of *The Paying Guest*. Moscow Lodge, a double-fronted house with white glazed brick, served as a model for the Mumfords' home, where the most part of the action takes place; also the double-fronted house with a close fence of unpainted lath is recreated in the book, and we recognise the asphalt pavement of the Brighton Road as well as the curious milestone which tells the passer-by that he is twelve miles from Westminster Bridge and thirteen from Standard and Cornhill. As for the titular phrase "paying guest" the O.E.D., which duly records Gissing's use of it, it was a rather snobbish coinage, to be carefully distinguished from the less pretentious "lodger"; it served as a (largely inefficient) screen from the snobbishly objectionable practice of taking in lodgers. The authorial satire on this point is devastating, but it was often lost on reviewers, particularly in America, where the English atmosphere of the novel put off more than one reader. The *Book Buyer* pyrrhically called the story an intaglio in putty and the *Overland Monthly*, which rejoiced that the characters were not American, pronounced it "a thrashing over and over of old straw." But Gissing, for better or for worse, remained ignorant of this.

What phrase could adequately encapsulate this lively tale of English life in a decadent age of waistcoats and cummerbunds which Gissing had first noted in his diary during the hot summer of 1893 brilliantly revived in his short story "The Day of Silence"? Perhaps it could be called a novel of the hot season that gives stupidity a sore back. *The Paying Guest* can be reduced to buffoonery in villadom or seen as a chastening social experiment, as a satire of enticing advertisements in the press, as a comic picture of an attempt at self-promotion which nearly makes of systematic bickering one of the fine arts. It could also be defined as a double love story from which genuine love is conspicuously absent, as are encounters without quarrelling.

Faithful to the promise contained in the title, Gissing made Louise Derrick, a surname suggestive of coarse materialism, the central figure around whom her familiars and the young couple who answer an attractively phrased announcement gravitate from beginning to end. The subject had the advantage of novelty allied to ambivalence, if not ambiguity, that attaching to the gender of the guest concerned, companionship being sought for by so many people of both sexes at any given moment. And the gravity of the subject found expression on the first page, fraught with the dangers of the initial risky operation contemplated.

Emmeline starts with a marked advantage over Clarence. Her native reticence if not distrust clearly points to the riskiness of the social adventure that her husband repeatedly plays down rather unconvincingly. His arguments partake of wishful thinking. As soon as Louise appears on the stage she reveals her unengaging personality, and difficulties are looming ahead. Emmeline's doubts about whether they (the Mumfords) will do are immediately confirmed though not for the reasons she had suspected: Louise promptly proves to be a vulgar, ill-educated, rowdy young woman at loggerheads with her relatives except her stepfather, who never appears in person and whose role is only that of a purveyor of funds for the benefit of quarrelsome females. Nor does Cissie Higgins, Louise's half-sister, ever show her face, remaining throughout the story a second rate agent in the art of bickering. Louise, whose bad manners manifest themselves in her movements as in her words and who is rightly called a savage by distant observers, is easily beaten by her ever-panting mother, the redoubtable Mrs. Higgins, whose inordinate self-satisfaction would reduce the most vocal of braggarts to silence. "People of that class," euphemistically declares the soft-spoken Clarence, "bring infection into the home." Mother and daughter nearly ruin the domestic peace which reigned in his. Clarence, influenced by one of the silly fashions that spread in the 1890s, made the ill-advised suggestion which set the ball of absurdity rolling.

The erotic quadrille in which Louise, the well-named Thomas Cobb, Cissie Higgins and Mr. Bowling are capriciously engaged largely contributes to give the narrative a comic dimension, the flexibility of which ranges from discreet irony to rowdy verbal exchanges. Louise, off and on, shows signs of amendment, even of making amends for her rude behaviour, but as her raw and unsmiling lover optimistically surmises she will gradually become more polished and learn the nuances of civilized behaviour. Cissie and Bowling are differentiated in a less purely psychological manner, the former being an angry sufferer, the latter a tepid tactician who mistakenly imagines that the younger sister would be a more bearable partner than the young woman he has only seen in the oppressive atmosphere of Coburg Lodge.

The story bears the stamp of the new south London suburb, where people were anxious to impress their neighbours with their new-fangled comfort. (It is characteristic that the Mumfords have a larger villa than they need; surely also more servants than are justified by their modest income.) Although discreet, Gissing's description of the environment of the Mumfords' home at Sutton is openly satirical. It probably derives additional force from its occurring at the beginning of chapter II, once four of the main characters have been introduced to the reader with a wealth of highly significant and humorous details. The name of the Mumfords' house points to their pretensions. "'Runnymede' [...] stood on its own little plot of ground in one of the tree-shadowed roads which persuade the inhabitants of Sutton that they live in the country. [...] Emmeline talked much of the delightful proximity of the Downs; one would have imagined her taking long walks over the breezy uplands to Banstead or Epsom, or yet further afield. The fact was, she saw no more of the country than if she had lived at Brixton." The name of the house, probably not chosen by its present occupants but by its owner, has genteel connotations which only uneducated people in the 1890s could have missed. There it was, in historic meadows near Egham in Surrey, that the negotiations between King John and the barons eventuated in the signing and sealing of Magna Carta in 1215, and the collocation of the remote past and the unseasoned present roused a perceptible twinkling of the author's pen.

Although *The Paying Guest* is in the nature of things an artistic creation where the author's opinions never transpire openly, they can be surmised in various places. Some of his deep-felt convictions relative to the differences between the conduct of men and women in critical circumstances are noticeable from the moment Clarence Mumford cautiously declares his intention to take in a paying guest likely to ease his mind about the family's resources. The fire caused by Cobb and his rowdy beloved reveals to Clarence's dismay that the veneer of good manners so far associated with his dear Emmeline is not quarrel proof. She responds to the domestic disaster in as uncontrolled a manner as the flighty parvenus who have intruded into her life. "Insolence," the narrator comments, "was no characteristic of Mrs. Mumford. But calamity had put her beside herself; she spoke, not in her own person, but as a woman whose carpets, curtains and bric-à-brac have ignominiously perished." Conversely Cobb, an electrical engineer by occupation, whose manners had seemed only passable in a previous scene, behaves with enviable dignity to the Mumfords once the flames have been put out and the damages can be reasonably assessed. His apologies to Mumford and his excited spouse are those of a young man who behaves responsibly to the couple whose life he has seriously disturbed. And his conduct to the end of the rampageous episode is that of a civil individual. Confirmation of Gissing's distrust of lower-class women is nowhere more strongly in evidence than in the character of Mrs. Higgins in whom a redeeming feature would be sought in vain. Her speech and actions offer the happiest of hunting grounds to stock takers of unfortunate remarks, embarrassing compliments, awkward mispronunciations of surnames and gaffes of the first magnitude. However, one reproach she flings at Emmeline's face which turns out to be justified – the Mumfords had been unable to introduce Louise to people of the very best society. The fact that Emmeline had expressed to her husband serious doubts about their ability to keep the promise requested in the alluring advertisement makes her writhe with remorse. Gissing was well aware that no character in this gallery of temperamentally fragile lower-middle-class individuals could be allowed to leave the stage unscathed. Emmeline's mortification raises in the reader a fear that the light-headed attempt made by Clarence to increase his household's income will never be entirely forgiven by Emmeline, all the less because of the narrator's warning at mid-narrative, even before Clarence is discovered by his wife through some friends' indiscreet remark to have been seen in the company of Louise: "When there enters the slightest possibility of jealousy, a man can never be sure that his wife will act as a rational being." This was a guarded statement, but one to which few men of experience would have taken exception in those days of rudimentary female education.

A briskly conducted short novel, *The Paying Guest* contains no thoroughly likable character. It is a cheering image of suburban life in times of change when vulgarity in the lower middle class was in the ascendant, which certainly made some readers ill at ease (*vide* the jibe at piano playing among uneducated young women on whose hands time hung heavy), suspecting as they might that they had been the writer's target. Popular language in its vocabulary, grammar and use of emphasis is rendered so truthfully that one could imagine Gissing had the assistance of some surreptitious recordings made in lower-class districts. Suspense is apparently maintained regarding the future of the unheroic heroine until the ultimate chapter, which relates in very concise terms the last known ups and downs of Louise's fate. She has become Mrs. Thomas Cobb, but naturally remains in essentials what she used to be when she descended ominously upon the Mumfords of Runnymede. The interim period has seen a good deal of that natural constituent of human life – quarrelling, but Tom has declared for Emmeline's benefit that immediate marriage might cure his "beloved" of her innate bickering mania, and it would indeed seem that physical love making is beneficent to her mental equilibrium, or at least will be for some time. Considering the uncertainty of human affairs and Louise's temperamental instability, her confession to Emmeline is perhaps truthful enough: "After [the marriage ceremony] was over, Tom and I had just a little disagreement about something, but of course he gave way, and I don't think we shall get on together at all badly." Her stepfather, aware that peace, domestic or otherwise, is a commodity which can often be bought, continues to act like a good fairy, doubtless saying to himself "Good riddance" after Louise has vacated Coburg Lodge.

Naturally it is not suggested that the couple will be happy ever after, even in some tongue-in-cheek authorial statement, and if Gissing had been pressed to conclude his novella with a proverb, he might have borrowed one from the French: "Chassez le naturel, il revient au galop," an ornate variant of the English "As nature made you, so you remain."

THREE NOVELLAS
by George Gissing

~ Eve's Ransom ~

~ *Chapter 1* ~

ON the station platform at Dudley Port, in the dusk of a February afternoon, half-a-dozen persons waited for the train to Birmingham. A south-west wind had loaded the air with moisture, which dripped at moments, thinly and sluggishly, from a featureless sky. The lamps, just lighted, cast upon wet wood and metal a pale yellow shimmer; voices sounded with peculiar clearness; so did the rumble of a porter's barrow laden with luggage. From a foundry hard by came the muffled, rhythmic thunder of mighty blows; this and the long note of an engine-whistle wailing far off seemed to intensify the stillness of the air as gloomy day passed into gloomier night.

In clear daylight the high, uncovered platform would have offered an outlook over the surrounding country, but at this hour no horizon was discernible. Buildings near at hand, rude masses of grimy brick, stood out against a grey confused background; among them rose a turret which vomited crimson flame. This fierce, infernal glare seemed to lack the irradiating quality of earthly fires; with hard, though fluctuating outline, it leapt towards the kindred night, and diffused a blotchy darkness. In the opposite direction, over towards Dudley Town, appeared spots of lurid glow. But on the scarred and barren plain which extends to Birmingham there had settled so thick an obscurity, vapours from above blending with earthly reek, that all the beacons of fiery toil were wrapped and hidden.

Of the waiting travellers, two kept apart from the rest, pacing this way and that, but independently of each other. They were men of dissimilar appearance; the one comfortably and expensively dressed, his age about fifty, his visage bearing the stamp of commerce; the other, younger by more than twenty years, habited in a way which made it difficult to ascertain his social standing, and looking about him with eyes suggestive of anything but prudence or content. Now and then they exchanged a glance: he of the high hat and caped ulster betrayed an interest in the younger man, who, in his turn, took occasion to observe the other from a distance, with show of dubious recognition.

The trill of an electric signal, followed by a clanging bell, brought them both to a pause, and they stood only two or three yards apart. Presently a light flashed through the thickening dusk; there was roaring, grinding, creaking and a final yell of brake-tortured wheels. Making at once for the nearest third-class carriage, the man in the seedy overcoat sprang to a place, and threw himself carelessly back; a moment, and he was followed by the second passenger, who seated himself on the opposite side of the compartment. Once more they looked at each other, but without change of countenance.

Tickets were collected, for there would be no stoppage before Birmingham: then the door slammed, and the two men were alone together.

Two or three minutes after the train had started, the elder man leaned forward, moved slightly, and spoke.

"Excuse me, I think your name must be Hilliard."

"What then?" was the brusque reply.

"You don't remember me?"

"Scoundrels are common enough," returned the other, crossing his legs, "but I remember you for all that."

The insult was thrown out with a peculiarly reckless air; it astounded the hearer, who sat for an instant with staring eyes and lips apart; then the blood rushed to his cheeks.

"If I hadn't just about twice your muscle, my lad," he answered angrily, "I'd make you repent that, and be more careful with your tongue in future. Now, mind what you say! We've a quiet quarter of an hour before us, and I might alter my mind."

The young man laughed contemptuously. He was tall, but slightly built, and had delicate hands.

"So you've turned out a blackguard, have you?" pursued his companion, whose name was Dengate. "I heard something about that."

"From whom?"

"You drink, I am told. I suppose that's your condition now."

"Well, no; not just now," answered Hilliard. He spoke the language of an educated man, but with a trace of the Midland accent. Dengate's speech had less refinement.

"What do you mean by your insulting talk, then? I spoke to you civilly."

"And I answered as I thought fit."

The respectable citizen sat with his hands on his knees, and scrutinised the other's sallow features.

"You've been drinking, I can see. I had something to say to you, but I'd better leave it for another time."

Hilliard flashed a look of scorn, and said sternly—

"I am as sober as you are."

"Then just give me civil answers to civil questions."

"Questions? What right have you to question me?"

"It's for your own advantage. You called me scoundrel. What did you mean by that?"

"That's the name I give to fellows who go bankrupt to get rid of their debts."

"Is it!" said Dengate, with a superior smile. "That only shows how little you know of the world, my lad. You got it from your father, I daresay; he had a rough way of talking."

"A disagreeable habit of telling the truth."

"I know all about it. Your father wasn't a man of business, and couldn't see things from a business point of view. Now, what I just want to say to you is this: there's all the difference in the world between commercial failure and rascality. If you go down to Liverpool, and ask men of credit for their opinion about Charles Edward Dengate, you'll have a lesson that would profit you. I can see you're one of the young chaps who think a precious deal of themselves; I'm often coming across them nowadays, and I generally give them a piece of my mind."

Hilliard smiled.

"If you gave them the whole, it would be no great generosity."

"Eh? Yes, I see you've had a glass or two, and it makes you witty. But wait a bit. I was devilish near thrashing you a few minutes ago; but I shan't do it, say what you like. I don't like vulgar rows."

"No more do I," remarked Hilliard; "and I haven't fought since I was a boy. But for your own satisfaction, I can tell you it's a wise resolve not to interfere with me. The temptation to rid the world of one such man as you might prove too strong."

There was a force of meaning in these words, quietly as they were uttered, which impressed the listener.

"You'll come to a bad end, my lad."

"Hardly. It's unlikely that I shall ever be rich."

"Oh! you're one of that sort, are you? I've come across Socialistic fellows. But look here. I'm talking civilly, and I say again it's for your advantage. I had a respect for your father, and I liked your brother – I'm sorry to hear he's dead."

"Please keep your sorrow to yourself."

"All right, all right! I understand you're a draughtsman at Kenn and Bodditch's?"

"I daresay you are capable of understanding that."

Hilliard planted his elbow in the window of the carriage and propped his cheek on his hand.

"Yes; and a few other things," rejoined the well-dressed man. "How to make money, for instance. – Well, haven't you any insult ready?"

The other looked out at a row of flaring chimneys, which the train was rushing past: he kept silence.

"Go down to Liverpool," pursued Dengate, "and make inquiries about me. You'll find I have as good a reputation as any man living."

He laboured this point. It was evident that he seriously desired to establish his probity and importance in the young man's eyes. Nor did anything in his look or speech conflict with such claims. He had hard, but not disagreeable features, and gave proof of an easy temper.

"Paying one's debts," said Hilliard, "is fatal to reputation."

"You use words you don't understand. There's no such thing as a debt, except what's recognised by the laws."

"I shouldn't wonder if you think of going into Parliament. You are just the man to make laws."

"Well, who knows? What I want you to understand is, that if your father were alive at this moment, I shouldn't admit that he had claim upon me for one penny."

"It was because I understood it already that I called you a scoundrel."

"Now be careful, my lad," exclaimed Dengate, as again he winced under the epithet. "My temper may get the better of me, and I should be sorry for it. I got into this carriage with you (of course I had a first-class ticket) because I wanted to form an opinion of your character. I've been told you drink, and I see that you do, and I'm sorry for it. You'll be losing your place before long, and you'll go down. Now look here; you've called me foul names, and you've done your best to rile me. Now I'm going to make you ashamed of yourself."

Hilliard fixed the speaker with his scornful eyes; the last words had moved him to curiosity.

"I can excuse a good deal in a man with an empty pocket," pursued the other. "I've been there myself; I know how it makes you feel – how much do you earn, by the bye?"

"Mind you own business."

"All right. I suppose it's about two pounds a week. Would you like to know what *my* income is? Well, something like two pounds an hour, reckoning eight hours as the working day. There's a difference, isn't there? It comes of minding my business, you see. You'll never make anything like it; you find it easier to abuse people who work than to work yourself. Now if you go down to Liverpool, and ask how I got to my present position, you'll find it's the result of hard and honest work. Understand that: honest work."

"And forgetting to pay your debts," threw in the young man.

"It's eight years since I owed any man a penny. The people I *did* owe money to were sensible men of business – all except your father, and he never could see things in the right light. I went through the bankruptcy court, and I made arrangements that satisfied my creditors. I should have satisfied your father too, only he died."

"You paid tuppence ha'penny in the pound."

"No, it was five shillings, and my creditors – sensible men of business – were satisfied. Now look here. I owed your father four hundred and thirty-six pounds, but he didn't rank as an ordinary creditor, and if I had paid him after my bankruptcy it would have been just because I felt a respect for him – not because he had any legal claim. I *meant* to pay him – understand that."

Hilliard smiled. Just then a block signal caused the train to slacken speed. Darkness had fallen, and lights glimmered from some cottages by the line.

"You don't believe me," added Dengate.

"I don't."

The prosperous man bit his lower lip, and sat gazing at the lamp in the carriage. The train came to a standstill; there was no sound but the throbbing of the engine.

"Well, listen to me," Dengate resumed. "You're turning out badly, and any money you get you're pretty sure to make a bad use of. But" – he assumed an air of great solemnity— "all the same – now listen—"

"I'm listening."

"Just to show you the kind of a man I am, and to make you feel ashamed of yourself, I'm going to pay you the money."

For a few seconds there was unbroken stillness. The men gazed at each other, Dengate superbly triumphant, Hilliard incredulous but betraying excitement.

"I'm going to pay you four hundred and thirty-six pounds," Dengate repeated. "No less and no more. It isn't a legal debt, so I shall pay no interest. But go with me when we get to Birmingham, and you shall have my cheque for four hundred and thirty-six pounds."

The train began to move on. Hilliard had uncrossed his legs, and sat bending forward, his eyes on vacancy.

"Does that alter your opinion of me?" asked the other.

"I shan't believe it till I have cashed the cheque."

"You're one of those young fellows who think so much of themselves they've no good opinion to spare for anyone else. And what's more, I've still half a mind to give you a good thrashing before I give you the cheque. There's just about time, and I shouldn't wonder if it did you good. You want some of the conceit taken out of you, my lad."

Hilliard seemed not to hear this. Again he fixed his eyes on the other's countenance.

"Do you say you are going to pay me four hundred pounds?" he asked slowly.

"Four hundred and thirty-six. You'll go to the devil with it, but that's no business of mine."

"There's just one thing I must tell you. If this is a joke, keep out of my way after you've played it out, that's all."

"It isn't a joke. And one thing I have to tell *you*. I reserve to myself the right of thrashing you, if I feel in the humour for it."

Hilliard gave a laugh, then threw himself back into the corner, and did not speak again until the train pulled up at New Street station.

~ *Chapter 2* ~

AN hour later he was at Old Square, waiting for the tram to Aston. Huge steam-driven vehicles came and went, whirling about the open space with monitory bell-clang. Amid a press of homeward-going workfolk, Hilliard clambered to a place on the top and lit his pipe. He did not look the same man who had waited gloomily at Dudley Port; his eyes gleamed with life; answering a remark addressed to him by a neighbour on the car, he spoke jovially.

No rain was falling, but the streets shone wet and muddy under lurid lamp-lights. Just above the house-tops appeared the full moon, a reddish disk, blurred athwart floating vapour. The car drove northward, speedily passing from the region of main streets and great edifices into a squalid district of factories and workshops and crowded by-ways. At Aston Church the young man alighted, and walked rapidly for five minutes, till he reached a row of small modern houses. Socially, they represented a step or two upwards in the gradation which, at Birmingham, begins with the numbered court and culminates in the mansions of Edgbaston.

He knocked at a door, and was answered by a girl, who nodded recognition. "Mrs. Hilliard in? Just tell her I'm here."

There was a natural abruptness in his voice, but it had a kindly note, and a pleasant smile accompanied it. After a brief delay he received permission to go upstairs, where the door of a sitting-room stood open. Within was a young woman, slight, pale, and pretty, who showed something of embarrassment, though her face made him welcome.

"I expected you sooner."

"Business kept me back. Well, little girl?"

The table was spread for tea, and at one end of it, on a high chair, sat a child of four years old. Hilliard kissed her, and stroked her curly hair, and talked with playful affection. This little girl was his niece, the child of his elder brother, who had died three years ago. The poorly furnished room and her own attire proved that Mrs. Hilliard had but narrow resources in her widowhood. Nor did she appear a woman of much courage; tears had thinned her cheeks, and her delicate hands had suffered noticeably from unwonted household work.

Hilliard remarked something unusual in her behaviour this evening. She was restless, and kept regarding him askance, as if in apprehension. A letter from her, in which she merely said she wished to speak to him, had summoned him hither from Dudley. As a rule, they saw each other but once a month.

"No bad news, I hope!" he remarked aside to her, as he took his place at the table.

"Oh, no. I'll tell you afterwards."

Very soon after the meal Mrs. Hilliard took the child away and put her to bed. During her absence the visitor sat brooding, a peculiar half-smile on his face. She came back, drew a chair up to the fire, but did not sit down.

"Well, what is it?" asked her brother-in-law, much as he might have spoken to the little girl.

"I have something very serious to talk about, Maurice."

"Have you? All right; go ahead."

"I – I am so very much afraid I shall offend you."

The young man laughed.

"Not very likely. I can take a good deal from you."

She stood with her hands on the back of the chair, and as he looked at her, Hilliard saw her pale cheeks grow warm.

"It'll seem very strange to you, Maurice."

"Nothing will seem strange after an adventure I've had this afternoon. You shall hear about it presently."

"Tell me your story first."

"That's like a woman. All right, I'll tell you. I met that scoundrel Dengate, and – he's paid me the money he owed my father."

"He has *paid* it? Oh! really?"

"See, here's a cheque, and I think it likely I can turn it into cash. The blackguard has been doing well at Liverpool. I'm not quite sure that I understand the reptile, but he seems to have given me this because I abused him. I hurt his vanity, and he couldn't resist the temptation to astonish me. He thinks I shall go about proclaiming him a noble fellow. Four hundred and thirty-six pounds; there it is." He tossed the piece of paper into the air with boyish glee, and only just caught it as it was fluttering into the fire.

"Oh, be careful!" cried Mrs. Hilliard.

"I told him he was a scoundrel, and he began by threatening to thrash me. I'm very glad he didn't try. It was in the train, and I know very well I should have strangled him. It would have been awkward, you know."

"Oh, Maurice, how *can* you—?"

"Well, here's the money; and half of it is yours."

"Mine? Oh, no! After all you have given me. Besides, I shan't want it."

"How's that?"

Their eyes met. Hilliard again saw the flush in her cheeks, and began to guess its explanation. He looked puzzled, interested.

"Do I know him?" was his next inquiry.

"Should you think it very wrong of me?" She moved aside from the line of his gaze. "I couldn't imagine how you would take it."

"It all depends. Who is the man?"

Still shrinking towards a position where Hilliard could not easily observe her, the young widow told her story. She had consented to marry a man of whom her brother-in-law knew little but the name, one Ezra Marr; he was turned forty, a widower without children, and belonged to a class of small employers of labour known in Birmingham as "little masters." The contrast between such a man and Maurice Hilliard's brother was sufficiently pronounced; but the widow nervously did her best to show Ezra Marr in a favourable light.

"And then," she added after a pause, while Hilliard was reflecting, "I couldn't go on being a burden on you. How very few men would have done what you have—"

"Stop a minute. Is *that* the real reason? If so—"

Hurriedly she interposed.

"That was only one of the reasons – only one."

Hilliard knew very well that her marriage had not been entirely successful; it seemed to him very probable that with a husband of the artisan class, a vigorous and go-ahead fellow, she would be better mated than in the former instance. He felt sorry for his little niece, but there again sentiment doubtless conflicted with common-sense. A few more questions, and it became clear to him that he had no ground of resistance.

"Very well. Most likely you are doing a wise thing. And half this money is yours; you'll find it useful."

The discussion of this point was interrupted by a tap at the door. Mrs. Hilliard, after leaving the room for a moment, returned with rosy countenance.

"He is here," she murmured. "I thought I should like you to meet him this evening. Do you mind?"

Mr. Marr entered; a favourable specimen of his kind; strong, comely, frank of look and speech. Hilliard marvelled somewhat at his choice of the frail and timid little widow, and hoped upon marriage would follow no repentance. A friendly conversation between the two men confirmed them in mutual good opinion. At length Mrs. Hilliard spoke of the offer of money made by her brother-in-law.

"I don't feel I've any right to it," she said, after explaining the circumstances. "You know what Maurice has done for me. I've always felt I was robbing him—"

"I wanted to say something about that," put in the bass-voiced Ezra. "I want to tell you, Mr. Hilliard, that you're a man I'm proud to know, and proud to shake hands with. And if my view goes for anything, Emily won't take a penny of what you're offering her. I should think it wrong and mean. It is about time – that's my way of thinking – that you looked after your own interests. Emily has no claim to a share in this money, and what's more, I don't wish her to take it."

"Very well," said Hilliard. "I tell you what we'll do. A couple of hundred pounds shall be put aside for the little girl. You can't make any objection to that."

The mother glanced doubtfully at her future husband, but Marr again spoke with emphasis.

"Yes, I do object. If you don't mind me saying it, I'm quite able to look after the little girl; and the fact is, I want her to grow up looking to me as her father, and getting all she has from me only. Of course, I mean nothing but what's friendly: but there it is; I'd rather Winnie didn't have the money."

This man was in the habit of speaking his mind; Hilliard understood that any insistence would only disturb the harmony of the occasion. He waved a hand, smiled good-naturedly, and said no more.

About nine o'clock he left the house and walked to Aston Church. While he stood there, waiting for the tram, a voice fell upon his ear that caused him to look round. Crouched by the entrance to the churchyard was a beggar in filthy rags, his face hideously bandaged, before him on the pavement a little heap of matchboxes; this creature kept uttering a meaningless sing-song, either idiot jabber, or calculated to excite attention and pity; it sounded something like "A-pah-pahky; pah-pahky; pah"; repeated a score of times, and resumed after a pause. Hilliard gazed and listened, then placed a copper in the wretch's extended palm, and turned away muttering, "What a cursed world!"

He was again on the tram-car before he observed that the full moon, risen into a sky now clear of grosser vapours, gleamed brilliant silver above the mean lights of earth. And round about it, in so vast a circumference that it was only detected by the wandering eye, spread a softly radiant halo. This vision did not long occupy his thoughts, but at intervals he again looked upward, to dream for a moment on the silvery splendour and on that wide halo dim-glimmering athwart the track of stars.

~ *Chapter 3* ~

INSTEAD of making for the railway station, to take a train back to Dudley, he crossed from the northern to the southern extremity of the town, and by ten o'clock was in one of the streets which lead out of Moseley Road. Here, at a house such as lodges young men in business, he made inquiry for "Mr. Narramore," and was forthwith admitted.

Robert Narramore, a long-stemmed pipe at his lips, sat by the fireside; on the table lay the materials of a satisfactory supper – a cold fowl, a ham, a Stilton cheese, and a bottle of wine.

"Hollo! You?" he exclaimed, without rising. "I was going to write to you; thanks for saving me the trouble. Have something to eat?"

"Yes, and to drink likewise."

"Do you mind ringing the bell? I believe there's a bottle of Burgundy left. If not, plenty of Bass."

He stretched forth a languid hand, smiling amiably. Narramore was the image of luxurious indolence; he had pleasant features, dark hair inclined to curliness, a well-built frame set off by good tailoring. His income from the commercial house in which he held a post of responsibility would have permitted him to occupy better quarters than these; but here he had lived for ten years, and he preferred a few inconveniences to the trouble of moving. Trouble of any kind was Robert's bugbear. His progress up the commercial ladder seemed due rather to the luck which favours amiable and good-looking young fellows than to any special ability or effort of his own. The very sound of his voice had a drowsiness which soothed – if it did not irritate – the listener.

"Tell them to lay out the truckle-bed," said Hilliard, when he had pulled the bell. "I shall stay here to-night."

"Good!"

Their talk was merely interjectional, until the visitor had begun to appease his hunger and had drawn the cork of a second bottle of bitter ale.

"This is a great day," Hilliard then exclaimed. "I left Dudley this afternoon feeling ready to cut my throat. Now I'm a free man, with the world before me."

"How's that?"

"Emily's going to take a second husband – that's one thing."

"Heaven be praised! Better than one could have looked for."

Hilliard related the circumstances. Then he drew from his pocket an oblong slip of paper, and held it out.

"Dengate?" cried his friend. "How the deuce did you get hold of this?"

Explanation followed. They debated Dengate's character and motives.

"I can understand it," said Narramore. "When I was a boy of twelve I once cheated an apple-woman out of three-halfpence. At the age of sixteen I encountered the old woman again, and felt immense satisfaction in giving her a shilling. But then, you see, I had done with petty cheating; I wished to clear my conscience, and look my fellow-woman in the face."

"That's it, no doubt. He seems to have got some sort of position in Liverpool society, and he didn't like the thought that there was a poor devil at Dudley who went about calling him a scoundrel. By-the-bye, someone told him that I had taken to liquor, and was on my way to destruction generally. I don't know who it could be."

"Oh, we all have candid friends that talk about us."

"It's true I have been drunk now and then of late. There's much to be said for getting drunk."

"Much," assented Narramore, philosophically.

Hilliard went on with his supper; his friend puffed tobacco, and idly regarded the cheque he was still holding.

"And what are you going to do?" he asked at length.

There came no reply, and several minutes passed in silence. Then Hilliard rose from the table, paced the floor once or twice, selected a cigar from a box that caught his eye, and, in cutting off the end, observed quietly— "I'm going to live."

"Wait a minute. We'll have the table cleared, and a kettle on the fire."

While the servant was busy, Hilliard stood with an elbow on the mantelpiece, thoughtfully smoking his cigar. At Narramore's request, he mixed two tumblers of whisky toddy, then took a draught from his own, and returned to his former position.

"Can't you sit down?" said Narramore.

"No, I can't."

"What a fellow you are! With nerves like yours, I should have been in my grave years ago. You're going to live, eh?"

"Going to be a machine no longer. Can I call myself a man? There's precious little difference between a fellow like me and the damned grinding mechanism that I spend my days in drawing – that roars all day in my ears and deafens me. I'll put an end to that. Here's four hundred pounds. It shall mean four hundred pounds'-worth of life. While this money lasts, I'll feel that I'm a human being."

"Dengate?" cried his friend. "How the deuce did you get hold of this?"

"Something to be said for that," commented the listener, in his tone of drowsy impartiality.

"I offered Emily half of it. She didn't want to take it, and the man Marr wouldn't let her. I offered to lay it aside for the child, but Marr wouldn't have that either. It's fairly mine."

"Undoubtedly."

"Think! The first time in my life that I've had money on which no one else had a claim. When the poor old father died, Will and I had to go shares in keeping up the home. Our sister couldn't earn anything; she had her work set in attending to her mother. When mother died, and Marian married, it looked as if I had only myself to look after: then came Will's death, and half my income went to keep his wife and child from the workhouse. You know very well I've never grudged it. It's my faith that we do what we do because anything else would be less agreeable. It was more to my liking to live on a pound a week than to see Emily and the little lass suffer want. I've no right to any thanks or praise for it. But the change has come none too soon. There'd have been a paragraph in the Dudley paper some rainy morning."

"Yes, I was rather afraid of that," said Narramore musingly.

He let a minute elapse, whilst his friend paced the room; then added in the same voice:

"We're in luck at the same time. My uncle Sol was found dead this morning."

"Do you come in for much?"

"We don't know what he's left, but I'm down for a substantial fraction in a will he made three years ago. Nobody knew it, but he's been stark mad for the last six months. He took a bed-room out Bordesley way, in a false name, and stored it with a ton or two of tinned meats and vegetables. There the landlady found him lying dead this morning; she learnt who he was from the papers in his pocket. It's come out that he had made friends with some old boozer of that neighbourhood; he told him that England was on the point of a grand financial smash, and that half the population would die of hunger. To secure himself, he began to lay in the stock of tinned provisions. One can't help laughing, poor old chap! That's the result, you see, of a life spent in sweating for money. As a young man he had hard times, and when his invention succeeded, it put him off balance a bit. I've often thought he had a crazy look in his eye. He may have thrown away a lot of his money in mad tricks: who knows?"

"That's the end the human race will come to," said Hilliard. "It'll be driven mad and killed off by machinery. Before long there'll be machines for washing and dressing people – machines for feeding them – machines for—"

His wrathful imagination led him to grotesque ideas which ended in laughter.

"Well, I have a year or two before me. I'll know what enjoyment means. And afterwards—"

"Yes; what afterwards?"

"I don't know. I may choose to come back; I may prefer to make an end. Impossible to foresee my state of mind after living humanly for a year or two. And what shall *you* do if you come in for a lot of money?"

"It's not likely to be more than a few thousands," replied Narramore. "And the chances are I shall go on in the old way. What's the good of a few thousands? I haven't the energy to go off and enjoy myself in your fashion. One of these days I may think of getting married, and marriage, you know, is devilish expensive. I should like to have three or four thousand a year; you can't start housekeeping on less, if you're not to be bored to death with worries. Perhaps I may get a partnership in our house. I began life in the brass bedstead line, and I may as well stick to brass bedsteads to the end: the demand isn't likely to fall off. Please fill my glass again."

Hilliard, the while, had tossed off his second tumbler. He began to talk at random.

"I shall go to London first of all. I may go abroad. Reckon a pound a day. Three hundred and – how many days are there in a year? Three hundred and sixty-five. That doesn't allow me two years. I want two years of life. Half a sovereign a day, then. One can do a good deal with half a sovereign a day – don't you think?"

"Not very much, if you're particular about your wine."

"Wine doesn't matter. Honest ale and Scotch whisky will serve well enough. Understand me; I'm not going in for debauchery, and I'm not going to play the third-rate swell. There's no enjoyment in making a beast of oneself, and none for me in strutting about the streets like an animated figure out of a tailor's window. I want to know the taste of free life, human life. I want to forget that I ever sat at a desk, drawing to scale – drawing damned machines. I want to—"

He checked himself. Narramore looked at him with curiosity.

"It's a queer thing to me, Hilliard," he remarked, when his friend turned away, "that you've kept so clear of women. Now, anyone would think you were just the fellow to get hobbled in that way."

"I daresay," muttered the other. "Yes, it *is* a queer thing. I have been saved, I suppose, by the necessity of supporting my relatives. I've seen so much of women suffering from poverty that it has got me into the habit of thinking of them as nothing but burdens to a man."

"As they nearly always are."

"Yes, nearly always."

Narramore pondered with his amiable smile; the other, after a moment's gloom, shook himself free again, and talked with growing exhilaration of the new life that had dawned before him.

~ *Chapter 4* ~

HILLIARD'S lodgings – they were represented by a single room—commanded a prospect which, to him a weariness and a disgust, would have seemed impressive enough to eyes beholding it for the first time. On the afternoon of his last day at Dudley he stood by the window and looked forth, congratulating himself, with a fierceness of emotion which defied misgiving, that he would gaze no more on this scene of his servitude. The house was one of a row situated on a terrace, above a muddy declivity marked with footpaths. It looked over a wide expanse of waste ground, covered in places with coarse herbage, but for the most part undulating in bare tracts of slag and cinder. Opposite, some quarter of a mile away, rose a lofty dome-shaped hill, tree-clad from base to summit, and rearing above the bare branches of its topmost trees the ruined keep of Dudley Castle. Along the foot of this hill ran the highway which descends from Dudley town – hidden by rising ground on the left – to the low-lying railway-station; there, beyond, the eye traversed a great plain, its limit the blending of earth and sky in lurid cloud. A ray of yellow sunset touched the height and its crowning ruin; at the zenith shone a space of pure pale blue: save for these points of relief the picture was colourless and uniformly sombre. Far and near, innumerable chimneys sent forth fumes of various density: broad-flung jets of steam, coldly white against the murky distance; wan smoke from lime-kilns, wafted in long trails; reek of solid blackness from pits and forges, voluming aloft and far-floated by the sluggish wind.

Born at Birmingham, the son of a teacher of drawing, Maurice Hilliard had spent most of his life in the Midland capital; to its grammar school he owed an education just sufficiently prolonged to unfit him for the tasks of an underling, yet not thorough enough to qualify him for professional life. In boyhood he aspired to the career of an artist, but his father, himself the wreck of a would-be painter, rudely discouraged this ambition; by way of compromise between the money-earning craft and the beggarly art, he became a mechanical-draughtsman. Of late years he had developed a strong taste for the study of architecture; much of his leisure was given to this subject, and what money he could spare went in the purchase of books and prints which helped him to extend his architectural knowledge. In moods of hope, he had asked himself whether it might not be possible to escape from bondage to the gods of iron, and earn a living in an architect's office. That desire was now forgotten in his passionate resolve to enjoy liberty without regard for the future.

All his possessions, save the articles of clothing which he would carry with him, were packed in a couple of trunks, to be sent on the morrow to Birmingham, where they would lie in the care of his friend Narramore. Kinsfolk he had none whom he cared to remember, except his sister; she lived at Wolverhampton, a wife and mother, in narrow but not oppressive circumstances, and Hilliard had taken leave of her in a short visit some days ago. He would not wait for the wedding of his sister-in-law; enough that she was provided for, and that his conscience would always be at ease on her account.

For he was troubled with a conscience – even with one unusually poignant. An anecdote from his twentieth year depicts this feature of the man. He and Narramore were walking one night in a very poor part of Birmingham, and for some reason they chanced to pause by a shop-window – a small window, lighted with one gas-jet, and laid out with a miserable handful of paltry wares; the shop, however, was newly opened, and showed a pathetic attempt at cleanliness and neatness. The friends asked each other how it could possibly benefit anyone to embark in such a business as that, and laughed over the display. While he was laughing, Hilliard became aware of a woman in the doorway, evidently the shopkeeper; she had heard their remarks and looked distressed. Infinitely keener was the pang which Maurice experienced; he could not forgive himself, kept exclaiming how brutally he had behaved, and sank into gloominess. Not very long after, he took Narramore to walk in the same direction; they came again to the little shop, and Hilliard surprised his companion with a triumphant shout. The window was now laid out in a much more promising way, with goods of modest value. "You remember?" said the young man. "I couldn't rest till I had sent her something. She'll wonder to the end of her life who the money came from. But she's made use of it, poor creature, and it'll bring her luck."

Only the hopeless suppression of natural desires, the conflict through years of ardent youth with sordid circumstances, could have brought him to the pass he had now reached – one of desperation centred in self. Every suggestion of native suavity and prudence was swept away in tumultuous revolt. Another twelvemonth of his slavery and he would have yielded to brutalising influences which rarely relax their hold upon a man. To-day he was prompted by the instinct of flight from peril threatening all that was worthy in him.

Just as the last glimmer of daylight vanished from his room there sounded a knock at the door.

"Your tea's ready, Mr. Hilliard," called a woman's voice.

He took his meals downstairs in the landlady's parlour. Appetite at present he had none, but the pretence of eating was a way of passing the time; so he descended and sat down at the prepared table.

His wandering eyes fell on one of the ornaments of the room – Mrs. Brewer's album. On first coming to live in the house, two years ago, he had examined this collection of domestic portraits, and subsequently, from time to time, had taken up the album to look at one photograph which interested him. Among an assemblage of types excelling in ugliness of feature and hideousness of costume – types of toil-worn age, of ungainly middle life, and of youth lacking every grace, such as are exhibited in the albums of the poor – there was discoverable one female portrait in which, the longer he gazed at it, Hilliard found an ever-increasing suggestiveness of those qualities he desired in woman. Unclasping the volume, he opened immediately at this familiar face. A month or two had elapsed since he last regarded it, and the countenance took possession of him with the same force as ever.

It was that of a young woman probably past her twentieth year. Unlike her neighbours in the album, she had not bedizened herself before sitting to be portrayed. The abundant hair was parted simply and smoothly from her forehead and tightly plaited behind; she wore a linen collar, and, so far as could be judged from the portion included in the picture, a homely cloth gown. Her features were comely and intelligent, and exhibited a gentleness, almost a meekness of expression which was as far as possible from seeming affected. Whether she smiled or looked sad Hilliard had striven vainly to determine. Her lips appeared to smile, but in so slight a degree that perchance it was merely an effect of natural line; whereas, if the mouth were concealed, a profound melancholy at once ruled the visage.

Who she was Hilliard had no idea. More than once he had been on the point of asking his landlady, but characteristic delicacies restrained him: he feared Mrs. Brewer's mental comment, and dreaded the possible disclosure that he had admired a housemaid or someone of yet lower condition. Nor could he trust his judgment of the face: perhaps it shone only by contrast with so much ugliness on either side of it; perhaps, in the starved condition of his senses, he was ready to find perfection in any female countenance not frankly repulsive.

Yet, no; it was a beautiful face. Beautiful, at all events, in the sense of being deeply interesting, in the strength of its appeal to his emotions. Another man might pass it slightingly; to him it spoke as no other face had ever spoken. It awakened in him a consciousness of profound sympathy. While he still sat at table his landlady came in. She was a worthy woman of her class, not given to vulgar gossip. Her purpose in entering the room at this moment was to ask Hilliard whether he had a likeness of himself which he could spare her, as a memento.

"I'm sorry I don't possess such a thing," he answered, laughing, surprised that the woman should care enough about him to make the request. "But, talking of photographs, would you tell me who this is?"

The album lay beside him, and a feeling of embarrassment, as he saw Mrs. Brewer's look rest upon it, impelled him to the decisive question.

"That? Oh! that's a friend of my daughter Martha's – Eve Madeley. I'm sure I don't wonder at you noticing her. But it doesn't do her justice; she's better looking than that. It was took better than two years ago – why, just before you came to me, Mr. Hilliard. She was going away – to London."

"Eve Madeley." He repeated the name to himself, and liked it.

"She's had a deal of trouble, poor thing," pursued the landlady. "We was sorry to lose sight of her, but glad, I'm sure, that she went away to do better for herself. She hasn't been home since then, and we don't hear of her coming, and I'm sure nobody can be surprised. But our Martha heard from her not so long ago – why, it was about Christmas-time."

"Is she" – he was about to add, "in service?" but could not voice the words. "She has an engagement in London?"

"Yes; she's a bookkeeper, and earns her pound a week. She was always clever at figures. She got on so well at the school that they wanted her to be a teacher, but she didn't like it. Then Mr. Reckitt, the ironmonger, a friend of her father's, got her to help him with his books and bills of an evening, and when she was seventeen, because his business was growing and he hadn't much of a head for figures himself, he took her regular into the shop. And glad she was to give up the school-teaching, for she could never abear it."

"You say she had a lot of trouble?"

"Ah, that indeed she had! And all her father's fault. But for him, foolish man, they might have been a well-to-do family. But he's had to suffer for it himself, too. He lives up here on the hill, in a poor cottage, and takes wages as a timekeeper at Robinson's when he ought to have been paying men of his own. The drink – that's what it was. When our Martha first

knew them they were living at Walsall, and if it hadn't a' been for Eve
they'd have had no home at all. Martha got to know her at the Sunday-
school; Eve used to teach a class. That's seven or eight years ago; she was
only a girl of sixteen, but she had the ways of a grown-up woman, and very
lucky it was for them belonging to her. Often and often they've gone for
days with nothing but a dry loaf, and the father spending all he got at the
public."

"Was it a large family?" Hilliard inquired.

"Well, let me see; at that time there was Eve's two sisters and her
brother. Two other children had died, and the mother was dead, too. I don't
know much about *her*, but they say she was a very good sort of woman,
and it's likely the eldest girl took after her. A quieter and modester girl than
Eve there never was. Our Martha lived with her aunt at Walsall – that's my
only sister, and she was bed-rid, poor thing, and had Martha to look after
her. And when she died, and Martha came back here to us, the Madeley
family came here as well, 'cause the father got some kind of work. But he
couldn't keep it, and he went off I don't know where, and Eve had the
children to keep and look after. We used to do what we could to help her,
but it was a cruel life for a poor thing of her age – just when she ought to
have been enjoying her life, as you may say."

Hilliard's interest waxed.

"Then," pursued Mrs. Brewer, "the next sister to Eve, Laura her name
was, went to Birmingham, into a sweetstuff shop, and that was the last ever
seen or heard of her. She wasn't a girl to be depended upon, and I never
thought she'd come to good, and whether she's alive or dead there's no
knowing. Eve took it to heart, that she did. And not six months after, the
other girl had the 'sipelas, and she died, and just as they was carrying her
coffin out of the house, who should come up but her father! He'd been
away for nearly two years, just sending a little money now and then, and
he didn't even know the girl had been ailing. And when he saw the coffin,
it took him so that he fell down just like a dead man. You wouldn't have
thought it, but there's no knowing what goes on in people's minds. Well,
if you'll believe it, from that day he was so changed we didn't seem to
know him. He turned quite religious, and went regular to chapel, and has
done ever since; and he wouldn't touch a drop of anything, tempt him who
might. It was a case of conversion, if ever there was one."

"So there remained only Eve and her brother?"

"Yes. He was a steady lad, Tom Madeley, and never gave his sister
much trouble. He earns his thirty shillings a week now. Well, and soon

after she saw her father going on all right, Eve left home. I don't wonder at it; it wasn't to be expected she could forgive him for all the harm and sorrows he'd caused. She went to Birmingham for a few months, and then she came back one day to tell us she'd got a place in London. And she brought that photo to give us to remember her by. But, as I said, it isn't good enough."

"Does she seem to be happier now?"

"She hasn't wrote more than once or twice, but she's doing well, and whatever happens she's not the one to complain. It's a blessing she's always had her health. No doubt she's made friends in London, but we haven't heard about them. Martha was hoping she'd have come for Christmas, but it seems she couldn't get away for long enough from business. I'd tell you her address, but I don't remember it. I've never been in London myself. Martha knows it, of course. She might look in to-night, and if she does I'll ask her."

Hilliard allowed this suggestion to pass without remark. He was not quite sure that he desired to know Miss Madeley's address.

But later in the evening, when, after walking for two or three hours about the cold, dark roads, he came in to have his supper and go to bed, Mrs. Brewer smilingly offered him a scrap of paper.

"There," she said, "that's where she's living. London's a big place, and you mayn't be anywhere near, but if you happened to walk that way, we should take it kindly if you'd just leave word that we're always glad to hear from her, and hope she's well."

With a mixture of reluctance and satisfaction the young man took the paper, glanced at it, and folded it to put in his pocket. Mrs. Brewer was regarding him, and he felt that his silence must seem ungracious.

"I will certainly call and leave your message," he said.

Up in his bed-room he sat for a long time with the paper lying open before him. And when he slept his rest was troubled with dreams of an anxious search about the highways and byways of London for that half-sad, half-smiling face which had so wrought upon his imagination.

Long before daylight he awoke at the sound of bells, and hootings, and whistlings, which summoned the Dudley workfolk to their labour. For the first time in his life he heard these hideous noises with pleasure: they told him that the day of his escape had come. Unable to lie still, he rose at once, and went out into the chill dawn. Thoughts of Eve Madeley no longer possessed him; a glorious sense of freedom excluded every recollection of his past life, and he wandered aimlessly with a song in his heart.

At breakfast, the sight of Mrs. Brewer's album tempted him to look once more at the portrait, but he did not yield.

"Shall we ever see you again, I wonder?" asked his landlady, when the moment arrived for leave-taking.

"If I am ever again in Dudley, I shall come here," he answered kindly.

But on his way to the station he felt a joyful assurance that fate would have no power to draw him back again into this circle of fiery torments.

~ *Chapter 5* ~

TWO months later, on a brilliant morning of May, Hilliard again awoke from troubled dreams, but the sounds about him had no association with bygone miseries. From the courtyard upon which his window looked there came a ringing of gay laughter followed by shrill, merry gossip in a foreign tongue. Somewhere in the neighbourhood a church bell was pealing. Presently footsteps hurried along the corridor, and an impatient voice shouted repeatedly, "Alphonse! Alphonse!"

He was in Paris; had been there for six weeks, and now awoke with a sense of loneliness, a desire to be back among his own people.

In London he had spent only a fortnight. It was not a time that he cared to reflect upon. No sooner had he found himself in the metropolis, alone and free, with a pocketful of money, than a delirium possessed him. Every resolution notwithstanding, he yielded to London's grossest lures. All he could remember, was a succession of extravagances, beneath a sunless sky, with chance companions whose faces he had forgotten five minutes after parting with them. Sovereign after sovereign melted out of his hand; the end of the second week found his capital diminished by some five-and-twenty pounds. In an hour of physical and moral nausea, he packed his travelling-bag, journeyed to Newhaven, and as a sort of penance, crossed the Channel by third-class passage. Arrived in Paris, he felt himself secure, and soon recovered sanity.

Thanks to his studious habits, he was equipped with book-French; now, both for economy's sake and for his mental advantage, he struggled with the spoken language, and so far succeeded as to lodge very cheaply in a rather disreputable hotel, and to eat at restaurants where dinner of several courses cost two francs and a half. His life was irreproachable; he studied the Paris of art and history. But perforce he remained companionless, and solitude had begun to weigh upon him.

This morning, whilst he sat over his bowl of coffee and *petit pain*, a certain recollection haunted him persistently. Yesterday, in turning out his pockets, he had come upon a scrap of paper, whereon was written:

"93, Belmont Street, Chalk Farm Road, London, N.W."

This formula it was which now kept running through his mind, like a refrain which will not be dismissed.

He reproached himself for neglect of his promise to Mrs. Brewer. More than that, he charged himself with foolish disregard of a possibility which might have boundless significance for him. Here, it seemed, was sufficient motive for a return to London. The alternative was to wander on, and see more of foreign countries; a tempting suggestion, but marred by the prospect of loneliness. He would go back among his own people and make friends. Without comradeship, liberty had little savour.

Still travelling with as small expense as might be, he reached London in the forenoon, left his luggage at Victoria Station, and, after a meal, betook himself in the northerly direction. It was a rainy and uncomfortable day, but this did not much affect his spirits; he felt like a man new risen from illness, seemed to have cast off something that had threatened his very existence, and marvelled at the state of mind in which it had been possible for him to inhabit London without turning his steps towards the address of Eve Madeley.

He discovered Belmont Street. It consisted of humble houses, and was dreary enough to look upon. As he sought for No. 93, a sudden nervousness attacked him; he became conscious all at once of the strangeness of his position. At this hour it was unlikely that Eve would be at home; an inquiry at the house and the leaving of a verbal message would discharge his obligation; but he proposed more than that. It was his resolve to see Eve herself, to behold the face which, in a picture, had grown so familiar to him. Yet till this moment he had overlooked the difficulties of the enterprise. Could he, on the strength of an acquaintance with Mrs. Brewer, claim the friendly regards of this girl who had never heard his name? If he saw her once, on what pretext could he seek for a second meeting?

Possibly he would not desire it. Eve in her own person might disenchant him.

Meanwhile he had discovered the house, and without further debate he knocked. The door was opened by a woman of ordinary type, slatternly, and with suspicious eye.

"Miss Madeley *did* live here," she said, "but she's been gone a month or more."

"Can you tell me where she is living now?"

After a searching look the woman replied that she could not. In the manner of her kind, she was anxious to dismiss the inquirer and get the door shut. Gravely disappointed, Hilliard felt unable to turn away without a further question.

"Perhaps you know where she is, or was, employed?"

But no information whatever was forthcoming. It very rarely is under such circumstances, for a London landlady, compounded in general of craft and caution, tends naturally to reticence on the score of her former lodgers. If she has parted with them on amicable terms, her instinct is to shield them against the menace presumed in every inquiry; if her mood is one of ill-will, she refuses information lest the departed should reap advantage. And then, in the great majority of cases she has really no information to give.

The door closed with that severity of exclusion in which London doors excel, and Hilliard turned despondently away. He was just consoling himself with the thought that Eve would probably, before long, communicate her new address to the friends at Dudley, and by that means he might hear of it, when a dirty-faced little girl, who had stood within earshot while he was talking, and who had followed him to the end of the street, approached him with an abrupt inquiry.

"Was you asking for Miss Madeley, Sir?"

"Yes, I was; do you know anything of her?"

"My mother did washing for her, and when she moved I had to take some things of hers to the new address."

"Then you remember it?"

"It's a goodish way from 'ere, Sir. Shall I go with you?"

Hilliard understood. Like the good Samaritan of old, he took out twopence. The face of the dirty little girl brightened wonderfully.

"Tell me the address; that will be enough."

"Do you know Gower Place, Sir?"

"Somewhere near Gower Street, I suppose?"

His supposition was confirmed, and he learnt the number of the house to which Miss Madeley had transferred herself. In that direction he at once bent his steps.

Gower Place is in the close neighbourhood of Euston Road; Hilliard remembered that he had passed the end of it on his first arrival in London, when he set forth from Euston Station to look for a lodging. It was a mere chance that he had not turned into this very street, instead of going further. Several windows displayed lodging-cards. On the whole, it looked a better locality than Belmont Street. Eve's removal hither might signify an improvement of circumstances.

The house which he sought had a clean doorstep and unusually bright windows. His knock was answered quickly, and by a young, sprightly woman, who smiled upon him.

"I believe Miss Madeley lives here?"

"Yes, she does."

"She is not at home just now?"

"No. She went out after breakfast, and I'm sure I can't say when she'll be back."

Hilliard felt a slight wonder at this uncertainty. The young woman, observing his expression, added with vivacious friendliness:

"Do you want to see her on business?"

"No; a private matter."

This occasioned a smirk.

"Well, she hasn't any regular hours at present. Sometimes she comes to dinner, sometimes she doesn't. Sometimes she comes to tea, but just as often she isn't 'ome till late. P'r'aps you'd like to leave your name?"

"I think I'll call again."

"Did you expect to find her at 'ome now?" asked the young woman, whose curiosity grew more eager as she watched Hilliard's countenance.

"Perhaps," he replied, neglecting the question, "I should find her here to-morrow morning?"

"Well, I can say as someone's going to call, you know."

"Please do so."

Therewith he turned away, anxious to escape a volley of interrogation for which the landlady's tongue was primed.

He walked into Gower Street, and pondered the awkward interview that now lay before him. On his calling to-morrow, Miss Madeley would doubtless come to speak with him at the door; even supposing she had a parlour at her disposal, she was not likely to invite a perfect stranger into the house. How could he make her acquaintance on the doorstep? To be sure, he brought a message, but this commission had been so long delayed that he felt some shame about discharging it. In any case, his delivery of the message would sound odd; there would be embarrassment on both sides.

Why was Eve so uncertain in her comings and goings? Necessity of business, perhaps. Yet he had expected quite the opposite state of things. From Mrs. Brewer's description of the girl's character, he had imagined her leading a life of clockwork regularity. The point was very trivial, but it somehow caused a disturbance of his thoughts, which tended to misgiving.

In the meantime he had to find quarters for himself. Why not seek them in Gower Place?

After ten minutes' sauntering, he retraced his steps, and walked down the side of the street opposite to that on which Eve's lodgings were situated. Nearly over against that particular house was a window with a card. Carelessly he approached the door, and carelessly asked to see the rooms that were to let. They were comfortless, but would suit his purpose for a time. He engaged a sitting-room on the ground-floor, and a bed-room above, and went to fetch his luggage from Victoria Station.

On the steamer last night he had not slept, and now that he was once more housed, an overpowering fatigue constrained him to lie down and close his eyes. Almost immediately he fell into oblivion, and lay sleeping on the cranky sofa, until the entrance of a girl with tea-things awakened him.

From his parlour window he could very well observe the houses opposite without fear of drawing attention from any one on that side; and so it happened that, without deliberate purpose of espial, he watched the door of Eve Madeley's residence for a long time; till, in fact, he grew weary of the occupation. No one had entered; no one had come forth. At half-past seven he took his hat and left the house.

Scarcely had he closed the door behind him when he became aware that a lightly tripping and rather showily dressed girl, who was coming down the other side of the way, had turned off the pavement and was plying the knocker at the house which interested him. He gazed eagerly. Impossible that a young person of that garb and deportment should be Eve Madeley. Her face was hidden from him, and at this distance he could not have recognised the features, even presuming that his familiarity with the portrait, taken more than two years ago, would enable him to identify Eve when he saw her. The door opened; the girl was admitted. Afraid of being noticed, he walked on.

The distance to the head of the street was not more than thirty yards; there lay Gower Street, on the right hand the Metropolitan station, to the left a long perspective southwards. Delaying in doubt as to his course, Hilliard glanced back. From the house which attracted his eyes he saw come forth the girl who had recently entered, and close following her another young woman. They began to walk sharply towards where he stood.

He did not stir, and the couple drew so near that he could observe their faces. In the second girl he recognised – or believed that he recognised – Eve Madeley.

She wore a costume in decidedly better taste than her companion's; for all that, her appearance struck him as quite unlike that he would have expected Eve Madeley to present. He had thought of her as very plainly, perhaps poorly, clad; but this attire was ornate, and looked rather expensive; it might be in the mode of the new season. In figure, she was altogether a more imposing young woman than he had pictured to himself. His pulses were sensibly quickened as he looked at her.

The examination was of necessity hurried. Walking at a sharp pace, they rapidly came close to where he stood. He drew aside to let them pass, and at that moment caught a few words of their conversation.

"I told you we should be late," exclaimed the unknown girl, in friendly remonstrance.

"What does it matter?" replied Eve – if Eve it were. "I hate standing at the doors. We shall find seats somewhere."

Her gay, careless tones astonished the listener. Involuntarily he began to follow; but at the edge of the pavement in Gower Street they stopped, and by advancing another step or two he distinctly overheard the continuation of their talk.

"The 'bus will take a long time."

"Bother the 'bus!" This was Eve Madeley again – if Eve it could really be. "We'll have a cab. Look, there's a crawler in Euston Road. I've stopped him!"

"I say, Eve, you *are* going it!"

This exclamation from the other girl was the last sentence that fell on Hilliard's ear. They both tripped off towards the cab which Eve's gesture had summoned. He saw them jump in and drive away.

"I say, Eve, you *are* going it!" Why, there his doubt was settled; the name confirmed him in his identification. But he stood motionless with astonishment.

They were going to a theatre, of course. And Eve spoke as if money were of no consequence to her. She had the look, the tones, of one bent on enjoying herself, of one who habitually pursued pleasure, and that in its most urban forms.

Her companion had a voice of thinner quality, of higher note, which proclaimed a subordinate character. It sounded, moreover, with the London accent, while Eve's struck a more familiar note to the man of the Midlands. Eve seemed to be the elder of the two; it could not be thought for a moment that her will was guided by that of the more trivial girl.

Eve Madeley – the meek, the melancholy, the long-suffering, the pious – what did it all mean?

Utterly bewildered, the young man walked on without thought of direction, and rambled dreamily about the streets for an hour or two. He could not make up his mind whether or not to fulfil the promise of calling to see Miss Madeley to-morrow morning. At one moment he regretted having taken lodgings in Gower Place; at another he determined to make use of his advantage, and play the spy upon Eve's movements without scruple. The interest she had hitherto excited in him was faint indeed compared with emotions such as this first glimpse of her had kindled and fanned. A sense of peril warned him to hold aloof; tumult of his senses rendered the warning useless.

At eleven o'clock he was sitting by his bedroom window, in darkness, watching the house across the way.

~ *Chapter 6* ~

IT was just upon midnight when Eve returned. She came at a quick walk, and alone; the light of the street-lamps showed her figure distinctly enough to leave the watcher in no doubt. A latchkey admitted her to the house. Presently there appeared a light at an upper window, and a shadow kept moving across the blind. When the light was extinguished Hilliard went to bed, but that night he slept little.

The next morning passed in restless debate with himself. He did not cross the way to call upon Eve: the thought of speaking with her on the doorstep of a lodging-house proved intolerable. All day long he kept his post of observation. Other persons he saw leave and enter the house, but Miss Madeley did not come forth. That he could have missed her seemed impossible, for even while eating his meals he remained by the window. Perchance she had left home very early in the morning, but it was unlikely.

Through the afternoon it rained: the gloomy sky intensified his fatigue and despondence. About six o'clock, exhausted in mind and body, he had allowed his attention to stray, when the sudden clang of a street organ startled him. His eyes turned in the wonted direction – and instantly he sprang up. To clutch his hat, to rush from the room and from the house, occupied but a moment. There, walking away on the other side, was Eve. Her fawn-coloured mantle, her hat with the yellow flowers, were the same as yesterday. The rain had ceased; in the western sky appeared promise of a fair evening.

Hilliard pursued her in a parallel line. At the top of the street she crossed towards him; he let her pass by and followed closely. She entered the booking-office of Gower Street station; he drew as near as possible and heard her ask for a ticket—

"Healtheries; third return."

The slang term for the Health Exhibition at Kensington was familiar to him from the English papers he had seen in Paris. As soon as Eve had passed on he obtained a like ticket and hastened down the steps in pursuit. A minute or two and he was sitting face to face with her in the railway carriage.

He could now observe her at his leisure and compare her features with those represented in the photograph. Mrs. Brewer had said truly that the portrait did not do her justice; he saw the resemblance, yet what a difference between the face he had brooded over at Dudley and that which lived before him! A difference not to be accounted for by mere lapse of time. She could not, he thought, have changed greatly in the last two or three years, for her age at the time of sitting for the photograph must have been at least one-and-twenty. She did not look older than he had expected: it was still a young face, but – and herein he found its strangeness – that of a woman who views life without embarrassment, without anxiety. She sat at her ease, casting careless glances this way and that. When her eyes fell upon him he winced, yet she paid no more heed to him than to the other passengers. Presently she became lost in thought; her eyes fell. Ah! now the resemblance to the portrait came out more distinctly. Her lips shaped themselves to that expression which he knew so well, the half-smile telling of habitual sadness.

His fixed gaze recalled her to herself, and immediately the countenance changed beyond recognition. Her eyes wandered past him with a look of cold if not defiant reserve; the lips lost all their sweetness. He was chilled with vague distrust, and once again asked himself whether this could be the Eve Madeley whose history he had heard.

Again she fell into abstraction, and some trouble seemed to grow upon her mind. It was difficult now to identify her with the girl who had talked and laughed so gaily last evening. Towards the end of the journey a nervous restlessness began to appear in her looks and movements. Hilliard felt that he had annoyed her by the persistency of his observation, and tried to keep his eyes averted. But no; the disturbance she betrayed was due to some other cause; probably she paid not the least regard to him.

At Earl's Court she alighted hurriedly. By this time Hilliard had begun to feel shame in the ignoble part he was playing, but choice he had none – the girl drew him irresistibly to follow and watch her. Among the crowd entering the Exhibition he could easily keep her in sight without risk of his espial being detected. That Eve had come to keep an appointment with some acquaintance he felt sure, and at any cost he must discover who the person was.

The event justified him with unexpected suddenness. No sooner had she passed the turnstile than a man stepped forward, saluting her in form. Eve shook hands with him, and they walked on.

Uncontrollable wrath seized on Hilliard and shook him from head to foot. A meeting of this kind was precisely what he had foreseen, and he resented it violently.

Eve's acquaintance had the external attributes of a gentleman. One could not easily imagine him a clerk or a shop-assistant smartened up for the occasion. He was plain of feature, but wore a pleasant, honest look, and his demeanour to the girl showed not only good breeding but unmistakable interest of the warmest kind. His age might perhaps be thirty; he was dressed well, and in all respects conventionally.

In Eve's behaviour there appeared a very noticeable reserve; she rarely turned her face to him while he spoke, and seemed to make only the briefest remarks. Her attention was given to the objects they passed.

Totally unconscious of the scenes through which he was moving, Hilliard tracked the couple for more than an hour. He noticed that the man once took out his watch, and from this trifling incident he sought to derive a hope; perhaps Eve would be quit ere long of the detested companionship. They came at length to where a band was playing, and sat down on chairs; the pursuer succeeded in obtaining a seat behind them, but the clamour of instruments overpowered their voices, or rather the man's voice, for Eve seemed not to speak at all. One moment, when her neighbour's head approached nearer than usual to hers, she drew slightly away.

The music ceased, whereupon Eve's companion again consulted his watch.

"It's a most unfortunate thing." He was audible now. "I can't possibly stay longer."

Eve moved on her chair, as if in readiness to take leave of him, but she did not speak.

"You think it likely you will meet Miss Ringrose?"

Eve answered, but the listener could not catch her words.

"I'm so very sorry. If there had been any—"

The voice sank, and Hilliard could only gather from observance of the man's face that he was excusing himself in fervent tones for the necessity of departure. Then they both rose and walked a few yards together. Finally, with a sense of angry exultation, Hilliard saw them part.

For a little while Eve stood watching the musicians, who were making ready to play a new piece. As soon as the first note sounded she moved slowly, her eyes cast down. With fiercely throbbing heart, thinking and desiring and hoping he knew not what, Hilliard once more followed her. Night had now fallen; the grounds of the Exhibition shone with many-coloured illumination; the throng grew dense. It was both easy and necessary to keep very near to the object of his interest.

There sounded a clinking of plates, cups, and glasses. People were sitting at tables in the open air, supplied with refreshments by the waiters who hurried hither and thither. Eve, after a show of hesitation, took a seat by a little round table which stood apart; her pursuer found a place whence he could keep watch. She gave an order, and presently there was brought to her a glass of wine with a sandwich.

Hilliard called for a bottle of ale: he was consumed with thirst.

"Dare I approach her?" he asked himself. "Is it possible? And, if possible, is it any use?"

The difficulty was to explain his recognition of her. But for that, he might justify himself in addressing her.

She had finished her wine and was looking round. Her glance fell upon him, and for a moment rested. With a courage not his own, Hilliard rose, advanced, and respectfully doffed his hat.

"Miss Madeley—"

The note was half interrogative, but his voice failed before he could add another syllable. Eve drew herself up, rigid in the alarm of female instinct.

"I am a stranger to you," Hilliard managed to say. "But I come from Dudley; I know some of your friends—"

His hurried words fell into coherence. At the name "Dudley" Eve's features relaxed.

"Was it you who called at my lodgings the day before yesterday?"

"I did. Your address was given me by Mrs. Brewer, in whose house I have lived for a long time. She wished me to call and to give you a kind message – to say how glad they would be to hear from you—"

"But you *didn't* leave the message."

The smile put Hilliard at his ease, it was so gentle and friendly.

"I wasn't able to come at the time I mentioned. I should have called to-morrow."

"But how is it that you knew me? I think," she added, without waiting for a reply, "that I have seen you somewhere. But I can't remember where."

"Perhaps in the train this evening?"

"Yes; so it was. You knew me then?"

"I thought I did, for I happened to come out from my lodgings at the moment you were leaving yours, just opposite, and we walked almost together to Gower Street station. I must explain that I have taken rooms in Gower Place. I didn't like to speak to you in the street; but now that I have again chanced to see you—"

"I still don't understand," said Eve, who was speaking with the most perfect ease of manner. "I am not the only person living in that house. Why should you take it for granted that I was Miss Madeley?"

Hilliard had not ventured to seat himself; he stood before her, head respectfully bent.

"At Mrs. Brewer's I saw your portrait."

Her eyes fell.

"My portrait. You really could recognise me from that?"

"Oh, readily! Will you allow me to sit down?"

"Of course. I shall be glad to hear the news you have brought. I couldn't imagine who it was had called and wanted to see me. But there's another thing. I didn't think Mrs. Brewer knew my address. I have moved since I wrote to her daughter."

"No; it was the old address she gave me. I ought to have mentioned that: it escaped my mind. First of all I went to Belmont Street."

"Mysteries still!" exclaimed Eve. "The people *there* couldn't know where I had gone to."

"A child who had carried some parcel for you to Gower Place volunteered information."

Outwardly amused, and bearing herself as though no incident could easily disconcert her, Eve did not succeed in suppressing every sign of nervousness. Constrained by his wonder to study her with critical attention, the young man began to feel assured that she was consciously acting a part. That she should be able to carry it off so well, therein lay the marvel. Of course, London had done much for her. Possessing no common gifts, she must have developed remarkably under changed conditions, and might, indeed, have become a very different person from the country girl who toiled to support her drunken father's family. Hilliard remembered the mention of her sister who had gone to Birmingham and disappeared; it suggested a characteristic of the Madeley blood, which possibly must be borne in mind if he would interpret Eve.

She rested her arms on the little round table.

"So Mrs. Brewer asked you to come and find me?"

"It was only a suggestion, and I may as well tell you how it came about. I used to have my meals in Mrs. Brewer's parlour, and to amuse myself I looked over her album. There I found your portrait, and – well, it interested me, and I asked the name of the original."

Hilliard was now in command of himself; he spoke with simple directness, as his desires dictated.

"And Mrs. Brewer," said Eve, with averted eyes, "told you about me?"

"She spoke of you as her daughter's friend," was the evasive answer. Eve seemed to accept it as sufficient, and there was a long silence.

"My name is Hilliard," the young man resumed. "I am taking the first holiday, worth speaking of, that I have known for a good many years. At Dudley my business was to make mechanical drawings, and I can't say that I enjoyed the occupation."

"Are you going back to it?"

"Not just yet. I have been in France, and I may go abroad again before long."

"For your pleasure?" Eve asked, with interest.

"To answer 'Yes' wouldn't quite express what I mean. I am learning to live."

She hastily searched his face for the interpretation of these words, then looked away, with grave, thoughtful countenance.

"By good fortune," Hilliard pursued. "I have become possessed of money enough to live upon for a year or two. At the end of it I may find myself in the old position, and have to be a living machine once more. But I shall be able to remember that I was once a man."

Eve regarded him strangely, with wide, intent eyes, as though his speech had made a peculiar impression upon her.

"Can you see any sense in that?" he asked, smiling.

"Yes. I think I understand you."

She spoke slowly, and Hilliard, watching her, saw in her face more of the expression of her portrait than he had yet discovered. Her soft tone was much more like what he had expected to hear than her utterances hitherto.

"Have you always lived at Dudley?" she asked.

He sketched rapidly the course of his life, without reference to domestic circumstances. Before he had ceased speaking he saw that Eve's look was directed towards something at a distance behind him; she smiled, and at length nodded, in recognition of some person who approached. Then a voice caused him to look round.

"Oh, there you are! I have been hunting for you ever so long."

As soon as Hilliard saw the speaker, he had no difficulty in remembering her. It was Eve's companion of the day before yesterday, with whom she had started for the theatre. The girl evidently felt some surprise at discovering her friend in conversation with a man she did not know; but Eve was equal to the situation, and spoke calmly.

"This gentleman is from my part of the world – from Dudley. Mr. Hilliard – Miss Ringrose."

Hilliard stood up. Miss Ringrose, after attempting a bow of formal dignity, jerked out her hand, gave a shy little laugh, and said with amusing abruptness—

"Do you really come from Dudley?"

"I do really, Miss Ringrose. Why does it sound strange to you?"

"Oh, I don't mean that it sounds strange." She spoke in a high but not unmusical note, very quickly, and with timid glances to either side of her collocutor. "But Eve – Miss Madeley – gave me the idea that Dudley people must be great, rough, sooty men. Don't laugh at me, please. You know very well, Eve, that you always talk in that way. Of course, I knew that there must be people of a different kind, but – there now, you're making me confused, and I don't know what I meant to say."

She was a thin-faced, but rather pretty girl, with auburn hair. Belonging to a class which, especially in its women, has little intelligence to boast of, she yet redeemed herself from the charge of commonness by a certain vivacity of feature and an agreeable suggestion of good feeling in her would-be frank but nervous manner. Hilliard laughed merrily at the vision in her mind of "great, rough, sooty men."

"I'm sorry to disappoint you, Miss Ringrose."

"No, but really – what sort of a place *is* Dudley? Is it true that they call it the Black Country?"

"Let us walk about," interposed Eve. "Mr. Hilliard will tell you all he can about the Black Country."

She moved on, and they rambled aimlessly; among cigar-smoking clerks and shopmen, each with the female of his kind in wondrous hat and drapery; among domestic groups from the middle-class suburbs, and from regions of the artisan; among the frankly rowdy and the solemnly superior; here and there a man in evening dress, generally conscious of his white tie and starched shirt, and a sprinkling of unattached young women with roving eyes. Hilliard, excited by the success of his advances, and by companionship after long solitude, became very unlike himself, talking and jesting freely. Most of the conversation passed between him and Miss Ringrose; Eve had fallen into an absent mood, answered carelessly when addressed, laughed without genuine amusement, and sometimes wore the look of trouble which Hilliard had observed whilst in the train.

Before long she declared that it was time to go home.

"What's the hurry?" said her friend. "It's nothing like ten o'clock yet – is it, Mr. Hilliard?"

"I don't wish to stay any longer. Of course you needn't go unless you like, Patty."

Hilliard had counted on travelling back with her; to his great disappointment, Eve answered his request to be allowed to do so with a coldly civil refusal which there was no misunderstanding.

"But I hope you will let me see you again?"

"As you live so near me," she answered, "we are pretty sure to meet. Are you coming or not, Patty?"

"Oh, of course I shall go if you do."

The young man shook hands with them; rather formally with Eve, with Patty Ringrose as cordially as if they were old friends. And then he lost sight of them amid the throng.

~ *Chapter 7* ~

HOW did Eve Madeley contrive to lead this life of leisure and amusement? The question occupied Hilliard well on into the small hours; he could hit upon no explanation which had the least plausibility.

Was she engaged to be married to the man who met her at the Exhibition? Her behaviour in his company by no means supported such a surmise; yet there must be something more than ordinary acquaintance between the two.

Might not Patty Ringrose be able and willing to solve for him the riddle of Eve's existence? But he had no idea where Patty lived. He recalled her words in Gower Street: "You *are* going it, Eve!" and they stirred miserable doubts; yet something more than mere hope inclined him to believe that the girl's life was innocent. Her look, her talk reassured him; so did her friendship with such a person as the ingenuous Patty. On learning that he dwelt close by her she gave no sign of an uneasy conscience.

In any case, the contrast between her actual life and that suggested by Mrs. Brewer's talk about her was singular enough. It supplied him with a problem of which the interest would not easily be exhausted. But he must pursue the study with due regard to honour and delicacy; he would act the spy no more. As Eve had said, they were pretty sure to meet before long; if his patience failed it was always possible for him to write a letter.

Four days went by and he saw nothing of her. On the fifth, as he was walking homeward in the afternoon, he came face to face with Miss Madeley in Gower Street. She stopped at once, and offered a friendly hand.

"Will you let me walk a little way with you?" he asked.

"Certainly. I'm just going to change a book at Mudie's." She carried a little handbag. "I suppose you have been going about London a great deal? Don't the streets look beautiful at this time of the year?"

"Beautiful? I'm not sure that I see much beauty."

"Oh, don't you? I delight in London. I had dreamt of it all my life before I came here. I always said to myself I should some day live in London."

Her voice to-day had a vibrant quality which seemed to result from some agreeable emotion. Hilliard remarked a gleam in her eyes and a colour in her cheeks which gave her an appearance of better health than a few days ago.

"You never go into the country?" he said, feeling unable to join in her praise of London, though it was intelligible enough to him.

"I go now and then as far as Hampstead Heath," Eve answered with a smile. "If it's fine I shall be there next Sunday with Patty Ringrose."

Hilliard grasped the opportunity. Would she permit him to meet her and Miss Ringrose at Hampstead? Without shadow of constraint or affectation, Eve replied that such a meeting would give her pleasure: she mentioned place and time at which they might conveniently encounter.

He walked with her all the way to the library, and attended her back to Gower Place. The result of this conversation was merely to intensify the conflict of feelings which Eve had excited in him. Her friendliness gave him no genuine satisfaction; her animated mood, in spite of the charm to which he submitted, disturbed him with mistrust. Nothing she said sounded quite sincere, yet it was more difficult than ever to imagine that she played a part quite alien to her disposition.

No word had fallen from her which threw light upon her present circumstances, and he feared to ask any direct question. It had surprised him to learn that she subscribed to Mudie's. The book she brought away with her was a newly published novel, and in the few words they exchanged on the subject while standing at the library counter she seemed to him to exhibit a surprising acquaintance with the literature of the day. Of his own shortcomings in this respect he was but too sensible, and he began to feel himself an intellectual inferior, where every probability had prepared him for the reverse.

The next morning he went to Mudie's on his own account, and came away with volumes chosen from those which lay on the counter. He was tired of wandering about the town, and might as well pass his time in reading.

When Sunday came, he sought the appointed spot at Hampstead, and there, after an hour's waiting, met the two friends. Eve was no longer in her vivacious mood; brilliant sunshine, and the breeze upon the heath, had no power to inspirit her; she spoke in monosyllables, and behaved with unaccountable reserve. Hilliard had no choice but to converse with Patty, who was as gay and entertaining as ever. In the course of their gossip he learnt that Miss Ringrose was employed at a music-shop, kept by her uncle, where she sold the latest songs and dances, and "tried over" on a piano any unfamiliar piece which a customer might think of purchasing. It was not easy to understand how these two girls came to be so intimate, for they seemed to have very little in common. Compared with Eve Madeley,

Patty was an insignificant little person; but of her moral uprightness Hilliard felt only the more assured the longer he talked with her, and this still had a favourable effect upon his estimate of Eve.

Again there passed a few days without event. But about nine o'clock on Wednesday evening, as he sat at home over a book, his landlady entered the room with a surprising announcement.

"There's a young lady wishes to see you, Sir. Miss Ringrose is the name."

Hilliard sprang up.

"Please ask her to come in."

The woman eyed him in a manner he was too excited to understand.

"She would like to speak to you at the door, Sir, if you wouldn't mind going out."

He hastened thither. The front door stood open, and a light from the passage shone on Patty's face. In the girl's look he saw at once that something was wrong.

"Oh, Mr. Hilliard – I didn't know your number – I've been to a lot of houses asking for you—"

"What is it?" he inquired, going out on to the doorstep.

"I called to see Eve, and – I don't know what it meant, but she's gone away. The landlady says she left this morning with her luggage – went away for good. And it's so strange that she hasn't let me know anything. I can't understand it. I wanted to ask if you know—"

Hilliard stared at the house opposite.

"I? I know nothing whatever about it. Come in and tell me—"

"If you wouldn't mind coming out—"

"Yes, yes. One moment; I'll get my hat."

He rejoined the girl, and they turned in the direction of Euston Square, where people were few.

"I couldn't help coming to see you, Mr. Hilliard," said Patty, whose manner indicated the gravest concern. "It has put me in such a fright. I haven't seen her since Sunday. I came to-night, as soon as I could get away from the shop, because I didn't feel easy in my mind about her."

"Why did you feel anxious? What has been going on?"

He searched her face. Patty turned away, kept silence for a moment, and at length, with one of her wonted outbursts of confidence, said nervously:

"It's something I can't explain. But as you were a friend of hers—"

A man came by, and Patty broke off.

~ *Chapter 8* ~

HILLIARD waited for her to continue, but Patty kept her eyes down and said no more.

"Did you think," he asked, "that I was likely to be in Miss Madeley's confidence?"

"You've known her a long time, haven't you?"

This proof of reticence, or perhaps of deliberate misleading, on Eve's part astonished Hilliard. He replied evasively that he had very little acquaintance with Miss Madeley's affairs, and added:

"May she not simply have changed her lodgings?"

"Why should she go so suddenly, and without letting me know?"

"What had the landlady to say?"

"She heard her tell the cab to drive to Mudie's – the library, you know."

"Why," said Hilliard; "that meant, perhaps, that she wanted to return a book before leaving London. Is there any chance that she has gone home – to Dudley? Perhaps her father is ill, and she was sent for."

Patty admitted this possibility, but with every sign of doubt.

"The landlady said she had a letter this morning."

"Did she? Then it may have been from Dudley. But you know her so much better than I do. Of course, you mustn't tell me anything you don't feel it right to speak of; still, did it occur to you that I could be of any use?"

"No, I didn't think; I only came because I was so upset when I found her gone. I knew you lived in Gower Place somewhere, and I thought you might have seen her since Sunday."

"I have not. But surely you will hear from her very soon. You may even get a letter to-night, or to-morrow morning."

Patty gave a little spring of hopefulness.

"Yes; a letter might come by the last post to-night. I'll go home at once."

"And I will come with you," said Hilliard. "Then you can tell me whether you have any news."

They turned and walked towards the foot of Hampstead Road, whence they could go by tram-car to Patty's abode in High Street, Camden Town. Supported by the hope of finding a letter when she arrived, Miss Ringrose grew more like herself.

"You must have wondered what*ever* I meant by calling to see you, Mr. Hilliard. I went to five or six houses before I hit on the right one. I do wish now that I'd waited a little, but I'm always doing things in that way and being sorry for them directly after. Eve is my best friend, you know, and that makes me so anxious about her."

"How long have you known her?"

"Oh, ever so long – about a year."

The temptation to make another inquiry was too strong for Hilliard.

"Where has she been employed of late?"

Patty looked up at him with surprise.

"Oh, don't you know? She isn't doing anything now. The people where she was went bankrupt, and she's been out of a place for more than a month."

"Can't find another engagement?"

"She hasn't tried yet. She's taking a holiday. It isn't very nice work, adding up money all day. I'm sure it would drive me out of my senses very soon. I think she might find something better than that."

Miss Ringrose continued to talk of her friend all the way to Camden Town, but the information he gathered did not serve to advance Hilliard in his understanding of Eve's character. That she was keeping back something of grave import the girl had already confessed, and in her chatter she frequently checked herself on the verge of an indiscretion. Hilliard took for granted that the mystery had to do with the man he had seen at Earl's Court. If Eve actually disappeared, he would not scruple to extract from Patty all that she knew; but he must see first whether Eve would communicate with her friend.

In High Street Patty entered a small shop which was on the point of being closed for the night.

Hilliard waited for her a few yards away; on her return he saw at once that she was disappointed.

"There's nothing!"

"It may come in the morning. I should like to know whether you hear or not."

"Would this be out of your way?" asked Patty. "I'm generally alone in the shop from half-past one to half-past two. There's very seldom any business going on then."

"Then I will come to-morrow at that time."

"Do, please? If I haven't heard anything I shall be that nervous."

They talked to no purpose for a few minutes, and bade each other good-night.

Next day, at the hour Patty had appointed, Hilliard was again in High Street. As he approached the shop he heard from within the jingle of a piano. A survey through the closed glass door showed him Miss Ringrose playing for her own amusement. He entered, and Patty jumped up with a smile of welcome.

"It's all right! I had a letter this morning. She *has* gone to Dudley."

"Ah! I am glad to hear it. Any reason given?"

"Nothing particular," answered the girl, striking a note on the piano with her forefinger. "She thought she might as well go home for a week or two before taking another place. She has heard of something in Holborn."

"So your alarm was groundless."

"Oh – I didn't really feel alarmed, Mr. Hilliard. You mustn't think that. I often do silly things."

Patty's look and tone were far from reassuring. Evidently she had been relieved from her suspense, but no less plainly did she seek to avoid an explanation of it. Hilliard began to glance about the shop.

"My uncle," resumed Patty, turning with her wonted sprightliness to another subject, "always goes out for an hour or two in the middle of the day to play billiards. I can tell by his face when he comes back whether he's lost or won; he does so take it to heart, silly man! Do *you* play billiards?"

The other shook his head.

"I thought not. You have a serious look."

Hilliard did not relish this compliment. He imagined he had cast away his gloom; he desired to look like the men who take life with easy courage. As he gazed through the glass door into the street, a figure suddenly blocked his prospect, and a face looked in. Then the door opened, and there entered a young man of clerkly appearance, who glanced from Miss Ringrose to her companion with an air of severity. Patty had reddened a little.

"What are *you* doing here at this time of day?" she asked familiarly.

"Oh – business – had to look up a man over here. Thought I'd speak a word as I passed."

Hilliard drew aside.

"Who has opened this new shop opposite?" added the young man, beckoning from the doorway.

A more transparent pretext for drawing Patty away could not have been conceived; but she readily lent herself to it, and followed. The door closed behind them. In a few minutes Patty returned alone, with rosy cheeks and mutinous lips.

"I'm very sorry to have been in the way," said Hilliard, smiling.

"*It's all right! I had a letter this morning. She* has *gone to Dudley.*"

"Oh, not you. It's all right. Someone I know. He can be sensible enough when he likes, but sometimes he's such a silly there's no putting up with him. Have you heard the new waltz – the Ballroom Queen?"

She sat down and rattled over this exhilarating masterpiece.

"Thank you," said Hilliard. "You play very cleverly."

"Oh, so can anybody – that's nothing."

"Does Miss Madeley play at all?"

"No. She's always saying she wishes she could; but I tell her, what does it matter? She knows no end of things that I don't, and I'd a good deal rather have that."

"She reads a good deal, I suppose?"

"Oh, I should think she does, just! And she can speak French."

"Indeed? How did she learn?"

"At the place where she was bookkeeper there was a young lady from Paris, and they shared lodgings, and Eve learnt it from her. Then her friend went to Paris again, and Eve wanted very much to go with her, but she didn't see how to manage it. Eve," she added, with a laugh, "is always wanting to do something that's impossible."

A week later, Hilliard again called at the music-shop, and talked for half an hour with Miss Ringrose, who had no fresh news from Eve. His visits were repeated at intervals of a few days, and at length, towards the end of June, he learnt that Miss Madeley was about to return to London; she had obtained a new engagement, at the establishment in Holborn of which Patty had spoken.

"And will she come back to her old lodgings?" he inquired.

Patty shook her head.

"She'll stay with me. I wanted her to come here before, but she didn't care about it. Now she's altered her mind, and I'm very glad."

Hilliard hesitated in putting the next question.

"Do you still feel anxious about her?"

The girl met his eyes for an instant.

"No. It's all right now."

"There's one thing I should like you to tell me – if you can."

"About Miss Madeley?"

"I don't think there can be any harm in your saying yes or no. Is she engaged to be married?"

Patty replied with a certain eagerness.

"No! Indeed she isn't. And she never has been."

"Thank you." Hilliard gave a sigh of relief. "I'm very glad to know that."

"Of course you are," Patty answered, with a laugh.

As usual, after one of her frank remarks, she turned away and struck chords on the piano. Hilliard meditated the while, until his companion spoke again.

"You'll see her before long, I dare say?"

"Perhaps. I don't know."

"At all events, you'll *want* to see her."

"Most likely."

"Will you promise me something?"

"If it's in my power to keep the promise."

"It's only – I should be so glad if you wouldn't mention anything about my coming to see you that night in Gower Place."

"I won't speak of it."

"Quite sure?"

"You may depend upon me. Would you rather she didn't know that I have seen you at all?"

"Oh, there's no harm in that. I should be sure to let it out. I shall say we met by chance somewhere."

"Very well. I feel tempted to ask a promise in return."

Patty stood with her hands behind her, eyes wide and lips slightly apart.

"It is this," he continued, lowering his voice. "If ever you should begin to feel anxious again about her will you let me know?"

Her reply was delayed; it came at length in the form of an embarrassed nod. Thereupon Hilliard pressed her hand and departed.

He knew the day on which Eve would arrive in London; from morning to night a feverish unrest drove him about the streets. On the morrow he was scarcely more at ease, and for several days he lived totally without occupation, save in his harassing thoughts. He paced and repaced the length of Holborn, wondering where it was that Eve had found employment; but from Camden Town he held aloof.

One morning there arrived for him a postcard on which was scribbled: "We are going to the Savoy on Saturday night. Gallery." No signature, no address; but of course the writer must be Patty Ringrose. Mentally, he thanked her with much fervour. And on the stated evening, nearly an hour before the opening of the doors, he climbed the stone steps leading to the gallery entrance of the Savoy Theatre. At the summit two or three persons were already waiting – strangers to him. He leaned against the wall, and read an evening paper. At every sound of approaching feet his eyes watched with covert eagerness. Presently he heard a laugh, echoing from below, and recognised Patty's voice; then Miss Ringrose appeared round the winding in the staircase, and was followed by Eve Madeley. Patty glanced up, and smiled consciously as she discovered the face she had expected to see; but Eve remained for some minutes unaware of her acquaintance's proximity. Scrutinising her appearance, as he could at his ease, Hilliard thought she looked far from well: she had a tired, dispirited expression, and paid no heed to the people about her. Her dress was much plainer than that she wore a month ago.

He saw Patty whispering to her companion, and, as a result, Eve's eyes turned in his direction. He met her look, and had no difficulty in making his way down two or three steps, to join her. The reception she gave him was one of civil indifference. Hilliard made no remark on what seemed the chance of their encounter, nor did he speak of her absence from London; they talked, as far as talk was possible under the circumstances, of theatrical and kindred subjects. He could not perceive that the girl was either glad or sorry to have met him again; but by degrees her mood brightened a little, and she exclaimed with pleasure when the opening of the door caused an upward movement.

"You have been away," he said, when they were in their places, he at one side of Eve, Patty on the other.

"Yes. At Dudley."

"Did you see Mrs. Brewer?"

"Several times. She hasn't got another lodger yet, and wishes you would go back again. A most excellent character she gave you."

This sounded satirical.

"I deserved the best she could say of me," Hilliard answered.

Eve glanced at him, smiled doubtfully, and turned to talk with Patty Ringrose. Through the evening there was no further mention of Dudley. Eve could with difficulty be induced to converse at all, and when the entertainment was over she pointedly took leave of him within the theatre. But while shaking hands with Patty, he saw something in that young lady's face which caused him to nod and smile.

~ *Chapter 9* ~

THERE came an afternoon early in July when Hilliard, tired with a long ramble in search of old City churches – his architectural interests never failed – sought rest and coolness in a Fleet Street tavern of time-honoured name. It was long since he had yielded to any extravagance; to-day his palate demanded wine, and with wine he solaced it. When he went forth again into the roaring highway things glowed before him in a mellow light: the sounds of Fleet Street made music to his ears; he looked with joyous benignity into the faces of men and women, and nowhere discovered a countenance inharmonious with his gallant mood.

No longer weary, he strolled westward, content with the satisfactions of each passing moment. "This," he said to himself, "is the joy of life. Past and future are alike powerless over me; I live in the glorious sunlight of this summer day, under the benediction of a great-hearted wine. Noble wine! Friend of the friendless, companion of the solitary, lifter-up of hearts that are oppressed, inspirer of brave thoughts in them that fail beneath the burden of being. Thanks to thee, O priceless wine!"

A bookseller's window arrested him. There, open to the gaze of every pedestrian, stood a volume of which the sight made him thrill with rapture; a finely illustrated folio, a treatise on the Cathedrals of France. Five guineas was the price it bore. A moment's lingering, restrained by some ignoble spirit of thrift which the wine had not utterly overcome, and he entered the shop. He purchased the volume. It would have pleased him to carry it away, but in mere good-nature he allowed the shopman's suggestion to prevail, and gave his address that the great tome might be sent to him.

How cheap it was – five guineas for so much instant delight and such boundless joy of anticipation!

On one of the benches in Trafalgar Square he sat for a long time watching the fountains, and ever and anon letting them lead his eyes upwards to the great snowy clouds that gleamed upon the profound blue. Some ragged children were at play near him; he searched his pocket, collected coppers and small silver, and with a friendly cry of "Holloa, you ragamuffins!" scattered amazement and delight.

St. Martin's Church told him that the hour was turned of six. Then a purpose that had hung vaguely in his mind like a golden mist took form and substance. He set off to walk northward, came out into Holborn, and loitered in the neighbourhood of a certain place of business, which of late he had many times observed. It was not long that he had to wait. Presently there came forth someone whom he knew, and with quick steps he gained her side.

Eve Madeley perceived him without surprise.

"Yes," he said, "I am here again. If it's disagreeable to you, tell me, and I will go my own way at once."

"I have no wish to send you away," she answered, with a smile of self-possession. "But all the same, I think it would be wiser if you did go."

"Ah, then, if you leave me to judge for myself—! You look tired this evening. I have something to say to you; let us turn for a moment up this byway."

"No, let us walk straight on."

"I beg of you! – Now you are kind. I am going to dine at a restaurant. Usually, I eat my dinner at home – a bad dinner and a cheerless room. On such an evening as this I can't go back and appease hunger in that animal way. But when I sit down in the restaurant I shall be alone. It's miserable to see the groups of people enjoying themselves all round and to sit lonely. I can't tell you how long it is since I had a meal in company. Will you come and dine with me?"

"I can't do that."

"Where's the impossibility?"

"I shouldn't like to do it."

"But would it be so very disagreeable to sit and talk? Or, I won't ask you to talk; only to let me talk to you. Give me an hour or two of your time – that's what I ask. It means so much to me, and to you, what does it matter?"

Eve walked on in silence; his entreaties kept pace with her. At length she stopped.

"It's all the same to me – if you wish it—"

"Thank you a thousand times!"

They walked back into Holborn, and Hilliard, talking merely of trifles, led the way to a great hall, where some scores of people were already dining. He selected a nook which gave assurance of privacy, sketched to the waiter a modest but carefully chosen repast, and from his seat on the opposite side of the table laughed silently at Eve as she leaned back on the plush cushions. In no way disconcerted by the show of luxury about her, Eve seemed to be reflecting, not without enjoyment.

"You would rather be here than going home in the Camden Town 'bus?"

"Of course."

"That's what I like in you. You have courage to tell the truth. When you said that you couldn't come, it was what you really thought. Now that you have learnt your mistake, you confess it."

"I couldn't have done it if I hadn't made up my mind that it was all the same, whether I came or refused."

"All the same to you. Yes; I'm quite willing that you should think it so. It puts me at my ease. I have nothing to reproach myself with. Ah, but how good it is to sit here and talk!"

"Don't you know anyone else who would come with you? Haven't you made any friends?"

"Not one. You and Miss Ringrose are the only persons I know in London."

"I can't understand why you live in that way."

"How should I make friends – among men? Why, it's harder than making money – which I have never done yet, and never shall, I'm afraid."

Eve averted her eyes, and again seemed to meditate.

"I'll tell you," pursued the young man "how the money came to me that I am living on now. It'll fill up the few moments while we are waiting."

He made of it an entertaining narrative, which he concluded just as the soup was laid before them. Eve listened with frank curiosity, with an amused smile. Then came a lull in the conversation. Hilliard began his dinner with appetite and gusto; the girl, after a few sips, neglected her soup and glanced about the neighbouring tables.

"In my position," said Hilliard at length, "what would you have done?"

"It's a difficult thing to put myself in your position."

"Is it, really? Why, then, I will tell you something more of myself. You say that Mrs. Brewer gave me an excellent character?"

"I certainly shouldn't have known you from her description."

Hilliard laughed.

"I seem to you so disreputable?"

"Not exactly that," replied Eve thoughtfully. "But you seem altogether a different person from what you seemed to her."

"Yes, I can understand that. And it gives me an opportunity for saying that you, Miss Madeley, are as different as possible from the idea I formed of you when I heard Mrs. Brewer's description."

"She described me? I should so like to hear what she said."

The changing of plates imposed a brief silence. Hilliard drank a glass of wine and saw that Eve just touched hers with her lips.

"You shall hear that – but not now. I want to enable you to judge me, and if I let you know the facts while dinner goes on it won't be so tiresome as if I began solemnly to tell you my life, as people do in novels."

He erred, if anything, on the side of brevity, but in the succeeding quarter of an hour Eve was able to gather from his careless talk, which sedulously avoided the pathetic note, a fair notion of what his existence had been from boyhood upward. It supplemented the account of himself she had received from him when they met for the first time. As he proceeded she grew more attentive, and occasionally allowed her eyes to encounter his.

"There's only one other person who has heard all this from me," he said at length. "That's a friend of mine at Birmingham – a man called Narramore. When I got Dengate's money I went to Narramore, and I told him what use I was going to make of it."

"That's what you haven't told me," remarked the listener.

"I will, now that you can understand me. I resolved to go right away from all the sights and sounds that I hated, and to live a man's life, for just as long as the money would last."

"What do you mean by a man's life?"

"Why, a life of enjoyment, instead of a life not worthy to be called life at all. This is part of it, this evening. I have had enjoyable hours since I left Dudley, but never yet one like this. And because I owe it to you, I shall remember you with gratitude as long as I remember anything at all."

"That's a mistake," said Eve. "You owe the enjoyment, whatever it is, to your money, not to me."

"You prefer to look at it in that way. Be it so. I had a delightful month in Paris, but I was driven back to England by loneliness. Now, if *you* had been there! If I could have seen you each evening for an hour or two, had dinner with you at the restaurant, talked with you about what I had seen in the day – but that would have been perfection, and I have never hoped for more than moderate, average pleasure – such as ordinary well-to-do men take as their right."

"What did you do in Paris?"

"Saw things I have longed to see any time the last fifteen years or so. Learned to talk a little French. Got to feel a better educated man than I was before."

"Didn't Dudley seem a long way off when you were there?" asked Eve half absently.

"In another planet. – You thought once of going to Paris; Miss Ringrose told me."

Eve knitted her brows, and made no answer.

~ *Chapter 10* ~

WHEN fruit had been set before them – and as he was peeling a banana:

"What a vast difference," said Hilliard, "between the life of people who dine, and of those who don't! It isn't the mere pleasure of eating, the quality of the food – though that must have a great influence on mind and character. But to sit for an hour or two each evening in quiet, orderly enjoyment, with graceful things about one, talking of whatever is pleasant – how it civilises! Until three months ago I never dined in my life, and I know well what a change it has made in me."

"I never dined till this evening," said Eve.

"Never? This is the first time you have been at a restaurant?"

"For dinner – yes."

Hilliard heard the avowal with surprise and delight. After all, there could not have been much intimacy between her and the man she met at the Exhibition.

"When I go back to slavery," he continued, "I shall bear it more philosophically. It was making me a brute, but I think there'll be no more danger of that. The memory of civilisation will abide with me. I shall remind myself that I was once a free man, and that will support me."

Eve regarded him with curiosity.

"Is there no choice?" she asked. "While you have money, couldn't you find some better way of earning a living?"

"I have given it a thought now and then, but it's very doubtful. There's only one thing at which I might have done well, and that's architecture. From studying it just for my own pleasure, I believe I know more about architecture than most men who are not in the profession; but it would take a long time before I could earn money by it. I could prepare myself to be an architectural draughtsman, no doubt, and might do as well that way as drawing machinery. But—"

"Then why don't you go to work! It would save you from living in hideous places."

"After all, does it matter much? If I had anything else to gain. Suppose I had any hope of marriage, for instance—"

He said it playfully. Eve turned her eyes away, but gave no other sign of self-consciousness.

"I have no such hope. I have seen too much of marriage in poverty."

"So have I," said his companion, with quiet emphasis.

"And when a man's absolutely sure that he will never have an income of more than a hundred and fifty pounds—"

"It's a crime if he asks a woman to share it," Eve added coldly.

"I agree with you. It's well to understand each other on that point. – Talking of architecture, I bought a grand book this afternoon."

He described the purchase, and mentioned what it cost.

"But at that rate," said Eve, "your days of slavery will come again very soon."

"Oh! it's so rarely that I spend a large sum. On most days I satisfy myself with the feeling of freedom, and live as poorly as ever I did. Still, don't suppose that I am bent on making my money last a very long time. I can imagine myself spending it all in a week or two, and feeling I had its worth. The only question is, how can I get most enjoyment? The very best of a lifetime may come within a single day. Indeed, I believe it very often does."

"I doubt that – at least, I know that it couldn't be so with me."

"Well, what do you aim at?" Hilliard asked disinterestedly.

"Safety," was the prompt reply.

"Safety? From what?"

"From years of struggle to keep myself alive, and a miserable old age."

"Then you might have said – a safety-match."

The jest, and its unexpectedness, struck sudden laughter from Eve. Hilliard joined in her mirth.

After that she suggested, "Hadn't we better go?"

"Yes. Let us walk quietly on. The streets are pleasant after sunset."

On rising, after he had paid the bill, Hilliard chanced to see himself in a mirror. He had flushed cheeks, and his hair was somewhat disorderly. In contrast with Eve's colourless composure, his appearance was decidedly bacchanalian; but the thought merely amused him.

They crossed Holborn, and took their way up Southampton Row, neither speaking until they were within sight of Russell Square.

"I like this part of London," said Hilliard at length, pointing before him. "I often walk about the squares late at night. It's quiet, and the trees make the air taste fresh."

"I did the same, sometimes, when I lived in Gower Place."

"Doesn't it strike you that we are rather like each other in some things?"

"Oh, yes!" Eve replied frankly. "I have noticed that."

"You have? Even in the lives we have led there's a sort of resemblance, isn't there?"

"Yes, I see now that there is."

In Russell Square they turned from the pavement, and walked along the edge of the enclosure.

"I wish Patty had been with us," said Eve all at once. "She would have enjoyed it so thoroughly."

"To be sure she would. Well, we can dine again, and have Patty with us. But, after all, dining in London can't be quite what it is in Paris. I wish you hadn't gone back to work again. Do you know what I should have proposed?"

She glanced inquiringly at him.

"Why shouldn't we all have gone to Paris for a holiday? You and Patty could have lived together, and I should have seen you every day."

Eve laughed.

"Why not? Patty and I have both so much more money than we know what to do with," she answered.

"Money? Oh, what of that! I have money."

She laughed again.

Hilliard was startled.

"You are talking rather wildly. Leaving myself out of the question, what would Mr. Dally say to such a proposal?"

"Who's Mr. Dally?"

"Don't you know? Hasn't Patty told you that she is engaged?"

"Ah! No; she hasn't spoken of it. But I think I must have seen him at the music-shop one day. Is she likely to marry him?"

"It isn't the wisest thing she could do, but that may be the end of it. He's in an auctioneer's office, and may have a pretty good income some day."

A long silence followed. They passed out of Russell into Woburn Square. Night was now darkening the latest tints of the sky, and the lamps shone golden against dusty green. At one of the houses in the narrow square festivities were toward; carriages drew up before the entrance, from which a red carpet was laid down across the pavement; within sounded music.

"Does this kind of thing excite any ambition in you?" Hilliard asked, coming to a pause a few yards away from the carriage which was discharging its occupants.

"Yes, I suppose it does. At all events, it makes me feel discontented."

"I have settled all that with myself. I am content to look on as if it were a play. Those people have an idea of life quite different from mine. I shouldn't enjoy myself among them. You, perhaps, would."

"I might," Eve replied absently. And she turned away to the other side of the square.

"By-the-bye, you *have* a friend in Paris. Do you ever hear from her?"

"She wrote once or twice after she went back; but it has come to an end."

"Still, you might find her again, if you were there."

Eve delayed her reply a little, then spoke impatiently.

"What is the use of setting my thoughts upon such things? Day after day I try to forget what I most wish for. Talk about yourself, and I will listen with pleasure; but never talk about me."

"It's very hard to lay that rule upon me. I want to hear you speak of yourself. As yet, I hardly know you, and I never shall unless you—"

"Why should you know me?" she interrupted, in a voice of irritation.

"Only because I wish it more than anything else, I have wished it from the day when I first saw your portrait."

"Oh! that wretched portrait! I should be sorry if I thought it was at all like me."

"It is both like and unlike," said Hilliard. "What I see of it in your face is the part of you that most pleases me."

"And that isn't my real self at all."

"Perhaps not. And yet, perhaps, you are mistaken. That is what I want to learn. From the portrait, I formed an idea of you. When I met you, it seemed to me that I was hopelessly astray; yet now I don't feel sure of it."

"You would like to know what has changed me from the kind of girl I was at Dudley?"

"*Are* you changed?"

"In some ways, no doubt. You, at all events, seem to think so."

"I can wait. You will tell me all about it some day."

"You mustn't take that for granted. We have made friends in a sort of way just because we happened to come from the same place, and know the same people. But—"

He waited.

"Well, I was going to say that there's no use in our thinking much about each other."

"I don't ask you to think of me. But I shall think a great deal about you for long enough to come."

"That's what I want to prevent."

"Why?"

"Because, in the end, it might be troublesome to me."

Hilliard kept silence awhile, then laughed. When he spoke again, it was of things indifferent.

~ *Chapter 11* ~

LAZIEST of men and worst of correspondents, Robert Narramore had as yet sent no reply to the letters in which Hilliard acquainted him with his adventures in London and abroad; but at the end of July he vouchsafed a perfunctory scrawl. "Too bad not to write before, but I've been floored every evening after business in this furious heat. You may like to hear that my uncle's property didn't make a bad show. I have come in for a round five thousand, and am putting it into brass bedsteads. Shan't be able to get away until the end of August. May see you then." Hilliard mused enviously on the brass bedstead business.

On looking in at the Camden Town music-shop about this time he found Patty Ringrose flurried and vexed by an event which disturbed her prospects. Her uncle the shopkeeper, a widower of about fifty, had announced his intention of marrying again, and, worse still, of giving up his business.

"It's the landlady of the public-house where he goes to play billiards," said Patty with scornful mirth; "a great fat woman! Oh! And he's going to turn publican. And my aunt and me will have to look out for ourselves."

This aunt was the shopkeeper's maiden sister who had hitherto kept house for him. "She had been promised an allowance," said Patty, "but a very mean one."

"I don't care much for myself," the girl went on; "there's plenty of shops where I can get an engagement, but of course it won't be the same as here, which has been home for me ever since I was a child. There! the things that men will do! I've told him plain to his face that he ought to be ashamed of himself, and so has aunt. And he *is* ashamed, what's more. Don't you call it disgusting, such a marriage as that?"

Hilliard avoided the delicate question.

"I shouldn't wonder if it hastens another marriage," he said with a smile.

"I know what you mean, but the chances are that marriage won't come off at all. I'm getting tired of men; they're so selfish and unreasonable. Of course I don't mean you, Mr. Hilliard, but – oh! you know what I mean."

"Mr. Dally has fallen under your displeasure?"

"Please don't talk about him. If he thinks he's going to lay down the law to me he'll find his mistake; and it's better he should find it out before it's too late."

They were interrupted by the entrance of Patty's amorous uncle, who returned from his billiards earlier than usual to-day. He scowled at the stranger, but passed into the house without speaking. Hilliard spoke a hurried word or two about Eve and went his way.

Something less than a week after this he chanced to be away from home throughout the whole day, and on returning he was surprised to see a telegram upon his table. It came from Patty Ringrose, and asked him to call at the shop without fail between one and two that day. The hour was now nearly ten; the despatch had arrived at eleven in the morning.

Without a minute's delay he ran out in search of a cab, and was driven to High Street. Here, of course, he found the shop closed, but it was much too early for the household to have retired to rest; risking an indiscretion, he was about to ring the house bell when the door opened, and Patty showed herself.

"Oh, is it *you*, Mr. Hilliard!" she exclaimed, in a flurried voice. "I heard the cab stop, and I thought it might be—You'd better come in – quick!"

He followed her along the passage and into the shop, where one gas-jet was burning low.

"Listen!" she resumed, whispering hurriedly. "If Eve comes – she'll let herself in with the latchkey – you must stand quiet here. I shall turn out the gas, and I'll let you out after she's gone upstairs? Couldn't you come before?"

Hilliard explained, and begged her to tell him what was the matter. But Patty kept him in suspense.

"Uncle won't be in till after twelve, so there's no fear. Aunt has gone to bed – she's upset with quarrelling about this marriage. Mind! You won't stir if Eve comes in. Don't talk loud; I must keep listening for the door."

"But what is it? Where is Eve?"

"I don't know. She didn't come home till very late last night, and I don't know where she was. You remember what you asked me to promise?"

"To let me know if you were anxious about her."

"Yes, and I am. She's in danger. I only hope—"

"What?"

"I don't like to tell you all I know. It doesn't seem right. But I'm so afraid for Eve."

"I can only imagine one kind of danger—"

"Yes – of course, it's that – you know what I mean. But there's more than you could fancy."

"Tell me, then, what has alarmed you?"

"When did you see her last?" Patty inquired.

"More than a week ago. Two or three days before I came here."

"Had you noticed anything?"

"Nothing unusual."

"No more did I, till last Monday night. Then I saw that something was wrong. Hush!"

She gripped his arm, and they listened. But no sound could be heard.

"And since then," Patty pursued, with tremulous eagerness, "she's been very queer. I know she doesn't sleep at night, and she's getting ill, and she's had letters from – someone she oughtn't to have anything to do with."

"Having told so much, you had better tell me all," said Hilliard impatiently. There was a cold sweat on his forehead, and his heart beat painfully.

"No. I can't. I can only give you a warning."

"But what's the use of that? What can I do? How can I interfere?"

"I don't know," replied the girl, with a helpless sigh. "She's in danger, that's all I call tell you."

"Patty, don't be a fool! Out with it! Who is the man? Is it some one you know?"

"I don't exactly know him. I've seen him."

"Is he – a sort of gentleman?"

"Oh, yes, he's a gentleman. And you'd never think to look at him that he could do anything that wasn't right."

"Very well. What reason have you for supposing that he's doing wrong?"

Patty kept silence. A band of rowdy fellows just then came shouting along the street, and one of them crashed up against the shop door, making Patty jump and scream. Oaths and foul language followed; and then the uproar passed away.

"Look here," said Hilliard. "You'll drive me out of my senses. Eve is in love with this man, is she?"

"I'm afraid so. She was."

"Before she went away, you mean. And, of course, her going away had something to do with it?"

"Yes, it had."

Hilliard laid his hands on the girl's shoulders.

"You've got to tell me the plain truth, and be quick about it. I suppose you haven't any idea of the torments I'm suffering. I shall begin to think you're making a fool of me, and that there's nothing but – though that's bad enough for me."

"Very well, I'll tell you. She went away because it came out that the man was married."

"Oh, that's it?" He spoke from a dry throat. "She told you herself?"

"Yes, not long after she came back. She said, of course, she could have no more to do with him. She used to meet him pretty often—"

"Stay, how did she get to know him first?"

"Just by chance – somewhere."

"I understand," said Hilliard grimly. "Go on."

"And his wife got someone to spy on him, and they found out he was meeting Eve, and she jumped out on them when they were walking somewhere together, and told Eve everything. He wasn't living with his wife, and hasn't been for a long time."

"What's his position?"

"He's in business, and seems to have lots of money; but I don't exactly know what it is he does."

"You are afraid, then, that Eve is being drawn back to him?"

"I feel sure she is – and it's dreadful."

"What I should like to know," said Hilliard, harshly, "is whether she really cares for him, or only for his money."

"Oh! How horrid you are! I never thought you could say such a thing!"

"Perhaps you didn't. All the same, it's a question. I don't pretend to understand Eve Madeley, and I'm afraid you are just as far from knowing her."

"I don't know her? Why, what are you talking about, Mr. Hilliard?"

"What do you think of her, then? Is she a good-hearted girl or—"

"Or what? Of course she's good-hearted. The things that men do say! They seem to be all alike."

"Women are so far from being all alike that one may think she understands another, and be utterly deceived. Eve has shown her best side to you, no doubt. With me, she hasn't taken any trouble to do so. And if—"

"Hush!"

This time the alarm was justified. A latchkey rattled at the house-door, the door opened, and in the same moment Patty turned out the light.

"It's my uncle," she whispered, terror-stricken. "Don't stir."

~ *Chapter 12* ~

A HEAVY footstep sounded in the passage, and Hilliard, to whose emotions was now added a sense of ludicrous indignity, heard talk between Patty and her uncle.

"You mustn't lock up yet," said the girl, "Eve is out."

"What's she doing?"

"I don't know. At the theatre with friends, I dare say."

"If we'd been staying on here, that young woman would have had to look out for another lodging. There's something I don't like about her, and if you take my advice, Patty, you'll shake her off. She'll do you no good, my girl."

They passed together into the room behind the shop, and though their voices were still audible, Hilliard could no longer follow the conversation. He stood motionless, just where Patty had left him, with a hand resting on the top of the piano, and it seemed to him that at least half an hour went by. Then a sound close by made him start; it was the snapping of a violin string; the note reverberated through the silent shop. But by this time the murmur of conversation had ceased, and Hilliard hoped that Patty's uncle had gone upstairs to bed.

As proved to be the case. Presently the door opened, and a voice called to him in a whisper. He obeyed the summons, and, not without stumbling, followed Patty into the open air.

"She hasn't come yet."

"What's the time?"

"Half-past eleven. I shall sit up for her. Did you hear what my uncle said? You mustn't think anything of that; he's always finding fault with people."

"Do you think she will come at all?" asked Hilliard.

"Oh, of course she will!"

"I shall wait about. Don't stand here. Good-night."

"You won't let her know what I've told you?" said Patty, retaining his hand.

"No, I won't. If she doesn't come back at all, I'll see you to-morrow."

He moved away, and the door closed.

Many people were still passing along the street. In his uncertainty as to the direction by which Eve would return – if return she did—Hilliard ventured only a few yards away. He had waited for about a quarter of an hour, when his eye distinguished a well-known figure quickly approaching. He hurried forward, and Eve stopped before he had quite come up to her.

"Where have you been to-night?" were his first words, sounding more roughly than he intended.

"I wanted to see you, I passed your lodgings and saw there was no light in the windows, else I should have asked for you."

She spoke in so strange a voice, with such show of agitation, that Hilliard stood gazing at her till she again broke silence.

"Have you been waiting here for me?"

"Yes. Patty told me you weren't back."

"Why did you come?"

"Why do I ever come to meet you?"

"We can't talk here," said Eve, turning away. "Come into a quieter place."

They walked in silence to the foot of High Street, and there turned aside into the shadowed solitude of Mornington Crescent. Eve checked her steps and said abruptly—

"I want to ask you for something."

"What is it?"

"Now that it comes to saying it, I – I'm afraid. And yet if I had asked you that evening when we were at the restaurant—"

"What is it?" Hilliard repeated gruffly.

"That isn't your usual way of speaking to me."

"Will you tell me where you have been tonight?"

"Nowhere – walking about—"

"Do you often walk about the streets till midnight?"

"Indeed I don't."

The reply surprised him by its humility. Her voice all but broke on the words. As well as the dim light would allow, he searched her face, and it seemed to him that her eyes had a redness, as if from shedding tears.

"You haven't been alone?"

"No – I've been with a friend."

"Well, I have no claim upon you. It's nothing to me what friends you go about with. What were you going to ask of me?"

"You have changed so all at once. I thought you would never talk in this way."

"I didn't mean to," said Hilliard. "I have lost control of myself, that's all. But you can say whatever you meant to say – just as you would have done at the restaurant. I'm the same man I was then."

Eve moved a few steps, but he did not follow her, and she returned. A policeman passing threw a glance at them.

"It's no use asking what I meant to ask," she said, with her eyes on the ground. "You won't grant it me."

"How can I say till I know what it is? There are not many things in my power that I wouldn't do for you."

"I was going to ask for money."

"Money? Why, it depends what you are going to do with it. If it will do you any good, all the money I have is yours, as you know well enough. But I must understand why you want it."

"I can't tell you that. I don't want you to give me money – only to lend it. You shall have it back again, though I can't promise the exact time. If you hadn't changed so, I should have found it easy enough to ask. But I don't know you to-night; it's like talking to a stranger. What has happened to make you so different?"

"I have been waiting a long time for you, that's all," Hilliard replied, endeavouring to use the tone of frank friendliness in which he had been wont to address her. "I got nervous and irritable. I felt uneasy about you. It's all right now. Let us walk on a little. You want money. Well, I have three hundred pounds and more. Call it mine, call it yours. But I must know that you're not going to do anything foolish. Of course, you don't tell me everything; I have no right to expect it. You haven't misled me; I knew from the first that – well, a girl of your age, and with your face, doesn't live alone in London without adventures. I shouldn't think of telling you all mine, and I don't ask to know yours – unless I begin to have a part in them. There's something wrong: of course, I can see that. I think you've been crying, and you don't shed tears for a trifle. Now you come and ask me for money. If it will do you good, take all you want. But I've an uncomfortable suspicion that harm may come of it."

"Why not treat me just like a man-friend? I'm old enough to take care of myself."

"You think so, but I know better. Wait a moment. How much money do you want?"

"Thirty-five pounds."

"Exactly thirty-five? And it isn't for your own use?"

"I can't tell you any more. I am in very great need of the money, and if you will lend it me I shall feel very grateful."

"I want no gratitude, I want nothing from you, Eve, except what you can't give me. I can imagine a man in my position giving you money in the hope that it might be your ruin just to see you brought down, humiliated. There's so much of the brute in us all. But I don't feel that desire."

"Why should you?" she asked, with a change to coldness. "What harm have I done you?"

"No harm at all, and perhaps a great deal of good. I say that I wish you nothing but well. Suppose a gift of all the money I have would smooth your whole life before you, and make you the happy wife of some other man. I would give it you gladly. That kind of thing has often been said, when it meant nothing: it isn't so with me. It has always been more pleasure to me to give than to receive. No merit of mine; I have it from my father. Make clear to me that you are to benefit by this money, and you shall have the cheque as soon as you please."

"I shall benefit by it, because it will relieve me from a dreadful anxiety."

"Or, in other words, will relieve someone else?"

"I can speak only of myself. The kindness will be done to me."

"I must know more than that. Come now, we assume that there's someone in the background. A friend of yours, let us say. I can't imagine why this friend of yours wants money, but so it is. You don't contradict me?"

Eve remained mute, her head bent.

"What about your friend and you in the future? Are you bound to this friend in any irredeemable way?"

"No – I am not," she answered, with emotion.

"There's nothing between you but – let us call it mere friendship."

"Nothing – nothing!"

"So far, so good." He looked keenly into her face. "But how about the future?"

"There will never be anything more – there can't be."

"Let us say that you think so at present. Perhaps I don't feel quite so sure of it. I say again, it's nothing to me, unless I get drawn into it by you yourself. I am not your guardian. If I tell you to be careful, it's an impertinence. But the money; that's another affair. I won't help you to misery."

"You will be helping me *out* of misery!" Eve exclaimed.

"Yes, for the present. I will make a bargain with you."

She looked at him with startled eyes.

"You shall have your thirty-five pounds on condition that you go to live, for as long as I choose, in Paris. You are to leave London in a day or two. Patty shall go with you; her uncle doesn't want her, and she seems to have quarrelled with the man she was engaged to. The expenses are my affair. I shall go to Paris myself, and be there while you are, but you need see no more of me than you like. Those are the terms."

"I can't think you are serious," said Eve.

"Then I'll explain why I wish you to do this. I've thought about you a great deal; in fact, since we first met, my chief occupation has been thinking about you. And I have come to the conclusion that you are suffering from an illness, the result of years of hardship and misery. We have agreed, you remember, that there are a good many points of resemblance between your life and mine, and perhaps between your character and mine. Now I myself, when I escaped from Dudley, was thoroughly ill – body and soul. The only hope for me was a complete change of circumstances – to throw off the weight of my past life, and learn the meaning of repose, satisfaction, enjoyment. I prescribe the same for you. I am your physician; I undertake your cure. If you refuse to let me, there's an end of everything between us; I shall say good-bye to you tonight, and to-morrow set off for some foreign country."

"How can I leave my work at a moment's notice?"

"The devil take your work – for he alone is the originator of such accursed toil!"

"How can I live at your expense?"

"That's a paltry obstacle. Oh, if you are too proud, say so, and there's an end of it. You know me well enough to feel the absolute truth of what I say, when I assure you that you will remain just as independent of me as you ever were. I shall be spending my money in a way that gives me pleasure; the matter will never appear to me in any other light. Why, call it an additional loan, if it will give any satisfaction to you. You are to pay me back some time. Here in London you perish; across the Channel there, health of body and mind is awaiting you; and are we to talk about money? I shall begin to swear like a trooper; the thing is too preposterous."

Eve said nothing: she stood half turned from him.

"Of course," he pursued, "you may object to leave London. Perhaps the sacrifice is too great. In that case, I should only do right if I carried you off by main force; but I'm afraid it can't be; I must leave you to perish."

"I am quite willing to go away," said Eve in a low voice. "But the shame of it – to be supported by you."

"Why, you don't hate me?"

"You know I do not."

"You even have a certain liking for me. I amuse you; you think me an odd sort of fellow, perhaps with more good than bad in me. At all events, you can trust me?"

"I can trust you perfectly."

"And it isn't as if I wished you to go alone. Patty will be off her head with delight when the thing is proposed to her."

"But how can I explain to her?"

"Don't attempt to. Leave her curiosity a good hard nut to crack. Simply say you are off to Paris, and that if she'll go with you, you will bear all her expenses."

"It's so difficult to believe that you are in earnest."

"You must somehow bring yourself to believe it. There will be a cheque ready for you to-morrow morning, to take or refuse. If you take it, you are bound in honour to leave England not later than – we'll say Thursday. That you are to be trusted, I believe, just as firmly as you believe it of me."

"I can't decide to-night."

"I can give you only till to-morrow morning. If I don't hear from you by midday, I am gone."

"You shall hear from me – one way or the other."

"Then don't wait here any longer. It's after midnight, and Patty will be alarmed about you. No, we won't shake hands; not that till we strike a bargain."

Eve seemed about to walk away, but she hesitated and turned again.

"I will do as you wish – I will go."

"Excellent! Then speak of it to Patty as soon as possible, and tell me what she says when we meet to-morrow – where and when you like."

"In this same place, at nine o'clock."

"So be it. I will bring the cheque."

"But I must be able to cash it at once."

"So you can. It will be on a London bank. I'll get the cash myself if you like."

Then they shook hands and went in opposite directions.

~ *Chapter 13* ~

ON THE evening of the next day, just after he had lit his lamp, Hilliard's attention was drawn by a sound as of someone tapping at the window. He stood to listen, and the sound was repeated – an unmistakable tap of fingers on the glass. In a moment he was out in the street, where he discovered Patty Ringrose.

"Why didn't you come to see me?" she asked excitedly.

"I was afraid *she* might be there. Did she go to business, as usual?"

"Yes. At least I suppose so. She only got home at the usual time. I've left her there: I was bound to see you. Do you know what she told me last night when she came in?"

"I dare say I could guess."

Hilliard began to walk down the street. Patty, keeping close at his side, regarded him with glances of wonder.

"Is it true that we're going to Paris? I couldn't make out whether she meant it, and this morning I couldn't get a word from her."

"Are you willing to go with her?"

"And have all my expenses paid?"

"Of course."

"I should think I am! But I daren't let my uncle and aunt know; there'd be no end of bother. I shall have to make up some sort of tale to satisfy my aunt, and get my things sent to the station while uncle's playing billiards. How long is it for?"

"Impossible to say. Three months – half-a-year – I don't know. What about Mr. Dally?"

"Oh, I've done with *him*!"

"And you are perfectly sure that you can get employment whenever you need it?"

"Quite sure: no need to trouble about that. I'm very good friends with aunt, and she'll take me in for as long as I want when I come back. But it's easy enough for anybody like me to get a place. I've had two or three offers the last half-year, from good shops where they were losing their young ladies. We're always getting married, in our business, and places have to be filled up."

"That settles it, then."

"But I want to know – I can't make it out – Eve won't tell me how she's managing to go. Are *you* going to pay for her?"

"We won't talk of that, Patty. She's going; that's enough."

"You persuaded her, last night?"

"Yes, I persuaded her. And I am to hear by the first post in the morning whether she will go to-morrow or Thursday. She'll arrange things with you to-night, I should think."

"It didn't look like it. She's shut herself in her room."

"I can understand that. She is ill. That's why I'm getting her away from London. Wait till we've been in Paris a few weeks, and you'll see how she changes. At present she is downright ill – ill enough to go to bed and be nursed, if that would do any good. It's your part to look after her. I don't want you to be her servant."

"Oh, I don't mind doing anything for her."

"No, because you are a very good sort of girl. You'll live at a hotel, and what you have to do is to make her enjoy herself. I shouldn't wonder if you find it difficult at first, but we shall get her round before long."

"I never thought there was anything the matter with her."

"Perhaps not, but I understand her better. Of course you won't say a word of this to her. You take it as a holiday – as good fun. No doubt I shall be able to have a few words in private with you now and then. But at other times we must talk as if nothing special had passed between us."

Patty mused. The lightness of her step told in what a spirit of gaiety she looked forward to the expedition.

"Do you think," she asked presently, "that it'll all come to an end – what I told you of?"

"Yes, I think so."

"You didn't let her know that I'd been talking—"

"Of course not. And, as I don't want her to know that you've seen me to-night, you had better stay no longer. She's sure to have something to tell you to-night or to-morrow morning. Get your packing done, and be ready at any moment. When I hear from Eve in the morning, I shall send her a telegram. Most likely we shan't see each other again until we meet at Charing Cross. I hope it may be to-morrow; but Thursday is the latest."

So Patty took her departure, tripping briskly homeward. As for Hilliard, he returned to his sitting-room, and was busy for some time with the pencilling of computations in English and French money. Towards midnight, he walked as far as High Street, and looked at the windows above the music-shop. All was dark.

He rose very early next morning, and as post-time drew near he walked about the street in agonies of suspense. He watched the letter-carrier from house to house, followed him up, and saw him pass the number at which he felt assured that he would deliver a letter. In frenzy of disappointment a fierce oath burst from his lips. "That's what comes of trusting a woman! – she is going to cheat me. She has gained her end, and will put me off with excuses." But perhaps a telegram would come. He made a pretence of breakfasting, and paced his room for an hour like a caged animal. When the monotony of circulating movement had all but stupefied him, he was awakened by a double postman's knock at the front door, the signal that announces a telegram.

Again from Patty, and again a request that he would come to the shop at mid-day.

"Just as I foresaw – excuses – postponement. What woman ever had the sense of honour!"

To get through the morning he drank – an occupation suggested by the heat of the day, which blazed cloudless. The liquor did not cheer him, but inspired a sullen courage, a reckless resolve. And in this frame of mind he presented himself before Patty Ringrose.

"She can't go to-day," said Patty, with an air of concern. "You were quite right – she is really ill."

"Has she gone out?"

"No, she's upstairs, lying on the bed. She says she has a dreadful headache, and if you saw her you'd believe it. She looks shocking. It's the second night she hasn't closed her eyes."

A savage jealousy was burning Hilliard's vitals. He had tried to make light of the connection between Eve and that unknown man, even after her extraordinary request for money, which all but confessedly she wanted on his account. He had blurred the significance of such a situation, persuading himself that neither was Eve capable of a great passion, nor the man he had seen able to inspire one. Now he rushed to the conviction that Eve had fooled him with a falsehood.

"Tell her this." He glared at Patty with eyes which made the girl shrink in alarm. "If she isn't at Charing Cross Station by a quarter to eleven to-morrow, there's an end of it. I shall be there, and shall go on without her. It's her only chance."

"But if she really *can't*—"

"Then it's her misfortune – she must suffer for it. She goes to-morrow or not at all. Can you make her understand that?"

"I'll tell her."

"Listen, Patty. If you bring her safe to the station to-morrow you shall have a ten-pound note, to buy what you like in Paris."

The girl reddened, half in delight, half in shame.

"I don't want it – she shall come—"

"Very well; good-bye till to-morrow, or for good."

"No, no; she shall come."

He was drenched in perspiration, yet walked for a mile or two at his topmost speed. Then a consuming thirst drove him into the nearest place where drink was sold. At six o'clock he remembered that he had not eaten since breakfast; he dined extravagantly, and afterwards fell asleep in the smoking-room of the restaurant. A waiter with difficulty aroused him, and persuaded him to try the effect of the evening air. An hour later he sank in exhaustion on one of the benches near the river, and there slept profoundly until stirred by a policeman.

"What's the time?" was his inquiry, as he looked up at the starry sky.

He felt for his watch, but no watch was discoverable. Together with the gold chain it had disappeared.

"Damnation! someone has robbed me."

The policeman was sympathetic, but reproachful.

"Why do you go to sleep on the Embankment at this time of night? Lost any money?"

Yes, his money too had flown; luckily, only a small sum. It was for the loss of his watch and chain that he grieved; they had been worn for years by his father, and on that account had a far higher value for him than was represented by their mere cost.

As a matter of form, he supplied the police with information concerning the theft. Of recovery there could be little hope.

Thoroughly awakened and sober, he walked across London to Gower Place arriving in the light of dawn. Too spiritless to take off his clothing, he lay upon the bed, and through the open window watched a great cloud that grew rosy above the opposite houses.

Would Eve be at the place of meeting to-day? It seemed to him totally indifferent whether she came or not; nay, he all but hoped that she would not. He had been guilty of prodigious folly. The girl belonged to another man; and even had it not been so, what was the use of flinging away his money at this rate? Did he look for any reward correspondent to the sacrifice? She would never love him, and it was not in his power to complete the work he had begun, by freeing her completely from harsh circumstances, setting her in a path of secure and pleasant life.

But she would not come, and so much the better. With only himself to provide for he had still money enough to travel far. He would see something of the great world, and leave his future to destiny.

He dozed for an hour or two.

Whilst he was at breakfast a letter arrived for him. He did not know the handwriting on the envelope, but it must be Eve's. Yes. She wrote a couple of lines:

"I will be at the station to-morrow at a quarter to eleven.—E. M."

~ *Chapter 14* ~

ONE travelling bag was all he carried. Some purchases that he had made in London – especially the great work on French cathedrals – were already despatched to Birmingham, to lie in the care of Robert Narramore.

He reached Charing Cross half an hour before train-time, and waited at the entrance. Several cabs that drove up stirred his expectation only to disappoint him. He was again in an anguish of fear lest Eve should not come. A cab arrived, with two boxes of modest appearance. He stepped forward and saw the girls' faces.

Between him and Eve not a word passed. They avoided each other's look. Patty, excited and confused, shook hands with him.

"Go on to the platform," he said. "I'll see after everything. This is all the luggage?"

"Yes. One box is mine, and one Eve's. I had to face it out with the people at home," she added, between laughing and crying. "They think I'm going to the seaside, to stay with Eve till she gets better. I never told so many fibs in my life. Uncle stormed at me, but I don't care."

"All right; go on to the platform."

Eve was already walking in that direction. Undeniably she looked ill; her step was languid; she did not raise her eyes. Hilliard, when he had taken tickets and booked the luggage through to Paris, approached his travelling companions. Seeing him, Eve turned away.

"I shall go in a smoking compartment," he said to Patty. "You had better take your tickets."

"But when shall we see you again?"

"Oh, at Dover, of course."

"Will it be rough, do you think? I do wish Eve would talk. I can't get a word out of her. It makes it all so miserable, when we might be enjoying ourselves."

"Don't trouble: leave her to herself. I'll get you some papers."

On returning from the bookstall, he slipped loose silver into Patty's hands.

"Use that if you want anything on the journey. And – I haven't forgot my promise."

"Nonsense!"

"Go and take your places now: there's only ten minutes to wait."

He watched them as they passed the barrier. Neither of the girls was dressed very suitably for travelling; but Eve's costume resembled that of a lady, while Patty's might suggest that she was a lady's-maid. As if to confirm this distinction, Patty had burdened herself with several small articles, whereas her friend carried only a sunshade. They disappeared among people upon the platform. In a few minutes Hilliard followed, glanced along the carriages till he saw where the girls were seated, and took his own place. He wore a suit which had been new on his first arrival in London, good enough in quality and cut to give his features the full value of their intelligence; a brown felt hat, a russet necktie, a white flannel shirt. Finding himself with a talkative neighbour in the carriage, he chatted freely. As soon as the train had started, he lit his pipe and tasted the tobacco with more relish than for a long time.

On board the steamer Eve kept below from first to last. Patty walked the deck with Hilliard, and vastly to her astonishment, achieved the voyage without serious discomfort. Hilliard himself, with the sea wind in his nostrils, recovered that temper of buoyant satisfaction which had accompanied his first escape from London. He despised the weak misgivings and sordid calculations of yesterday. Here he was, on a Channel steamer, bearing away from disgrace and wretchedness the woman whom his heart desired. Wild as the project had seemed to him when first he conceived it, he had put it into execution. The moment was worth living for. Whatever the future might keep in store for him of dreary, toilsome, colourless existence, the retrospect would always show him this patch of purple – a memory precious beyond all the possible results of prudence and narrow self-regard.

The little she-Cockney by his side entertained him with the flow of her chatter; it had the advantage of making him feel a travelled man.

"I didn't cross this way when I came before," he explained to her. "From Newhaven it's a much longer voyage."

"You like the sea, then?"

"I chose it because it was cheaper – that's all."

"Yet you're so extravagant now," remarked Patty, with eyes that confessed admiration of this quality.

"Oh, because I am rich," he answered gaily. "Money is nothing to me."

"Are you really rich? Eve said you weren't."

"Did she?"

"I don't mean she said it in a disagreeable way. It was last night. She thought you were wasting your money upon us."

"If I choose to waste it, why not? Isn't there a pleasure in doing as you like?"

"Oh, of course there is," Patty assented. "I only wish I had the chance. But it's awfully jolly, this! Who'd have thought, a week ago, that I should be going to Paris? I have a feeling all the time that I shall wake up and find I've been dreaming."

"Suppose you go down and see whether Eve wants anything? You needn't say I sent you."

From Calais to Paris he again travelled apart from the girls. Fatigue overcame him, and for the last hour or two he slept, with the result that, on alighting at the Gare du Nord, he experienced a decided failure of spirits. Happily, there was nothing before him but to carry out a plan already elaborated. With the aid of his guide-book he had selected an hotel which seemed suitable for the girls, one where English was spoken, and thither he drove with them from the station. The choice of their rooms, and the settlement of details took only a few minutes; then, for almost the first time since leaving Charing Cross, he spoke to Eve.

"Patty will do everything she can for you," he said; "I shall be not very far away, and you can always send me a message if you wish. To-morrow morning I shall come at about ten to ask how you are – nothing more than that – unless you care to go anywhere."

The only reply was "Thank you," in a weary tone. And so, having taken his leave he set forth to discover a considerably less expensive lodging for himself. In this, after his earlier acquaintance with Paris, he had no difficulty; by half-past eight his business was done, and he sat down to dinner at a cheap restaurant. A headache spoilt his enjoyment of the meal. After a brief ramble about the streets, he went home and got into a bed which was rather too short for him, but otherwise promised sufficient comfort.

The first thing that came into his mind when he awoke next morning was that he no longer possessed a watch; the loss cast a gloom upon him. But he had slept well, and a flood of sunshine that streamed over his scantily carpeted floor, together with gladly remembered sounds from the street, soon put him into an excellent humour. He sprang up, partly dressed himself, and unhasped the window. The smell of Paris had become associated in his mind with thoughts of liberty; a grotesque dance about the bed-room expressed his joy.

As he anticipated, Patty alone received him when he called upon the girls. She reported that Eve felt unable to rise.

"What do you think about her?" he asked. "Nothing serious, is it?"

"She can't get rid of her headache."

"Let her rest as long as she likes. Are you comfortable here?"

Patty was in ecstasies with everything, and chattered on breathlessly. She wished to go out; Eve had no need of her – indeed had told her that above all she wished to be left alone.

"Get ready, then," said Hilliard, "and we'll have an hour or two."

They walked to the Madeleine and rode thence on the top of a tram-car to the Bastille. By this time Patty had come to regard her strange companion in a sort of brotherly light; no restraint whatever appeared in her conversation with him. Eve, she told him, had talked French with the chambermaid.

"And I fancy it was something she didn't want *me* to understand."

"Why should you think so?"

"Oh, something in the way the girl looked at me."

"No, no; you were mistaken. She only wanted to show that she knew some French."

But Hilliard wondered whether Patty could be right. Was it not possible that Eve had gratified her vanity by representing her friend as a servant – a lady's-maid? Yet why should he attribute such a fault to her? It was an odd thing that he constantly regarded Eve in the least favourable light, giving weight to all the ill he conjectured in her, and minimising those features of her character which, at the beginning, he had been prepared to observe with sympathy and admiration. For a man in love his reflections followed a very unwonted course. And, indeed, he had never regarded his love as of very high or pure quality; it was something that possessed him and constrained him – by no means a source of elevating emotion.

"Do you like Eve?" he asked abruptly, disregarding some trivial question Patty had put to him.

"Like her? Of course I do."

"And *why* do you like her?"

"Why? – ah – I don't know. Because I do."

And she laughed foolishly.

"Does Eve like *you*?" Hilliard continued.

"I think she does. Else I don't see why she kept up with me."

"Has she ever done you any kindness?"

"I'm sure I don't know. Nothing particular. She never gave anything, if you mean that. But she has paid for me at theatres and so on."

Hilliard quitted the subject.

"If you like to go out alone," he told her before they parted, "there's no reason why you shouldn't – just as you do in London. Remember the way back, that's all, and don't be out late. And you'll want some French money."

"But I don't understand it, and how can I buy anything when I can't speak a word?"

"All the same, take that and keep it till you are able to make use of it. It's what I promised you."

Patty drew back her hand, but her objections were not difficult to overcome.

"I dare say," Hilliard continued, "Eve doesn't understand the money much better than you do. But she'll soon be well enough to talk, and then I shall explain everything to her. On this piece of paper is my address; please let Eve have it. I shall call to-morrow morning again."

He did so, and this time found Eve, as well as her companion, ready to go out. No remark or inquiry concerning her health passed his lips; he saw that she was recovering from the crisis she had passed through, whatever its real nature. Eve shook hands with him, and smiled, though as if discharging an obligation.

"Can you spare time to show us something of Paris?" she asked.

"I am your official guide. Make use of me whenever it pleases you."

"I don't feel able to go very far. Isn't there some place where we could sit down in the open air?"

A carriage was summoned, and they drove to the Fields Elysian. Eve benefited by the morning thus spent. She left to Patty most of the conversation, but occasionally made inquiries, and began to regard things with a healthy interest. The next day they all visited the Louvre, for a light rain was falling, and here Hilliard found an opportunity of private talk with Eve; they sat together whilst Patty, who cared little for pictures, looked out of a window at the Seine.

"Do you like the hotel I chose?" he began.

"Everything is very nice."

"And you are not sorry to be here?"

"Not in one way. In another I can't understand how I come to be here at all."

"Your physician has ordered it."

"Yes – so I suppose it's all right."

"There's one thing I'm obliged to speak of. Do you understand French money?"

~ *Eve's Ransom* ~

Eve averted her face, and spoke after a slight delay.

"I can easily learn."

"Yes. You shall take this Paris guide home with you. You'll find all information of that sort in it. And I shall give you an envelope containing money – just for your private use. You have nothing to do with the charges at the hotel."

"I've brought it on myself; but I feel more ashamed than I can tell you."

"If you tried to tell me I shouldn't listen. What you have to do now is to get well. Very soon you and Patty will be able to find your way about together; then I shall only come with you when you choose to invite me. You have my address."

He rose and broke off the dialogue.

For a week or more Eve's behaviour in his company underwent little change. In health she decidedly improved, but Hilliard always found her reserved, coldly amicable, with an occasional suggestion of forced humility which he much disliked. From Patty he learnt that she went about a good deal and seemed to enjoy herself.

"We don't always go together," said the girl. "Yesterday and the day before Eve was away by herself all the afternoon. Of course she can get on all right with her French. She takes to Paris as if she'd lived here for years."

On the day after, Hilliard received a postcard in which Eve asked him to be in a certain room of the Louvre at twelve o'clock. He kept the appointment, and found Eve awaiting him alone.

"I wanted to ask whether you would mind if we left the hotel and went to live at another place?"

He heard her with surprise.

"You are not comfortable?"

"Quite. But I have been to see my friend Mlle. Roche – you remember. And she has shown me how we can live very comfortably at a quarter of what it costs now, in the same house where she has a room. I should like to change, if you'll let me."

"Pooh! You're not to think of the cost—"

"Whether I am to or not, I do, and can't help myself. I know the hotel is fearfully expensive, and I shall like the other place much better. Miss Roche is a very nice girl, and she was glad to see me; and if I'm near her, I shall get all sorts of advantages – in French, and so on."

Hilliard wondered what accounts of herself Eve had rendered to the Parisienne, but he did not venture to ask.

"Will Patty like it as well?"

"Just as well. Miss Roche speaks English, you know, and they'll get on very well together."

"Where is the place?"

"Rather far off – towards the Jardin des Plantes. But I don't think that would matter, would it?"

"I leave it entirely to you."

"Thank you," she answered, with that intonation he did not like. "Of course, if you would like to meet Miss Roche, you can."

"We'll think about it. It's enough that she's an old friend of yours."

~ *Chapter 15* ~

WHEN this change had been made Eve seemed to throw off a burden. She met Hilliard with something like the ease of manner, the frank friendliness, which marked her best moods in their earlier intercourse. At a restaurant dinner, to which he persuaded her in company with Patty, she was ready in cheerful talk, and an expedition to Versailles, some days after, showed her radiant with the joy of sunshine and movement. Hilliard could not but wonder at the success of his prescription.

He did not visit the girls in their new abode, and nothing more was said of his making the acquaintance of Mlle. Roche. Meetings were appointed by post-card – always in Patty's hand if the initiative were female; they took place three or four times a week. As it was now necessary for Eve to make payments on her own account, Hilliard despatched to her by post a remittance in paper money, and of this no word passed between them. Three weeks later he again posted the same sum. On the morrow they went by river to St. Cloud – it was always a trio, Hilliard never making any other proposal – and the steam-boat afforded Eve an opportunity of speaking with her generous friend apart.

"I don't want this money," she said, giving him an envelope. "What you sent before isn't anything like finished. There's enough for a month more."

"Keep it all the same. I won't have any pinching."

"There's nothing of the kind. If I don't have my way in this I shall go back to London."

He put the envelope in his pocket, and stood silent, with eyes fixed on the river bank.

"How long do you intend us to stay?" asked Eve.

"As long as you find pleasure here."

"And – what am I to do afterwards?"

He glanced at her.

"A holiday must come to an end," she added, trying, but without success, to meet his look.

"I haven't given any thought to that," said Hilliard, carelessly; "there's plenty of time. It will be fine weather for many weeks yet."

"But I have been thinking about it. I should be crazy if I didn't."

"Tell me your thoughts, then."

"Should you be satisfied if I got a place at Birmingham?"

There again was the note of self-abasement. It irritated the listener.

"Why do you put it in that way? There's no question of what satisfies me, but of what is good for you."

"Then I think it had better be Birmingham."

"Very well. It's understood that when we leave Paris we go there."

A silence. Then Eve asked abruptly:

"You will go as well?"

"Yes, I shall go back."

"And what becomes of your determination to enjoy life as long as you can?"

"I'm carrying it out. I shall go back satisfied, at all events."

"And return to your old work?"

"I don't know. It depends on all sorts of things. We won't talk of it just yet."

Patty approached, and Hilliard turned to her with a bright, jesting face.

Midway in August, on his return home one afternoon, the concierge let him know that two English gentlemen had been inquiring for him; one of them had left a card. With surprise and pleasure Hilliard read the name of Robert Narramore, and beneath it, written in pencil, an invitation to dine that evening at a certain hotel in the Rue de Provence. As usual, Narramore had neglected the duties of a correspondent; this was the first announcement of his intention to be in Paris. Who the second man might be Hilliard could not conjecture.

He arrived at the hotel, and found Narramore in company with a man of about the same age, his name Birching, to Hilliard a stranger. They had reached Paris this morning, and would remain only for a day or two, as their purpose was towards the Alps.

"I couldn't stand this heat," remarked Narramore, who, in the very lightest of tourist garbs, sprawled upon a divan, and drank something iced out of a tall tumbler. "We shouldn't have stopped here at all if it hadn't been for you. The idea is that you should go on with us."

"Can't – impossible—"

"Why, what are you doing here – besides roasting?"

"Eating and drinking just what suits my digestion."

"You look pretty fit – a jolly sight better than when we met last. All the same, you will go on with us. We won't argue it now; it's dinner-time. Wait till afterwards."

At table, Narramore mentioned that his friend Birching was an architect.

"Just what this fellow ought to have been," he said, indicating Hilliard. "Architecture is his hobby. I believe he could sit down and draw to scale a front elevation of any great cathedral in Europe – couldn't you, Hilliard?"

Laughing the joke aside, Hilliard looked with interest at Mr. Birching, and began to talk with him. The three young men consumed a good deal of wine, and after dinner strolled about the streets, until Narramore's fatigue and thirst brought them to a pause at a café on the Boulevard des Italiens. Birching presently moved apart, to reach a newspaper, and remained out of earshot while Narramore talked with his other friend.

"What's going on?" he began. "What are you doing here? Seriously, I want you to go along with us. Birching is a very good sort of chap, but just a trifle heavy – takes things rather solemnly for such hot weather. Is it the expense? Hang it! You and I know each other well enough, and, thanks to my old uncle—"

"Never mind that, old boy," interposed Hilliard. "How long are you going for?"

"I can't very well be away for more than three weeks. The brass bedsteads, you know—"

Hilliard agreed to join in the tour.

"That's right: I've been looking forward to it," said his friend heartily. "And now, haven't you anything to tell me? Are you alone here? Then, what the deuce do you do with yourself?"

"Chiefly meditate."

"You're the rummest fellow I ever knew. I've wanted to write to you, but – hang it! – what with hot weather and brass bedsteads, and this and that—Now, what *are* you going to do? Your money won't last for ever. Haven't you any projects? It was no good talking about it before you left Dudley. I saw that. You were all but fit for a lunatic asylum, and no wonder. But you've pulled round, I see. Never saw you looking in such condition. What is to be the next move?"

"I have no idea."

"Well, now, *I* have. This fellow Birching is partner with his brother, in Brum, and they're tolerably flourishing. I've thought of you ever since I came to know him; I think it was chiefly on your account that I got thick with him – though there was another reason. I'll tell you about that some time. Now, why shouldn't you go into their office? Could you manage to pay a small premium? I believe I could square it with them. I haven't said anything. I never hurry – like things to ripen naturally. Suppose you saw your way, in a year or two, to make only as much in an architect's office as you did in that—machine-shop, wouldn't it be worth while?"

Hilliard mused. Already he had a flush on his cheek, but his eyes sensibly brightened.

"Yes," he said at length with deliberation. "It would be worth while."

"So I should think. Well, wait till you've got to be a bit chummy with Birching. I think you'll suit each other. Let him see that you do really know something about architecture – there'll be plenty of chances."

Hilliard, still musing, repeated with mechanical emphasis:

"Yes, it would be worth while."

Then Narramore called to Birching, and the talk became general again.

The next morning they drove about Paris, all together. Narramore, though it was his first visit to the city, declined to see anything which demanded exertion, and the necessity for quenching his thirst recurred with great frequency. Early in the afternoon he proposed that they should leave Paris that very evening.

"I want to see a mountain with snow on it. We're bound to travel by night, and another day of this would settle me. Any objection, Birching?"

The architect agreed, and time-tables were consulted. Hilliard drove home to pack. When this was finished, he sat down and wrote a letter:

"Dear Miss Madeley,

My friend Narramore is here, and has persuaded me to go to Switzerland with him. I shall be away for a week or two, and will let you hear from me in the meantime. Narramore says I am looking vastly better, and it is you I have to thank for this. Without you, my attempts at 'enjoying life' would have been a poor business. We start in an hour or two.

Yours ever,
"Maurice Hilliard."

~ *Chapter 16* ~

HE WAS absent for full three weeks, and arrived with his friends at the Gare de Lyon early one morning of September. Narramore and the architect delayed only for a meal, and pursued their journey homeward; Hilliard returned to his old quarters, despatched a post-card asking Eve and Patty to dine with him that evening, and thereupon went to bed, where for some eight hours he slept the sleep of healthy fatigue.

The place he had appointed for meeting with the girls was at the foot of the Boulevard St. Michel. Eve came alone.

"And where's Patty?" he asked, grasping her hand heartily in return for the smile of unfeigned pleasure with which she welcomed him.

"Ah, where indeed? Getting near to Charing Cross by now, I think."

"She has gone back?"

"Went this very morning, before I had your card – let us get out of the way of people. She has been dreadfully home-sick. About a fortnight ago a mysterious letter came for her; she hid it away from me. A few days after another came, and she shut herself up for a long time, and when she came out again I saw she had been crying. Then we talked it over. She had written to Mr. Dally and got an answer that made her miserable; that was the *first* letter. She wrote again, and had a reply that made her still more wretched; and that was the *second*. Two or three more came, and yesterday she could bear it no longer."

"Then she has gone home to make it up with him?"

"Of course. He declared that she has utterly lost her character and that no honest man could have anything more to say to her! I shouldn't wonder if they are married in a few weeks' time."

Hilliard laughed light-heartedly.

"I was to beg you on my knees to forgive her," pursued Eve. "But I can't very well do that in the middle of the street, can I? Really, she thinks she has behaved disgracefully to you. She wouldn't write a letter – she was ashamed. 'Tell him to forget all about me!' she kept saying."

"Good little girl! And what sort of a husband will this fellow Dally make her?"

"No worse than husbands in general, I dare say – but how well you look! How you must have been enjoying yourself!"

"I can say exactly the same about you!"

"Oh, but you are sunburnt, and look quite a different man!"

"And you have an exquisite colour in your cheeks, and eyes twice as bright as they used to be; and one would think you had never known a care."

"I feel almost like that," said Eve, laughing.

He tried to meet her eyes; she eluded him.

"I have an Alpine hunger; where shall we dine?"

The point called for no long discussion, and presently they were seated in the cool restaurant. Whilst he nibbled an olive, Hilliard ran over the story of his Swiss tour.

"If only *you* had been there! It was the one thing lacking."

"You wouldn't have enjoyed yourself half so much. You amused me by your description of Mr. Narramore, in the letter from Geneva."

"The laziest rascal born! But the best-tempered, the easiest to live with. A thoroughly good fellow; I like him better than ever. Of course he is improved by coming in for money – who wouldn't be, that has any good in him at all? But it amazes me that he can be content to go back to Birmingham and his brass bedsteads. Sheer lack of energy, I suppose. He'll grow dreadfully fat, I fear, and by when he becomes really a rich man – it's awful to think of."

Eve asked many questions about Narramore; his image gave mirthful occupation to her fancy. The dinner went merrily on, and when the black coffee was set before them:

"Why not have it outside?" said Eve. "You would like to smoke, I know."

Hilliard assented, and they seated themselves under the awning. The boulevard glowed in a golden light of sunset; the sound of its traffic was subdued to a lulling rhythm.

"There's a month yet before the leaves will begin to fall," murmured the young man, when he had smoked awhile in silence.

"Yes," was the answer. "I shall be glad to have a little summer still in Birmingham."

"Do you wish to go?"

"I shall go to-morrow, or the day after," Eve replied quietly.

Then again there came silence.

"Something has been proposed to me," said Hilliard, at length, leaning forward with his elbows upon the table. "I mentioned that our friend Birching is an architect. He's in partnership with his brother, a much older man. Well, they have offered to take me into their office if I pay a premium of fifty guineas. As soon as I can qualify myself to be of use to them, they'll give me a salary. And I shall have the chance of eventually doing much better than I ever could at the old grind, where, in fact, I had no prospect whatever."

"That's very good news," Eve remarked, gazing across the street.

"You think I ought to accept?"

"I suppose you can pay the fifty guineas, and still leave yourself enough to live upon?"

"Enough till I earn something," Hilliard answered with a smile.

"Then I should think there's no doubt."

"The question is this – are you perfectly willing to go back to Birmingham?"

"I'm *anxious* to go."

"You feel quite restored to health?"

"I was never so well in my life."

Hilliard looked into her face, and could easily believe that she spoke the truth. His memory would no longer recall the photograph in Mrs. Brewer's album; the living Eve, with her progressive changes of countenance, had obliterated that pale image of her bygone self. He saw her now as a beautiful woman, mysterious to him still in many respects, yet familiar as though they had been friends for years.

"Then, whatever life is before me," he said. "I shall have done *one* thing that is worth doing."

"Perhaps – if everyone's life is worth saving," Eve answered in a voice just audible.

"Everyone's is not; but yours was."

Two men who had been sitting not far from them rose and walked away. As if more at her ease for this secession, Eve looked at her companion, and said in a tone of intimacy:

"How I must have puzzled you when you first saw me in London!"

He answered softly:

"To be sure you did. And the thought of it puzzles me still."

"Oh, but can't you understand? No; of course you can't – I have told you so little. Just give me an idea of what sort of person you expected to find."

"Yes, I will. Judging from your portrait, and from what I was told of you, I looked for a sad, solitary, hard-working girl – rather poorly dressed – taking no pleasure – going much to chapel – shrinking from the ordinary world."

"And you felt disappointed?"

"At first, yes; or, rather, bewildered – utterly unable to understand you."

"You are disappointed still?" she asked.

"I wouldn't have you anything but what you are."

"Still, that other girl was the one you *wished* to meet."

"Yes, before I had seen you. It was the sort of resemblance between her life and my own. I thought of sympathy between us. And the face of the portrait – but I see better things in the face that is looking at me now."

"Don't be quite sure of that – yes, perhaps. It's better to be healthy, and enjoy life, than broken-spirited and hopeless. The strange thing is that you were right – you fancied me just the kind of a girl I was: sad and solitary, and shrinking from people – true enough. And I went to chapel, and got comfort from it – as I hope to do again. Don't think that I have no religion. But I was so unhealthy, and suffered so in every way. Work and anxiety without cease, from when I was twelve years old. You know all about my father? If I hadn't been clever at figures, what would have become of me? I should have drudged at some wretched occupation until the work and the misery of everything killed me."

Hilliard listened intently, his eyes never stirring from her face.

"The change in me began when father came back to us, and I began to feel my freedom. Then I wanted to get away, and to live by myself. I thought of London – I've told you how much I always thought of London – but I hadn't the courage to go there. In Birmingham I began to change my old habits; but more in what I thought than what I did. I wished to enjoy myself like other girls, but I couldn't. For one thing, I thought it wicked; and then I was so afraid of spending a penny – I had so often known what it was to be in want of a copper to buy food. So I lived quite alone; sat in my room every evening and read books. You could hardly believe what a number of books I read in that year. Sometimes I didn't go to bed till two or three o'clock."

"What sort of books?"

"I got them from the Free Library – books of all kinds; not only novels. I've never been particularly fond of novels; they always made me feel my own lot all the harder. I never could understand what people mean when they say that reading novels takes them 'out of themselves.' It was never so with me. I liked travels and lives of people, and books about the stars. Why do you laugh?"

"You escaped from yourself *there*, at all events."

"At last I saw an advertisement in a newspaper – a London paper in the reading-room – which I was tempted to answer; and I got an engagement in London. When the time came for starting I was so afraid and low-spirited that I all but gave it up. I should have done, if I could have known what was before me. The first year in London was all loneliness and ill-health. I didn't make a friend, and I starved myself, all to save money. Out of my pound a week I saved several shillings – just because it was the habit of my whole life to pinch and pare and deny myself. I was obliged to dress decently, and that came out of my food. It's certain I must have a very good constitution to have gone through all that and be as well as I am to-day."

"It will never come again," said Hilliard.

"How can I be sure of that? I told you once before that I'm often in dread of the future. It would be ever so much worse, after knowing what it means to enjoy one's life. How do people feel who are quite sure they can never want as long as they live? I have tried to imagine it, but I can't; it would be too wonderful."

"You may know it some day."

Eve reflected.

"It was Patty Ringrose," she continued, "who taught me to take life more easily. I was astonished to find how much enjoyment she could get out of an hour or two of liberty, with sixpence to spend. She did me good by laughing at me, and in the end I astonished *her*. Wasn't it natural that I should be reckless as soon as I got the chance?"

"I begin to understand."

"The chance came in this way. One Sunday morning I went by myself to Hampstead, and as I was wandering about on the Heath I kicked against something. It was a cash-box, which I saw couldn't have been lying there very long. I found it had been broken open, and inside it were a lot of letters – old letters in envelopes; nothing else. The addresses on the envelopes were all the same – to a gentleman living at Hampstead. I thought the best I could do was to go and inquire for this address; and I found it, and rang the door-bell. When I told the servant what I wanted – it was a large house – she asked me to come in, and after I had waited a little she took me into a library, where a gentleman was sitting. I had to answer a good many questions, and the man talked rather gruffly to me. When he had made a note of my name and where I lived, he said that I should hear from him, and so I went away. Of course I hoped to have a reward, but for two or three days I heard nothing; then, when I was at business, someone asked to see me – a man I didn't know. He said he had come from Mr. So and So, the gentleman at Hampstead, and had brought something for me – four five-pound notes. The cash-box had been stolen by someone, with other things, the night before I found it, and the letters in it, which disappointed the thief, had a great value for their owner. All sorts of inquiries had been made about me and no doubt I very nearly got into the hands of the police, but it was all right, and I had twenty pounds reward. Think! Twenty pounds!"

Hilliard nodded.

"I told no one about it – not even Patty. And I put the money into the Post Office savings bank. I meant it to stay there till I might be in need; but I thought of it day and night. And only a fortnight after, my employers shut up their place of business, and I had nothing to do. All one night I lay awake, and when I got up in the morning I felt as if I was no longer my old self. I saw everything in a different way – felt altogether changed. I had made up my mind not to look for a new place, but to take my money out of the Post Office – I had more than twenty-five pounds there altogether – and spend it for my pleasure. It was just as if something had enraged me, and I was bent on avenging myself. All that day I walked about the town, looking at shops, and thinking what I should like to buy: but I only spent a shilling or two, for meals. The next day I bought some new clothing. The day after that I took Patty to the theatre, and astonished her by my extravagance; but I gave her no explanation, and to this day she doesn't understand how I got my money. In a sort of way, I *did* enjoy myself. For one thing, I took a subscription at Mudie's, and began to read once more. You can't think how it pleased me to get my books – new books – where rich people do. I changed a volume about every other day – I had so many hours I didn't know what to do with. Patty was the only friend I had made, so I took her about with me whenever she could get away in the evening."

"Yet never once dined at a restaurant," remarked Hilliard, laughing. "There's the difference between man and woman."

"My ideas of extravagance were very modest, after all."

Hilliard, fingering his coffee-cup, said in a lower voice:

"Yet you haven't told me everything."

Eve looked away, and kept silence.

"By the time I met you" – he spoke in his ordinary tone – "you had begun to grow tired of it."

"Yes – and—" She rose. "We won't sit here any longer."

When they had walked for a few minutes:

"How long shall you stay in Paris?" she asked.

"Won't you let me travel with you?"

"I do whatever you wish," Eve answered simply.

~ *Chapter 17* ~

HER accent of submission did not affect Hilliard as formerly; with a nervous thrill, he felt that she spoke as her heart dictated. In his absence Eve had come to regard him, if not with the feeling he desired, with something that resembled it; he read the change in her eyes. As they walked slowly away she kept nearer to him than of wont; now and then her arm touched his, and the contact gave him a delicious sensation. Askance he observed her figure, its graceful, rather languid, movement; to-night she had a new power over him, and excited with a passion which made his earlier desires seem spiritless.

"One day more of Paris?" he asked softly.

"Wouldn't it be better—?" she hesitated in the objection.

"Do you wish to break the journey in London?"

"No; let us go straight on."

"To-morrow, then?"

"I don't think we ought to put it off. The holiday is over."

Hilliard nodded with satisfaction. An incident of the street occupied them for a few minutes, and their serious conversation was only resumed when they had crossed to the south side of the river, where they turned eastwards and went along the quays.

"Till I can find something to do," Eve said at length, "I shall live at Dudley. Father will be very glad to have me there. He wished me to stay longer."

"I am wondering whether it is really necessary for you to go back to your drudgery."

"Oh, of course it is," she answered quickly. "I mustn't be idle. That's the very worst thing for me. And how am I to live?"

"I have still plenty of money," said Hilliard, regarding her.

"No more than you will need."

"But think – how little more it costs for two than for one—"

He spoke in spite of himself, having purposed no such suggestion. Eve quickened her step.

"No, no, no! You have a struggle before you; you don't know what—"

"And if it would make it easier for me? – there's no real doubt about my getting on well enough—"

"Everything is doubtful." She spoke in a voice of agitation. "We can't see a day before us. We have arranged everything very well—"

Hilliard was looking across the river. He walked more and more slowly, and turned at length to stand by the parapet. His companion remained apart from him, waiting. But he did not turn towards her again, and she moved to his side.

"I know how ungrateful I must seem." She spoke without looking at him. "I have no right to refuse anything after all you—"

"Don't say that," he interrupted impatiently. "That's the one thing I shall never like to think of."

"I shall think of it always, and be glad to remember it—"

"Come nearer – give me your hand—"

Holding it, he drew her against his side, and they stood in silence looking upon the Seine, now dark beneath the clouding night.

"I can't feel sure of you," fell at length from Hilliard.

"I promise—"

"Yes; here, now, in Paris. But when you are back in that hell—"

"What difference can it make in me? It can't change what I feel now. You have altered all my life, my thoughts about everything. When I look back, I don't know myself. You were right; I must have been suffering from an illness that affected my mind. It seems impossible that I could ever have done such things. I ought to tell you. Do you wish me to tell you everything?"

Hilliard spoke no answer, but he pressed her hand more tightly in his own.

"You knew it from Patty, didn't you?"

"She told me as much as she knew that night when I waited for you in High Street. She said you were in danger, and I compelled her to tell all she could."

"I *was* in danger, though I can't understand now how it went so far as that. It was he who came to me with the money, from the gentleman at Hampstead. That was how I first met him. The next day he waited for me when I came away from business."

"It was the first time that anything of that kind had happened?"

"The first time. And you know what the state of my mind was then. But to the end I never felt any – I never really loved him. We met and went to places together. After my loneliness – you can understand. But I distrusted him. Did Patty tell you why I left London so suddenly?"

"Yes."

"When that happened I knew my instinct had been right from the first. It gave me very little pain, but I was ashamed and disgusted. He hadn't tried to deceive me in words; he never spoke of marriage; and from what I found out then, I saw that he was very much to be pitied."

"You seem to contradict yourself," said Hilliard. "Why were you ashamed and disgusted?"

"At finding myself in the power of such a woman. He married her when she was very young, and I could imagine the life he had led with her until he freed himself. A hateful woman!"

"Hateful to you, I see," muttered the listener, with something tight at his heart.

"Not because I felt anything like jealousy. You must believe me. I should never have spoken if I hadn't meant to tell you the simple truth."

Again he pressed her hand. The warmth of her body had raised his blood to fever-heat.

"When we met again, after I came back, it was by chance. I refused to speak to him, but he followed me all along the street, and I didn't know it till I was nearly home. Then he came up again, and implored me to hear what he had to say. I knew he would wait for me again in High Street, so I had no choice but to listen, and then tell him that there couldn't be anything more between us. And, for all that, he followed me another day. And again I had to listen to him."

Hilliard fancied that he could feel her heart beat against his arm.

"Be quick!" he said. "Tell all, and have done with it."

"He told me, at last, that he was ruined. His wife had brought him into money difficulties; she ran up bills that he was obliged to pay, and left him scarcely enough to live upon. And he had used money that was not his own – he would have to give an account of it in a day or two. He was trying to borrow, but no one would lend him half what he needed—"

"That's enough," Hilliard broke in, as her voice became inaudible.

"No, you ought to know more than I have told you. Of course he didn't ask me for money; he had no idea that I could lend him even a pound. But what I wish you to know is that he hadn't spoken to me again in the old way. He said he had done wrong, when he first came to know me; he begged me to forgive him that, and only wanted me to be his friend."

"Of course."

"Oh, don't be ungenerous: that's so unlike you."

"I didn't mean it ungenerously. In his position I should have done exactly as he did."

"Say you believe me. There was not a word of love between us. He told me all about the miseries of his life – that was all; and I pitied him so. I felt he was so sincere."

"I believe it perfectly."

"There was no excuse for what I did. How I had the courage – the shamelessness – is more than I can understand now."

Hilliard stirred himself, and tried to laugh.

"As it turned out, you couldn't have done better. Well, there's an end of it. Come."

He walked on, and Eve kept closely beside him, looking up into his face.

"I am sure he will pay the money back," she said presently.

"Hang the money!"

Then he stood still.

"How is he to pay it back? I mean, how is he to communicate with you?"

"I gave him my address at Dudley."

Again Hilliard moved on.

"Why should it annoy you?" Eve asked. "If ever he writes to me, I shall let you know at once: you shall see the letter. It is quite certain that he *will* pay his debt; and I shall be very glad when he does."

"What explanation did you give him?"

"The true one. I said I had borrowed from a friend. He was in despair, and couldn't refuse what I offered."

"We'll talk no more of it. It was right to tell me. I'm glad now it's all over. Look at the moon rising – harvest moon, isn't it?"

Eve turned aside again, and leaned on the parapet. He, lingering apart for a moment, at length drew nearer. Of her own accord she put her hands in his.

"In future," she said, "you shall know everything I do. You can trust me: there will be no more secrets."

"Yet you are afraid—"

"It's for your sake. You must be free for the next year or two. I shall be glad to get to work again. I am well and strong and cheerful."

Her eyes drew him with the temptation he had ever yet resisted. Eve did not refuse her lips.

"You must write to Patty," she said, when they were at the place of parting. "I shall have her new address in a day or two."

"Yes, I will write to her."

~ *Chapter 18* ~

BY THE end of November Hilliard was well at work in the office of Messrs. Birching, encouraged by his progress and looking forward as hopefully as a not very sanguine temperament would allow. He lived penuriously, and toiled at professional study night as well as day. Now and then he passed an evening with Robert Narramore, who had moved to cozy bachelor quarters a little distance out of town, in the Halesowen direction. Once a week, generally on Saturday, he saw Eve. Other society he had none, nor greatly desired any.

But Eve had as yet found no employment. Good fortune in this respect seemed to have deserted her, and at her meetings with Hilliard she grew fretful over repeated disappointments. Of her day-to-day life she made no complaint, but Hilliard saw too clearly that her spirits were failing beneath a burden of monotonous dullness. That the healthy glow she had brought back in her cheeks should give way to pallor was no more than he had expected, but he watched with anxiety the return of mental symptoms which he had tried to cheat himself into believing would not reappear. Eve did not fail in pleasant smiles, in hopeful words; but they cost her an effort which she lacked the art to conceal. He felt a coldness in her, divined a struggle between conscience and inclination. However, for this also he was prepared; all the more need for vigour and animation on his own part.

Hilliard had read of the woman who, in the strength of her love and loyalty, heartens a man through all the labours he must front; he believed in her existence, but had never encountered her – as indeed very few men have. From Eve he looked for nothing of the kind. If she would permit herself to rest upon his sinews, that was all he desired. The mood of their last night in Paris might perchance return, but only with like conditions. Of his workaday passion she knew nothing; habit of familiarity and sense of obligation must supply its place with her until a brightening future once more set her emotions to the gladsome tune.

Now that the days of sun and warmth were past, it was difficult to arrange for a meeting under circumstances that allowed of free comfortable colloquy. Eve declared that her father's house offered no sort of convenience; it was only a poor cottage, and Hilliard would be altogether out of place there. To his lodgings she could not come. Of necessity they had recourse to public places in Birmingham, where an hour or two of talk under shelter might make Eve's journey hither worth while. As Hilliard lived at the north end of the town, he suggested Aston Hall as a possible rendezvous, and here they met, early one Saturday afternoon in December.

From the eminence which late years have encompassed with a proletarian suburb, its once noble domain narrowed to the bare acres of a stinted breathing ground, Aston Hall looks forth upon joyless streets and fuming chimneys, a wide welter of squalid strife. Its walls, which bear the dints of Roundhead cannonade, are blackened with ever-driving smoke; its crumbling gateway, opening aforetime upon a stately avenue of chestnuts, shakes as the steam-tram rushes by. Hilliard's imagination was both attracted and repelled by this relic of what he deemed a better age. He enjoyed the antique chambers, the winding staircases, the lordly gallery, with its dark old portraits and vast fireplaces, the dim-lighted nooks where one could hide alone and dream away the present; but in the end, reality threw scorn upon such pleasure. Aston Hall was a mere architectural relic, incongruous and meaningless amid its surroundings; the pathos of its desecrated dignity made him wish that it might be destroyed, and its place fittingly occupied by some People's Palace, brand new, aglare with electric light, ringing to the latest melodies of the street. When he had long gazed at its gloomy front, the old champion of royalism seemed to shrink together, humiliated by Time's insults.

It was raining when he met Eve at the entrance.

"This won't do," were his first words. "You can't come over in such weather as this. If it hadn't seemed to be clearing up an hour or two ago, I should have telegraphed to stop you."

"Oh, the weather is nothing to me," Eve answered, with resolute gaiety. "I'm only too glad of the change. Besides, it won't go on much longer. I shall get a place."

Hilliard never questioned her about her attempts to obtain an engagement; the subject was too disagreeable to him.

"Nothing yet," she continued, as they walked up the muddy roadway to the Hall. "But I know you don't like to talk about it."

"I have something to propose. How if I take a couple of cheap rooms in some building let out for offices, and put in a few sticks of furniture? Would you come to see me there?"

He watched her face as she listened to the suggestion, and his timidity seemed justified by her expression.

"You would be so uncomfortable in such a place. Don't trouble. We shall manage to meet somehow. I am certain to be living here before long."

"Even when you are," he persisted, "we shall only be able to see each other in places like this. I can't talk – can't say half the things I wish to—"

"We'll think about it. Ah, it's warm in here!"

This afternoon the guardians of the Hall were likely to be troubled with few visitors. Eve at once led the way upstairs to a certain suite of rooms, hung with uninteresting pictures, where she and Hilliard had before this spent an hour safe from disturbance. She placed herself in the recess of a window: her companion took a few steps backward and forward.

"Let me do what I wish," he urged. "There's a whole long winter before us. I am sure I could find a couple of rooms at a very low rent, and some old woman would come in to do all that's necessary."

"If you like."

"I may? You would come there?" he asked eagerly.

"Of course I would come. But I shan't like to see you in a bare, comfortless place."

"It needn't be that. A few pounds will make a decent sort of sitting-room."

"Anything to tell me?" Eve asked, abruptly quitting the subject.

She seemed to be in better spirits than of late, notwithstanding the evil sky; and Hilliard smiled with pleasure as he regarded her.

"Nothing unusual. Oh, yes; I'm forgetting. I had a letter from Emily, and went to see her."

Hilliard had scarcely seen his quondam sister-in-law since she became Mrs. Marr. On the one occasion of his paying a call, after his return from Paris, it struck him that her husband offered no very genial welcome. He had expected this, and willingly kept aloof.

"Read the letter."

Eve did so. It began, "My dear Maurice," and ended, "Ever affectionately and gratefully yours." The rest of its contents ran thus:

"I am in great trouble – dreadfully unhappy. It would be such a kindness if you would let me see you. I can't put in a letter what I want to say, and I do hope you won't refuse to come. Friday afternoon, at three, would do, if you can get away from business for once. How I look back on the days when you used to come over from Dudley and have tea with us in the dear little room. Do come!"

"Of course," said Hilliard, laughing as he met Eve's surprised look. "I knew what *that* meant. I would much rather have got out of it, but it would have seemed brutal. So I went. The poor simpleton has begun to find that marriage with one man isn't necessarily the same thing as marriage with another. In Ezra Marr she has caught a Tartar."

"Surely he doesn't ill-use her?"

"Not a bit of it. He is simply a man with a will, and finds it necessary to teach his wife her duties. Emily knows no more about the duties of life than her little five-year-old girl. She thought she could play with a second husband as she did with the first, and she was gravely mistaken. She complained to me of a thousand acts of tyranny – every one of them, I could see, merely a piece of rude commonsense. The man must be calling himself an idiot for marrying her. I could only listen with a long face. Argument with Emily is out of the question. And I shall take good care not to go there again."

Eve asked many questions, and approved his resolve.

"You are not the person to console and instruct her. But she must look upon you as the best and wisest of men. I can understand that."

"You can understand poor, foolish Emily thinking so—"

"Put all the meaning you like into my words," said Eve, with her pleasantest smile. "Well, I too have had a letter. From Patty. She isn't going to be married, after all."

"Why, I thought it was over by now."

"She broke it off less than a week before the day. I wish I could show you her letter, but, of course, I mustn't. It's very amusing. They had quarrelled about every conceivable thing – all but one, and this came up at last. They were talking about meals, and Mr. Dally said that he liked a bloater for breakfast every morning. 'A bloater!' cried Patty. 'Then I hope you won't ask me to cook it for you. I can't bear them.' 'Oh, very well: if you can't cook a bloater, you're not the wife for me.' And there they broke off, for good and all."

"Which means for a month or two, I suppose."

"Impossible to say. But I have advised her as strongly as I could not to marry until she knows her own mind better. It is too bad of her to have gone so far. The poor man had taken rooms, and all but furnished them. Patty's a silly girl, I'm afraid."

"Wants a strong man to take her in hand – like a good many other girls."

Eve paid no attention to the smile.

"Paris spoilt her for such a man as Mr. Dally. She got all sorts of new ideas, and can't settle down to the things that satisfied her before. It isn't nice to think that perhaps we did her a great deal of harm."

"Nonsense! Nobody was ever harmed by healthy enjoyment."

"Was it healthy – for *her*? That's the question."

Hilliard mused, and felt disinclined to discuss the matter.

"That isn't the only news I have for you," said Eve presently. "I've had another letter."

Her voice arrested Hilliard's step as he paced near her.

"I had rather not have told you anything about it, but I promised. And I have to give you something."

She held out to him a ten-pound note.

"What's this?"

"He has sent it. He says he shall be able to pay something every three months until he has paid the whole debt. Please to take it."

After a short struggle with himself, Hilliard recovered a manly bearing.

"It's quite right he should return the money, Eve, but you mustn't ask me to have anything to do with it. Use it for your own expenses. I gave it to you, and I can't take it back."

She hesitated, her eyes cast down,

"He has written a long letter. There's not a word in it I should be afraid to show you. Will you read it – just to satisfy me? Do read it!"

Hilliard steadily refused, with perfect self-command.

"I trust you – that's enough. I have absolute faith in you. Answer his letter in the way you think best, and never speak to me of the money again. It's yours; make what use of it you like."

"Then I shall use it," said Eve, after a pause, "to pay for a lodging in Birmingham. I couldn't live much longer at home. If I'm here, I can get books out of the library, and time won't drag so. And I shall be near you."

"Do so, by all means."

As if more completely to dismiss the unpleasant subject, they walked into another room. Hilliard began to speak again of his scheme for providing a place where they could meet and talk at their ease. Eve now entered into it with frank satisfaction.

"Have you said anything yet to Mr. Narramore?" she asked at length.

"No. I have never felt inclined to tell him. Of course I shall some day. But it isn't natural to me to talk of this kind of thing, even with so intimate a friend. Some men couldn't keep it to themselves: for me the difficulty is to speak."

"I asked again, because I have been thinking – mightn't Mr. Narramore be able to help me to get work?"

Hilliard repelled the suggestion with strong distaste. On no account would he seek his friend's help in such a matter. And Eve said no more of it.

On her return journey to Dudley, between eight and nine o'clock, she looked cold and spiritless. Her eyelids dropped wearily as she sat in the corner of the carriage with some papers on her lap, which Hilliard had given her. Rain had ceased, and the weather seemed turning to frost. From Dudley station she had a walk of nearly half an hour, to the top of Kate's Hill.

Kate's Hill is covered with an irregular assemblage of old red-tiled cottages, grimy without, but sometimes, as could be seen through an open door admitting into the chief room, clean and homely-looking within. The steep, narrow alleys leading upward were scarce lighted; here and there glimmered a pale corner-lamp, but on a black night such as this the oil-lit windows of a little shop, and the occasional gleam from doors, proved very serviceable as a help in picking one's path. Towards the top of the hill there was no paving, and mud lay thick. Indescribable the confusion of this toilers' settlement – houses and workshops tumbled together as if by chance, the ways climbing and winding into all manner of pitch-dark recesses, where cats prowled stealthily. In one spot silence and not a hint of life; in another, children noisily at play amid piles of old metal or miscellaneous rubbish. From the labyrinth which was so familiar to her, Eve issued of a sudden on to a sort of terrace, where the air blew shrewdly: beneath lay cottage roofs, and in front a limitless gloom, which by daylight would have been an extensive northward view, comprising the towns of Bilston and Wolverhampton. It was now a black gulf, without form and void, sputtering fire. Flames that leapt out of nothing, and as suddenly disappeared; tongues of yellow or of crimson, quivering, lambent, seeming to snatch and devour and then fall back in satiety. When a cluster of these fires shot forth together, the sky above became illumined with a broad glare, which throbbed and pulsed in the manner of sheet-lightning, though more lurid, and in a few seconds was gone.

She paused here for a moment, rather to rest after her climb than to look at what she had seen so often, then directed her steps to one of the houses within sight. She pushed the door, and entered a little parlour, where a fire and a lamp made cheery welcome. By the hearth, in a round-backed wooden chair, sat a grizzle-headed man, whose hard features proclaimed his relation to Eve, otherwise seeming so improbable. He looked up from the volume open on his knee – a Bible – and said in a rough, kind voice:

"I was thinkin' it 'ud be about toime for you. You look starved, my lass."

"Yes; it has turned very cold."

"I've got a bit o' supper ready for you. I don't want none myself; there's food enough for me *here*." He laid his hand on the book. "D'you call to mind the eighteenth of Ezekiel, lass? – 'But if the wicked will turn from all his sins that he hath committed—' "

Eve stood motionless till he had read the verse, then nodded and began to take off her out-of-door garments. She was unable to talk, and her eyes wandered absently.

~ *Chapter 19* ~

AFTER a week's inquiry, Hilliard discovered the lodging that would suit his purpose. It was at Camp Hill; two small rooms at the top of a house, the ground-floor of which was occupied as a corn-dealer's shop, and the story above that tenanted by a working optician with a blind wife. On condition of papering the rooms and doing a few repairs necessary to make them habitable, he secured them at the low rent of four shillings a week.

Eve paid her first visit to this delectable abode on a Sunday afternoon; she saw only the sitting-room, which would bear inspection; the appearance of the bed-room was happily left to her surmise. Less than a five-pound note had paid for the whole furnishing. Notwithstanding the reckless invitation to Eve to share his fortunes straightway, Hilliard, after paying his premium of fifty guineas to the Birching Brothers, found but a very small remnant in hand of the money with which he had set forth from Dudley some nine months ago. Yet not for a moment did he repine; he had the value of his outlay; his mind was stored with memories and his heart strengthened with hope.

At her second coming – she herself now occupied a poor little lodging not very far away – Eve beheld sundry improvements. By the fireside stood a great leather chair, deep, high-backed, wondrously self-assertive over against the creaky cane seat which before had dominated the room. Against the wall was a high bookcase, where Hilliard's volumes, previously piled on the floor, stood in loose array; and above the mantelpiece hung a framed engraving of the Parthenon.

"This is dreadful extravagance!" she exclaimed, pausing at the threshold, and eying her welcomer with mock reproof.

"It is, but not on my part. The things came a day or two ago, simply addressed to me from shops."

"Who was the giver, then?"

"Must be Narramore, of course. He was here not long ago, and growled a good deal because I hadn't a decent chair for his lazy bones."

"I am much obliged to him," said Eve, as she sank back in the seat of luxurious repose. "You ought to hang his portrait in the room. Haven't you a photograph?" she added carelessly.

"Such a thing doesn't exist. Like myself, he hasn't had a portrait taken since he was a child. A curious thing, by-the-bye, that you should have had yours taken just when you did. Of course it was because you were going far away for the first time; but it marked a point in your life, and put on record the Eve Madeley whom no one would see again. If I can't get that photograph in any other way I shall go and buy, beg, or steal it from Mrs. Brewer."

"Oh, you shall have one if you insist upon it."

"Why did you refuse it before?"

"I hardly know – a fancy – I thought you would keep looking at it, and regretting that I had changed so."

As on her previous visit, she soon ceased to talk, and, in listening to Hilliard, showed unconsciously a tired, despondent face.

"Nothing yet," fell from her lips, when he had watched her silently.

"Never mind; I hate the mention of it."

"By-the-bye," he resumed, "Narramore astounded me by hinting at marriage. It's Miss Birching, the sister of my man. It hasn't come to an engagement yet, and if it ever does I shall give Miss Birching the credit for it. It would have amused you to hear him talking about her, with a pipe in his mouth and half asleep. I understand now why he took young Birching with him to Switzerland. He'll never carry it through; unless, as I said, Miss Birching takes the decisive step."

"Is she the kind of girl to do that?" asked Eve, waking to curiosity.

"I know nothing about her, except from Narramore's sleepy talk. Rather an arrogant beauty, according to him. He told me a story of how, when he was calling upon her, she begged him to ring the bell for something or other, and he was so slow in getting up that she went and rang it herself. 'Her own fault,' he said; 'she asked me to sit on a chair with a seat some six inches above the ground, and how can a man hurry up from a thing of that sort?' "

"He must be a strange man. Of course he doesn't care anything about Miss Birching."

"But I think he does, in his way."

"How did he ever get on at all in business?"

"Oh, he's one of the lucky men." Hilliard replied, with a touch of good-natured bitterness. "He never exerted himself; good things fell into his mouth. People got to like him – that's one explanation, no doubt."

"Don't you think he may have more energy than you imagine?"

"It's possible. I have sometimes wondered."

"What sort of life does he lead? Has he many friends I mean?"

"Very few. I should doubt whether there's anyone he talks with as he does with me. He'll never get much good out of his money; but if he fell into real poverty – poverty like mine – it would kill him. I know he looks at me as an astonishing creature, and marvels that I don't buy a good dose of chloral and have done with it."

Eve did not join in his laugh.

"I can't bear to hear you speak of your poverty," she said in an undertone. "You remind me that I am the cause of it."

"Good Heavens! As if I should mention it if I were capable of such a thought!"

"But it's the fact," she persisted, with something like irritation. "But for me, you would have gone into the architect's office with enough to live upon comfortably for a time."

"That's altogether unlikely," Hilliard declared. "But for you, it's improbable that I should have gone to Birching's at all. At this moment I should be spending my money in idleness, and, in the end, should have gone back to what I did before. You have given me a start in a new life."

This, and much more of the same tenor, failed to bring a light upon Eve's countenance. At length she asked suddenly, with a defiant bluntness—

"Have you ever thought what sort of a wife I am likely to make?"

Hilliard tried to laugh, but was disagreeably impressed by her words and the look that accompanied them.

"I have thought about it, to be sure," he answered carelessly.

"And don't you feel a need of courage?"

"Of course. And not only the need but the courage itself."

"Tell me the real, honest truth." She bent forward, and gazed at him with eyes one might have thought hostile. "I demand the truth of you: I have a right to know it. Don't you often wish you had never seen me?"

"You're in a strange mood."

"Don't put me off. Answer!"

"To ask such a question," he replied quietly, "is to charge me with a great deal of hypocrisy. I did *once* all but wish I had never seen you. If I lost you now I should lose what seems to me the strongest desire of my life. Do you suppose I sit down and meditate on your capacity as cook or housemaid? It would be very prudent and laudable, but I have other thoughts – that give me trouble enough."

"What thoughts?"

"Such as one doesn't talk about – if you insist on frankness."

Her eyes wandered.

"It's only right to tell you," she said, after silence, "that I dread poverty as much as ever I did. And I think poverty in marriage a thousand times worse than when one is alone."

"Well, we agree in that. But why do you insist upon it just now? Are *you* beginning to be sorry that we ever met?"

"Not a day passes but I feel sorry for it."

"I suppose you are harping on the old scruple. Why will you plague me about it?"

"I mean," said Eve, with eyes down, "that you are the worse off for having met me, but I mean something else as well. Do you think it possible that anyone can owe too much gratitude, even to a person one likes?"

He regarded her attentively.

"You feel the burden?"

She delayed her answer, glancing at him with a new expression – a deprecating tenderness.

"It's better to tell you. I *do* feel it, and have always felt it."

"Confound this infernal atmosphere!" Hilliard broke out wrathfully. "It's making you morbid again. Come here to me! Eve – come!"

As she sat motionless, he caught her hands and drew her forward, and sat down again with her passive body resting upon his knees. She was pale, and looked frightened.

"Your gratitude be hanged! Pay me back with your lips – so – and so! Can't you understand that when my lips touch yours, I have a delight that would be well purchased with years of semi-starvation? What is it to me how I won you? You are mine for good and all – that's enough."

She drew herself half away, and stood brightly flushed, touching her hair to set it in order again. Hilliard, with difficulty controlling himself, said in a husky voice—

"Is the mood gone?"

Eve nodded, and sighed.

~ *Chapter 20* ~

AT THE time appointed for their next meeting, Hilliard waited in vain. An hour passed, and Eve, who had the uncommon virtue of punctuality, still did not come. The weather was miserable – rain, fog, and slush – but this had heretofore proved no obstacle, for her lodgings were situated less than half a mile away. Afraid of missing her if he went out, he fretted through another hour, and was at length relieved by the arrival of a letter of explanation. Eve wrote that she had been summoned to Dudley; her father was stricken with alarming illness, and her brother had telegraphed.

For two days he heard nothing; then came a few lines which told him that Mr. Madeley could not live many more hours. On the morrow Eve wrote that her father was dead.

To the letter which he thereupon despatched Hilliard had no reply for nearly a week. When Eve wrote, it was from a new address at Dudley. After thanking him for the kind words with which he had sought to comfort her, she continued—

"I have at last found something to do, and it was quite time, for I have been very miserable, and work is the best thing for me. Mr. Welland, my first employer, when I was twelve years old, has asked me to come and keep his books for him, and I am to live in his house. My brother has gone into lodgings, and we see no more of the cottage on Kate's Hill. It's a pity I have to be so far from you again, but there seems to be no hope of getting anything to do in Birmingham, and here I shall be comfortable enough, as far as mere living goes. On Sunday I shall be quite free, and will come over as often as possible; but I have caught a bad cold, and must be content to keep in the house until this dreadful weather changes. Be more careful of yourself than you generally are, and let me hear often. In a few months' time we shall be able to spend pleasant hours on the Castle Hill. I have heard from Patty, and want to tell you about her letter, but this cold makes me feel too stupid. Will write again soon."

It happened that Hilliard himself was just now blind and voiceless with a catarrh. The news from Dudley by no means solaced him. He crouched over his fire through the long, black day, tormented with many miseries, and at eventide drank half a bottle of whisky, piping hot, which at least assured him of a night's sleep.

Just to see what would be the result of his silence, he wrote no reply to this letter. A fortnight elapsed; he strengthened himself in stubbornness, aided by the catarrh, which many bottles of whisky would not overcome. When his solitary confinement grew at length insufferable, he sent for Narramore, and had not long to wait before his friend appeared. Narramore was rosy as ever: satisfaction with life beamed from his countenance.

"I've ordered you in some wine," he exclaimed genially, sinking into the easy-chair which Hilliard had vacated for him – an instance of selfishness in small things which did not affect his generosity in greater. "It isn't easy to get good port nowadays, but they tell me that this is not injurious. Hasn't young Birching been to see you? No, I suppose he would think it *infra dig*. to come to this neighbourhood. There's a damnable self-conceit in that family: you must have noticed it, eh? It comes out very strongly in the girl. By-the-bye I've done with her – haven't been there for three weeks, and don't think I shall go again, unless it's for the pleasure of saying or doing something that'll irritate her royal highness."

"Did you quarrel?"

"Quarrel? I never quarrel with anyone; it's bad for one's nerves."

"Did you get as far as proposing?"

"Oh, I left *her* to do that. Women are making such a row about their rights nowadays, that it's as well to show you grant them perfect equality. I gave her every chance of saying something definite. I maintain that she trifled with my affections. She asked me what my views in life were. Ah, thought I, now it's coming; and I answered modestly that everything depended on circumstances. I might have said it depended on the demand for brass bedsteads; but perhaps that would have verged on indelicacy – you know that I am delicacy personified. 'I thought,' said Miss Birching, 'that a man of any energy made his own circumstances?' 'Energy!' I shouted. 'Do you look for energy in *me*? It's the greatest compliment anyone ever paid me.' At that she seemed desperately annoyed, and wouldn't pursue the subject. That's how it always was, just when the conversation grew interesting."

"I'm sorry to see you so cut up about it," remarked Hilliard.

"None of your irony, old fellow. Well, the truth is, I've seen someone I like better."

"Not surprised."

"It's a queer story; I'll tell it you some day, if it comes to anything. I'm not at all sure that it will, as there seems to be a sort of lurking danger that I may make a damned fool of myself."

"Improbable?" commented the listener. "Your blood is too temperate."

"So I thought; but one never knows. Unexpected feelings crop up in a fellow. We won't talk about it just now. How have things been going in the architectural line?"

"Not amiss. Steadily, I think."

Narramore lay back at full length, his face turned to the ceiling.

"Since I've been living out yonder, I've got a taste for the country. I have a notion that, if brass bedsteads keep firm, I shall some day build a little house of my own; an inexpensive little house, with a tree or two about it. Just make me a few sketches, will you? When you've nothing better to do, you know."

He played with the idea, till it took strong hold of him, and he began to talk with most unwonted animation.

"Five or six thousand pounds – I ought to be able to sink that in a few years. Not enough, eh? But I don't want a mansion. I'm quite serious about this, Hilliard. When you're feeling ready to start on your own account, you shall have the job."

Hilliard laughed grimly at the supposition that he would ever attain professional independence, but his friend talked on, and overleaped difficulties with a buoyancy of spirit which ultimately had its effect upon the listener. When he was alone again, Hilliard felt better, both in body and mind, and that evening, over the first bottle of Narramore's port, he amused himself with sketching ideal cottages.

"The fellow's in love, at last. When a man thinks of pleasant little country houses, 'with a tree or two' about them—"

He sighed, and ground his teeth, and sketched on.

Before bedtime, a sudden and profound shame possessed him. Was he not behaving outrageously in neglecting to answer Eve's letter? For all he knew the cold of which she complained might have caused her more suffering than he himself had gone through from the like cause, and that was bad enough. He seized paper and wrote to her as he had never written before, borne on the very high flood of passionate longing. Without regard to prudence he left the house at midnight and posted his letter.

"It never occurred to me to blame you for not writing," Eve quickly replied; "I'm afraid you are more sensitive than I am, and, to tell the truth, I believe men generally *are* more sensitive than women in things of this kind. It pleased me very much to hear of the visit you had had from Mr. Narramore, and that he had cheered you. I do so wish I could have come, but I have really been quite ill, and I must not think of risking a journey till the weather improves. Don't trouble about it; I will write often.

"I told you about a letter I had had from poor Patty, and I want to ask you to do something. Will you write to her? Just a nice, friendly little letter. She would be so delighted, she would indeed. There's no harm in copying a line or two from what she sent me. 'Has Mr. Hilliard forgotten all about me?' she says. 'I would write to him, but I feel afraid. Not afraid of *you*, dear Eve, but he might feel I was impertinent. What do you think? We had such delicious times together, he and you and I, and I really don't want him to forget me altogether?' Now I have told her that there is no fear whatever of your forgetting her, and that we often speak of her. I begin to think that I have been unjust to Patty in calling her silly, and making fun of her. She was anything but foolish in breaking off with that absurd Mr. Dally, and I can see now that she will never give a thought to him again. What I fear is that the poor girl will never find any one good enough for her. The men she meets are very vulgar, and vulgar Patty is *not* – as you once said to me, you remember. So, if you can spare a minute, write her a few lines, to show that you still think of her. Her address is—, etc."

To Hilliard all this seemed merely a pleasant proof of Eve's amiability, of her freedom from that acrid monopolism which characterises the ignoble female in her love relations. Straightway he did as he was requested, and penned to Miss Ringrose a chatty epistle, with which she could not but be satisfied. A day or two brought him an answer. Patty's handwriting lacked distinction, and in the matter of orthography she was not beyond reproach, but her letter chirped with a prettily expressed gratitude. "I am living with my aunt, and am likely to for a long time. And I get on very well at my new shop, which I have no wish to leave." This was her only allusion to the shattered matrimonial project: "I wish there was any chance of you and Eve coming to live in London, but I suppose that's too good to hope for. We don't get many things as we wish them in this world. And yet I oughtn't to say that either, for if it hadn't been for you I should never have seen Paris, which was so awfully jolly! But you'll be coming for a holiday, won't you? I should so like just to see you, if ever you do. It isn't like it was at the old shop. There's a great deal of business done here, and very little time to talk to anyone in the shop. But many girls have worse things to put up with than I have, and I won't make you think I'm a grumbler."

The whole of January went by before Hilliard and Eve again saw each other. The lover wrote at length that he could bear it no longer, that he was coming to Dudley, if only for the mere sight of Eve's face; she must meet him in the waiting-room at the railway station. She answered by return of post, "I will come over next Sunday, and be with you at twelve o'clock, but I must leave very early, as I am afraid to be out after nightfall." And this engagement was kept.

The dress of mourning became her well; it heightened her always noticeable air of refinement, and would have constrained to a reverential tenderness even had not Hilliard naturally checked himself from any bolder demonstration of joy. She spoke in a low, soft voice, seldom raised her eyes, and manifested a new gentleness very touching to Hilliard, though at the same time, and he knew not how or why, it did not answer to his desire. A midday meal was in readiness for her; she pretended to eat, but in reality scarce touched the food.

"You must taste old Narramore's port wine," said her entertainer. "The fellow actually sent a couple of dozen."

She was not to be persuaded; her refusal puzzled and annoyed Hilliard, and there followed a long silence. Indeed, it surprised him to find how little they could say to each other to-day. An unknown restraint had come between them.

"Well," he exclaimed at length, "I wrote to Patty, and she answered."

"May I see the letter?"

"Of course. Here it is."

Eve read it, and smiled with pleasure.

"Doesn't she write nicely! Poor girl!"

"Why have you taken so to commiserating her all at once?" Hilliard asked. "She's no worse off than she ever was. Rather better, I think."

"Life isn't the same for her since she was in Paris," said Eve, with peculiar softness.

"Well, perhaps it improved her."

"Oh, it certainly did! But it gave her a feeling of discontent for the old life and the people about her."

"A good many of us have to suffer that. She's nothing like as badly off as you are, my dear girl."

Eve coloured, and kept silence.

"We shall hear of her getting married before long," resumed the other. "She told me herself that marriage was the scourge of music-shops – it carries off their young women at such a rate."

"She told you that? It was in one of your long talks together in London? Patty and you got on capitally together. It was very natural she shouldn't care much for men like Mr. Dally afterwards."

Hilliard puzzled over this remark, and was on the point of making some impatient reply, but discretion restrained him. He turned to Eve's own affairs, questioned her closely about her life in the tradesman's house, and so their conversation followed a smoother course. Presently, half in jest, Hilliard mentioned Narramore's building projects.

"But who knows? It *might* come to something of importance for me. In two or three years, if all goes well, such a thing might possibly give me a start."

A singular solemnity had settled upon Eve's countenance. She spoke not a word, and seemed unaccountably ill at ease.

"Do you think I am in the clouds?" said Hilliard.

"Oh, no! Why shouldn't you get on – as other men do?"

But she would not dwell upon the hope, and Hilliard, not a little vexed, again became silent.

Her next visit was after a lapse of three weeks. She had again been suffering from a slight illness, and her pallor alarmed Hilliard. Again she began with talk of Patty Ringrose.

"Do you know, there's really a chance that we may see her before long! She'll have a holiday at Easter, from the Thursday night to Monday night, and I have all but got her to promise that she'll come over here. Wouldn't it be fun to let her see the Black Country? You remember her talk about it. I could get her a room, and if it's at all bearable weather, we would all have a day somewhere. Wouldn't you like that?"

"Yes; but I should greatly prefer a day with you alone."

"Oh, of course, the time is coming for that. Would you let us come here one day?"

With a persistence not to be mistaken Eve avoided all intimate topics; at the same time her manner grew more cordial. Through February and March, she decidedly improved in health. Hilliard saw her seldom, but she wrote frequent letters, and their note was as that of her conversation, lively, all but sportive. Once again she had become a mystery to her lover; he pondered over her very much as in the days when they were newly acquainted. Of one thing he felt but too well assured. She did not love him as he desired to be loved. Constant she might be, but it was the constancy of a woman unaffected with ardent emotion. If she granted him her lips they had no fervour respondent to his own; she made a sport of it, forgot it as soon as possible. Upon Hilliard's vehement nature this acted provocatively; at times he was all but frenzied with the violence of his sensual impulses. Yet Eve's control of him grew more assured the less she granted of herself; a look, a motion of her lips, and he drew apart, quivering but subdued. At one such moment he exclaimed:

"You had better not come here at all. I love you too insanely."

Eve looked at him, and silently began to shed tears. He implored her pardon, prostrated himself, behaved in a manner that justified his warning. But Eve stifled the serious drama of the situation, and forced him to laugh with her.

In these days architectural study made little way.

Patty Ringrose was coming for the Easter holidays. She would arrive on Good Friday. "As the weather is so very bad still," wrote Eve to Hilliard, "will you let us come to see you on Saturday? Sunday may be better for an excursion of some sort."

And thus it was arranged. Hilliard made ready his room to receive the fair visitors, who would come at about eleven in the morning. As usual nowadays, he felt discontented, but, after all, Patty's influence might be a help to him, as it had been in worse straits.

~ *Chapter 21* ~

TO-DAY he had the house to himself. The corn-dealer's shop was closed, as on a Sunday; the optician and his blind wife had locked up their rooms and were spending Easter-tide, it might be hoped, amid more cheerful surroundings. Hilliard sat with his door open, that he might easily hear the knock which announced his guests at the entrance below.

It sounded, at length, but timidly. Had he not been listening, he would not have perceived it. Eve's handling of the knocker was firmer than that, and in a different rhythm. Apprehensive of disappointment, he hurried downstairs and opened the door to Patty Ringrose – Patty alone. With a shy but pleased laugh, her cheeks warm and her eyes bright, she jerked out her hand to him as in the old days.

"I know you won't be glad to see me. I'm so sorry. I said I had better not come."

"Of course I am glad to see you. But where's Eve?"

"It's so unfortunate – she has such a bad headache!" panted the girl. "She couldn't possibly come, and I wanted to stay with her, I said. I should only disappoint you."

"It's a pity, of course; but I'm glad you came, for all that." Hilliard stifled his dissatisfaction and misgivings. "You'll think this a queer sort of place. I'm quite alone here to-day. But after you have rested a little we can go somewhere else."

"Yes. Eve told me you would be so kind as to take me to see things. I'm not tired. I won't come in, if you'd rather—"

"Oh, you may as well see what sort of a den I've made for myself."

He led the way upstairs. When she reached the top, Patty was again breathless, the result of excitement more than exertion. She exclaimed at sight of the sitting-room. How cosy it was! What a scent from the flowers! Did he always buy flowers for his room? No doubt it was to please Eve. What a comfortable chair! Of course Eve always sat in this chair?

Then her babbling ceased, and she looked up at Hilliard, who stood over against her, with nervous delight. He could perceive no change whatever in her, except that she was better dressed than formerly. Not a day seemed to have been added to her age; her voice had precisely the intonations that he remembered. After all, it was little more than half a year since they were together in Paris; but to Hilliard the winter had seemed of interminable length, and he expected to find Miss Ringrose a much altered person.

"When did this headache begin?" he inquired, trying to speak without over-much concern.

"She had a little yesterday, when she met me at the station. I didn't think she was looking at all well."

"I'm surprised to hear that. She looked particularly well when I saw her last. Had you any trouble in making your way here?"

"Oh, not a bit. I found the tram, just as Eve told me. But I'm so sorry! And a fine day too! You don't often have fine days here, do you, Mr. Hilliard?"

"Now and then. So you've seen Dudley at last. What do you think of it?"

"Oh, I like it! I shouldn't mind living there a bit. But of course I like Birmingham better."

"Almost as fine as Paris, isn't it?"

"You don't mean that, of course. But I've only seen a few of the streets, and most of the shops are shut up to-day. Isn't it a pity Eve has to live so far off? Though, of course, it isn't really very far – and I suppose you see each other often?"

Hilliard took a seat, crossed his legs, and grasped his knee. The girl appeared to wait for an answer to her last words, but he said nothing, and stared at the floor.

"If it's fine to-morrow," Patty continued, after observing him furtively, "are you coming to Dudley?"

"Yes, I shall come over. Did she send any message?"

"No – nothing particular—"

Patty looked confused, stroked her dress, and gave a little cough.

"But if it rains – as it very likely will – there's no use in my coming."

"No, she said not."

"Or if her headache is still troubling her—"

"Let's hope it will be better. But – in any case, she'll be able to come with me to Birmingham on Monday, when I go back. I must be home again on Monday night."

"Don't you think," said Hilliard carelessly, "that Eve would rather have you to herself, just for the short time you are here?"

Patty made vigorous objection.

"I don't think that at all. It's quite settled that you are to come over to-morrow, if it's fine. Oh, and I *do* hope it will be! It would be so dreadful to be shut up in the house all day at Dudley. How very awkward that there's no place where she can have you there! If it rains, hadn't we better come here? I'm sure it would be better for Eve. She seems to get into such low spirits – just like she was sometimes in London."

"That's quite news to me," said the listener gravely.

"Doesn't she let you know? Then I'm so sorry I mentioned it. You won't tell her I said anything?"

"Wait a moment. Does she say that she is often in low spirits?"

Patty faltered, stroking her dress with the movement of increasing nervousness.

"It's better I should know," Hilliard added, "I'm afraid she keeps all this from me. For several weeks I have thought her in particularly good health."

"But she tells me just the opposite. She says—"

"Says what?"

"Perhaps it's only the place that doesn't agree with her. I don't think Dudley is *very* healthy, do you?"

"I never heard of doctors sending convalescents there. But Eve must be suffering from some other cause, I think. Does it strike you that she is at all like what she used to be when – when you felt so anxious about her?"

He met the girl's eyes, and saw them expand in alarm.

"I didn't think – I didn't mean—" she stammered.

"No, but I have a reason for asking. Is it so or not?"

"Don't frighten me, Mr. Hilliard! I do so wish I hadn't said anything. She isn't in good health, that's all. How can you think—? That was all over long ago. And she would never – I'm *sure* she wouldn't, after all you've done for her."

Hilliard ground the carpet with his foot, and all but uttered a violent ejaculation.

"I know she is all gratitude," were the words that became audible.

"She is indeed!" urged Patty. "She says that – even if she wished – she could never break off with you; as I am *sure* she would never wish!"

"Ah! that's what she says," murmured the other. And abruptly he rose. "There's no use in talking about this. You are here for a holiday, and not to be bored with other people's troubles. The sun is trying to shine. Let us go and see the town, and then – yes, I'll go back with you to Dudley, just to hear whether Eve is feeling any better. You could see her, and then come out and tell me."

"Mr. Hilliard, I'm quite sure you are worrying without any cause – you are, indeed!"

"I know I am. It's all nonsense. Come along, and let us enjoy the sunshine."

They spent three or four hours together, Hilliard resolute in his discharge of hospitable duties, and Miss Ringrose, after a brief spell of unnatural gravity, allowing no reflection to interfere with her holiday mood. Hilliard had never felt quite sure as to the limits of Patty's intelligence; he could not take her seriously, and yet felt unable to treat her altogether as a child or an imbecile. To-day, because of his preoccupied thoughts, and the effort it cost him to be jocose, he talked for the most part in a vein of irony which impressed, but did not much enlighten, his hearer.

"This," said he, when they had reached the centre of things, "is the Acropolis of Birmingham. Here are our great buildings, of which we boast to the world. They signify the triumph of Democracy – and of money. In front of you stands the Town Hall. Here, to the left, is the Midland Institute, where a great deal of lecturing goes on, and the big free library, where you can either read or go to sleep. I have done both in my time. Behind yonder you catch a glimpse of the fountain that plays to the glory of Joseph Chamberlain – did you ever hear of him? And further back still is Mason College, where young men are taught a variety of things, including discontent with a small income. To the right there, that's the Council Hall – splendid, isn't it! We bring our little boys to look at it, and tell them if they make money enough they may some day go in and out as if it were their own house. Behind it you see the Art Gallery. We don't really care for pictures; a great big machine is our genuine delight; but it wouldn't be nice to tell everybody that."

"What a lot I have learnt from you!" exclaimed the girl ingenuously, when at length they turned their steps towards the railway station. "I shall always remember Birmingham. You like it much better than London, don't you?"

"I glory in the place!"

Hilliard was tired out. He repented of his proposal to make the journey to Dudley and back, but his companion did not suspect this.

"I'm sure Eve will come out and have a little walk with us," she said comfortingly. "And she'll think it so kind of you."

At Dudley station there were crowds of people; Patty asked leave to hold by her companion's arm as they made their way to the exit. Just outside Hilliard heard himself hailed in a familiar voice; he turned and saw Narramore.

"I beg your pardon," said his friend, coming near. "I didn't notice – I thought you were alone, or, of course I shouldn't have shouted. Shall you be at home to-morrow afternoon?"

"If it rains."

"It's sure to rain. I shall look in about four."

~ *Chapter 22* ~

WITH a glance at Miss Ringrose, he raised his hat and passed on. Hilliard, confused by the rapid rencontre, half annoyed at having been seen with Patty, and half wishing he had not granted the appointment for to-morrow, as it might interfere with a visit from the girls, walked forward in silence.

"So we really shan't see you if it's wet to-morrow," said Patty.

"Better not. Eve would be afraid to come, she catches cold so easily."

"It may be fine, like to-day. I do hope—"

She broke off and added:

"Why, isn't that Eve in front?"

Eve it certainly was, walking slowly away from the station, a few yards in advance of them. They quickened their pace, and Patty caught her friend by the arm. Eve, startled out of abstraction, stared at her with eyes of dismay and bloodless cheeks.

"Did I frighten you? Mr. Hilliard has come back with me to ask how you are. Is your head better?"

"I've just been down to the station – for something to do," said Eve, her look fixed on Hilliard with what seemed to him a very strange intensity. "The afternoon was so fine."

"We've had a splendid time," cried Patty. "Mr. Hilliard has shown me everything."

"I'm so glad. I should only have spoilt it if I had been with you. It's wretched going about with a headache, and I can't make believe to enjoy Birmingham."

Eve spoke hurriedly, still regarding Hilliard, who looked upon the ground.

"Have you been alone all day?" he asked, taking the outer place at her side, as they walked on.

"Of course – except for the people in the house," was her offhand reply.

"I met Narramore down at the station; he must have passed you. What has brought him here to-day, I wonder?"

Appearing not to heed the remark, Eve glanced across at Patty, and said with a laugh:

"It's like Paris again, isn't it – we three? You ought to come and live here, Patty. Don't you think you could get a place in Birmingham? Mr. Hilliard would get a piano for his room, and you could let him have some music. I'm too old to learn."

"I'm sure he wouldn't want *me* jingling there."

"Wouldn't he? He's very fond of music indeed."

Hilliard stopped.

"Well, I don't think I'll go any further," he said mechanically. "You're quite well again, Eve, and that's all I wanted to know."

"What about to-morrow?" Eve asked.

The sun had set, and in the westward sky rose a mountain of menacing cloud. Hilliard gave a glance in that direction before replying.

"Don't count upon me. Patty and you will enjoy the day together, in any case. Yes, I had rather have it so. Narramore said just now he might look in to see me in the afternoon. But come over on Monday. When does Patty's train go from New Street?"

Eve was mute, gazing at the speaker as if she did not catch what he had said. Patty answered for herself.

"Then you can either come to my place," he continued, "or I'll meet you at the station."

Patty's desire was evident in her face; she looked at Eve.

"We'll come to you early in the afternoon," said the latter, speaking like one aroused from reverie. "Yes, we'll come whatever the weather is."

The young man shook hands with them, raised his hat, and walked away without further speech. It occurred to him that he might overtake Narramore at the station, and in that hope he hastened; but Narramore must have left by a London and North-Western train which had just started; he was nowhere discoverable. Hilliard travelled back by the Great Western, after waiting about an hour; he had for companions half-a-dozen beer-muddled lads, who roared hymns and costers' catches impartially.

His mind was haunted with deadly suspicions: he felt sick at heart.

Eve's headache, undoubtedly, was a mere pretence for not accompanying Patty to-day. She had desired to be alone, and – this he discovered no less clearly – she wished the friendship between him and Patty to be fostered. With what foolish hope? Was she so shallow-natured as to imagine that he might transfer his affections to Patty Ringrose? It proved how strong her desire had grown to be free from him.

The innocent Patty (*was* she so innocent?) seemed not to suspect the meaning of her friend's talk. Yet Eve must have all but told her in so many words that she was weary of her lover. That hateful harping on "gratitude"! Well, one cannot purchase a woman's love. He had missed the right, the generous, line of conduct. That would have been to rescue Eve from manifest peril, and then to ask nothing of her. Could he but have held his passions in leash, something like friendship – rarest of all relations between man and woman – might have come about between him and Eve. She, too, certainly had never got beyond the stage of liking him as a companion; her senses had never answered to his appeal. He looked back upon the evening when they had dined together at the restaurant in Holborn. Could he but have stopped at *that* point! There would have been no harm in such avowals as then escaped him, for he recognised without bitterness that the warmth of feeling was all on one side, and Eve, in the manner of her sex, could like him better for his love without a dream of returning it. His error was to have taken advantage – perhaps a mean advantage – of the strange events that followed. If he restrained himself before, how much more he should have done so when the girl had put herself at his mercy, when to demand her love was the obvious, commonplace, vulgar outcome of the situation? Of course she harped on "gratitude." What but a sense of obligation had constrained her?

Something had taken place to-day; he felt it as a miserable certainty. The man from London had been with her. She expected him, and had elaborately planned for a day of freedom. Perhaps her invitation of Patty had no other motive.

That Patty was a conspirator against him he could not believe. No! She was merely an instrument of Eve's subtlety. And his suspicion had not gone beyond the truth. Eve entertained the hope that Patty might take her place. Perchance the silly, good-natured girl would feel no objection; though it was not very likely that she foresaw or schemed for such an issue.

At Snow Hill station it cost him an effort to rise and leave the carriage. His mood was sluggish; he wished to sit still and think idly over the course of events.

He went by way of St. Philip's Church, which stands amid a wide graveyard, enclosed with iron railings, and crossed by paved walks. The locality was all but forsaken; the church rose black against the grey sky, and the lofty places of business round about were darkly silent. A man's footstep sounded in front of him, and a figure approached along the narrow path between the high bars. Hilliard would have passed without attention, but the man stopped his way.

"Hollo! Here we are again!"

He stared at the speaker, and recognised Mr. Dengate.

"So you've come back?"

"Where from?" said Hilliard. "What do you know of me?"

"As much as I care to," replied the other with a laugh. "So you haven't quite gone to the devil yet? I gave you six months. I've been watching the police news in the London papers."

In a maddening access of rage, Hilliard clenched his fist and struck fiercely at the man. But he did no harm, for his aim was wild, and Dengate easily warded off the blows.

"Hold on! You're drunk, of course. Stop it, my lad, or I'll have you locked up till Monday morning. Very obliging of you to offer me the pleasure I was expecting, but you *will* have it, eh?"

A second blow was repaid in kind, and Hilliard staggered back against the railings. Before he could recover himself, Dengate, whose high hat rolled between their feet, pinned his arms.

"There's someone coming along. It's a pity. I should enjoy thrashing you and then running you in. But a man of my position doesn't care to get mixed up in a street row. It wouldn't sound well at Liverpool. Stand quiet, will you!"

A man and a woman drew near, and lingered for a moment in curiosity. Hilliard already amazed at what he had done, became passive, and stood with bent head.

"I must have a word or two with you," said Dengate, when he had picked up his hat. "Can you walk straight? I didn't notice you were drunk before I spoke to you. Come along this way."

To escape the lookers-on, Hilliard moved forward.

"I've always regretted," resumed his companion, "that I didn't give you a sound thrashing that night in the train. It would have done you good. It might have been the making of you. I didn't hurt you, eh?"

"You've bruised my lips – that's all. And I deserved it for being such a damned fool as to lose my temper."

"You look rather more decent than I should have expected. What have you been doing in London?"

"How do you know I have been in London?"

"I took that for granted when I knew you'd left your work at Dudley."

"Who told you I had left it?"

"What does it matter?"

"I should like to know," said Hilliard, whose excitement had passed and left him cold. "And I should like to know who told you before that I was in the habit of getting drunk?"

"Are you drunk now, or not?"

"Not in the way you mean. Do you happen to know a man called Narramore?"

"Never heard the name."

Hilliard felt ashamed of his ignoble suspicion. He became silent.

"There's no reason why you shouldn't be told," added Dengate; "it was a friend of yours at Dudley that I came across when I was making inquiries about you: Mullen his name was."

A clerk at the ironworks, with whom Hilliard had been on terms of slight intimacy.

"Oh, that fellow," he uttered carelessly. "I'm glad to know it was no one else. Why did you go inquiring about me?"

"I told you. If I'd heard a better account I should have done a good deal more for you than pay that money. I gave you a chance, too. If you'd shown any kind of decent behaviour when I spoke to you in the train – but it's no good talking about that now. This is the second time you've let me see what a natural blackguard you are. It's queer, too, you didn't get that from your father. I could have put you in the way of something good at Liverpool. Now, I'd see you damned first. Well, have you run through the money?"

"Every penny of it gone in drink."

"And what are you doing?"

"Walking with a man I should be glad to be rid of."

"All right. Here's my card. When you get into the gutter, and nobody'll give you a hand out, let me know."

With a nod, Dengate walked off. Hilliard saw him smooth his silk hat as he went; then, without glancing at the card, he threw it away.

The next morning was cold and wet. He lay in bed till eleven o'clock, when the charwoman came to put his rooms in order. At mid-day he left home, had dinner at the nearest place he knew where a meal could be obtained on Sunday, and afterwards walked the streets for an hour under his umbrella. The exercise did him good; on returning he felt able to sit down by the fire, and turn over the plates of his great book on French Cathedrals. This, at all events, remained to him out of the wreck, and was a joy that could be counted upon in days to come.

He hoped Narramore would keep his promise, and was not disappointed. On the verge of dusk his friend knocked and entered.

"The blind woman was at the door below," he explained, "looking for somebody."

"It isn't as absurd as it sounds. She does look for people – with her ears. She knows a footstep that no one else can hear. What were you doing at Dudley yesterday?"

Narramore took his pipe out of its case and smiled over it.

"Colours well, doesn't it?" he remarked. "You don't care about the colouring of a pipe? I get a lot of satisfaction out of such little things! Lazy fellows always do; and they have the best of life in the end. By-the-bye, what were *you* doing at Dudley?"

"Had to go over with a girl."

"Rather a pretty girl, too. Old acquaintance?"

"Someone I got to know in London. No, no, not at all what you suppose."

"Well, I know you wouldn't talk about it. It isn't my way, either, to say much about such things. But I half-promised, not long ago, to let you know of something that was going on – if it came to anything. And it rather looks as if it might. What do you think! Birching has been at me, wanting to know why I don't call. I wonder whether the girl put him up to it?"

"You went rather far, didn't you?"

"Oh, I drew back in time. Besides, those ideas are old-fashioned. It'll have to be understood that marriageable girls have nothing specially sacred about them. They must associate with men on equal terms. The day has gone by for a hulking brother to come asking a man about his 'intentions.' As a rule, it's the girl that has intentions. The man is just looking round, anxious to be amiable without making a fool of himself. We're at a great disadvantage. A girl who isn't an idiot can very soon know all about the men who interest her; but it's devilish difficult to get much insight into *them* – until you've hopelessly committed yourself – won't you smoke? I've something to tell you, and I can't talk to a man who isn't smoking, when my own pipe's lit."

Hilliard obeyed, and for a few moments they puffed in silence, twilight thickening about them.

"Three or four months ago," resumed Narramore, "I was told one day – at business – that a lady wished to see me. I happened to have the room to myself, and told them to show the lady in. I didn't in the least know who it could be, and I was surprised to see rather a good-looking girl – not exactly a lady – tallish, and with fine dark eyes – what did you say?"

"Nothing."

"A twinge of gout?"

"Go on."

Narramore scrutinised his friend, who spoke in an unusual tone.

"She sat down, and began to tell me that she was out of work – wanted a place as a bookkeeper, or something of the kind. Could I help her? I asked her why she came to *me*. She said she had heard of me from someone who used to be employed at our place. That was flattering. I showed my sense of it. Then I asked her name, and she said it was Miss Madeley."

A gust threw rain against the windows. Narramore paused, looking into the fire, and smiling thoughtfully.

~ *Chapter 23* ~

"YOU foresee the course of the narrative?"

"Better tell it in detail," muttered Hilliard.

"Why this severe tone? Do you anticipate something that will shock your moral sense? I didn't think you were so straitlaced."

"Do you mean to say—"

Hilliard was sitting upright; his voice began on a harsh tremor, and suddenly failed. The other gazed at him in humorous astonishment.

"What the devil do you mean? Even suppose – who made you a judge and a ruler? This is the most comical start I've known for a long time. I was going to tell you that I have made up my mind to marry the girl."

"I see – it's all right—"

"But do you really mean," said Narramore, "that anything else would have aroused your moral indignation?"

Hilliard burst into a violent fit of laughter. His pipe fell to the floor, and broke; whereupon he interrupted his strange merriment with a savage oath.

"It was a joke, then?" remarked his friend.

"Your monstrous dulness shows the state of your mind. This is what comes of getting entangled with women. You need to have a sense of humour."

"I'm afraid there's some truth in what you say, old boy. I've been conscious of queer symptoms lately – a disposition to take things with absurd seriousness, and an unwholesome bodily activity now and then."

"Go on with your tragic story. The girl asked you to find her a place—"

"I promised to think about it, but I couldn't hear of anything suitable. She had left her address with me, so at length I wrote her a line just saying I hadn't forgotten her. I got an answer on black-edged paper. Miss Madeley wrote to tell me that her father had recently died, and that she had found employment at Dudley; with thanks for my kindness – and so on. It was rather a nicely written letter, and after a day or two I wrote again. I heard nothing – hardly expected to; so in a fortnight's time I wrote once more. Significant, wasn't it? I'm not fond of writing letters, as you know. But I've written a good many since then. At last it came to another meeting. I went over to Dudley on purpose, and saw Miss Madeley on the Castle Hill. I had liked the look of her from the first, and I liked it still better now. By dint of persuasion, I made her tell me all about herself."

"Did she tell you the truth?"

"Why should you suppose she didn't?" replied Narramore with some emphasis. "You must look at this affair in a different light, Hilliard. A joke is a joke, but I've told you that the joking time has gone by. I can make allowance for you: you think I have been making a fool of myself, after all."

"The beginning was ominous."

"The beginning of our acquaintance? Yes, I know how it strikes you. But she came in that way because she had been trying for months—"

"Who was it that told her of you?"

"Oh, one of our girls, no doubt. I haven't asked her – never thought again about it."

"And what's her record?"

"Nothing dramatic in it, I'm glad to say. At one time she had an engagement in London for a year or two. Her people, 'poor but honest' – as the stories put it. Father was a timekeeper at Dudley; brother, a mechanic there. I was over to see her yesterday; we had only just said good-bye when I met you. She's remarkably well educated, all things considered: very fond of reading; knows as much of books as I do – more, I daresay. First-rate intelligence; I guessed that from the first. I can see the drawbacks, of course. As I said, she isn't what *you* would call a lady; but there's nothing much to find fault with even in her manners. And the long and the short of it is, I'm in love with her."

"And she has promised to marry you?"

"Well, not in so many words. She seems to have scruples – difference of position, and that kind of thing."

"Very reasonable scruples, no doubt."

"Quite right that she should think of it in that way, at all events. But I believe it was practically settled yesterday. She isn't in very brilliant health, poor girl! I want to get her away from that beastly place as soon as possible. I shall give myself a longish holiday, and take her on to the Continent. A thorough change of that kind would set her up wonderfully.

"She has never been on to the Continent?"

"What a preposterous question! You're going to sleep, sitting here in the dark. Oh, don't trouble to light up for me; I can't stay much longer."

Hilliard had risen, but instead of lighting the lamp he turned to the window and stood there drumming with his fingers on a pane.

"Are you seriously concerned for me?" said his friend. "Does it seem a piece of madness?"

"You must judge for yourself, Narramore."

"When you have seen her I think you'll take my views. Of course it's the very last thing I ever imagined myself doing; but I begin to see that the talk about fate isn't altogether humbug. I want this girl for my wife, and I never met any one else whom I really *did* want. She suits me exactly. It isn't as if I thought of marrying an ordinary, ignorant, low-class girl. Eve – that's her name – is very much out of the common, look at her how you may. She's rather melancholy, but that's a natural result of her life."

"No doubt, as you say, she wants a thorough change," remarked Hilliard, smiling in the gloom.

"That's it. Her nerves are out of order. Well, I thought I should like to tell you this, old chap. You'll get over the shock in time. I more than half believe, still, that your moral indignation was genuine. And why not? I ought to respect you for it."

"Are you going?"

"I must be in Bristol Road by five – promised to drink a cup of Mrs. Stocker's tea this afternoon. I'm glad now that I have kept up a few homely acquaintances; they may be useful. Of course I shall throw over the Birchings and that lot. You see now why my thoughts have been running on a country house!"

He went off laughing, and his friend sat down again by the fireside.

Half an hour passed. The fire had burnt low, and the room was quite dark. At length, Hilliard bestirred himself. He lit the lamp, drew down the blind, and seated himself at the table to write. With great rapidity he covered four sides of note-paper, and addressed an envelope. But he had no postage-stamp. It could be obtained at a tobacconist's.

So he went out, and turned towards a little shop hard by. But when he had stamped the letter he felt undecided about posting it. Eve had promised to come to-morrow with Patty. If she again failed him it would be time enough to write. If she kept her promise the presence of a third person would be an intolerable restraint upon him. Yet why? Patty might as well know all, and act as judge between them. There needed little sagacity to arbitrate in a matter such as this.

To sit at home was impossible. He walked for the sake of walking, straight on, without object. Down the long gas-lit perspective of Bradford Street, with its closed, silent workshops, across the miserable little river Rea – canal rather than river, sewer rather than canal – up the steep ascent to St. Martin's and the Bull Ring, and the bronze Nelson, dripping with dirty moisture; between the big buildings of New Street, and so to the centre of the town. At the corner by the Post Office he stood in idle contemplation. Rain was still falling, but lightly. The great open space gleamed with shafts of yellow radiance reflected on wet asphalt from the numerous lamps. There was little traffic. An omnibus clattered by, and a tottery cab, both looking rain-soaked. Near the statue of Peel stood a hansom, the forlorn horse crooking his knees and hanging his hopeless head. The Town Hall colonnade sheltered a crowd of people, who were waiting for the rain to stop, that they might spend their Sunday evening, as usual, in rambling about the streets. Within the building, which showed light through all its long windows, a religious meeting was in progress, and hundreds of voices peeled forth a rousing hymn, fortified with deeper organ-note.

Hilliard noticed that as rain-drops fell on the heated globes of the street-lamps they were thrown off again in little jets and puffs of steam. This phenomenon amused him for several minutes. He wondered that he had never observed it before.

Easter Sunday. The day had its importance for a Christian mind. Did Eve think about that? Perhaps her association with him, careless as he was in all such matters, had helped to blunt her religious feeling. Yet what hope was there, in such a world as this, that she would retain the pieties of her girlhood?

Easter Sunday. As he walked on, he pondered the Christian story, and tried to make something out of it. Had it any significance for *him*? Perhaps, for he had never consciously discarded the old faith; he had simply let it fall out of his mind. But a woman ought to have religious convictions. Yes; he saw the necessity of that. Better for him if Eve were in the Town Hall yonder, joining her voice with those that sang.

Better for *him*. A selfish point of view. But the advantage would be hers also. Did he not desire her happiness? He tried to think so, but after all was ashamed to play the sophist with himself. The letter he carried in his pocket told the truth. He had but to think of her as married to Robert Narramore and the jealous fury of natural man drove him headlong.

Monday was again a holiday. When would the cursed people get back to their toil, and let the world resume its wonted grind and clang? They seemed to have been making holiday for a month past.

He walked up and down on the pavement near his door, until at the street corner there appeared a figure he knew. It was Patty Ringrose, again unaccompanied.

~ *Chapter 24* ~

THEY shook hands without a word, their eyes meeting for an instant only. Hilliard led the way upstairs; and Patty, still keeping an embarrassed silence, sat down on the easy-chair. Her complexion was as noticeably fresh as Hilliard's was wan and fatigued. Where Patty's skin showed a dimple, his bore a gash, the result of an accident in shaving this morning.

With hands behind he stood in front of the girl.

"She chose not to come, then?"

"Yes. She asked me to come and see you alone."

"No pretence of headache this time."

"I don't think it was a pretence," faltered Patty, who looked very ill at ease, for all the bloom on her cheeks and the clear, childish light in her eyes.

"Well, then, why hasn't she come to-day?"

"She has sent a letter for you, Mr. Hilliard."

Patty handed the missive, and Hilliard laid it upon the table.

"Am I to read it now?"

"I think it's a long letter."

"Feels like it. I'll study it at my leisure. You know what it contains?"

Patty nodded, her face turned away.

"And why has she chosen to-day to write to me?" Patty kept silence. "Anything to do with the call I had yesterday from my friend Narramore?"

"Yes – that's the reason. But she has meant to let you know for some time."

Hilliard drew a long breath. He fixed his eyes on the letter.

"She has told me everything," the girl continued, speaking hurriedly.

"Did you know about it before yesterday?"

"I'm not so good an actor as all that. Eve has the advantage of me in that respect. She really thought it possible that Narramore had spoken before?"

"She couldn't be sure."

"H'm! Then she didn't know for certain that Narramore was going to talk to me about her yesterday?"

"She knew it *must* come."

"Patty, our friend Miss Madeley is a very sensible person – don't you think so?"

"You mustn't think she made a plan to deceive you. She tells you all about it in the letter, and I'm quite sure it's all true, Mr. Hilliard. I was astonished when I heard of it, and I can't tell you how sorry I feel—"

"I'm not at all sure that there's any cause for sorrow," Hilliard interrupted, drawing up a chair and throwing himself upon it. "Unless you mean that you are sorry for Eve."

"I meant that as well."

"Let us understand each other. How much has she told you?"

"Everything, from beginning to end. I had no idea of what happened in London before we went to Paris. And she does so repent of it! She doesn't know how she could do it. She wishes you had refused her."

"So do I."

"But you saved her – she can never forget that. You mustn't think that she only pretends to be grateful. She will be grateful to you as long as she lives. I know she will."

"On condition that I – what?"

Patty gave him a bewildered look.

"What does she ask of me now?"

"She's ashamed to ask anything. She fears you will never speak to her again."

Hilliard meditated, then glanced at the letter.

"I had better read this now, I think, if you will let me."

"Yes – please do—"

He tore open the envelope, and disclosed two sheets of note-paper, covered with writing. For several minutes there was silence; Patty now and then gave a furtive glance at her companion's face as he was reading. At length he put the letter down again, softly.

"There's something more here than I expected. Can you tell me whether she heard from Narramore this morning?"

"She has had no letter."

"I see. And what does she suppose passed between Narramore and me yesterday?"

"She is wondering what you told him."

"She takes it for granted, in this letter, that I have put an end to everything between them. Well, hadn't I a right to do so?"

"Of course you had," Patty replied, with emphasis. "And she knew it must come. She never really thought that she could marry Mr. Narramore. She gave him no promise."

"Only corresponded with him, and made appointments with him, and allowed him to feel sure that she would be his wife."

"Eve has behaved very strangely. I can't understand her. She ought to have told you that she had been to see him, and that he wrote to her. It's always best to be straightforward. See what trouble she has got herself into!"

Hilliard took up the letter again, and again there was a long silence.

"Have you said good-bye to her?" were his next words.

"She's going to meet me at the station to see me off."

"Did she come from Dudley with you?"

"No."

"It's all very well to make use of you for this disagreeable business—"

"Oh, I didn't mind it!" broke in Patty, with irrelevant cheerfulness.

"A woman who does such things as this should have the courage to go through with it. She ought to have come herself, and have told me that. She was aiming at much better things than *I* could have promised her. There would have been something to admire in that. The worst of it is she is making me feel ashamed of her. I'd rather have to do with a woman who didn't care a rap for my feelings than with a weak one, who tried to spare me to advantage herself at the same time. There's nothing like courage, whether in good or evil. What do you think? Does she like Narramore?"

"I think she does," faltered Patty, nervously stroking her dress.

"Is she in love with him?"

"I – I really don't know!"

"Do you think she ever was in love with anyone, or ever will be?"

Patty sat mute.

"Just tell me what you think."

"I'm afraid she never – Oh, I don't like to say it, Mr. Hilliard!"

"That she never was in love with *me*? I know it."

His tone caused Patty to look up at him, and what she saw in his face made her say quickly:

"I am so sorry; I am indeed! You deserve—"

"Never mind what I deserve," Hilliard interrupted with a grim smile. "Something less than hanging, I hope. That fellow in London; she was fond of *him*?"

The girl whispered an assent.

"A pity I interfered."

"Ah! But think what—"

"We won't discuss it, Patty. It's a horrible thing to be mad about a girl who cares no more for you than for an old glove; but it's a fool's part to try to win her by the way of gratitude. When we came back from Paris I

ought to have gone my way, and left her to go hers. Perhaps just possible
– if I had seemed to think no more of her—"

Patty waited, but he did not finish his speech.

"What are you going to do, Mr. Hilliard?"

"Yes, that's the question. Shall I hold her to her promise? She says here
that she will keep her word if I demand it."

"She says that!" Patty exclaimed, with startled eyes.

"Didn't you know?"

"She told me it was impossible. But perhaps she didn't mean it. Who
can tell *what* she means?"

For the first time there sounded a petulance in the girl's voice. Her lips
closed tightly, and she tapped with her foot on the floor.

"Did she say that the other thing was also impossible – to marry
Narramore?"

"She thinks it is, after what you've told him."

"Well, now, as a matter of fact I told him nothing."

Patty stared, a new light in her eyes.

"You told him – nothing?"

"I just let him suppose that I had never heard the girl's name before."

"Oh, how kind of you! How—"

"Please to remember that it wasn't very easy to tell the truth. What sort
of figure should I have made?"

"It's too bad of Eve! It's cruel! I can never like her as I did before."

"Oh, she's very interesting. She gives one such a lot to talk about."

"I don't like her, and I shall tell her so before I leave Birmingham. What
right has she to make people so miserable?"

"Only one, after all."

"Do you mean that you will let her marry Mr. Narramore?" Patty asked
with interest.

"We shall have to talk about that."

"If I were you I should never see her again!"

"The probability is that we shall see each other many a time."

"Then *you* haven't much courage, Mr. Hilliard!" exclaimed the girl,
with a flush on her cheeks.

"More than you think, perhaps," he answered between his teeth.

"Men are very strange," Patty commented in a low voice of scorn,
mitigated by timidity.

"Yes, we play queer pranks when a woman has made a slave of us. I
suppose you think I should have too much pride to care any more for her.

The truth is that for years to come I shall tremble all through whenever she is near me. Such love as I have felt for Eve won't be trampled out like a spark. It's the best and the worst part of my life. No woman can ever be to me what Eve is."

Abashed by the grave force of this utterance, Patty shrank back into the chair, and held her peace.

"You will very soon know what comes of it all," Hilliard continued with a sudden change of voice. "It has to be decided pretty quickly, one way or another."

"May I tell Eve what you have said to me?" the girl asked with diffidence.

"Yes, anything that I have said."

Patty lingered a little, then, as her companion said no more, she rose.

"I must say good-bye, Mr. Hilliard."

"I am afraid your holiday hasn't been as pleasant as you expected."

"Oh, I have enjoyed myself very much. And I hope" – her voice wavered – "I do hope it'll be all right. I'm sure you'll do what seems best."

"I shall do what I find myself obliged to, Patty. Good-bye. I won't offer to go with you, for I should be poor company."

He conducted her to the foot of the stairs, again shook hands with her, put all his goodwill into a smile, and watched her trip away with a step not so light as usual. Then he returned to Eve's letter. It gave him a detailed account of her relations with Narramore. "I went to him because I couldn't bear to live idle any longer; I had no other thought in my mind. If he had been the means of my finding work, I should have confessed it to you at once. But I was tempted into answering his letters.... I knew I was behaving wrongly; I can't defend myself.... I have never concealed my faults from you – the greatest of them is my fear of poverty. I believe it is this that has prevented me from returning your love as I wished to do. For a long time I have been playing a deceitful part, and the strange thing is that I *knew* my exposure might come at any moment. I seem to have been led on by a sort of despair. Now I am tired of it; whether you were prepared for this or not, I must tell you.... I don't ask you to release me. I have been wronging you and acting against my conscience, and if you can forgive me I will try to make up for the ill I have done...."

How much of this could he believe? Gladly he would have fooled himself into believing it all, but the rational soul in him cast out credulity. Every phrase of the letter was calculated for its impression. And the very risk she had run, was not that too a matter of deliberate speculation? She *might* succeed in her design upon Narramore; if she failed, the poorer man was still to be counted upon, for she knew the extent of her power over him. It was worth the endeavour. Perhaps, in her insolent self-confidence, she did not fear the effect on Narramore of the disclosure that might be made to him. And who could say that her boldness was not likely to be justified?

He burned with wrath against her, the wrath of a hopelessly infatuated man. Thoughts of revenge, no matter how ignoble, harassed his mind. She counted on his slavish spirit, and even in saying that she did not ask him to release her, she saw herself already released. At each reperusal of her letter he felt more resolved to disappoint the hope that inspired it. When she learnt from Patty that Narramore was still ignorant of her history how would she exult! But that joy should be brief. In the name of common honesty he would protect his friend. If Narramore chose to take her with his eyes open—

Jealous frenzy kept him pacing the room for an hour or two. Then he went forth and haunted the neighbourhood of New Street station until within five minutes of the time of departure of Patty's train. If Eve kept her promise to see the girl off he might surprise her upon the platform.

From the bridge crossing the lines he surveyed the crowd of people that waited by the London train, a bank-holiday train taking back a freight of excursionists. There-amid he discovered Eve, noted her position, descended to the platform, and got as near to her as possible. The train moved off. As Eve turned away among the dispersing people, he stepped to meet her.

~ *Chapter 25* ~

SHE gave no sign of surprise. Hilliard read in her face that she had prepared herself for this encounter.

"Come away where we can talk," he said abruptly.

She walked by him to a part of the station where only a porter passed occasionally. The echoings beneath the vaulted roof allowed them to speak without constraint, for their voices were inaudible a yard or two off. Hilliard would not look into her face, lest he should be softened to foolish clemency.

"It's very kind of you," he began, with no clear purpose save the desire of harsh speech, "to ask me to overlook this trifle, and let things be as before."

"I have said all I *can* say in the letter. I deserve all your anger."

That was the note he dreaded, the too well remembered note of pathetic submission. It reminded him with intolerable force that he had never held her by any bond save that of her gratitude.

"Do you really imagine," he exclaimed, "that I could go on with make-believe – that I could bring myself to put faith in you again for a moment?"

"I don't ask you to," Eve replied, in firmer accents. "I have lost what little respect you could ever feel for me. I might have repaid you with honesty – I didn't do even that. Say the worst you can of me, and I shall think still worse of myself."

The voice overcame him with a conviction of her sincerity, and he gazed at her, marvelling.

"Are you honest *now*? Anyone would think so; yet how am I to believe it?"

Eve met his eyes steadily.

"I will never again say one word to you that isn't pure truth. I am at your mercy, and you may punish me as you like."

"There's only one way in which I can punish you. For the loss of *my* respect, or of my love, you care nothing. If I bring myself to tell Narramore disagreeable things about you, you will suffer a disappointment, and that's all. The cost to me will be much greater, and you know it. You pity yourself. You regard me as holding you ungenerously by an advantage you once gave me. It isn't so at all. It is I who have been held by bonds I couldn't break, and from the day when you pretended a love you never felt, all the blame lay with you."

"What could I do?"

"Be truthful – that was all."

"You were not content with the truth. You forced me to think that I could love you. Only remember what passed between us."

"Honesty was still possible, when you came to know yourself better. You should have said to me in so many words: 'I can't look forward to our future with any courage; if I marry it must be a man who has more to offer.' Do you think I couldn't have endured to hear that? You have never understood me. I should have said: 'Then let us shake hands, and I am your friend to help you all I can.'"

"You say that *now*—"

"I should have said it at any time."

"But I am not so mean as you think me. If I loved a man I could face poverty with him, much as I hate and dread it. It was because I only liked you, and could not feel more—"

"Your love happens to fall upon a man who has solid possessions."

"It's easy to speak so scornfully. I have not pretended to love the man you mean."

"Yet you have brought him to think that you are willing to marry him."

"Without any word of love from me. If I had been free I would have married him – just because I am sick of the life I lead, and long for the kind of life he offered me."

"When it's too late you are frank enough."

"Despise me as much as you like. You want the truth, and you shall hear nothing else from me."

"Well, we get near to understanding each other. But it astonishes me that you spoilt your excellent chance. How could you hope to carry through this—"

Eve broke in impatiently.

"I told you in the letter that I had no hope of it. It's your mistake to think me a crafty, plotting, selfish woman. I'm only a very miserable one – it went on from this to that, and I meant nothing. I didn't scheme; I was only tempted into foolishness. I felt myself getting into difficulties that would be my ruin, but I hadn't strength to draw back."

"You do yourself injustice," said Hilliard, coldly. "For the past month you have acted a part before me, and acted it well. You seemed to be reconciling yourself to my prospects, indifferent as they were. You encouraged me – talked with unusual cheerfulness – showed a bright face. If this wasn't deliberate acting what did it mean?"

"Yes, it was put on," Eve admitted, after a pause. "But I couldn't help that. I was obliged to keep seeing you, and if I had looked as miserable as I felt—" She broke off. "I tried to behave just like a friend. You can't charge me with pretending – anything else. I *could* be your friend: that was honest feeling."

"It's no use to me. I must have more, or nothing."

The flood of passion surged in him again. Some trick of her voice, or some indescribable movement of her head – the trifles which are all-powerful over a man in love – beat down his contending reason.

"You say," he continued, "that you will make amends for your unfair dealing. If you mean it, take the only course that shows itself. Confess to Narramore what you have done; you owe it to him as much as to me."

"I can't do that," said Eve, drawing away. "It's for you to tell him – if you like."

"No. I had my opportunity, and let it pass. I don't mean that you are to inform him of all there has been between us; that's needless. We have agreed to forget everything that suggests the word I hate. But that you and I have been lovers and looked – I, at all events – to be something more, this you must let him know."

"I can never do that."

"Without it, how are you to disentangle yourself?"

"I promise you he shall see no more of me."

"Such a promise is idle, and you know it. Remember, too, that Narramore and I are friends. He will speak to me of you, and I can't play a farce with him. It would be intolerable discomfort to me, and grossly unfair to him. Do, for once, the simple, honourable thing, and make a new beginning. After that, be guided by your own interests. Assuredly I shall not stand in your way."

Eve had turned her eyes in the direction of crowd and bustle. When she faced Hilliard again, he saw that she had come to a resolve.

"There's only one way out of it for me," she said impulsively. "I can't talk any longer. I'll write to you."

She moved from him; Hilliard followed. At a distance of half-a-dozen yards, just as he was about to address her again, she stopped and spoke—

"You hate to hear me talk of 'gratitude.' I have always meant by it less than you thought. I was grateful for the money, not for anything else. When you took me away, perhaps it was the unkindest thing you could have done."

An unwonted vehemence shook her voice. Her muscles were tense; she stood in an attitude of rebellious pride.

"If I had been true to myself then—But it isn't too late. If I am to act honestly, I know very well what I must do. I will take your advice."

Hilliard could not doubt of her meaning. He remembered his last talk with Patty. This was a declaration he had not foreseen, and it affected him otherwise than he could have anticipated.

"My advice had nothing to do with *that*," was his answer, as he read her face. "But I shall say not a word against it. I could respect you, at all events."

"Yes, and I had rather have your respect than your love."

With that, she left him. He wished to pursue, but a physical languor held him motionless. And when at length he sauntered from the place, it was with a sense of satisfaction at what had happened. Let her carry out that purpose: he faced it, preferred it. Let her be lost to him in that way rather than any other. It cut the knot, and left him with a memory of Eve that would efface her dishonouring weakness.

Late at night, he walked about the streets near his home, debating with himself whether she would act as she spoke, or had only sought to frighten him with a threat. And still he hoped that her resolve was sincere. He could bear that conclusion of their story better than any other – unless it were her death. Better a thousand times than her marriage with Narramore.

In the morning, fatigue gave voice to conscience. He had bidden her go, when, perchance, a word would have checked her. Should he write, or even go to her straightway and retract what he had said? His will prevailed, and he did nothing.

The night that followed plagued him with other misgivings. It seemed more probable now that she had threatened what she would never have the courage to perform. She meant it at the moment – it declared a truth but an hour after she would listen to commonplace morality or prudence. Narramore would write to her; she might, perhaps, see him again. She would cling to the baser hope.

Might but the morrow bring him a letter from London!

It brought nothing; and day after day disappointed him. More than a week passed: he was ill with suspense, but could take no step for setting his mind at rest. Then, as he sat one morning at his work in the architect's office, there arrived a telegram addressed to him—

"I must see you as soon as possible. Be here before six. – Narramore."

~ *Chapter 26* ~

"WHAT the devil does this mean, Hilliard?"

If never before, the indolent man was now thoroughly aroused. He had an open letter in his hand. Hilliard, standing before him in a little office that smelt of ledgers and gum, and many other commercial things, knew that the letter must be from Eve, and savagely hoped that it was dated London.

"This is from Miss Madeley, and it's all about you. Why couldn't you speak the other day?"

"What does she say about me?"

"That she has known you for a long time; that you saw a great deal of each other in London; that she has led you on with a hope of marrying her, though she never really meant it; in short, that she has used you very ill, and feels obliged now to make a clean breast of it."

The listener fixed his eye upon a copying-press, but without seeing it. A grim smile began to contort his lips.

"Where does she write from?"

"From her ordinary address – why not? I think this is rather too bad of you. Why didn't you speak, instead of writhing about and sputtering? That kind of thing is all very well – sense of honour and all that – but it meant that I was being taken in. Between friends – hang it! Of course I have done with her. I shall write at once. It's amazing; it took away my breath. No doubt, though she doesn't say it, it was from you that she came to know of me. She began with a lie. And who the devil could have thought it! Her face – her way of talking! This will cut me up awfully. Of course, I'm sorry for you, too, but it was your plain duty to let me know what sort of a woman I had got hold of. Nay, it's she that has got hold of me, confound her! I don't feel myself! I'm thoroughly knocked over!"

Hilliard began humming an air. He crossed the room and sat down.

"Have you seen her since that Saturday?"

"No; she has made excuses, and I guessed something was wrong. What has been going on? *You* have seen her?"

"Of course."

Narramore glared.

"It's devilish underhand behaviour! Look here, old fellow, we're not going to quarrel. No woman is worth a quarrel between two old friends. But just speak out – can't you? What did you mean by keeping it from me?"

"It meant that I had nothing to say," Hilliard replied, through his moustache.

"You kept silence out of spite, then? You said to yourself, 'Let him marry her and find out afterwards what she really is!' "

"Nothing of the kind." He looked up frankly. "I saw no reason for speaking. She accuses herself without a shadow of reason; it's mere hysterical conscientiousness. We have known each other for half a year or so, and I have made love to her, but I never had the least encouragement. I knew all along she didn't care for me. How is she to blame? A girl is under no obligation to speak of all the men who have wanted to marry her, provided she has done nothing to be ashamed of. There's just one bit of insincerity. It's true she knew of you from me. But she looked you up because she despaired of finding employment; she was at an end of her money, didn't know what to do. I have heard this since I saw you last. It wasn't quite straightforward, but one can forgive it in a girl hard driven by necessity."

Narramore was listening with eagerness, his lips parted, and a growing hope in his eyes.

"There never was anything serious between you?"

"On her side, never for a moment. I pursued and pestered her, that was all."

"Do you mind telling me who the girl was that I saw you with at Dudley?"

"A friend of Miss Madeley's, over here from London on a holiday. I have tried to make use of her – to get her influence on my side—"

Narramore sprang from the corner of the table on which he had been sitting.

"Why couldn't she hold her tongue! That's just like a woman, to keep a thing quiet when she ought to speak of it, and bring it out when she had far better say nothing. I feel as if I had treated you badly, Hilliard. And the way you take it – I'd rather you eased your mind by swearing at me."

"I could swear hard enough. I could grip you by the throat and jump on you—"

"No, I'm hanged if you could!" He forced a laugh. "And I shouldn't advise you to try. Here, give me your hand instead." He seized it. "We're going to talk this over like two reasonable beings. Does this girl know her own mind? It seems to me from this letter that she wants to get rid of me."

"You must find out whether she does or not."

"Do you *think* she does?"

"I refuse to think about it at all."

"You mean she isn't worth troubling about? Tell the truth, and be hanged to you! Is she the kind of a girl a man may marry?"

"For all I know."

"Do you suspect her?" Narramore urged fiercely.

"She'll marry a rich man rather than a poor one – that's the worst I think of her."

"What woman won't?"

When question and answer had revolved about this point for another quarter of an hour, Hilliard brought the dialogue to an end. He was clay-colour, and perspiration stood on his forehead.

"You must make her out without any more help from me. I tell you the letter is all nonsense, and I can say no more."

He moved towards the exit.

"One thing I must know, Hilliard – Are you going to see her again?"

"Never – if I can help it."

"Can we be friends still?"

"If you never mention her name to me."

Again they shook hands, eyes crossing in a smile of shamed hostility. And the parting was for more than a twelvemonth.

Late in August, when Hilliard was thinking of a week's rest in the country, after a spell of harder and more successful work than he had ever previously known, he received a letter from Patty Ringrose.

"Dear Mr. Hilliard," wrote the girl, "I have just heard from Eve that she is to be married to Mr. Narramore in a week's time. She says you don't know about it; but I think you *ought* to know. I haven't been able to make anything of her two last letters, but she has written plainly at last. Perhaps she means me to tell you. Will you let me have a line? I should like to know whether you care much, and I do so hope you don't! I felt sure it would come to this, and if you'll believe me, it's just as well. I haven't answered her letter, and I don't know whether I shall. I might say disagreeable things. Everything is the same with me and always will be, I suppose." In conclusion, she was his sincerely. A postscript remarked: "They tell me I play better. I've been practising a great deal, just to kill the time."

"Dear Miss Ringrose," he responded, "I am very glad to know that Eve is to be comfortably settled for life. By all means answer her letter, and by all means keep from saying disagreeable things. It is never wise to quarrel with prosperous friends, and why should you? With every good wish—" he remained sincerely hers.

~ *Chapter 27* ~

WHEN Hilliard and his friend again shook hands it was the autumn of another year. Not even by chance had they encountered in the interval and no written message had passed between them. Their meeting was at a house newly acquired by the younger of the Birching brothers, who, being about to marry, summoned his bachelor familiars to smoke their pipes in the suburban abode while yet his rule there was undisputed. With Narramore he had of late resumed the friendship interrupted by Miss Birching's displeasure, for that somewhat imperious young lady, now the wife of an elderly ironmaster, moved in other circles; and Hilliard's professional value, which was beginning to be recognised by the Birchings otherwise than in the way of compliment, had overcome the restraints at first imposed by his dubious social standing.

They met genially, without a hint of estrangement.

"Your wife well?" Hilliard took an opportunity of asking apart.

"Thanks, she's getting all right again. At Llandudno just now. Glad to see that you're looking so uncommonly fit."

Hilliard had undoubtedly improved in personal appearance. He grew a beard, which added to his seeming age, but suited with his features; his carriage was more upright than of old.

A week or two after this, Narramore sent a friendly note—

"Shall I see you at Birching's on Sunday? My wife will be there, to meet Miss Marks and some other people. Come if you can, old fellow. I should take it as a great kindness."

And Hilliard went. In the hall he was confronted by Narramore, who shook hands with him rather effusively, and said a few words in an undertone.

"She's out in the garden. Will be delighted to see you. Awfully good of you, old boy! Had to come sooner or later, you know."

Not quite assured of this necessity, and something less than composed, Hilliard presently passed through the house into the large walled garden behind it. Here he was confusedly aware of a group of ladies, not one of whom, on drawing nearer, did he recognise. A succession of formalities discharged, he heard his friend's voice saying—

"Hilliard, let me introduce you to my wife."

There before him stood Eve. He had only just persuaded himself of her identity; his eyes searched her countenance with wonder which barely allowed him to assume a becoming attitude. But Mrs. Narramore was perfect in society's drill. She smiled very sweetly, gave her hand, said what the occasion demanded. Among the women present – all well bred – she suffered no obscurement. Her voice was tuned to the appropriate harmony; her talk invited to an avoidance of the hackneyed.

Hilliard revived his memories of Gower Place – of the streets of Paris. Nothing preternatural had come about; nothing that he had not forecast in his hours of hope. But there were incidents in the past which this moment blurred away into the region of dreamland, and which he shrank from the effort of reinvesting with credibility.

"This is a pleasant garden."

Eve had approached him as he stood musing, after a conversation with other ladies.

"Rather new, of course; but a year will do wonders. Have you seen the chrysanthemums?"

She led him apart, as they stood regarding the flowers, Hilliard was surprised by words that fell from her.

"Your contempt for me is beyond expression, isn't it?"

"It is the last feeling I should associate with you," he answered.

"Oh, but be sincere. We have both learnt to speak another language – you no less than I. Let me hear a word such as you used to speak. I know you despise me unutterably."

"You are quite mistaken. I admire you very much."

"What – my skill? Or my dress?"

"Everything. You have become precisely what you were meant to be."

"Oh, the scorn of that!"

"I beg you not to think it for a moment. There was a time when I might have found a foolish pleasure in speaking to you with sarcasm. But that has long gone by."

"What am I, then?"

"An English lady – with rather more intellect than most."

Eve flushed with satisfaction.

"It's more than kind of you to say that. But you always had a generous spirit. I never thanked you. Not one poor word. I was cowardly – afraid to write. And you didn't care for my thanks."

"I do now."

"Then I thank you. With all my heart, again and again!"

Her voice trembled under fulness of meaning.

"You find life pleasant?"

"You do, I hope?" she answered, as they paced on.

"Not unpleasant, at all events. I am no longer slaving under the iron gods. I like my work, and it promises to reward me."

Eve made a remark about a flower-bed. Then her voice subdued again. "How do you look back on your great venture – your attempt to make the most that could be made of a year in your life?"

"Quite contentedly. It was worth doing, and is worth remembering."

"Remember, if you care to," Eve resumed, "that all I am and have I owe to you. I was all but lost – all but a miserable captive for the rest of my life. You came and ransomed me. A less generous man would have spoilt his work at the last moment. But you were large-minded enough to support my weakness till I was safe."

Hilliard smiled for answer.

"You and Robert are friends again?"

"Perfectly."

She turned, and they rejoined the company.

A week later Hilliard went down into the country, to a quiet spot where he now and then refreshed his mind after toil in Birmingham. He slept at a cottage, and on the Sunday morning walked idly about the lanes.

A white frost had suddenly hastened the slow decay of mellow autumn. Low on the landscape lay a soft mist, dense enough to conceal everything at twenty yards away, but suffused with golden sunlight; overhead shone the clear blue sky. Roadside trees and hedges, their rich tints softened by the medium through which they were discerned, threw shadows of exquisite faintness. A perfect quiet possessed the air, but from every branch, as though shaken by some invisible hand, dead foliage dropped to earth in a continuous shower; softly pattering from beech or maple, or with the heavier fall of ash-leaves, while at long intervals sounded the thud of apples tumbling from a crab-tree. Thick-clustered berries arrayed the hawthorns, the briar was rich in scarlet fruit; everywhere the frost had left the adornment of its subtle artistry. Each leaf upon the hedge shone silver-outlined; spiders' webs, woven from stem to stem, glistened in the morning radiance; the grasses by the wayside stood stark in gleaming mail.

And Maurice Hilliard, a free man in his own conceit, sang to himself a song of the joy of life.

Bibliography

1. Bibliographical Note

C. K. Shorter, the editor of the *Illustrated London News*, originally commissioned Gissing in January 1894 to write a story for a weekly serialization scheduled to take place at the end of the year. Eventually, because the prospective illustrator Fred Barnard could not be ready in time, Walter Paget replaced him, and the novel, which Gissing had written at Clevedon in 25 days from 4 to 29 June, ran in Shorter's magazine from 5 January to 30 March 1895, publication in volume form by Lawrence and Bullen taking place about 8 April. *Eve's Ransom* was Gissing's fourteenth published novel and the first to appear in one volume, in the vertically ribbed maroon cloth favoured by H. W. Lawrence and A. H. Bullen. The original edition was followed by a "second edition" in May 1895. A. H. Bullen reissued the novel in 1901 after the dissolution of his partnership with Lawrence. Using the old Lawrence and Bullen plates, Sidgwick and Jackson brought out in 1911 a new edition in red cloth uniform with the seven other titles formerly available from Lawrence and Bullen, an edition which they reissued in 1915. The last English edition proper was that of Ernest Benn Ltd (1929).

Simultaneously with the first English edition, George Bell and Sons included the book in their Indian and Colonial Library.

The history of the novel in America is circumscribed to the first edition published by Appletons in 1895, reprinted in 1912, a photographic reprint by AMS of New York of the first English edition issued in 1969, and a reset paperback edition by Dover (1980), which was available in England from Constable.

Five translations are on record. A Russian version was serialized in the weekly periodical *Zhivopisnoe Obozrenie*, nos. 29-36, that is, apparently, from late July to mid-September 1895, with no subsequent publication in volume form. In France, after serialization in four instalments in the *Revue de Paris* from 1 April to 15 May 1898, Calmann-Lévy brought out Georges Art's translation, *La Rançon d'Eve*, in 1898. The original price, 3.50 francs, was reduced to 60 centimes in 1907. Georges Art's translation also appeared in the *Gazette de Lausanne* from 26 February to 4 April 1900. In Denmark *Eva Madeley* first appeared serially in the Copenhagen daily *Samfundet* from 2 January to 18 February 1900, before publication in volume form by O. C. Olsen & Co. in the same year. A Dutch version by Johanna F. J. J. Buijtendijk, entitled *Eve's Losprijs*, came out under the imprint of De Erven F. Bohn in Harlem in 1904. Lastly Maria Teresa Chialant published an Italian translation, *Il riscatto di Eva* in October 2005 (Naples: Liguori Editore). The volume was reprinted in 2008.

The manuscript is held by the Huntington Library. The few corrections made by Gissing in his own copy of the first English edition (Coustillas collection) have been incorporated in the present edition.

~ Bibliography ~

2. List of Reviews

1895

Glasgow Herald, 11 April, p. 9
Speaker, 13 April, pp. 416-17
Union and Advertiser (Rochester NY), 13 April, p. 2 (John Northern Hilliard)
Scotsman, 15 April, p. 3
Star, 18 April, p. 1 (Guthlac Strong)
Daily Telegraph, 19 April, p. 6
Publishers' Circular, 20 April, p. 427
Daily News, 23 April, p. 6
Sketch, 24 April, p. 697
Literary World (London), 26 April, p. 386
Saturday Review (Supplement), 27 April, p. 531 [H. G. Wells]
New York Times, 27 April, p. 3
Globe, 29 April, p. 3
Manchester Guardian, 30 April, p. 10
World, 1 May, p. 27 (P. and Q.)
Woman, 1 May, p. 7 (Barbara, i.e. Arnold Bennett)
Daily Chronicle, 9 May, p. 3
Athenæum, 11 May, p. 605 [Lewis Sargeant]
Chicago Evening Post, 11 May, p. 5
Pall Mall Gazette, 14 May, p. 4
Academy, 18 May, p. 422 (George Cotterell)
National Observer, 18 May, p. 26
San Francisco Chronicle, 19 May, p. 4
Guardian, 22 May, p. 765
Morning Post, 24 May, p. 7
Wave (San Francisco), 25 May, p. 13
Bookman (New York), May, p. 265
Bookman (London), May, pp. 54-5
Literary Era (Philadelphia), May
Bookseller, 8 June, p. 509
Canterbury Times (New Zealand), 13 June, p. 41
Chicago Times Herald, 28 June, p. 12 (Mary Abbott)
Sydney Morning Herald, 6 July, p. 4
Nation (New York), 11 July, p. 32 (Annie R. M. Logan)
New York Daily Tribune, 21 July, p. 24
New Zealand Graphic, 3 August, p. 136
Leader (Melbourne), 29 August, p. 5
Sun (Melbourne), 30 August, p. 3
Spectator, 14 September, pp. 344-5
Critic (New York), 19 October, p. 218

~ Bibliography ~

3. Articles and later Comments

Adeline R. Tintner, "Eve Madeley: Gissing's Mona Lisa," *Gissing Newsletter*, January 1981, pp. 1-8

Terry L. Spaise, "Eve's Ransom and the Mutability of Freedom and Repression," *Gissing Newsletter*, October 1989, pp. 2-15

Constance Harsh, "The Text of *Eve's Ransom*: Insights from the *Illustrated London News* serialization," *Gissing Journal*, July 2005, pp. 1-9

Selected Reviews

Eve's Ransom — Five First Edition Reviews and One Later Comment

Manchester Guardian, 30 April 1895, p. 10

Eve's Ransom, Mr Gissing's last novel, is not only fully up to the intellectual level of Mr Gissing's former work, but it is for the first time, to our thinking, possessed of just that subtle power of arresting the attention and arousing the sympathies of the reader which such work as *In the Year of Jubilee* or *The Emancipated* lacked. The central figure, Maurice Hilliard, is a study of great and unusual interest. When the story opens he is a mechanical draughtsman on a salary of £100 a year, of which he gives £50 away to his brother's widow. His work is uncongenial to him; he has no prospect of ever being able to gratify the rather fastidious tastes with which he was born; life stretches before him like an arid waste; and in order to blind his eyes to the prospect and to dull his nerves he is beginning to drink. Just at this moment a former creditor of his father's, being seized with qualms of conscience, sends him a cheque for £400. In a moment everything is changed and he becomes a new man. 'And what are you going to do?' asks his friend. 'I'm going to live,' replies Hilliard; 'going to be a machine no longer. Can I call myself a man? There's precious little difference between a fellow like me and the damned grinding mechanism that I spend all my days in drawing. I'll put an end to that. Here's £400. It shall mean four hundred pounds of life. While this money lasts I'll feel that I'm a human being.' And so he does. The craving for drink, born of monotony and hopelessness, disappears, swallowed up in the satisfaction of long-repressed and rational desires. In the use to which Maurice Hilliard puts his freedom is to be found the story of the book, while the effect of freedom upon a nature so constituted forms its central and underlying idea. The first impression left by the book is one of acute depression. Is it really true, one asks oneself, that the average clerk leads the consciously repressed starved life of Maurice Hilliard before his emancipation? In other words, is the case selected by Mr Gissing for presentation typical? At first, so complete is the illusion produced, one feels inclined to believe that it is, following therein the natural inclination to argue from the particular to the general. And while this impression lasts depression is inevitable, for were it really so it would prove beyond doubt that this is the worst of all possible worlds. But in the end the conviction that Maurice Hilliard is and always will be an exception wins the day, though that he should exist at all is bad enough. The real *amor intellectualis* is as rare as the passionate desire for freedom. Most men hug their chains, and if you gave the average man £400 and his liberty the chances are that he would gamble it away on the nearest racecourse. As a rule man fits his environment, and it is only rarely that a square individual finds himself in a round hole, though when it has so happened the individual has generally had his angles remorselessly pared to make him fit like the rest. But we are coming to see that the helping of the square individuals out of round holes into square ones is one of our principal duties as human beings, even though it should involve the gradual reconstruction of human society.

Chicago Evening Post, 11 May 1895, p. 5, "Books of the Week: Tried to Ransom a Woman"

George Gissing is the historian of the lower middle class, who finds his inspiration in the tragic dullness of its life. He has accustomed us to expect excellent work from his pen, and if his last book, 'Eve's Ransom' (Appleton & Co.) is not poignant and powerful as are some of its predecessors it carries on every page the same imprint of unexaggerated truth. Written throughout in a lighter key, it is less sordid, sunnier and pleasanter in effect. The hero, Hilliard, is a mechanical draughtsman. When we meet him first he is sick to death of his life of drudgery; and in his passionate longing to escape from bondage, his mood of desperation, centered in self, is leading him to yield to brutalizing influences. By an unlooked-for chance the man who ruined his father pays the son a long-standing debt of £400. Hilliard, thirsting to have a taste of freedom, vows that the money will purchase him £400 worth of life. "While this money lasts I'll feel that I'm a human being." Fortunately he has a conscience and the sanity of taste that finds "no enjoyment in making a beast of oneself." In holiday mood he goes in quest of Eve Madeley, whose photograph in his landlady's album haunts his fancy. When at last he meets her Eve, by a curious coincidence, has become possessed of £25, and is spending it in securing a span of "repose, satisfaction, enjoyment." The resemblance in the condition of their lives, in their aims, in their passionate longing to touch life, draws the two together. Unfortunately the shadow of an unhappy love casts its gloom over Eve's spirit. Her ways perplex Hilliard, but he becomes her friend and conducts himself toward her with chivalric delicacy. The larger part of the £400 is spent in the ransom of Eve from bondage. How it is paid and what comes of the generous expenditure we shall leave our readers to discover for themselves. The end comes somewhat as a surprise, but it has the convincing unexpectedness of truth. Eve acts as such a woman would act. Without being ignoble, she has lost the finer sensibilities in her struggle for existence, and her strongest feeling is terror of the poverty that once dragged her down to be one of life's miserable captives. The character Patty Ringrose, who is employed in her uncle's music shop, is a life-like sketch of a sprightly, superficial, yet thoroughly human girl. Every character in the book bears the stamp of being observed from life. If not the most characteristic, the story is one of the most attractive of Mr Gissing's books.

Academy, 18 May 1895, p. 422,
"New Novels" (George Cotterell)

Mr George Gissing, in *Eve's Ransom*, writes of sad things without being pathetic, of mean circumstances without being sordid. Down in the Black Country, whose lurid nights and smoky days and barren wastes Mr Gissing knows so well, there lives a young man, Hilliard by name, fettered by poverty to an occupation he does not like, and by generosity to his poor and unsupported sister-in-law. A stroke of luck sets him free for a time, and he goes to London to "live" – and to meet Eve Madeley, who alters his whole existence. Earlier in the book Hilliard rather loudly proclaims to a more amorous friend that he shall never love or marry. You are notified of no change in his sentiments until he suddenly surprises you by making violent love to Eve. The story is curiously rather the history of events and utterances than a record of feelings as they lead up to acts. Eve herself is absolutely objective. You see her through the eyes of the other persons: hardly at all do you look at the world or at herself through her own eyes. She is at once impalpable and life-like. Her actions are quite consistent with what you gather of her character, but the fascination she has for Hilliard rarely extends to you who know her so little. The book is extremely interesting, as being a love-story in the subdued tones of lower middle-class life, without any of the misleading glamour of romance, and as, in its own way, achieving realism without nastiness.

Bookman (New York), May 1895, p. 265

Mr Gissing's last volume is much slighter, both in conception and in execution, than *In the Year of Jubilee*, which we had occasion to notice two months ago. It is to be hoped that he is not going the way of so many writers, and producing too rapidly for his own reputation. Nevertheless, although inferior to his greatest work, *Eve's Ransom* is a strong and impressive story, and one that holds the attention of the reader to the end. The principal male character is a young mechanical draughtsman from the Black Country, who works from morning to night for a meagre salary of two pounds a week, and with nothing to relieve the monotony of existence. Becoming unexpectedly possessed of a few hundred pounds, he resolves, as he says, at any rate for a few months, to discover how it feels really to live, so that he may at least have something to remember in after years. He casts aside his work and rushes up to London, visits Paris, and plunges into various forms of distractions, but at first in utter loneliness. At this stage of his career, he makes the acquaintance of a more or less attractive young woman, who, like himself, has led a narrow, provincial life, and longs for a glimpse of the world of luxury. It is easy to see to what end one of the decadent school of fiction would have conducted this affair; but Mr Gissing, though pessimistic, is no decadent. His heroine is very unconventional, but nothing worse. The book deals largely with the development in the man of a perfectly unselfish affection, and with the conflict in the woman between unselfishness and motives that are mercenary. The latter are made to win. The psychology of Eve Madeley is a very curious study, and perhaps involves a certain amount of paradox; but the analysis is carried out very convincingly by Mr Gissing, and the book on the whole will detract nothing from his reputation.

Sun (Melbourne), 30 August 1895, p. 3

Eve's Ransom, published by Lawrence and Bullen, is a novel that is likely to be much in evidence for a time at least. The author touches most tellingly upon the longing desire that seems to animate all beings in this present age for a broader, fuller, and perhaps freer life. The hero Maurice Hilliard, an ill-paid draughtsman, comes to feel his position in life unbearable. A windfall of £400 comes to him and full of new zeal, new hopes and aspirations he goes to that city to which all roads lead and there meets his fate in the person of a young girl who has longings and desires like his own. One feels on reading this work how hard it is for poverty and morality to go hand in hand. By morality do not interpret the word in its present limited meaning, but in its wider, fuller and larger acceptation.

Comment on *Eve's Ransom* from chapter XIV, "The Creed of George Gissing," in Cornelius Weygandt's *A Century of the English Novel* (New York: The Century Co.), 1925, pp. 246-47

Eve's Ransom has, from my first reading of it, seemed to me the most original of Gissing's novels. It is the story of a woman who cannot forgive the man who loves her for saving her from a liaison with a married man. After Eve Madeley is saved, after she has accepted from Hilliard everything he has to give, his money, his devotion, all of him that matters, and given him nothing in return, not even real friendship, she marries a rich friend of his, Narramore. Eve has all along cherished a grudge against Hilliard. This affair with the married man she looked back upon as true love, and for it the world had been well lost. She says to Hilliard, "When you took me away, perhaps it was the unkindest thing you could have done." Eve, of course, had never loved Hilliard. Why, then, should she marry him, when she did not love him, and he a poor man? She was not grateful to him. She was afraid of poverty. Now that her real love was over, her fear of poverty was her ruling passion. Why, then, should she not marry Narramore? She did not love him any more than she loved Hilliard, but with the rich man she could avoid poverty for ever.

There is a remarkable scene, unemphasized, almost slurred over, at the end of *Eve's Ransom*, in which, as Narramore's wife, Eve thanks Hilliard for saving her. Are we to assume a weather-vane has shifted? I think not. We are to suppose that now in the position of an English lady of fortune her girlish dream of a grand passion has shrunk to scant proportions and that she is sincere in saying, "I was all but lost—all but a miserable captive for the rest of my life." It is the close ironic, always dangerous to a story of emotions deeply stirred, but Gissing dares a last page even more unsentimental. It is a week later than the scene in Narramore's garden. Going down into the country Hilliard experiences in the "golden sunlight" of Autumn the last stages of his freeing from the dominance of Eve, a dominance that was almost obsessive. The last words of the book are "And Maurice Hilliard, a free man in his own conceit, sang to himself a song of the joy of life." Not even Hardy goes so far as to show you his hero losing the captivating heroine and crying, "Thank God," for such luck!

THREE NOVELLAS

by George Gissing

~ Sleeping Fires ~

~ *Chapter 1* ~

THE rain was over. As he sat reading Langley saw the page illumined with a flood of sunshine, which warmed his face and hand. For a few minutes he read on, then closed his Aristophanes with a laugh – faint echo of the laughter of more than two thousand years ago.

He had passed the winter at Athens, occupying rooms, chosen for the prospects they commanded, in a hotel unknown to his touring countrymen, where the waiters had no English, and only a smattering of French or Italian. No economic necessity constrained him. Within sight of the Acropolis he did not care to be constantly reminded of Piccadilly or the Boulevard – that was all. He consumed *pilafi*[1] and meats generously enriched with the native oil, drank resinated wine, talked such Greek as Heaven permitted. At two and forty, whether by choice or pressure of circumstance, a man may be doing worse.

The cup and plate of his early breakfast were still on the table, with volumes many, in many languages, heaped about them. Langley looked at his watch, rose with deliberation, stretched himself, and walked to the window. Hence, at a southern angle, he saw the Parthenon, honey-coloured against a violet sky, and at the opposite limit of his view the peak of Lycabettus; between and beyond, through the pellucid air which at once reveals and softens its barren ruggedness, Hymettus basking in the light of spring.[2] He could not grow weary of such a scene, which he had watched through changes innumerable of magic gleam and shade since the sunsets of autumn fired it with solemn splendour; but his gaze this morning was directed merely by habit. With the laugh he had forgotten Aristophanes, and now, as his features told, was possessed with thought of some modern, some personal interest, a care, it seemed, and perchance that one, woven into the fabric of his life, which accounted for deep lines on a face otherwise expressing the contentment of manhood in its prime.

A second time he consulted his watch – perhaps because he had no appointment, nor any call whatever upon his time. Then he left the room, crossed a corridor, and entered his bedchamber to make ready for going forth. Thus equipped he presented a recognisable type of English gentleman, without eccentricity of garb, without originality, clad for ease and for the southern climate, but obviously by a London tailor. Ever so slight a bend of shoulders indicated the bookman, but he walked, even in sauntering, with free, firm step, and looked about him like a man of this world. The face was pleasant to encounter, features handsome and genial, moustache and beard, in hue something like the foliage of a copper-beech, peculiarly well trimmed. At a little distance one judged him on the active side of forty. His lineaments provoked another estimate, but with no painful sense of disillusion.

Careless of direction, he strolled to the public market – the Bazaar, as it is called – where, as in the Athens of old, men, not women, were engaged in marketing, and where fish seemed a commodity no less important than when it nourished the sovereign Demos. Thence, by the Street of Athena, head bent in thought, to the street of Hermes, where he loitered as if in uncertainty, indifference leading him at length to the broad sunshine of that dusty, desolate spot where stands the Temple of Theseus.[3] So nearly perfect that it can scarce be called a ruin, there, on the ragged fringe of modern Athens, hard by the station of the Piræus Railway,[4] its marble majesty consecrates the ravaged soil. A sanctuary still, so old, so wondrous in its isolation, that all the life of to-day around it seems a futility and an impertinence.

Looking dreamily before him, Langley saw a man who drew near – a man with a book under one arm, an umbrella under the other, and an open volume in his hands – a tourist, of course, and probably an Englishman, for his garb was such as no native of a civilised country would exhibit among his own people. His eccentric straw hat, with a domed crown and an immense brim, shadowed a long, thin visage disguised with blue spectacles. A grey Norfolk jacket moulded itself to his meagre form; below were flannel trousers, very baggy at the knees, and a pair of sand-shoes. This individual, absorbed in study of the book he held open, moved forward with a slow, stumbling gait. He was arrested at length, and all but overthrown, by coming in contact with the sword-pointed leaf of a great agave. Langley, now close at hand, barely refrained from laughter. He had averted his eyes, when, with no little astonishment, he heard himself called by name. The stranger – for Langley tried in vain to recognise him – hurried forward with a hand of greeting.

"Don't you remember me? – Worboys."

"Of course! In another moment your voice would have declared you to me. I seemed to hear some one calling from an immense distance – knew I ought to know the voice—"

They shook hands cordially.

"Good heavens, Langley! To think that we should meet in the

Kerameikos![5] You know that we are in the Kerameikos? I've got Pausanias[6]
here, but it really is so extremely difficult to identify the sites—"

Fifteen years had elapsed since their last meeting; but Worboys,
oblivious of the trifle, plunged forthwith into a laborious statement of his
topographic and archæologic perplexities. He talked just as at Cambridge,
where his ponderous pedantry had been wont to excite Langley's
amusement, at the same time that the sterling qualities of the man attracted
his regard. Anything but brilliantly endowed, Worboys, by dint of
plodding, achieved academic repute, got his fellowship, and pursued a
career of erudition. He was known to schools and colleges by his
exhaustive editing of the "Cyropædia".[7] Langley, led by fate into other
paths, gradually lost sight of his entertaining friend. That their
acquaintance should be renewed "in the Kerameikos" was appropriate
enough, and Langley's mood prepared him to welcome the incident.

"Are you here alone?" he asked, when civility allowed him to wave
Pausanias aside.

"No; I am bear-leading. Last autumn, I regret to say, I had a rather
serious illness, and travel was recommended. It happened at the same time
that Lord Henry Strands – I was his young brother's tutor, by the by –
spoke to me of a lady who wished to find a travelling companion for a
young fellow, a ward of hers. I somewhat doubted my suitability – the
conditions of the case were peculiar – but after an interview with Lady
Revill—"

The listener's half-absent smile changed of a sudden to a look of
surprise and close attention.

"– I gave my assent. He's a lad of eighteen without parents to look after
him, and really a difficult subject. I much fear that he finds my
companionship wearisome; at all events, he gets out of my way as often as
he can. Louis Reed is his name. I'm afraid he has caused his guardian a great
deal of anxiety. And Lady Revill – such an admirable person, I really can't
tell you how I admire and respect her – she regards him quite as her son."

"Lady Revill has no child of her own, I believe?" said Langley.

"No. You are acquainted with her?"

"I knew her before her marriage."

"Indeed! What a delightful coincidence! I can't tell you how she
impresses me. Of course I am not altogether unaccustomed to the society
of such people, but Lady Revill – I really regard her as the very best type
of aristocratic woman, I do indeed. She must have been most interesting in
her youth."

"Do you think of her as old?" Langley asked, with a grave smile.

"Oh, not exactly old – oh, dear no! I imagine that her age – well, I never gave the matter a thought."

"Does she seem—?" Langley hesitated, dropping his look. "Should you say that her life has been a pleasant one?"

"Oh, undoubtedly! Well, that is to say, we must remember that she has suffered a sad loss. I believe Sir Thomas Revill was a most admirable man."

"She speaks of him?"

"Not to me. But I have heard from others. Not a distinguished man, of course; silent, as a member of Parliament, I believe, but admirable in all private relations. To be sure, I have only heard of him casually. You knew him?"

"By repute. I should say you are quite right about him. And this boy gives you a good deal of trouble?"

"No, no!" Worboys exclaimed hurriedly. "I didn't wish to convey that impression. To begin with, one can hardly call him a boy. No, he is singularly mature for his age. And yet I don't mean mature; on the contrary, he abounds in youthful follies. I don't wish to convey an impression – really it's very difficult to describe him. But of course you will come and have lunch with us, Langley? He'll be at the hotel by one o'clock, no doubt. I left him writing letters – he's always writing letters. Really, I am tempted to imagine some – but he doesn't confide in me, and I seldom allow myself to talk of anything but serious subjects."

They were moving in the townward direction. Langley, divided between his own thoughts and attention to what his companion was saying, walked with eyes on the ground.

"And what have you been doing all these years?" Worboys inquired. "Strange how completely we have drifted apart. I knew you on the instant. You have changed wonderfully little. And how pleasant it is to hear your voice again! Life is so short; friends ought not to lose sight of each other. *Soles occidere et redire possunt*[8] – you know."

The other gave a brief and good-humoured account of himself.

"And you have lived here alone all the winter," said Worboys. "Not like you; you were so sociable; the life and soul of our old symposia – though I don't know that I ought to say *our*, for I seldom found time to join in such relaxations. A pity; I regret it. The illness of last autumn made me all at once an old man. And no doubt that's why Louis finds me so unsympathetic. Though I like him; yes, I really like him. Don't imagine that he is illiterate.

He'll make a notable man, if he lives. Yes, I regret to say that his health leaves much to be desired. In Italy he had a troublesome fever – not grave, but difficult to shake off. He lives at such high pressure; perpetual fever of the mind. Our project was to spend a whole twelvemonth abroad. We ought not to have reached Athens till the autumn of this year; yet here we are. Louis can't stay in any place more than a week or so, and to resist him is really dangerous – I mean for his health. Lady Revill allows me complete discretion, but it's really Louis who directs our travel. I wanted to devote at least a month to the antiquities at Rome. There are several questions I should like to have settled for myself. For instance—"

He went off into Roman archæology, and his companion, excused from listening, walked in reverie. Thus they ascended the long street of Hermes, which brought them to the Place of the Constitution,[9] and in view of Mr. Worboys' hotel, the approved resort which Langley had taken trouble to avoid. As they drew near to the entrance, a young man, walking briskly, approached from the opposite quarter, and of a sudden Worboys exclaimed:

"Ha! here comes our young friend."

~ *Chapter 2* ~

"LOUIS, let me introduce you to a very old friend of mine, Mr. Langley. We were contemporaries at Cambridge, and after many years we meet unexpectedly in the Kerameikos!"

The young man stepped forward with peculiarly frank and pleasant address. It was evident at a glance that his physique would support no serious strain; he had a very light and graceful figure, with narrow shoulders, small hands and feet, and a head which for beauty and poise would not have misbecome the youthful Hermes.[10] Grotesque indeed was the aspect of his blue-spectacled tutor standing side by side with Louis. On the other hand, when he and Langley came together, a certain natural harmony appeared in the two figures; it might even have been observed that their faces offered a mutual resemblance, sufficient to excuse a stranger for supposing them akin. Louis, though only a golden down appeared upon his chin, and the mere suggestion of a moustache on his lip, looked older than he was by two or three years; perhaps the result of that slight frown, a fixed but not unamiable characteristic of his physiognomy, which was noticeable also on Langley's visage. The elder man bearing his age so lightly, they might have been taken for brothers.

"I have been to the Cemetery," was Louis's first remark. "Do you know it, Mr. Langley? The monuments are nearly as hideous as those at Naples. There's a marble life-sized medallion of a man in his habit as he lived, and, by Jove, if they haven't gilded the studs in his shirt-front!"

"How interesting!" exclaimed the tutor. "The sculptors of the great age were just as realistic."

"With a difference," Langley interposed.

"And something else that will delight you, Mr. Worboys," the youth continued. "There's a public notice, painted on a board, in continuous lettering, without spaces – just like the *Codices!*"[11]

His emphasis on the last word evidently had humorous reference to Mr. Worboys' habits of speech. Langley smiled, but Worboys was delighted.

"But they stick a skull and crossbones on their tombs," pursued Louis. "That's hideously degenerate. Your ancient friends, Mr. Worboys, knew better how to deal with death."

To Langley's ears this remark had an unexpectedness which made him regard the speaker more closely. Louis had something more in him than youthful vivacity and sprightliness; his soft-glancing eyes could look below the surface of things.

"You observe, Langley," said the tutor, "that he speaks of *my* ancient friends. Louis is a terribly modern young man. I can't get him to care much about the classical civilisations. The idea of his running off to see a new cemetery, when he hasn't yet seen the Theseion![12] And that reminds me, Langley; I am strongly tempted to believe with some of the Germans that the Theseion isn't a temple of Theseus at all. I'll show you my reasons."

He did so, with *Ausführlichkeit* and *Gründlichkeit*,[13] as they ascended the steps of the hotel. Langley, the while, continued observant of Louis Reed, with whom, presently, he was able to converse at his ease; for Worboys recognized that the costume in which it delighted him to roam among ruins would be inappropriate at the luncheon-table. Louis, when the waiter in the vestibule had dusted him from head to heel – a necessary service performed for all who entered – needed to make no change of dress; he wore the clothing which would have suited him on a warm spring day in England, and the minutiæ of his attire denoted a quiet taste, a sense of social propriety, agreeable to Langley's eye. They had no difficulty in exchanging reflections on things Continental. Louis talked with animation, yet with deference. It was easy to perceive his pleasure in finding an acquaintance more sympathetic than the erudite but hidebound Worboys. When all three sat down to the meal, Worboys drew attention to the wine that was put before him, Côtes de Parnès, with the brand of "Solon and Co."

"We cannot drink the wine of the gods," he observed with a chuckle, "but here is the next best thing – the wine of the philosophers."

Louis averted his face. It was the fifth day since their arrival at Athens, and his tutor had indulged in this joke at least once daily.

"By the by, Langley, where are you staying?"

Langley named the hotel, and briefly described it.

"How interesting! Yes, that's much better."

"I should think so!" exclaimed Louis. "Why shouldn't we go there, Mr. Worboys? Living like this, what can we get to know of the life of the country? That's what I care about, Mr. Langley. I want to see how the people live nowadays. It matters very little what they did ages ago. It seems to me that life isn't long enough to live in the past as well as in the present."

"Yet you concern yourself a great deal with the future, my dear boy," remarked Worboys,

"Yes; I can't help that. Isn't the future growing in us? And surely it's a duty to—"

Either incapacity to express himself, or a modest self-restraint, caused him to break off and bend over his plate. For some minutes after this he kept silence, whilst Mr. Worboys pleaded, in set phrase, for the study of the classics and all that appertained thereto. Langley observed that the young man ate delicately and sparingly, but that he was by no means so moderate in his use of the philosophic beverage. Louis drank glass after glass of undiluted wine, a practice which his tutor's classic sympathies ought surely to have disapproved. But possibly Mr. Worboys, even without his coloured spectacles, had not become aware of it.

They repaired to the smoking room, where Louis lit a cigarette. The wine had not made him talkative; rather it seemed to lull his vivacious temper, to wrap him in meditation or day-dream. He lay back and watched the curling of the smoke; on his emotional lips a smile of gentle melancholy, his eyes wide and luminous in mental vision. When he had sat thus for a few minutes, he was approached by a waiter, who handed him two letters. Instantly his countenance flashed into vivid life; having glanced at the writing on the envelopes, he held them with a tight grasp; and very shortly, seeing that his friends were conversing, he walked from the room.

"There now," remarked Worboys. "He's been wild with impatience for letters. One of them, no doubt, is from Lady Revill, but it isn't *that* he was waiting for. Do you know a certain Mrs. Tresilian?"

"What – *the* Mrs. Tresilian?"

"Really, I never heard the name till Louis spoke of her. Is she distinguished? A lady of so-called advanced opinions."

"Yes, yes; the Mrs. Tresilian of public fame, no doubt," said Langley, with interest. "I don't know her personally. Is she a friend of his?"

"My dear Langley, it sounds very absurd, but I'm afraid the poor boy has quite lost his head about her. And I suspect – I only *suspect* – that Lady Revill wished to remove him beyond the sphere of her malign influence. She spoke to me of 'unfortunate influences' in his life, but mentioned no name. Who is this lady? What is her age?"

"I know very little of her, except that she addresses meetings on political and humanitarian subjects. A woman with a head, I believe, and rather eloquent. Her age? Oh, five and thirty, perhaps, to judge from her portraits. Handsome, undeniably. How can he have got into her circle?"

"I have no idea," Worboys replied, with a gesture of helplessness. "I know nothing of that sphere."

"And they correspond?"

"I am convinced they do; though Louis has never said so. I surmise it from his talk in – in moments of unusual expansiveness. And imagine how it must distress such a person as Lady Revill!"

Langley mused before he spoke again.

"You mean that she fears for his – or the lady's – morals?"

"Oh, dear me, I didn't mean that! But the effects on a young, excitable nature of such principles as Mrs. Tresilian appears to hold! Perhaps you are not aware of the strong conservatism of Lady Revill's mind?"

"I see," faltered the other. "She seriously desires to guard him from 'advanced opinion'?"

"Most seriously. I have told you that she has almost a maternal affection for the boy. How it must shock her to see him going off into those wild speculations – seeking to undermine all she reverences!"

"Is he such a revolutionist?" Langley asked, with a smile.

"Well, I have sometimes thought him a sort of Shelley," ventured the tutor, with amusing diffidence. "Though I don't know that he writes verses. However, you see the points of similarity? A strange youth, altogether. As I said, I can't help liking him. I daresay he'll outgrow his follies."

Langley smoked and was silent. The other, thinking the subject dismissed, uttered a remark tending to matters archaic; but Langley disregarded it and spoke again.

"What's his origin – do you know?"

"Really, I don't. He never speaks of it – Lady Revill only said that he was an orphan, and her ward."

"Where has he been educated?"

"Private tutors, and private schools. Of course Lady Revill wishes him to pass to a University, but it seems he is set against it. He has some extraordinary idea that he is old enough, and educated sufficiently, to begin the serious business of life; though I don't gather what he means exactly by that. I conceive that Mrs. Tresilian is responsible for such vagaries. He appears to reprobate the thought of being connected with the aristocracy – part of his Shelleyism, of course. I almost believe that he would like to take some active part in democratic politics."

"H'm – the type is familiar," murmured Langley. "Nothing very abnormal about him, I daresay. And it occurred to Lady Revill that your companionship might abate these ecstasies?"

"That," Worboys replied, with modesty, "appears to have been her view.

A student who has given some proof of solid attainment might naturally seem—"

"To be sure," interposed the other, suavely. "But our young friend seems cut out for rather obstinate independence."

"I really fear so." And Mr. Worboys shook his sage head.

At this moment Louis re-entered the room. He had a flushed face, and an air of exaltation. Stepping rapidly up to the two men, he threw himself upon a chair beside them, and said with a boyish laugh:

"Well, Mr. Worboys, I'm quite ready for the Theseion or the Kerameikos, or anything you like to propose. But when are we going to Salamis – and to Marathon – and to climb Pentelikon?[14] I should really like to see Marathon. And Thermopylæ better still.[15] Of course we must get to Thermopylæ."

This led to a discussion with Langley of facilities for travel in the remoter parts of Greece. It ended in their all strolling out together, and having a drive to Phaleron, on the white dusty road which is the fashionable course for carriages and equestrians at Athens. Worboys talked about the "Long Walls";[16] Louis Reed was in a sportive spirit, and found mirth in everything. Their companion said little, but listened good-naturedly and smiled. Once, too, when his eyes had been fixed for a moment on the boy's bright countenance, he seemed to sigh.

~ *Chapter 3* ~

IN the view of most of his acquaintances, Edmund Langley's life seemed to have followed a very smooth and ordinary course. There was no break of continuity, no sudden change in himself or his circumstances, in the retrospect of two and twenty years: that is to say, since he began to disappoint the friends who had looked to him for a brilliant career at Cambridge. Brilliant, in a manner, it was; in his undergraduate group he shone as a leading light, and later his reputation as a man of clever and imposing talk, held good with those who regretted his failure in the contests of scholarship. He left the University with a mere degree, and went to London to read law.

It was very leisurely reading, for no necessity spurred him on. His ambitions at that time were political, and he enjoyed a private income which allowed him to think of Parliament; personally devoted to a liberal culture, he was prepared to take the popular-progressive side, and to accept with genial humour those articles of the popular creed which he no longer held with his early enthusiasm. But nothing came of it. When, in his twenty-sixth year, an opportunity of candidature offered itself, he declined for rather vague reasons, and soon after it became known that he was to accompany on extensive travels a young nobleman, who had been his contemporary at Cambridge. Six months after their departure from England, the luckless Peer suffered a perilous accident, which lamed him for life. They returned, and Langley, for some fifteen years, remained with his friend as private secretary. In that capacity he had very little to do, but the life was agreeable; he found satisfaction in the society of a liberal-minded circle, learned to smile at the projects of his early manhood, and soothed his leisure with studies utterly remote from any popular or progressive programme. The nobleman's death enriched him with a legacy of which he stood in no need whatever, and murmuring to himself, "To him that hath shall be given," he wandered off to spend a year or two abroad.

Beneath this placid flow of existence lay hidden a sorrow of which he spoke to no one. The occasion of it was far behind him, in the years of turbulent youth; for a long time it had troubled him little, and only when his spirits invited care; but these latter months of solitude tended to revive the old distress, with new features attributable to the stage of life that he had reached. He knew not whether to be glad or sorry, when a casual meeting at Athens brought vividly before his mind the bygone things he had so long tried to forget.

After the drive with Worboys and Louis Reed, he returned to his hotel in a mood of melancholy. The evening, usually a pleasant enough time over his books, dragged with something worse than tedium; and the night that followed was such as he had not known for many years. Out of the darkness, a tormenting memory evoked two faces; the one pale and blurred, refusing distinct presentment, even to the obstinate efforts which, in spite of himself, he repeated hour after hour; the other so distinct, so living, that at moments it thrilled him as with a touch of the supernatural – a light on the features, a play of expression, all but a voice from the moving lips. Faces of character much unlike, though both female, and both young. The one which haunted him elusively had but a superficial charm: no depth in the smiling eyes, no intellectual beauty on the brows; the moment's fancy of sensual youth; powerless to subdue, to retain. The other, clear upon the gloom, spoke a finer womanhood, so much more nobly endowed in qualities of flesh and spirit that its beauty seemed to scorn comparison. Animation, self-command, the dignity of breeding and intelligence, lighted its lineaments. It was the woman whom a man in his maturity desires unashamed.

In these visions of the troubled night he saw also a large house, old and pleasant to the eye, which stood beyond the limits of a manufacturing town, planted about with fair trees, and walled from the frequented highway. He heard a soft roll of carriage wheels on the drive, the sound of cheery voices beneath the portico; he felt the languid, scented air of an old-time garden, where fruits hung ripe. And in the garden walked Agnes Forrest, youngest of the children of the house, but already in her twenty-first year. Her father was no man of yesterday's uprising, but the son and grandson of substantial merchants; he sat among his family and his guests, a reverend potentate.

The suggestion of her name did not well accord with Agnes' character. Had humility been her distinguishing virtue, Langley would never have made her his ideal of womanhood. He knew her strong of will, and found her opinions frequently at variance with his own; all the more delightful to perceive his influence in the directing of her mind. She was no great student, and took her full share in the active pleasures of life; rode as well as she danced; seemed to have admirable judgment in dress; enjoyed society, and liked to shine in it. Her ridicule of sentimentalities by no means discouraged the lover; it suited his taste, and could throw no doubt upon the capacity for strong feeling which he had often noted in her. The general conservatism of her thought was far from distasteful to him, smile as he might at some of its manifestations; she never opposed reason with mere feminine prejudice, and Langley was disposed to regard woman as the natural safeguard of traditions that have an abiding value. She was not a girl to be lightly wooed, and won as a matter of course. Her beauty and her brilliant social qualities cost him many an anxious hour, even when he believed himself gently encouraged. She did not conceal her ambitions; happily, he felt that she credited him with abilities of the conquering kind.

The old-time garden, and two who walked there, with long silences between the words that still disguised their deeper meaning. Langley knew himself peculiarly welcome to the parents, and felt a reasonable assurance that Agnes wished him to speak. On this same day, as it chanced, Sir Thomas Revill, the borough member, a widower of middle age, was one of the guests. Mr. Forrest seemed less cordial to the baronet than to the friend of lower rank. But Langley let the day pass, for a scruple restrained his tongue. After a night when temptation had all but vanquished conscience, he sought a private interview with Agnes' father.

"Mr. Forrest," he began frankly, yet with diffidence, "you cannot but see that I love your daughter, and that I wish to ask her if she will be my wife."

"I have suspected it, my dear Langley," was the old man's reply, as he smiled with satisfaction.

"I dare not speak to her until I have told you something, which perhaps you will think ought to have forbidden me to approach Miss Forrest at all. – Three years ago, in London, I formed a connection which resulted in my becoming the father of a child. The mother subsequently married, and left England, taking this child with her – her own desire, and with the consent of her husband. I could not oppose it; perhaps I hardly felt any desire to do so, though I need not say that mother and child both had a claim upon me which I never dreamt of disputing. Her place in life was below my own, and she married a man of her own class. When she last took leave of me – we had lived apart for more than a year – I told her that, if circumstances ever made it necessary, she was to look to me again for aid, and that, if ever she desired it, I would bring up the child in every way as my own – short of public acknowledgment. She went to South Africa, and I have since heard nothing. But there is still the possibility that I may be called upon to keep my word. This I am obliged to tell you. I cannot speak of it to Miss Forrest."

He paused with eyes cast down, and Mr. Forrest kept a short silence.

"An unpleasant business, Langley," the old man remarked at length, in a perplexed, but not a severe voice. "Of course you are right to speak of it. A very awkward matter."

He mused again, then began to interrogate. Langley answered with all frankness. He was not responsible for the girl's lapse from virtue; that must be laid to the account of the man who at length married her. In every respect, save for this trouble of conscience, he was honourably free.

"The deuce of it is," exclaimed Mr. Forrest, at last, "that women have a way of their own of regarding this sort of thing. For my own part – well, a young man is a young man. You were three and twenty. I can understand and excuse. But women—"

It did not occur to him to ask who the girl was, and on this point Langley offered no information beyond what he had said of her social position.

"I know quite well, Langley, that this, as it regards yourself, forms no presumption whatever against your making Agnes a good husband, if you married her. Your self-respect won't allow you to urge assurances of that; I know it all the same, because I have a pretty fair knowledge of you. But women think differently. There's nothing for it, I fear: I must talk with my wife about it."

Langley bowed to the decision he had foreseen. He went away with misery in his heart, cursing the honesty that had made him speak. Mr. Forrest's liberality of view might, only too probably, be explained by his certainty that Agnes' mother would never consent to the proposed marriage. "Should I myself give my daughter to a man who came with such a story?"

A day passed, and again he was closeted with the old man.

"Langley, my wife won't hear of this being mentioned to Agnes."

Oh, cursed folly! And it seemed, now, such an easy thing to have kept silence.

"It's my own fault. I ought never to have dared—"

"Remember, Langley, how very recently these things have happened."

"I know – I see all the folly, and worse, that I have been guilty of. Pardon it, if you can, Mr. Forrest, to one who is for the first time in love – and with Agnes."

Ten minutes, and all was over. Langley turned from the house, thinking to see its occupants no more.

But to the relief of misery came common-sense. What right had he thus to turn his back on Agnes without a word of explanation? His mysterious behaviour could not but result in confidences of some kind between Agnes and her parents. They, worthy people, assuredly would spare him; but, short of telling the truth, how could they avoid misrepresentation which in Agnes' mind must have all the effect of calumny? Impossible to let the matter end thus. He wrote to Mr. Forrest, and urged, with all respect, his claim to be judged by Agnes herself. Was she yet one and twenty? In any case she had attained responsible womanhood. He begged that this point might receive consideration.

"We were obliged to speak to Agnes," replied the father. "We have told her that something has happened which unexpectedly makes it impossible for you to think of marriage. This was all. I fear you have no choice but to preserve absolute silence. Agnes is just of age, but her mother and I feel very strongly that, out of regard for her happiness, you ought to think of her no more. Our friends, of course, shall never surmise anything disagreeable from our manner when you are spoken of. At the worst it will be imagined that Agnes has declined to marry you."

Regard for his old friends kept Langley silent for a week; then his passion overcame him. He wrote two letters – one to Agnes, simply offering marriage; the other to Mr. Forrest, saying what he had done, asserting his right, and begging that Agnes might be told the plain facts of the case before she answered him. The next day brought Mr. Forrest's reply, a few coldly civil lines, stating that Agnes had been informed of everything. Another day, and Agnes herself wrote, just as briefly – a courteous refusal.

Then Langley left England with his friend the nobleman. He had battled through amorous despair, but the disaster seemed to drain his life of hope and purpose; succumbing to fatality, he must make the best of sunless years.

A few months of travel dispelled this unnatural gloom. He began to foster the thought that Agnes' parents were both aged; it could not be expected that either would be alive ten years hence, and half that period might see both removed. If Agnes cared much for him, she would wait on the future. If he had been mistaken, and her heart were not gravely wounded, she would make proof of liberty by marrying another man. In which case—

Langley knew not how securely he had come to count upon Miss Forrest's fidelity, until one day the news reached him that she was Miss Forrest no longer. Agnes had married the middle-aged member of

Parliament, and henceforth must be thought of as Lady Revill. That chapter of life, whether or not the doom of his existence, was finally closed. She had waited barely a twelvemonth, so that, in all likelihood his timid love-making had but feebly impressed her. Another twelvemonth, and Mr. Forrest was dead; two years later Agnes' mother followed him. Oh, the folly of it all! The imbecile hesitation where common-sense pointed his path! She liked him well enough to marry him, and probably her life, as well as his own, must miss its consummation because he had played the pedant in morals.

This regret had long lost its poignancy, though it imparted a sober tinge to the epicureanism whereby Langley thought to direct his otherwise purposeless life. But the course of years shaped into conscious sorrow that loss which, as a young man, he had hardly regarded as a loss at all. He grew to an understanding of the wantonness with which he had acted in so lightly abandoning his child. Whilst the petty casuistry of his relations with Agnes Forrest was capable of compelling him into perverse heroism, he had committed what now seemed to him a much graver recklessness – perhaps, indeed, a crime – with but the faintest twinge of conscience. His child, his son, would now be grown up – a young man, about the same age as Louis Reed; and in such companionship how different would the world appear to him! In love with Agnes, he had been glad to rid himself of a troublesome and dangerous responsibility. For the mother – and this fact he had withheld in his confession – belonged to the town in which the Forrests were practically resident, and where he had other friends; a coincidence unknown to him when he made her acquaintance in London. Rescued from the evil of sense only to be rapt aloft by romantic passion, what thought had he of the duties and the rewards of paternity? Now, a sobered and somewhat lonely man, he saw the result of his hasty act in a very different light. Perchance the boy was dead; if living, better perchance that he should have died. What future could be hoped for him, delivered into such hands?

For the disregard of duty conscience offered excuse. His relations with the girl had worn no semblance of conjugality; they never lived together; he had seen the child but once or twice; every obligation imposed by the worldly code of honour he had abundantly discharged. The girl, moreover, had not loved him; he found her (though ignorant of the circumstances till long afterwards) on the brink of hopeless degradation, the result of her having been forsaken by the man for whom she strayed, and whom she subsequently married. As far as *she* was concerned he might reasonably be at rest, for in all probability his conduct saved her from the abyss. But such reasoning did not help him to forget that he had had a son, and that he had wantonly made himself childless. It were well if the child did not at this moment think with bitterness of an unknown parent, or, thinking not at all, live basely amid base companions.

He had never sought for tidings of them; it was possible, and merely possible, that inquiries in the town he never revisited might have had results. But if the child's mother had wished to communicate with him she could always have done so; that was provided for at their parting. It might be that neither she nor the boy had ever needed him; the man she married, a petty traveller in commerce, perhaps behaved well to them in the new country; that the girl was permitted to take her child seemed in her husband's favour. For her, too, did it not speak well that she would not forsake the little one? A weak, silly girl, but not without good traits; he remembered her, though dimly, with kindness – nay, with a certain respect. After all—

Well, it was the sight of Louis Reed that had turned him to melancholy musing. A son of that age, a handsome intelligent lad, overflowing with the zeal and the zest of life; with such a one at his side how lightly and joyously would he walk among these ruins of the old world! What flow of talk! What happiness of silent sympathy!

So passed the night.

~ *Chapter 4* ~

THE window of Langley's bedroom opened on to a balcony, pleasant to him in early morning for the air and the view. Over the straggling outskirts of Athens he looked upon the plain, or broad valley, where Cephisus, with scant and precious flow, draws seaward through grey-green olive gardens, down from Acharnæ of the poet, past the bare hillock which is called Colonus, to the blue Phaleric bay.[17] His eye loved to follow a far-winding track, mile after mile, away to the slope of Aigaleos, where the white road vanished in a ravine; for this was the Sacred Way, pursued of old by the procession of the Mysteries from Athens to Eleusis.[18]

Here, on a morning when earth and sky were mated in unutterable calm and loveliness, he stood dreaming with unquiet heart. "They lived their life, enjoyed to the uttermost the golden day that was granted them. And I, whose day is passing, can only try to forget myself in the tale of their vanished glory. Is it too late? Are the hopes and energies of life for ever withdrawn?"

A voice called to him from below; he looked down into the street and saw Louis waving a friendly hand.

"Do you feel disposed to climb Lycabettus?" shouted the young man.

"Gladly! With you in a moment."

It was ten days since their first meeting, and in the meanwhile they had been much together; occasionally without Worboys, whose archæologic zeal delighted in solitude. Langley found an increasing pleasure in Louis' society, evinced by the readiness with which he hastened forth to meet him. This companionship revived in him some of the fervours of youth; even – strange as it seemed to him – turned his mind to some of the old ambitions. Yet he tried to subdue the symptoms of febrile temperament which overcame Louis in sympathetic conversation; good-humouredly, almost affectionately, he struck the note of disillusioned age; and it gratified him to see how the young man put restraint upon himself to listen patiently and answer with respect. Already, in a measure, he was succeeding where Worboys had so signally failed.

At a vigorous pace they breasted the hillside, turning often to gaze at the dazzling whiteness of Athens below them, and at the wondrous panorama spreading around as they ascended. On reaching the quarries Louis pointed with indignation to the girls and women who toiled at breaking up stone.

"That's the kind of thing that makes me detest these countries!"

"What about cotton-mills and match factories?" said Langley. "It's better breaking stone on Lycabettus."

"Well, both are alike damnable. Women shouldn't work in such ways at all."

"Doesn't your friend Mrs. Tresilian prefer it to idle dependence upon men?"

"Perhaps so," Louis replied, with the brightness of countenance which always accompanied a thought of Mrs. Tresilian. "But that's only for the present, until society can be civilised. Talking of that reminds me of something I wanted to ask you. Wouldn't it be possible for me to get – some day – an inspectorship of factories? How are they appointed?"

"Good heavens! This is your latest inspiration?"

"Please don't be contemptuous, Mr. Langley. I see no reason why I shouldn't be able to qualify myself. It's the kind of thing that would suit me exactly."

"Oh, admirably! Ordained from eternity, in the fitness of things! Pray, has Mrs. Tresilian suggested it?"

"No. But she certainly would approve it. The difficulty is to find an employment in which I can be of some use to the world. I hate the idea of the professions and the businesses, with nothing before me but money-making. And I've tried incessantly to think of something respectable – you know what I mean by that – which I could hope to do effectually. It would delight me to get an inspectorship of factories and workshops. The satisfaction of coming down on brutes who break the laws – every kind of law – just to save their pockets! Don't you feel how glorious it would be to prosecute such scoundrels?"

Langley glanced at the glowing face and smiled.

"Yes, I can sympathise with that. But I believe an inspector has to be a man of long practical experience."

"I must make inquiries. I would gladly go and work at some mechanical trade to qualify myself."

"What would Lady Revill think of the suggestion?"

For a moment Louis hesitated. His features were a little clouded.

"I don't think she would seriously object – when she saw my motives."

"But you have told me that such motives make very little appeal to Lady Revill."

"The fact is, Mr. Langley, I am as far from understanding her as she is from understanding me. It would be outrageous ingratitude if I said, or thought, that she has any but the best and kindest intentions. You know, I daresay, how much I owe to her. But there it is; there is no getting over the fact that we can't see things from the same point of view. She isn't by any means an obstinate aristocrat; she can talk liberally about all sorts of things, and I know she has the kindest heart. Well, why should she take such care of *me*, the son of insignificant people except out of mere goodness? But she has such strong personal antipathies. I've never mentioned it, but she hates the name of Mrs. Tresilian. Now, of course I can't be ruled by such prejudices in her. You don't think I ought to be, do you?"

"It's a delicate point," answered Langley, looking far off. "As you say, you have great obligations—"

He paused, and Louis continued abruptly:

"Yes. That's why I am so anxious not to incur more. That's why I don't want to go to Oxford. I should do her no credit there, for one thing; study isn't my bent. I want to be *doing* something. I seem to be acting inconsiderately, but I feel so sure that Lady Revill will admit before long that I did right. Remember that I don't want to get up in public and rail against all the things she values. I couldn't do that. All I aim at is some work of quiet usefulness; something, too, which will make me independent. When I was a boy it didn't matter so much – I mean my obstinate self-will. Often enough I behaved very badly; I know it, and I'm ashamed of it; but then I *was* only a boy. Now it's very different; and in the future—"

Louis broke off, as if checked by a thought he found it difficult to utter.

"I haven't asked you," he added, when his companion kept walking silently on, "whether you know Lord Henry Strands."

"I knew nothing but his name, until Mr. Worboys spoke of him."

"Did he say—?"

Langley encouraged him with interrogative look.

"I've never spoken about it to Mr. Worboys, and I don't know whether—. But it's so important to me that, if I am to talk of myself at all I can't help mentioning it. And in Lady Revill's circle I don't see how it can help being talked about. I believe that she will marry Lord Henry."

Langley stopped, but immediately turned his eyes upon the landscape, and spoke as if it alone had arrested him.

"You see the dark mountain top far away there – to the right of Salamis. That's Akrokorinthos.[19] – Ah, you were saying that Lady Revill may marry again. And in that case, you think your position might be still more difficult?"

"If she married Lord Henry Strands. He and I can't get on together. Now he is an obstinate aristocrat, and the kind of man – well, I'd better not say how I feel towards him. It astonishes me that Lady Revill can endure such a man. People with titles are often very pleasant to get on with; but *he*—. I wish you knew him, Mr. Langley. I should so like to hear what you thought of him."

"You have no reason" – Langley spoke slowly – "for thinking that this marriage will take place, except your own surmise?"

"Well – he comes so often. And his sister is so intimate with Lady Revill. I'm sure it's taken for granted by lots of people."

"I see."

Something in the tone of this brevity caused Louis to look at the speaker with uneasiness.

"I'm afraid you think I oughtn't to have mentioned it. – But really, it's very much like talking about royal marriages. One somehow doesn't feel—"

"I meant no reproof," said Langley. "Stop; here's a good place to rest. I see there are a lot of people up at the Chapel. – It's a month since I was here."

His eyes wandered over the vast scene, where natural beauty and historic interest vied for the beholder's enthusiasm. Plain and mountain; city and solitude; harbour and wild shore; craggy islands and the far expanse of sea: a miracle of lights and hues, changing ever as cloudlets floated athwart the sun. From Parnes to the Argolic hills, what flight of gaze and of memory! The companions stood mute, but it was the younger man who betrayed a lively pleasure.

"What's the use," he exclaimed at length, "of reading history in books! Standing here I learn more in five minutes than through all the grind of my school-time. Ægina – Salamis – Munychia – nothing but names and boredom; now I shall delight to remember them as long as I live! Look at the white breakers on the shore of Salamis. – It's all so real to me now; and yet I never saw anything like these Greek landscapes for suggesting unreality. I felt something of that in Italy, but this is more wonderful. It struck me at the first sight of Greece, as we sailed in early morning along the Peloponnesus. It's the landscape you pick out of the clouds, at home in England. Again and again I have had to remind myself that these are real mountains and coasts."

Langley roused himself from oppressive abstraction, and put into better words this common sense of mirage due to the air and light of Greece. He spoke deliberately, and as if his thoughts were still half occupied with things remote. The frown imprinted on his features conveyed an impression of gloom; which was rarely its effect.

"How do you like the smoking mill-chimneys at Piræus?" he asked suddenly.

"Oh, of course that's abomination."

"Ah, I thought you would perhaps defend it. The Greeklings of to-day would be only too glad if their whole country blackened with such fumes."

"Well, they have their lives to live. They can't feed on the past."

Louis apologised with a smile for his matter-of-fact remark; but Langley surprised him by saying abruptly:

"You're quite right. They have their lives to live; and if they want mill-chimneys, let them be built from Olympus to Tænarum."[20]

Wherewith he turned away, and moved a few paces with restless step. Louis followed slowly, his eyes cast down, and did not speak until the other gave him a glance of singular moodiness.

"I'm afraid I often disgust you, Mr. Langley."

"Nay, my dear fellow; that you have never done," was the kindly-toned answer. "I meant what I said. You are right – a thousand times right – in pleading for to-day. It's good to be able to appreciate such a view as this; but it's infinitely better to make the most of one's own little life. I get a black fit now and then when I remember how much of mine has been wasted – that's all."

Concession such as this from a man he had quickly learned to like and respect stirred all the modesty in Louis.

"My trouble is," he said, "that I haven't knowledge enough to make me feel secure, when I take my own way. I may be blundering as all very young men are apt to do."

"Don't be in a hurry, that's the main thing. Above all, don't act in disregard of Lady Revill."

"That's what I wish never to do," Louis answered fervently. "And I should like to tell you that Mrs. Tresilian has always spoken in the same way. Lady Revill dislikes her – can't bear the mention of her name. She thinks I have got a great deal of harm from Mrs. Tresilian. Not long before I left England, she told me as much, in plain words, and it made me so angry that I said things I'm sorry for now. – I am hasty-tempered; I flare up, and call people names, and that kind of thing. It's a bad fault, I know; but surely it's a fault also to hate people out of mere prejudice."

"You can hardly call it mere prejudice, in this case," objected Langley, walking with head bent again.

"But I do! Lady Revill has never taken the trouble to inquire what sort of woman Mrs. Tresilian is, and what she really aims at. When I told her – too violently, I admit – that Mrs. Tresilian had begged me always to think first of what I owed to my guardian, she simply didn't believe it. Of course she didn't say so, but I saw she *wouldn't* believe it, and that enraged me. – There is no better, nobler woman living than Mrs. Tresilian! Every day of her life she does beautiful, admirable things. Her friendship would honour any man or woman under the sun!"

The listener restrained a smile.

"I can quite believe you. But I am equally convinced that Lady Revill is, in her own way, as good and conscientious. They would never like each other—"

"The fault would be entirely on Lady Revill's side," broke in Louis, now glowing with the ardour of his scarcely disguised passion. "Mrs. Tresilian is incapable of prejudice; but Lady Revill—"

"You must remember," interposed Langley, "that I once knew her. I don't suppose she has altered very much, in essentials."

"I beg your pardon, Mr. Langley. I am forgetting myself again."

"No, no; speak as you think. It's a long time ago; Lady Revill may have altered very much. You think her hopelessly prejudiced in matters such as this."

"I only mean, after all," said the young man, "that she belongs to her class."

"There's a good deal of enlightenment among the aristocracy nowadays," rejoined Langley, with a smile.

"No doubt. I have seen signs of it here and there. But Lady Revill—"

"Is altogether old-fashioned, you were going to say."

"Not those words; but it's true; she prides herself on being old-fashioned. And really, I should like to know why. It isn't as if she were a silly or ill-educated woman."

Langley laughed.

"After all," he said, with humorous gravity, "the old ways of thinking didn't invariably come of folly or ignorance. Never mind; I know what you mean, and I can sympathise with you. I think it very likely, too, that the habits of her life have prevented her mind from developing, as it once promised to. For many years Lady Revill has taken a great part in – we won't say social life, but in the life of society."

"And the surprising thing," exclaimed Louis, "is that she doesn't care for it."

"Why do you think she doesn't!" his companion asked, with a look of keen interest.

"From observing her at various times. Society far more often bores her than not. I have seen her tired and disgusted after being among people, and she has often spoken to me contemptuously of society life on the whole. That's the contradiction in her character."

"No contradiction, necessarily, of her old-fashioned views."

"I mean," Louis explained, "that despise it as she may, she allows herself to be society's slave. She would perish rather than commit some trifling breach of etiquette. Another inconsistency: she is profoundly religious."

"Life is made up of such incongruities," said Langley.

"Evidently; and they astound me. I believe that if Lady Revill acted on her convictions, she would have to give all she possesses to the poor, and join a sisterhood, or something of the kind. And I really think she is often much troubled by her conscience. All the more astonishing to me that she feels such a hatred of the people who try to carry religion into practice – such as Mrs. Tresilian."

The boy talked on, and Langley kept a long silence.

"On the whole, then," he said at length, absently, "you don't think Lady Revill has found much satisfaction in life."

"Indeed I don't!" Louis replied with emphasis. "And, what's more, I am convinced that if she marries Lord Henry Strands she will have less happiness than ever."

Langley walked on a little, then, as if shaking off reverie, spoke with sudden change of tone.

"I forgot to ask you what Mr. Worboys is doing this morning."

"Oh, he is busy writing-up his notes. It's a tremendous business always."

"Well, I envy him. He has a purpose in life. You and I, Louis, have still our vocations to discover."

It was the first time that he had used this familiar address. The young man reddened a little, and looked pleased.

"You, Mr. Langley!"

"You think me too old to have anything before me? – Do I strike you as a decrepit senior?"

"Of course not," answered the other, laughing. "I meant that I thought your vocation was scholarship."

"Nothing of the kind. I am no more a scholar than you are. To be sure,

I like the old Greeks. The mischief is that I haven't paid enough heed to them."

Louis gave an inquiring glance.

"What do you suppose it amounts to," asked Langley, "all we know of Greek life? What's the use of it to us?"

"That's what I have never been able to learn. It seems to me to have no bearing whatever on our life to-day. That's why I hate the thought of giving years more to such work—"

"You'll see it in a different light some day," said Langley. "The world never had such need of the Greeks as in our time. Vigour, sanity, and joy – that's their gospel."

"And of what earthly use," cried the other, "to all but a fraction of mankind?"

"Why, as the ideal, my dear fellow. And lots of us, who might make it a reality, mourn through life. I am thinking of myself."

Louis walked on with a meditative, unsatisfied smile.

~ *Chapter 5* ~

A DAY or two after this Langley had a morning appointment with Worboys at the Central Museum, where the archæologist wished to invite his friend's "very serious attention" to certain minutiæ of the small copy of the Athena Parthenos.[21] Nearly half an hour after the time mentioned Worboys had not arrived, yet he prided himself on habitual punctuality. Impatient, and beset with thoughts which ill prepared him to discuss the work of Pheidias, Langley loitered among the sepulchral marbles. These relics of the golden age of Hellas had always possessed a fascination for him; he had spent hours among them, dwelling with luxury of emotion on this or that favourite group, on a touching face or exquisite figure; ever feeling as he departed that on these simple tablets was graven the noblest thought of man confronting death. No horror, no gloom, no unavailing lamentation; a tenderness of memory clinging to the homely life of those who live no more; a clasp of hands, the humane symbolism of drooping eyes or face averted; all touched with that supreme yet simplest pathos of mortality resigned to fate. But he could not see it as he was wont, and he knew not whether this inability argued an ignoble turmoil of being, or yet another step in that reasonable unrest of manhood which had come upon him like an awakening after sluggish sleep.

A rapid step approached him. It was Worboys at last, and wearing a look of singular perturbation.

"A thousand apologies, my dear Langley, for this seeming neglect. I couldn't get here before. Something very troublesome has happened. I must beg your advice – your help."

They walked apart, for other visitors had just come within earshot.

"By this morning's post," pursued Worboys, "Louis has had a letter – I don't know from whom, though I suspect – which has upset him terribly. He came to me at once, after reading it, and declared that he must return to England immediately. In vain I begged for an explanation; he would tell me nothing except that go he must, and go he would. Straightway he began making inquiries about steamboats. I am bound to say that he treats me in very inconsiderate fashion. Of course I could not dream of letting him go back alone; my responsibility to Lady Revill is of the gravest. In this state of mind he is as likely as not to fall ill: in fact, when he came to me an hour ago, I thought he was in a high fever. Now, what *am* I to do, Langley? Happily he can't get off to-day, but—"

"Who do you suspect the letter was from?"

"Mrs. Tresilian, that source of all our woes. I'm sure the occasion is unspeakably preposterous. The idea of this lad believing himself in love with a woman of that age and position! And what's the good of his going? Really, one is tempted to imagine very strange things. I shouldn't like to calumniate Mrs. Tresilian—"

"The letter may not be from her at all. Just as likely, I should say, that it is from Lady Revill. Well, I don't see how you are to detain him if he's determined to go."

"Lady Revill will be exceedingly displeased," said Worboys, at the height of nervous exasperation. "In her very last letter she said that we were not, in any case, to return before midsummer, though discretion was accorded me as to how and where we should spend the time. I should be ashamed to face her. It's monstrous that a man in my position should find himself powerless over a boy of eighteen! And to leave Greece just when I am—"

"It's confoundedly annoying," the other interrupted, absently.

"Will you see him? Will you try what you can do?"

"If you don't think he'll bid me mind my own business."

"Nothing of that sort to fear. He always behaves like a gentleman – in words, at all events. But for that I'm afraid I should never have got on with him at all. He's a thoroughly good fellow, you know; it's only his outrageous excitability, and this unaccountable affair with—. Well, well, as you say, I may be mistaken. But I don't like the way he looks when I plead Lady Revill's directions."

"Does he defy them?"

"Simply declares that he has no power to obey her, but he looks savagely. Will you come to the hotel?"

Langley consulted his watch.

"No. I'll send a note as quickly as possible asking him to come and see me early in the afternoon. Better to let him calm down a little. You say no steamer leaves the Piræus to-day?"

"None. And he's too late for the train that would take him to Patras. He won't sneak off; that isn't his way. It'll all be done openly and vehemently, depend upon it."

They parted, and Langley soon dispatched his note of invitation. At three o'clock, as he sat in the book-cumbered room, smoking his longest pipe – for he wished to receive the visitor with every appearance of philosophic repose – Louis joined him. So troublous was the expression of the pale, handsome face; so pathetic its presentment of the eternal tragedy

– youth, ignorant alike of itself and of the world, in passionate revolt against it knows not what; that the older man could not begin conversation as he had purposed, with tranquil pleasantry. He rose, offered his hand, pressed the other's warmly, and said, in a grave voice:

"I'm very sorry to hear that you are going away."

"I must. I, too, am sorry, Mr. Langley. But I must go to Patras to-morrow, and leave by the steamer which sails for Brindisi at midnight."[22]

The voice quivered in its effort to express unchangeable purpose without undignified vehemence.

"That's most unfortunate. If we had been longer acquainted I should have felt tempted to ask whether a deputy could save you this trouble, for I myself am leaving for England very soon."

"Thank you, Mr. Langley; it is impossible. I must go."

"Let us sit down. It's no use pretending that I don't see how upset you are. You have had bad news, and your journey will be no pleasant one. At your age, Louis, it's no joke to be travelling for a week with misery for one's companion."

The young man was sitting bent forward, his hands locked together between his knees.

"Nor at any age, I should think," he answered, trying to smile.

"Oh, well, one takes things more resignedly later on. I suppose Mr. Worboys will go with you?"

"He says he feels obliged to. It's too bad, I know. I seem to be acting selfishly. But" – his voice faltered on a boyish note – "I simply can't help it. Something has happened – I can't go on living here – at any cost I must get back to London—"

Gradually, patiently, with infinite tact, always assuming that the journey was a settled thing, Langley brought him to disclose the disastrous necessity. That morning, said Louis, he had heard from Mrs. Tresilian; a short letter, which it drove him frantic to read. Mrs. Tresilian wrote a good-bye. She informed him that a gentleman – name unmentioned – had called upon her with a strange request – that she would hold no more communication with Louis Reed. This person represented to her that, however innocently, she had made serious mischief between Louis and the lady to whom he owed everything, upon whom his future depended. The explanation that followed allowed her no choice; she must say farewell to her dear young friend, though hoping that the severance would not be final. It was her simple duty, out of regard for him, to do so. So she begged that he would not write again, and that, on his return to England, he would not see her.

"And I know who has done this!" the young man exclaimed passionately. "Lady Revill would never have done it herself. I can't believe that she knows of it – I can't! I have told her frankly that I corresponded with Mrs. Tresilian, and she said only that she regretted the acquaintance. No; it's that man I have spoken of to you: Lord Henry Strands."

"That sounds a trifle improbable."

"I dare say, but I *know* it! He has done this, thinking it would please Lady Revill. Of course she tells him everything about me. Well, it only drives me into what must have come before long. I must ask Lady Revill to give me my independence. I shall go out into the world and work for my own living. I'm going back to tell her this."

"And to tell Mrs. Tresilian also," remarked Langley, with his kindest smile.

Louis averted his face.

"I have told you how I regard her," he said, in a tone of forced firmness. "Her friendship is more valuable to me than—Why should I be called upon to give it up? The thought of her is the best motive in my life. Without that, I don't know what may become of me. I should very likely go headlong—"

Langley checked the hurrying sentences.

"Don't strike that note, my dear boy. I know what you mean by it, but it isn't in harmony with the rest of you; it isn't manly."

Louis accepted the rebuke; he coloured, and said nothing. Thereupon his friend began to talk in an impressive strain; with gravity, with kindliness that almost had the warmth of affection, with wisdom which would not be denied a hearing. He pointed out that no harm whatever had been done by the officious stranger. Mrs. Tresilian's friendship had merely proved itself anew, and in a way that did her credit. Now, which of two possible courses was the more likely to commend itself to her respect: a wild rush from abroad, with youthful heroics to follow, or a calm, manly acceptance of her own view of the situation, with assurance that their mutual regard could not suffer by a temporary silence?

"If you find anything reasonable in all this, let me go on to make a proposal. For purposes of my own I must go to England, and I may as well start to-morrow as a week hence. I shall see Lady Revill as soon as I arrive. I mean" – he lowered his voice, and spoke with peculiar deliberation – "I have a reason of my own for wishing to see her. It is sixteen years since we met, but our acquaintance was intimate, and there's no possibility of her receiving me as a stranger. Now, will you allow me to speak for you to Lady Revill? No word shall pass my lips which you would disown. Will you stay in Greece, or, at all events, on the Continent, until you have heard from me, and from her?"

He paused, knowing the first reply that trembled on his hearer's lips. Impossible! Louis declared that it would be misery beyond endurance. His relations with Lady Revill had grown intolerable. He could not permit even the kindest friend to act for him in such circumstances.

Langley watched the flush that deepened on the face wrung with impetuous emotions. His sympathy grew painful; he was on the point of saying, "Well, then, we will travel together." But other thoughts prevailed with him; he struggled to support the aspect of equanimity, and talked on with a resolve to impose his reasonable will, if by any effort it might be done. Louis was reminded that the post would still convey his letters whithersoever he pleased.

"I dare say you have already replied to Mrs. Tresilian?"

"Yes."

"And told her that you were coming straightway? Now, if I were Mrs Tresilian (don't laugh scornfully), nothing would please me better after receiving that piping-hot epistle, than to get another couched in far more thoughtful language. You don't forget that this admirable lady will suffer a good deal if she is compelled to believe that her friendship has really been a cause of injury to you?"

That stroke told. The young man fixed his eyes on a distant point and became silent. Langley talked on, calmly, irresistibly. Little by little he permitted himself a half authoritative tone, which the listener seemed very far from resenting. Langley had learnt from his sympathetic imagination that the repose of acquiescence would seem sweet to one in Louis's state of mind, if only perfect confidence were instilled together with it. He spoke long and familiarly, revealing much of himself, at the same time that he displayed his complete understanding of the trouble he strove to soothe. And in the end Louis yielded.

"In that case," he said, his voice hoarse with nervous exhaustion, "I can't stay at Athens. I must be moving. I should perish here."

"We'll settle that with Mr. Worboys. You had better go and 'sail among the Isles Aegean.' Do you know Landor's 'Pericles'?[23] Oh, you must read it. Here, I'll lend it you. Return it when we meet in England."

Louis took the volume mechanically.

"I know it will all be useless. You will write and tell me what I already know. If you imagine that Lady Revill can be persuaded by reasoning—"

"I don't," interrupted the other, with a peculiar smile.

"I feel convinced, Mr. Langley, that you will find her very different from the lady you knew so many years ago. Even since I was old enough to observe such things, I have noticed a change in her; she is colder, harder—"

Langley still smiled.

"Yet, you say, not happy in her coldness and hardness. Bear in mind that I am something of an old-fashioned Tory myself; perhaps we shall find points of sympathy to start from."

"You are the most advanced of Radicals compared with Lady Revill."

Langley mused.

"By the by," he said, as his companion rose, "there seems to have been an understanding that you were not to return, in any case, till after midsummer."

"Yes. And the reason is plain."

"Indeed?"

"It means, of course, that on my return I shall find her married."

"It is the merest conjecture on your part," said Langley, knitting his brows. "As likely as not you are altogether mistaken in that matter."

Louis smiled with youthful confidence.

"We shall see."

His friend moved across the room, and turned again, restlessly.

"You admit that you have absolutely no authority but your own surmises?"

"True. But it's sure as fate – and very wretched fate. I don't speak selfishly; pray don't imagine anything of that kind; I'm not capable of it. Whatever I say of Lady Revill, I" – he hesitated – "I have a son's love for her. And that's why I loathe the thought of her marrying such a man. But for him, with his hateful pride, things would never have come to this pass between us. He has made her dislike me, and I regard him as my worst enemy. She puts me out of her way – she is sorry she ever had anything to do with me – and yet I have no one else—"

The emotion which broke his voice, as far as possible from unmanly complaint, touched the listener profoundly.

"Give me your hand, Louis. I pledge you my word that this shall be settled in some way satisfactory to you. Be of good heart, old fellow, and trust me."

"You will do all that any one can, Mr. Langley."

"Perhaps more than any one else could. We shall see."

~ *Chapter 6* ~

IN the morning Langley had a talk with Worboys. The tutor, far from exhibiting jealousy of his friend's superior influence, was delighted at the unhoped-for turn of things.

"It would have cut me to the heart," he declared, "to go away without having visited either Delphi or Olympia. We shall be able to take them on the homeward route. I agree with you that it will be well to spend a week or so in travel among the islands. We will go to Suros (Syra, they call it), whence, I understand, we can get to Delos. Thence to Euboea, to Thermopylæ, and perhaps as far north as the Pagasæan Gulf (Gulf of Volo, they barbarously name it), which would allow us a glimpse of Pelion."[24]

The greater part of the night Langley spent in packing and letter-writing. His heavy luggage would follow him to England. When he looked around him on trunks and portmanteaux ready for removal, it wanted but an hour of daybreak; from his sitting-room window he saw a pale pearly rift in the sky above Hymettus. Merely to rest his limbs, for sleep he could not, he threw himself on the bed.

"Thanks to you, friend Louis! You have given me the push for which I waited, and it will impel me – who knows how far? Perhaps at this time next year – but that lies in the lap of the gods."

Worboys came to him after breakfast, and announced that Louis would be at the railway station to see him off.

"He looks a ghost this morning, poor fellow. What a calamity to have such nerves! I can't remember that I was anything like that at his time of life. My father used to call me the young philosopher."

They reached the station a quarter of an hour before train-time, and found Louis pacing the platform. Drawing Langley aside, he talked with feverish energy, repeating all his requests and demands of the day before. When the traveller entered the shaky little carriage Louis still kept near to him; silent now, but with anxious eyes watching his countenance. As the train began to move they looked for a moment fixedly at each other. In that moment the two faces were strangely alike.

The line makes a circuit over the plain of Attica, and turns westward through the hollow between Aigaleos and Parnes. Thence, in view of the bay so closely guarded by lofty Salamis as to seem an inland water, it runs to Eleusis, and a railway porter shouts the name once so reverently uttered.

A little beyond rise abruptly those jagged peaks which were the limit of Attic soil; and then comes Megara, its white houses clustered over the two round hills; silent, sleepy, ignorant of its immortal fame. On by the enchanted shore, looking now across a broader sea to softly-limned Ægina and the far mountains of Troezene; until the isthmus is reached, and the train passes over that delved link of west and eastern gulfs which the ancient world cared not to complete. *"Non cuivis homini,"* murmured Langley to himself, as he stretched his limbs on the platform at Corinth;[25] gazing now at the mighty bulk of Geraneion, dark, cloud-capped; now at the noble heights of the ancient citadel, Akrokorinthos. Once more he could enjoy these visions, for with movement there had come to him a cheery quietude, a happiness of resolve.

Forward now by the coast of Peloponnesus, through mile after mile of currant fields and olive plantations, riven here and there by deep track of torrents which at times rush from the Achæan mountains. Through a long afternoon his gaze turned across the blue strip of sea, beholding as in a magic mirror those forms which appear to be bodied forth by the imagination rather than viewed with common sight: Helicon, shapen like a summer cloud, vast yet incorporeal, far-folded, melting from hue to hue; and more remote Parnassus,[26] glimmering on the liquid heaven with its rosy wreath.

At Patras he was in the world again. A clamour of porters and hotel-touts; a drive through choking dust; dinner at a table where he heard all languages save Greek; then the purchase of his ticket for Brindisi. Exhausted in mind and body, he shipped himself as soon as possible, and slept for many hours. On awaking he found himself within sight of Corfu – Corcyra,[27] as he remembered with a smile, thinking of Worboys. But it was the modern world; he could now give little thought to Homer or to Thucydides. In his last glimpse of Parnassus he had bidden farewell to the old dreams. English people were on board, and their talk sounded not unpleasant to him.

Another night (to his impatience, the whole day was spent at Corfu), and he rose early for a view of the Italian shore. There it lay, a long yellow line, whereon, presently, a harbour became visible. Not Brundisium, but Brindisi. A great English steamship was putting forth, bound for India; he watched it with a glow of pleasure, even of pride.

A brief delay at the port, then onward by rail once more. By sunny-golden sands of Calabria, where yet linger the Hellenic names; northward through rugged mountains, to Salerno throned above her azure bay; by the vine-clad slopes of Vesuvius, by the dead city of the menaced shore, into a regal sunset burning upon Naples.

~ *Chapter 7* ~

HIS arrival in London was at mid-day; the sky heavily clouded, and the streets lashed with a cold rain. Until late in the evening he sat idly at his hotel reading newspapers, but before going to bed he wrote a few lines addressed to Lady Revill. A formal note, constructed in the third person. Would Lady Revill grant an interview to Mr. Edmund Langley, who was newly returned from Athens? No more.

Were the lady in town he might receive an answer by the evening of next day. But the day passed, and no letter arrived for him. A second day went by; and only on the morning of the third was there put into his hand a small envelope, which he knew at a glance to be the reply he awaited. He opened it with nervous haste. Lady Revill apologised for her delay; she was in the west of England, and would not be back in town until Saturday evening. But if Mr. Langley could conveniently call at eleven on Monday morning, it would give her pleasure to see him.

Friday, to-day. By way of killing an hour he wrote to his friends at Athens. It was long since time had dragged with him so drearily, for he did not care to seek any of his acquaintance, and could fix his attention on nothing more serious than the daily news. To his surprise, the last post on Saturday brought him a letter with a Greek stamp. Figuring ill, he struggled with the cacography of Mr. Worboys, which conveyed disagreeable intelligence.

"We were to have sailed from the Piræus for Syra on the afternoon of the day after you left us, but I grieve to say that this was rendered impossible by an attack of illness which befell our young friend. He could neither sleep nor eat, and was obliged to confess – when we had absolutely reached the harbour – that he felt unable to go on board. I felt his pulse, and found him in a high fever. One circumstance contributing to this was doubtless a long and exhausting walk which he took on the day of your departure; if you can believe it, he positively walked for some nine hours, on an empty stomach, returning in a great perspiration long after sunset. This, in one of his constitution, was sheer madness, as I forthwith told him. From the Piræus we returned as quickly as possible to Athens, and medical aid was summoned. Our excellent doctor seems not to regard the crisis as alarming, but he forbids any movement. How often I have tried to impress upon Louis that these southern climates do not permit of the excesses in bodily exertion which may with impunity be indulged in at home! I have telegraphed to Lady Revill, as she desired me always to do in case of illness. I shall send other dispatches from time to time, and you will thus, probably, be aware of what is going on before you receive this letter."

"Poor lad! poor lad!" was the burden of Langley's thought for the rest of the evening.

On the morrow, precisely at the appointed hour, he made his call in Cornwall Gardens. It was long since he had stood at any door with an uncomfortable beating of the heart. The sensation revived, with hardly less than their original intensity, those pains with which he had entered old Mr. Forrest's presence for the fatal interview sixteen years ago.

The door opened, and solemnly, behind a solemn footman, he ascended the stairs, vaguely percipient of the marks of wealth and taste about him, breathing a fragrance which increased the trouble of his blood. In vain he strove to command himself. It was like the ascent of a scaffold; every step lengthened his physical and mental distress.

A murmur of the footman's voice; a vision of tempered sunlight on many rich and beautiful things; a graceful figure rising before him. It was over. The mist cleared from his eyes, and he was a man again.

Lady Revill received him with grave formality, almost as though they met for the first time. He had not expected her to smile, but her absolute self-control, the perfection of her stately reserve, excited his wonder. On him, it was clear, lay the necessity of breaking silence; but the phrases he had prepared were all forgotten. Their greeting was mere exchange of bows; he must plunge straightway into the business which brought him here.

"I have just returned from Greece." A motion bade him be seated, and he took the nearest chair. "At Athens I encountered by chance an old friend of mine, Mr. Worboys, and thus I was led into acquaintance with Mr. Louis Reed."

Lady Revill sat still and mute. When the speaker paused, she regarded him with an air of expectancy which puzzled Langley; it was an intense look, calm yet suggesting concealed emotion.

"I am sorry to hear," he continued, straying from a tenor of speech which threatened to be both stiff and vague, "that Mr. Reed fell ill just after I left. I had a letter on Saturday from Mr. Worboys."

The lady spoke.

"I received a telegram on Friday. Mr. Reed was then better; but his illness, I fear, has been dangerous."

Her voice reassured Langley, so nearly was it the voice of days gone by. In face and figure Lady Revill retained more of youth than he had allowed himself to expect; on the other hand, her beauty appeared to him of less sympathetic type than that which his memory preserved. She was thirty-seven, and, like most handsome women who have lived to that age amid the numberless privileges of wealth, had lost no attribute of her sex; feminine at every point, she still, merely as a woman, discomposed the man who approached her. Yet her features had undergone a change, and of the kind that time alone would not account for. Langley defined it to himself as loss of sweetness, for which was substituted a cold dignity, capable of passing into austere pride. This was independent of her gravity assumed for the occasion; he saw it inseparable from her countenance. He felt sure that she did not often smile. In silence her lips were somewhat too closely set – a pity, seeing how admirable was their natural contour. She was so well dressed that Langley had no consciousness of what she wore, save that it shimmered pearly-grey. Her hair had not changed at all; now as then, she well understood how to make manifest its abundance, whilst subduing it to the fine shape of her head. Her hand bore only two rings, the plain circlet and the keeper; its beauty was but the more declared.

"I knew nothing of this illness when I wrote asking your permission to call. But it was of Louis that I wished to speak."

Again he saw the singular expectancy in Lady Revill's look. Her eyes fell before his scrutiny. He continued.

"When I learnt that he was your ward, I of course felt a greater interest in him. I told him I had known you before your marriage, and in that way we quickly formed a friendship. It is as his friend that I must now venture to speak to you. I came to England with this purpose, after persuading him, with great difficulty, to give up an intention he had of coming hurriedly back himself. The news of his illness hardly surprised me. I left him in a terribly excited state – the result of a letter he had received from London."

Langley talked on without constraint, but not without an uncomfortable sense that he must appear impertinent in the eyes of the mute, grave listener. Her coldness, however, had begun to touch his pride; he felt the possibility of braving considerations which would have embarrassed him seriously enough even had Lady Revill betrayed some tenderness for their common memories.

"A letter from me?" she asked, in deliberate tones.

"From Mrs. Tresilian."

A shadow crossed her face. Her lips grew harder.

"In a boy's spirit of confidence," Langley pursued, "he had talked to me of Mrs. Tresilian, whom I know only by name. He had told me that he regarded her as a very dear friend, and told me also that it was a friendship of which his guardian disapproved. Then, one morning, Mr. Worboys asked me to aid him in opposing this resolve. I did so, and successfully, but not until Louis had told me the facts of the case. Mrs. Tresilian had written to him that their friendship must come to an end, the reason being that she had learnt how distasteful it was to you. A gentleman, unnamed, had called upon her, and begged her to make this sacrifice out of regard for the young man's welfare."

With satisfaction he perceived that his narrative was overcoming the listener's cold reserve. It became obvious that Lady Revill had no knowledge of these details.

"I cannot think," she said, "that any one known to me has behaved in that strange manner."

"Louis had no choice but to believe his friend's explanation. I thought it probable that he had written to you on the subject."

"He wrote a very short and vehement letter. But it contained no word of this." She paused for an instant, then added, "All he had to say to me was that he begged me to grant him his independence, that he wished to go forth into the world without assistance or advice from any one, and more to the same effect. I have had such letters from him before."

"You can understand now how he came to write in that strain."

Langley spoke, in spite of himself, with less scrupulous respect than hitherto – somewhat curtly. On Louis's behalf, he resented Lady Revill's unsympathetic tone.

"I can understand," she said, "that the person whom he calls his friend may have wrought cruelly upon his feelings; but I repeat that no acquaintance of mine can possibly have had any part in the matter."

Langley reflected, and controlled his tongue, which threatened to outrun discretion.

"In any case, Lady Revill, his feelings *were* cruelly wrought upon, and to that the poor boy's illness is due. May I speak now of something that had entered my mind even before this event? Louis talked a good deal to me of his position and of his aims. You will do me the justice to take for granted that I in no way encouraged him in discontent. On the contrary, I did my best to keep him reminded of how young he was, and how inexperienced. Happily there was no need to insist upon the deference he owed to your wishes; on that point he showed a right feeling. But at the age of eighteen, and with a temperament such as his, it is difficult always to act unselfishly, or even rationally. Whatever the source of it, he is possessed with a resolve to be – as he puts it – of some use in the world. You know the meaning of that formula on the lips of a young man nowadays. He is going through the stage of hot radicalism. Education for its own sake seems to him mere waste of time. The burden of the world is on his shoulders."

Langley's smile elicited no response. But Lady Revill had abandoned her statuesque pose, and her countenance reflected anxious thoughts.

"Mr. Worboys," she remarked coldly, "seems to have been unable to influence him."

"Quite unable, though I should say that travel had not been without its good effect. Mr. Worboys has too little understanding of his pupil's mind."

"What were you about to suggest, Mr. Langley?"

"Nothing very definite. But I think I can enter into Louis's feelings, and I seemed to attract his confidence, and this suggested to me that I might be of some service if other influences failed. I know that I am inviting a rebuke for officiousness. A word, and I efface myself again. But if you permit me to serve you, I would gladly do all I can."

"The difficulty is very great," said Lady Revill, "and I feel it as a kindness that you should wish to help me. But how? I am slow to catch your meaning."

"All I should ask of you would be a permission to continue, with your good will, the relations with Louis which began at Athens. I am an idle man, without engagements, without responsibilities. When Louis comes home, would you consent to my taking up, informally, the position Mr. Worboys will relinquish? It would give me a purpose in life – which I feel the want of – and it might, I think, afford you some relief from anxiety."

Lady Revill sat with eyes cast down; she kept so long a silence that Langley allowed himself to utter his impatient thought.

"You don't like to say that you think me unfit for such a charge?"

"I had nothing of that sort in mind, Mr. Langley," she answered, in a lowered and softened tone.

"You shrink from restoring me, thus far, to your friendly confidence."

"That is not the cause of my hesitation."

Langley winced at this reply, which was spoken with a return to the more distant manner.

"In brief, then," he said quietly, "my offer is unwelcome, and I must ask your pardon for venturing it."

"You misunderstand me. I am very willing that you should act as you propose."

It seemed to him, now, that Lady Revill assumed the tone of granting a suit for favour. Moment by moment her proximity, her voice, regained the old power over him, and with the revival of tender emotion he grew more sensitive to the meanings of her reserve.

"But," he remarked, "you foresee a number of practical difficulties?"

Very strangely, she again kept a long silence. Her visitor rose.

"I ought not to ask you to decide this matter at once, Lady Revill. Enough if you will give it your consideration."

"It is decided," she made answer, rising also, but with a hesitation, all but a timidity, which did not escape Langley's eye. "My difficulty is that I must acquaint you with certain facts concerning Louis which I don't feel able to speak of in this moment."

"If you will let me see you at another time—"

"Do you remain at the hotel?"

"For the present. I have no home."

"Believe, Mr. Langley, that I feel the kindness which has brought you here."

She seemed of a sudden anxious to atone for cold formalities. Her face, he thought, had a somewhat brighter colour, and the touch of diffidence in her bearing was more perceptible.

"If you knew how glad I am to speak with you once more—"

Suppressed emotion at length betrayed itself in his voice, and he stopped.

"I will let you hear very soon," said Lady Revill.

She offered her hand, and Langley at once withdrew. When he had left the house it surprised him to find how short the interview had been, and he was puzzled at the abruptness of its termination. He had imagined that they would talk either for a mere five minutes or for a couple of hours.

~ *Chapter 8* ~

BUT the worst of his suspense was over. He could now seek such congenial acquaintances as he had in town, and look to their society with the relish born of long solitude. Never a man of many friends, he knew himself welcome at all times in certain households of good standing; and for some years he had belonged to one of the most agreeable of literary clubs. It was early in the London season; a man who felt that he had somehow entered upon a new lease of life could not do better, whilst grave possibilities hung in the balance, than live as London prescribes to those who have means and leisure, taste and social connexions.

First of all, however, he dispatched a letter to Louis Reed; a letter warm with the kindest sympathy, and full of hopeful suggestiveness. All was going well, he assured Louis, and news more definite should come before long.

He thought it likely that some days would elapse before he heard from Lady Revill; and so, when he rose on the following morning, he had no special anxiety to inquire for letters. But on entering the coffee-room, he saw that the unexpected had happened; there was a letter for him, and from Lady Revill. Having given his order for breakfast, he broke the envelope. It contained several pages of writing, which, to his surprise, did not begin with any form of epistolary address; at the end, he saw, stood merely the signature, "Agnes Revill." In one whom he believed so careful of conventionalities, this seemed strange. Hastily he glanced over the first page; then he folded the letter, and cast a glance about him, a glance of bewilderment, of apprehension, as though afraid of a stranger's proximity. Catching a waiter's eye, he rose, and directed that his breakfast should be kept back till he again ordered it; then he went upstairs to his bedroom.

Sunshine flooded the room. Standing with his back to the window, and so that the morning glory streamed upon the paper in his hand, he read what follows: –

"In the autumn of 1877, a year after my marriage, I went to spend a fortnight with my parents, at their home. Whilst staying there, I heard, in family talk, that a middle-aged couple who were old friends of ours, their name Reed – people in a humble position, whom I think you never met, and perhaps never heard spoken of – had recently adopted a child, a little waif of three years old. I called upon them, and they told me, as far as they knew it, this child's history.

"A few years before, a young and parentless girl, whom they had known since her childhood, had disappeared from the town; her name was Eliza Morton. Suspicion arose that she had gone away with a man named Hollingdon, a commercial traveller, and some attempts were made to discover her whereabouts, but these efforts failed. But in the summer of 1877, Mrs. Reed one day received a message from the young woman, who had returned to the town, and lay ill at a lodging-house. Mrs. Reed went to see her, and found her in a dying state. The woman said that she was married, and to the man who had been suspected of leading her astray; the child she had with her, a little boy, was the offspring of this union. Hollingdon had taken her abroad, to South Africa, where eventually he deserted her, but not without leaving her sufficient means to return to England. For twelve months she had been in failing health, and it was with difficulty that she reached her native town. Fearing she might not recover, she appealed to Mrs. Reed on behalf of the child, whose name, she said, was Percival Louis Hollingdon. After a consultation with her husband, Mrs. Reed consented to take charge of the child should the mother die – an event which happened a few days later.

"The Reeds thought it doubtful whether the young woman had really been married; she wore a wedding-ring, but evaded questions as to the date and place of the ceremony. That, however, did not affect their promise on the child's behalf. Childless themselves, they were very willing to adopt this poor little boy, whose intelligence and prettiness made him interesting for his own sake. So he was taken into their home. As Mrs. Reed had no liking for the name Percival, she decided to use the child's second name, and call him Louis. For patronymic he received their own, and so grew up as Louis Reed.

"As years went on, I frequently saw this child, who grew much endeared to his adoptive parents. When he was seven, Mrs. Reed died. Her husband survived her for two years only, and in broken health. Shortly before his death, in 1882, I went to see him, and on this occasion he revealed to me a fact which had been known to him for about six months – a fact relating to Louis Reed's origin. He said that he had received a visit from the man Hollingdon, who, newly back from wanderings over the world, was making inquiries in the town concerning his wife, and had been directed to Mrs. Reed. On learning all that had happened, Hollingdon declared that the dead woman had spoken falsely in saying that her child was his also. It was true that he had married Eliza Morton, but only after she had lived, in London, with another man, to whom she had borne a child. He affirmed that, out of love for the girl, who had broken with her 'protector,' he permitted her to take the child when they were married and went abroad together. Subsequently, he confessed, he deserted his wife, partly because he wished for a child of his own, and felt jealous of her devotion to the little boy. Asked if he knew the name of this boy's father, he said that it was Langley.

"There seemed no reason to doubt the story. The dying woman had doubtless been ashamed to confess the whole truth to her friends; she wished to leave an honourable memory, and thought, no doubt, that she was doing the best thing for her child. With its father she either could not, or would not, communicate.

"As you have interested yourself in Louis Reed, I felt it necessary to inform you of these circumstances. On Mrs. Reed's death, I made myself responsible for the boy's future. A small sum of money was left for his use when he should come of age. Mrs. Reed had had him well taught at a day-school, and his education proceeded much as it would have done had he been my own child. During the last three years, he has regarded my house as his home, and me as legally his guardian. He knows that the Reeds were not his parents, having learnt that from the talk of his early schoolfellows; and on the one occasion when he asked me about his origin, I thought it the wisest course to profess total ignorance. From Mr. and Mrs. Reed, it appears, he had learnt nothing on this point."

After this came the simple signature.

An hour elapsed before Langley left the room, and went down to breakfast. The unobservant waiter remarked no change in him, but in truth the interval had changed his aspect wonderfully – had lent his features the vivacity of youth, and given him a lighter step, a more animated bearing. As he sat at the breakfast table and affected to read the newspaper, his vision was more than once dimmed with moisture; he smiled frequently.

After the meal, he wrote to Lady Revill, and, in imitation of her example, omitted epistolary forms.

"Will you let me see you very soon? May I come to-morrow morning, at the same hour as yesterday? – Edmund Langley."

He was engaged to lunch at Hampstead, and he walked all the way thither from Trafalgar Square; it seemed the pleasantest mode of passing so fine a morning. For he had an unfamiliar surplus of energy to work off, and the buoyancy of his spirits could not find adequate play save in the open air and the sunshine. After his climb up the northern heights, finding that he would have half an hour to spare, he executed a purpose which had only come into his mind when the beginning of fatigue enabled him to think more soberly; he went to the post-office and wrote a telegram addressed to Worboys at Athens. "Send me news of Louis without delay." This dispatched, he walked on in meditation. "All danger was over some days ago," ran his thoughts. "But I must know how he is. And to-morrow evening – yes, to-morrow evening – I start for Greece again!"

His hostess, a charming woman, as she talked with him after luncheon, paid a merry compliment to the health and brilliancy he had brought back from the classic land. Langley, absorbed at the moment in his own thoughts, said, as though replying:

"Do you know Mrs. Tresilian?"

"A singular question! Has she any credit for your air of happiness?"

"I am not acquainted with her, but I wish to find some one who is."

"Be your wish fulfilled. I know Mrs. Tresilian, and have known her for years."

"Yes," said Langley, with a smile, "I am fortune's favourite. Pray tell me something about her."

"Oh, she is delightful. Dine with us on Sunday, and I think I can promise you shall meet her."

"I shall probably be thousands of miles away. But what can you tell me of Mr. Tresilian?"

"Monsieur is a most estimable man," answered the lady, with a face of good-humour. "Somewhat older than his wife, it is true, but a model of the domestic virtues, and sincerely respected by all who know him – though I am bound to say they are few. His passion is for agriculture; he lives for the most part on his farm in Norfolk."

"And Mrs. Tresilian prefers the town?"

"She is a citizeness of the world, and lives wherever she can do good. I am quite serious. A great deal of nonsense is talked and believed about her. She is 'advanced,' but I wish all women were equally to the fore in work and spirit such as hers."

"I am very glad indeed to hear this," said Langley, in a grave tone. "I thought it probable."

"Oh, generous man! How your view of probabilities becomes you!"

"I am getting old, remember. Let the young enjoy the privilege of cynicism. And yet there are young people, even in our day, who can think with the generosity which ought to be the note of youth."

"Happily," returned the hostess, "I know one or two – girls, of course."

"Of course? Not a bit of it. I was thinking of a noble-spirited boy."

He dropped his eyes, for they dazzled

~ *Chapter 9* ~

HIS hope of receiving a telegram from Athens before night was disappointed. But he did not allow this to disturb him; it might be explained in several ways. The notorious uncertainty of postal matters in Greece made it possible that Worboys had not yet received the message. All was well; he looked forward with the steadfast gaze of a rapt visionary.

The morning would bring a reply from Lady Revill; and in this his confidence was justified. She expected him at eleven o'clock.

When he entered the drawing-room, it was vacant. He moved about, glancing at the pictures and other objects of interest; and presently his eye fell upon a photograph of Louis, which stood on a table. An excellent likeness; he regarded it with such intense delight that he was not aware of the entrance and approach of Lady Revill; her voice, bidding him good morning, called his startled attention, and he took with unthinking ardour the hand she offered.

"Have you any news from Athens?"

"None." She withdrew her hand, and retired a little, but did not sit down. "As the last telegram was so reassuring, I feel no uneasiness."

Her demeanour had more suavity than on the former occasion. Still reserved, still clad in her conscious dignity, and speaking with the voice of one who has much to pardon, she manifested relief; and Langley felt no check upon the impulses which demanded utterance.

"I telegraphed yesterday morning, but there was no reply when I left the hotel. No news is of course good news. As soon as I have heard, I shall start."

"For Athens?"

"Yes."

They exchanged a look. Lady Revill did not invite him to be seated, and her wandering eyes, as she stood in the unconsciously fine attitude of a tall, graceful woman, expectant, embarrassed, explained the neglect of forms.

"Why have you kept this from me?" he proceeded. "But for an accident, should I never have known it?"

"Perhaps, never. Perhaps, when Louis attained manhood."

"May I hope to know your reasons?"

"You do not doubt the truth of the story on which it all depends?" she asked, without regarding him.

"How can I doubt it? Every detail in your narrative is true – so far as they come within my own knowledge."

"Yet no suspicion crossed your mind – at Athens?"

"How could I have been led to such a thought? The name – Louis – but then it wasn't the name by which his mother called him – the name of her own choosing. And the fact of your guardianship; was that likely to turn my suspicions towards the truth?"

Lady Revill cast a glance towards Louis's portrait on the table.

"Did no one with whom you were in company perceive a personal likeness?"

"Worboys seems not to have observed anything of the kind. Is there a likeness?"

He turned to the photograph, and then again to Lady Revill, with a light of ingenuous pleasure on his face.

"I don't understand," she answered coldly, "how the resemblance escaped any one who saw you together."

Langley smiled, with difficulty repressing a laugh of joy.

"Mr. Worboys lives in the ancient world; modern trivialities make no impression upon him. And this likeness confirmed you in the belief of what you had been told?"

His voice, vibrant with glad feeling, fell to a note that was almost of intimacy.

"I am surprised," said Lady Revill, taking a few steps and laying her hand upon a chair, "that the revelation seems so welcome to you."

"It is more to me than I dare tell you," he answered with a fervour which seemed to resent her lack of sympathy. "How you yourself feel towards Louis, I cannot know; yet you must have some understanding of what it means to a man very much alone in the world when he finds that Louis is his own son."

"Have you ever tried to discover what had become of the child?"

"Never. Will you forgive a question I am obliged to ask you in return? It is this: Did your parents speak of me to you, when I went away, with absolute condemnation? or did they offer any excuses for my behaviour in their house? I took care that my story should be made known to you. But will you let me know in what shape it was related?"

Lady Revill seated herself; Langley remained standing. The great joy that had befallen him overcame his oppressive self-consciousness; and the thought that this beautiful woman, whom in his heart he still named "Agnes," had for years been mother to his son, gave him a right of intimate approach not to be denied by her stateliest gravity.

"I only knew," was her distant answer, "that you had a responsibility which forbade your marriage."

"That is extremely vague." He began to speak as one who demands, rather than requests, an explanation. "Besides, it was not true."

"How can you say that?" Lady Revill looked upon him for an instant with surprise. "You have acknowledged the truth of what I put in writing."

"There was no responsibility that forbade marriage. When I told your father my story, he took time to think about it, and I then heard from him that it was deemed impossible to speak to you of such things. I accepted this decision, but only for a day. Then I understood that respect for your parents must not make me unjust to myself – and perhaps to you. When I wrote, at length, asking you to be my wife, I wrote at the same time to your father, telling him of the step I had taken, and requesting that you should be informed of all I had let him know. It seemed my only course: rightly or wrongly, our habits forbid a man to speak of such things to the girl he wishes to marry. Is it possible that your father, in replying that you had heard 'everything,' did not tell the truth? I know what crimes good people will commit in the name of morality; but surely Mr. Forrest was incapable of such transaction with his honour?"

The listener's countenance grew fixed as a face in marble. Langley, unheeding its frigid reproof, went on.

"Did you know *all* the facts? Or only that I was father of a child? Or perhaps not even as much as that?"

The statue spoke.

"I knew of the child's existence. It was enough."

"From my point of view, far from enough. You were never told that the child's mother, of her own desire, had married another man and taken the child away?"

"The knowledge could not have affected my opinion."

It was spoken with undisguisable effort. Langley, watching her face intently, saw a quiver of the brows and of the hard-set lips.

"Ah, then you did *not* know. In telling you so much, and no more, your parents did me a grave wrong.

"Mr. Langley, your own wrong-doing was so much graver that I cannot see what right you have to reproach them."

His blood was now warm; his pride rose in contest with hers.

"In a case like this, Lady Revill, the question of right or wrong can only be decided on a most intimate acquaintance with the circumstances."

"I think otherwise. Admission of one fact is enough."

"There we are at issue, and I daresay neither of us would care to argue on the subject. But in one respect your natural kindness has overcome the severity of your creed. You did not visit upon the child the sins of the father."

Lady Revill was silent.

"If you had condemned me," proceeded Langley, "because I neglected my duty to the boy, I could have said little enough to excuse myself. There, indeed, I was guilty. The circumstances made it difficult for me to act otherwise than I did; but none the less I threw aside carelessly the gravest responsibility that can be laid upon a man. In your view, no doubt, it was my first duty to marry the mother. To have done that would have been to lay the foundation of life-long misery. My selfishness – if you like – saved me from worse than folly. But it is true that I ought not to have given up the child to an unknown fate. The mere ceremony of marriage is of no account; but a parent is bound by every kind of law in the interests of his child."

A movement in his hearer checked him. Turning, he saw that a servant had entered the room. The man silently approached, and presented a salver on which lay a telegram.

"I think this is from Athens," said Lady Revill, when they were alone again.

Langley waited, his pulse quickened with expectation. He watched the delicate hands as they broke the envelope, saw them unfold the paper, saw them suddenly fall.

"What news—?"

Her eyes had turned to him. In their stricken look, in the blanching of her cheeks and of her parted lips, he read what lay before her.

"Will you let me see?" he said quietly.

She gave him the telegram.

"Grieve to say that Louis died this morning. Painless and like a sleep. Please let me know your wishes."

He looked to the sunny window, but saw nothing. Dark wings seemed to beat over him, and chill him with their shadow. Lady Revill had risen; the sound of a sob escaped her, and she trembled, but her eyes were tearless. Then Langley faced her again.

"I must reply at once. What is your wish, Lady Revill?"

"My wish is yours. Would you like him to be brought to England?"

"Why? What does it matter?" he answered in a hard voice.

"It is yours to decide."

Her utterance echoed the note of his. They stood regarding each other distantly, their faces stricken with a grief which they strove to master.

"Let him be buried among the ruins," said Langley, with bitter emphasis. He laid the telegram on a table; stood for a moment in hesitancy; turned to his companion.

"Good-bye."

Her lips moved, as if to speak the same word; but another sob caught her breath. Commanding herself, she flashed a look at him, and said impulsively:

"Do you lay it to my charge?"

Langley was over-wrought; a flood of violent emotion broke through all restraint.

"Why have you stood for years between me and my son? What right had you to withhold him from me?"

"I see no shadow of right in your reproach. You cast him off when he was a little child. What claim had you upon him when he grew up?"

"Again you speak in ignorance of what happened. It was against my will that I let his mother take him away. She could pretend no love for me, but she loved her child, and I was unable to refuse her. There was an understanding that, if ever she needed help, she would let me know. In acting as she did, afterwards, she broke her promise to me. I foresaw the possibility of what came about. She knew how to communicate with me. The child would have been brought up under my care. But she wished to die in the odour of respectability."

"And does your conscience acquit you in all other respects?" Lady Revill asked, she, too, the mere mouthpiece of tumultuous feelings. "Have you no thought of the first sin – the source of all that followed, including your misery now?"

"Say what you will of that," he answered scornfully. "The moral folk of the world take good care that what they choose to call crimes shall not go unpunished, and then they point to an avenging Providence. You, no doubt, in keeping my son from me, considered yourself to be discharging a religious duty. You feared, perhaps, that his father would corrupt him. If the boy had died before I saw him, you would have written me a letter, pointing the moral of the tragedy. You have robbed me of years of happiness. And how much happier would his young life have been! As it was, you condemned him to a struggle with conditions utterly unsuited to his nature. Your prejudices of every kind, your lack of sympathy with all that is precious to a generous young mind in our time – did no perception of this ever trouble you? Perhaps, after all, I was wrong in what I granted just now. Perhaps you knew all that the boy was suffering, and accepted it as the penalty he had to pay for his father's vileness?"

"You don't know what you are saying!" exclaimed the other, shrinking before his vehemence, and now gazing at him with sorrowful rebuke.

"What reason had you?" He stepped nearer. His face had aged by many years, and showed wrinkles hitherto invisible; his eyelids were red and swollen, as though from weeping. "How do you justify yourself, Lady Revill?"

"The child was not yours," she answered, with troubled breath. "You gave him up to his mother, and it was her right, when dying, to choose what guardian she would."

"Even so, *you* were not the guardian chosen. When you learnt the truth from Mrs. Reed, it was your duty to communicate with me. – But you are right; I am talking wildly and foolishly. Nothing can be undone. The boy lies dead at Athens. Let him be buried there – among the ruins."

As he once more turned from her, his eye fell upon Louis's portrait. He moved towards it, and stood gazing at the ardent face; then, without looking round, said in a thick voice:

"Have you one of these that you can give me?"

"Take that. There are others that you shall have."

"Is there one taken long ago – when he was a little boy?"

"Several. You shall have them."

"Tell me this – speak frankly, plainly. Had you any true affection for him?"

"Why else should I have treated him as though he were a child of my own?"

"Did you? That is what I want to know. Or was it only the conscientious discharge of what you somehow came to think your duty?"

Lady Revill looked at him with searching eyes.

"Did he speak," she asked, "as if I had behaved to him without affection?"

"He spoke of you with respect."

"With nothing more?"

It was all but a cry of pain, and Langley subdued his voice in answering.

"Remember that we were strangers to each other; mere acquaintances, it seemed, and of such different ages. Remember, too, that he was at the time of life when a boy's simplicity is outgrown, and the man's thoughtfulness has not yet developed. I found in him – and it is saying much – not a trace of ungenerous feeling. He spoke with regret of the trouble and anxiety he had caused you."

"Never heartlessly," interrupted the listener. "Never in a way that could make me sorry I had—"

Her voice broke; she bent her head.

"He said more; and judge of the strength of his feeling, that he could overcome a boy's shame, and speak of such things. He confessed to me, in his bitterness, that he loved you with a son's love; and lamented that you had lost all kindness for him."

"It was not true! How could he think that?"

"What is the use of love that is never shown?"

"He turned from me – he made friends of people who taught him to rebel against my wish in everything."

"You were mistaken," said Langley. "I know who you are thinking of. That friend of his, from first to last, spoke no word disrespectful to you. She did not even know that you had found fault with him on her account. And when some one or other told her how serious the matter was getting, you know how she wrote to him."

"An easy magnanimity."

"It is you who seem to find the reverse of magnanimity so easy. I know nothing of this woman, except what I heard from Louis. Public report is worthless; though you, doubtless, make it the whole ground of your prejudice against her. I believe that she did act magnanimously, or at all events in honest kindness; out of regard both for him and for you. I know a lad can be fooled by the most worthless woman, but this is no such case."

"I bring no charge against her," said Lady Revill, coldly, "except that the result of her influence, whether she proposed it or not, was to set Louis's mind in opposition to all I desired."

"What did you desire?"

She seemed to disdain an answer.

"Perhaps," Langley went on, without harshness, "you had some memory of me – of views I used to hold – and your intention was to make of him a man as unlike me as possible. I am not what I was – unhappily. Life has killed off so many of my enthusiasms, as it does in most men. You did me the honour, perhaps, of imagining me still warm on the side of poor wretches – still cold to the aristocratic ideal. You sought to repress in the boy all that did him most credit – his unselfish aspirations, his bright zeal for justice and mercy – his contempt for idle and conceited worldlings. I once knew a woman who would never have done that – but the world has changed her."

"You talk in utter ignorance of me," Lady Revill replied.

"Whatever your motive, the result was the same."

Emotion again shook her.

"I tried to do my duty, and you are the last person who should reproach me if I mistook – if I failed to make his boyhood a time of happiness—"

"His life," said Langley, after a few moments of painful silence, "was not unhappy. His troubles came of no idle or shameful cause, and he was full of purpose. If he could have grown up at my side! If I could have led him on, taught him, watched the growth of his mind – what a companion! what a friend! And I have wasted my life, idled and sauntered through the years, whilst, unknown to me, that duty and that happiness lay within reach!"

Lady Revill gazed at him appealingly through tears.

"No," he continued, with a gesture of impatience, "I shall not forget myself again. I spoke in maddening pain; it was true, I didn't know what I said. I am ashamed to have spoken to you like that – to you. You had reasons for what you did; never mind what they were."

Again there was silence, and Lady Revill sank wearily upon a seat.

"Shall you go to Athens?" she asked.

"What use – to see a grave? But yes; I shall go."

"You do wish him to be buried there?"

"Yes. In the little cemetery by the Ilissus. Ah, you know nothing of all that."

"Is it beautiful – like the cemetery at Rome?"

"No; not in that way. A poor little patch of ground. But it lies close by the ruins of a great temple, and at evening the shadow of the Acropolis falls upon it. He was learning to love Athens; and if I could have gone back to him –. I should have started to-night. In a week I thought to be with him again."

When he paused Lady Revill asked under her breath:

"You would at once have told him?"

"You think I should have shrunk from it," he answered, with a revival of scornful emotion. "Oh, how the proprieties imprison you! How the pretty hypocrisies of life constrain the nobler part of you!"

"To you, then," she exclaimed, a hot flush upon her cheeks, "all decency, all shame, is the restraint of hypocrites?"

"No; but the false feelings that take their name. You would think it more becoming, I dare say, to have let him remain fatherless, than to confess that, twenty years ago, I was young, and had a young man's passions."

"Poor boy! I can hardly grieve that he is dead."

"At least, that is logical," said Langley, with answering bitterness, "for you would have liked him to feel a misery worse than death in the knowledge of his birth. And perhaps he would really have felt it. Perhaps the influence of his education, the moral lessons you have assiduously taught him –. Oh, let us make the best of what can't be helped; let us be content that he is dead."

Lady Revill rose from her chair.

"Mr. Langley, shall I reply to this telegram, or will you do so?"

"I will do so, in your name."

"Thank you."

It was a dismissal. Langley glanced at the photograph, but did not take it. Lady Revill, however, moved quickly, and put it into his hand.

"Your grief is very bitter," she said, in a shaken voice.

Their hands just touched, and he left her.

~ *Chapter 10* ~

THE day passed in a moody and fretful indecision. There was a telegram from Worboys, repeating the words of that addressed to Lady Revill; he carried it about with him, and read it times innumerable. The photograph he had put away; but the face it represented came before his mind persistently, and, by a morbid trick of the imagination, changed always to a deathly rigidness, with eyes closed and sunken cheeks.

From harassed sleep, he awoke when it was yet dark, and the sudden return of consciousness was a shock that left him quivering with shapeless fears. He did not know himself, could not recover his personality. It was as though a man should turn to the glass, and behold the visage of a stranger. So much had crowded into the two brief yesterdays: a joy undreamt, the glowing forecast of a life's happiness, a stroke of fate, and thereupon that whirling hour that made him think and speak so wildly. Trying to remember all he had said, he was racked with something worse than shame. It seemed impossible that a moment's anguish could so disfigure a ripened mind, stultify the self knowledge of philosophic years. What foolish insults had he uttered? It was like the behaviour of crude youth, stung into recklessness by a law of life unknown to him.

When day broke, he rose, half dressed himself, and sat down in the twilight with pen and paper.

"For all my frenzy of yesterday, I beg your forgiveness. I owed you gratitude, and behaved with brutality. Will you write a few words, and say that you can make allowance for what was spoken at such a time? Do not think that revealed myself as I am; that was the spirit of long years ago, which in truth I have outlived. Forgive me, and tell me that you do."

Whilst it was still very early, he went out and posted this. An hour after, there came regret for having done so; and through the morning he wandered miserably about unfamiliar streets.

Early in the afternoon, he despatched a telegram to Hampstead, asking for the address of Mrs. Tresilian. No sooner was it sent than he remembered that a glance at a Directory might perhaps have saved the trouble; so forthwith he searched the volume. "Tresilian, Frederick James," no other of the name appeared; and this gentleman's house was in Connaught Square. But Langley could not be sure that it was the residence of the lady he sought; after all, he must await the reply from his friend. It arrived in an hour's time, and astonished him.

"Mrs. Tresilian's address – 34, East Lane, Bermondsey."

Was she, then, even more enthusiastic in her cause than he had imagined? Did she positively dwell among the poor?

After brief hesitation he took a hansom, and was driven towards the glooming levels of South-east London. In Bermondsey the cabman had to ask his way. When East Lane was at length discovered Langley alighted at the end, dismissed his vehicle, and explored the by-way on foot. He found that No. 34 was a larger house than its neighbours; it had recently undergone repairs, and looked not only clean, but, to judge from the windows, comfortably furnished. In answer to his knock appeared a very pretty woman, very plainly dressed, whose face, unless he were mistaken, declared her name.

"I wish to see Mrs. Tresilian."

"Will you come in?" was the pleasantly toned invitation; and he followed to a sitting-room on the ground floor, a room simple as could be, but at the same time totally unlike the representative parlour of Bermondsey. There the pretty woman faced him with, "I am Mrs. Tresilian."

"My name is Langley—"

He could add no particulars, for at once his hostess exclaimed vivaciously:

"And you have come from Greece! You have been with Louis Reed!"

"Yes."

"But how did you find me? Louis doesn't know of this place, does he?"

Langley explained, and Mrs. Tresilian laughed at what she called the perfidy of their Hampstead friend.

"I know all about you from a letter of Louis's. How is he? Not ill, I hope?"

The pause which Langley made, and his dark look, alarmed her. In a few words he told what had befallen. The listener, clasping her hands in a gesture of sincere grief, stood for a moment voiceless; then her eyes filled.

"Oh, poor boy! poor boy! Do you know, Mr. Langley, what great friends we were? Oh, and I expected so much of him. He seemed so—"

She had to turn away. Langley, choking with a gentler sorrow than he had yet felt, regarded her through tears that would not be restrained. Often he had smiled at the name of Mrs. Tresilian, knowing only of certain extravagances which served to caricature her personality in the eye of the world; he saw her now as she had appeared to Louis, admiring scarcely less than he sympathised.

"Tell me about him, Mr. Langley. Was he quite well when you left him?"

"In fair health, I thought. But—" He changed the form of his sentence.

"Did he not write to you very recently?"

She exhibited much distress.

"Yes. I had a letter only a day or two ago. And how unhappy it will always make me to think that—Do tell me all you know. You seem to keep something back. If he said anything to you – I will explain my reasons—"

Langley related the events of his last two days at Athens, and the listener sat with bent head, her tears falling. When he ceased she made an effort to calm herself; then, with perfect simplicity, made known the reason for what she had done. It was a sacrifice imposed by her genuine affection for Louis. She had never known, until some one authorised to speak came and told her, that Louis's guardian looked with the strongest disapproval upon their friendship; the matter was represented to her so very gravely that there seemed no alternative, though it broke her heart to write as she did. And Louis's letter in reply was so manly, so noble—

"He wrote so?" Langley interrupted eagerly.

"How proud I should be to show you the letter, if it were not too sacred! And I seem to have only just read it, fresh from his hands. How is it *possible* that the poor boy can be dead? I can't believe it!"

"You speak, Mrs. Tresilian, of some one who came to you with authority. Now, when I mentioned this fact to Lady Revill, she utterly denied that any friend of hers could have taken such a step."

"Then I must justify myself, at any cost," answered the other, with dignity. "The gentleman who called was Lord Henry Strands. He came to the house in Connaught Square – it was the day before I left to come here – and went so far as to tell me in confidence that Lady Revill would shortly become his wife. Of that, Mr. Langley, I am sure you will not speak. I must tell you, for I can't bear that you should think I acted frivolously."

Langley kept silence. His habitual frown expressed a gloomy severity, and Mrs. Tresilian seemed unable to move her eyes from him.

"Are you well acquainted with Lady Revill?" she asked, diffidently.

"Till the other day it is years since we met."

"What I have said surprises you?"

"No. I have heard of Lord Henry Strands. But," he added slowly, "it is clear that he came to you without authority from Lady Revill."

"There seems no doubt of that." Mrs. Tresilian's eyes, still moist, gleamed with indignation. "I know Lady Revill only by name, but I have heard people say all sorts of pleasant things of her. Of course I was sorry to know how she thought of me, but I could not for a moment, considering Louis's age, countenance him in disregarding her wishes."

"Can you – forgive me for questioning you further – can you tell me anything of Lord Henry Strands?"

"I know nothing of him. He looks a man of forty, and seems well-bred, though perhaps a little conscious of his rank."

Their eyes met for a moment, and Mrs. Tresilian again seemed to discover something in the visitor's face which strongly held her attention.

"Do tell me, if you can," she continued, "whether it's true that Lady Revill has a *very* bad opinion of me?"

"She has conservative prejudices."

"And do you suppose that Louis had lost any of her favour on this account? Believe me, Mr. Langley, I never had a suspicion of it. He never spoke to me of any such thing."

"I fear there is no doubt that they differed on this point."

"And perhaps for that very reason he was sent abroad? Oh, how cruel it is! I must think myself in part the cause of his death!"

Her tears flowed again. But Langley, in his kindest voice, endeavoured to reassure her, representing that the actual and sufficient cause of Louis's being sent to travel was the young man's disinclination to enter upon a University career. For this self-will, as he knew, Mrs. Tresilian could in no way be held responsible; Louis's radicalism had begun to flourish before ever he met with her.

"You felt a great interest in him, I am sure?" said the lady, presently; and again her look fixedly encountered his.

"It was inevitable," Langley answered, in a low voice, "after once talking with him."

Their conversation lasted for an hour; before they parted Mrs. Tresilian explained the meaning of her residence in East Lane. She belonged to an informal sisterhood, who had recently undertaken to live, two or three together, and in turns, among this poor population, for example and for help. They kept no servants; all the work of the house was done by their own hands. Each of them took up her abode here for three weeks at a time.

"But I never spoke of it to Louis," she said sadly. "I ceased to tell him of such things when I found that it disturbed his thoughts. He was so good and generous. He wished to be doing something himself. But it was his time for study, and—Oh, but I shall always reproach myself! I did harm, great harm!"

Langley, standing in readiness to take his leave, murmured a few words of deep feeling; and as they shook hands Mrs. Tresilian looked into his face with eyes that thanked him.

~ *Chapter 11* ~

WHEN the next morning brought no letter from Lady Revill, Langley ground his teeth; he keenly repented his haste in sending off that passionate plea for her forgiveness. What was to be expected of a woman dyed to the core in conventionality? – the widow of Sir Thomas Revill – the plighted wife of Lord Henry Strands! In asking pardon he had been untrue to himself. Heaven forbid that he should have outlived that spirit of revolt which so offended her little soul! If to-morrow he heard nothing he would write once more, and in a more self-respectful strain; then back to Athens, to stand by his son's grave.

But in the evening came a reply. It was written on black-edged note-paper of the finest quality, and couched in terms of irreproachable correctness. "Dear Mr. Langley," it began. Yes; she would no longer countenance informalities; he was henceforth to be an acquaintance like any other. "This afternoon I am leaving town again, to stay for a time at my house in Somerset. You would no doubt like to have some of the things that belonged to Louis, such as books and papers; these shall be put at your disposal when you return to England. Moreover, as you know, I am trustee of a small fund which would have been his when he came of age; in this matter your wishes will be consulted by my solicitors. Believe me, dear Mr. Langley, faithfully yours,—."

How gracious! What delicate regard for his feelings!

He sat late in the smoking-room, turning over newspapers. His hand fell upon a journal of society, and he wondered idly whether it contained any mention of the names in which he was interested. Here was one. Lord Henry Strands, said a rumour, had it in mind to purchase the house in Hyde Park Gardens, vacant since the death of So-and-so. To be sure; a natural step. And, a little further on, the polite chronicler announced that Lady Revill had returned to town for the season, having spent the greater part of the winter at her delightful country home in the west of England. The name of her estate was Fallowfield, and it lay near the interesting and beautiful village of Norton St. Philip, in Somerset, celebrated as having been the resting-place of the ill-fated Duke of Monmouth just before the battle of Sedgmoor.[28] With other particulars; but on the leading point the newsman for once was wrong.

Norton St. Philip. To that part of England, Langley was a stranger. With purposeless curiosity he reached for Bradshaw, but the name of the village did not appear in the index. An out-of-the-way place. The estate had probably belonged to Sir Thomas. Langley yawned, and went to bed.

In the morning he paid an early visit to his club, and for the sole purpose of consulting a gazetteer or guide-book. He found that the village of Norton St. Philip lay some three miles from a little place named Wellow, which was a station on the Somerset and Dorset railway, only six miles from Bath. Again he referred to Bradshaw. The 1:15 express would land him at Bath by 3:30; and thence, after waiting an hour and a half, he could reach Wellow by half past five. He sat musing, and frowning, till the clock pointed to eleven; then returned to his hotel. Here again he mused and frowned, till nearly noon.

At one o'clock he drove up to Paddington, with a travelling-bag. The first part of his journey passed without pleasure or impatience; he watched the telegraph-wires in their seeming sway, up and down, up and down; saw the white steam of the engine float over green meadows, and was at Bath before he had time to unfold his newspaper. An unobservant stroll in the town, and a meal for which he had no appetite – though fasting since formal breakfast – killed the moments until he could proceed. At Wellow he found himself amid breezy uplands. There was no difficulty in procuring a conveyance to Norton St. Philip. He liked the drive, and liked, too, the appearance of the old inn, a fifteenth-century house, which at length received him.

Not till night had fallen did he go forth and ramble in the direction of Fallowfield, some half-hour's walk along a leafy road. Having looked at the closed gates, and the lighted windows of the lodge, he rambled back again. At bedtime he thought of nothing in particular – unless it were the Duke of Monmouth.

But the shining of a new day quickened his life. When he opened his window, spring breathed upon him with the fragrance of all her flowers, and birds sang to him their morning rapture. He no longer marvelled at the impulse which had brought him hither, but smiled to think that he had so much more of resolute manhood than in the prime of youth.

When the sun was high, he again walked over to Fallowfield, and by inquiry at the lodge ascertained that Lady Revill had in truth returned from town. By a winding drive of no great length he approached the house: a most respectable structure, which declared the hand of a Georgian architect. The garden at all events was beautiful, and lovely in their new leafage were the trees that stood about. In the imposing hall, he waited with no less painful tremor than on presenting himself at the house in Cornwall Gardens. When led at length into a room, he saw with satisfaction that it was no chamber of state, but small and cosy, with windows that opened upon a little lawn. Here again he had to endure some minutes of solitude, marked by heart-throbs. Then sounded a soft rustle behind the screen which concealed the door, and Lady Revill advanced to him. She wore a garb of mourning, admirable of course in its graceful effectiveness, and somehow, despite the suggestion of grief, not out of harmony with the bright spring day. Unsmiling, yet with the friendly welcome which became her as a country hostess, she offered her hand.

"I am so sorry that you should have had to make such a journey to see me. I thought you had left England. If I had known that there was anything you wished to speak of immediately—"

The civil address struck Langley mute. He had not imagined that, face to face with him, Lady Revill would adhere to the conventionalities of her last letter.

"Could it not have been done by correspondence?" she added, as they seated themselves.

"I had no choice but to come. I couldn't go away without seeing you again. The memory of our meeting in London is too painful to me."

Her mood, it seemed, was gentle, for she listened with bent head, and answered softly.

"Hadn't we better forget that, Mr. Langley?"

"I cannot forget that I gave you cause to think very ill of me."

"No. I have no such thought." She was gravely kind. "I did not reply directly to your letter, because I felt sure that you would understand my omission to do so. The blow that fell upon you was so sudden and so dreadful."

"But upon you also it fell," said Langley, when she paused.

"More heavily than perhaps you are willing to believe."

He searched her face for evidence of this, and a moment elapsed. Then, with a collected manner, Lady Revill again spoke.

"As the opportunity offers, let me ask whether you have seen Mrs. Tresilian."

"I called upon her."

"Before leaving town, I had a letter from her. We don't know each other, and I have never wished to know Mrs. Tresilian; but she wrote, seemingly, in great distress, reproaching herself with having contributed to Louis's fatal illness. Whether there can be any truth in that, I am unable to decide. As it was from you, I find, that she learnt the particulars, I am afraid you left her under the impression that she was to blame."

"I tried not to do so."

"In this letter," proceeded Lady Revill, "Mrs. Tresilian repeats what I was so surprised to learn from you, the story of some one having called upon her in my name. Please tell me, Mr. Langley, whether this was mentioned in your conversation."

"We spoke of it," he answered steadily.

"I believe I have a right to ask what you learnt from Mrs. Tresilian."

Langley faced the challenge, admiring the stern beauty of his questioner as she uttered it.

"Certain facts were mentioned in confidence," he said. "But it can hardly be a breach of confidence to repeat them – to you. The gentleman who called upon Mrs. Tresilian was Lord Henry Strands."

"Thank you."

Their eyes met unwaveringly. On Lady Revill's cheek mantled a soft glow, but she continued in the same voice, melodious always, though in the note of royal command.

"Did Lord Henry Strands offer any explanation of the step he had taken?"

"He did."

"Kindly tell me what it was."

"In confidence, he told Mrs. Tresilian that you would shortly be married to him."

"Thank you."

The colour had died out of her face. Without venturing even a glance, Langley waited for her next words; he could not surmise what they would be, for her "Thank you" was uttered in an uncertain, absent tone, very unlike that of the interrogator.

"It was not true," she said at length, coldly.

He raised his eyes. In the same moment Lady Revill stood up, and spoke once more with the self-possession of a friendly hostess.

"Would you like to see the gardens? If you will wait a moment."

Quickly she reappeared with covered head. She talked of flowers and trees, but her voice sounded to him only as distant music; he answered mechanically, or not at all. A direct question recalled him to himself.

"Do you return this afternoon?"

"I am uncertain. I haven't thought about it."

Utterly confused he could only stare at the shadow upon the grass. Lady Revill walked on, and again drew his attention to some detail of gardening. Able at length to answer in ordinary tones, he met her look, and for the first time she smiled. A smile of no meaning; the mere play of facial muscles trained to express suavity.

"You are alone here?" he asked.

"At present. But I am expecting guests this afternoon – two little nieces, who will stay for a few weeks with me."

Reviving his recollections of her family, Langley was about to ask whose children these were; but Lady Revill spoke again, and on another subject.

"Will you tell me something of Mrs. Tresilian? I am afraid I have done her injustice. Probably I have been misled by public opinion. You are well acquainted with her?"

"Not at all. I had never met her before."

He continued vaguely; careful to avoid specific eulogy, yet suggesting a favourable estimate. And even whilst speaking, he was dissatisfied with himself, for he knew that to any one else he would have given a much bolder description of Mrs. Tresilian. Conscience rebuked him for cowardice.

Conversing thus, they had passed through a shrubbery, and reached an open spot, sheltered with larch trees, where stood a small building of no very graceful design. Lady Revill explained that it was a mortuary chapel, built by the original owner of Fallowfield to contain his wife's tomb. The family was Roman Catholic. Nothing of general interest marked the interior; it had been converted to the uses of Protestantism, and a clerical guest or the incumbent of the parish, occasionally read service here.

"This path," she added, with her hand upon a little wicket which opened into the consecrated spot, "leads through the plantation to the high road – in the direction of the village."

Was it a dismissal? Langley stood in miserable embarrassment; he seemed to have lost all his tact, all his breeding; he could behave neither as a man of the world nor as an impassioned lover. A boobyish boy could not have been more at a loss how to act or speak. Then he saw that Lady Revill was again smiling.

"Will you give me the pleasure of your company at luncheon?" she said.

This excessive courtesy restored command of his tongue. He answered, in a matter-of-fact phrase, that he feared the time at his disposal was too short; he had better follow this path to the village.

"I mentioned in my letter," began Lady Revill; and then paused, her eyes wandering.

"Thank you; it was very kind. You will let me write to you – when I have decided where I shall live."

She offered her hand, gravely; the dismissal was now in form. Without word of leave-taking, Langley touched her fingers, and passed through the little gate.

~ *Chapter 12* ~

HE travelled back to London. With no intention of remaining there, and with no settled purpose of going further; rest he could not, and the railway journey at all events consumed what else must have been hours of intolerable idleness. For the fire that so long had slept within him, hidden beneath the accumulating habits of purposeless, self-indulgent life, denied by his smiling philosophy, thought of as a mere flash amid the ardours of youth – the fire of a life's passion, no longer to be disguised or resisted, burst into consuming flame. He had accustomed himself to believe that his senses were subdued by reason, if not by time; and nature mocked at his security. No hapless lad, tortured by his twentieth year, suffered keener pains than Langley through the night that followed.

It was solace to him that Lady Revill had expressly declared herself a free woman. The very fact of her having done so seemed to crush his hope: for the dismissal that fell from her lips signified, more probably than not, a passing anger with the indiscreet Lord Henry; she would shame the man and bring him to his knees, but only for the pleasure of forgiving him. Such a suitor was not likely to have so far presumed without solid assurance; and Agnes Revill was not the woman to cast away, for so trifling a cause, the hope of high dignities.

A few days passed, and in the meanwhile he again communicated by telegraph with Worboys. The archæologist made known his intention of remaining in Greece; he had written to Lady Revill, and at the same time to Langley. Thereupon Langley addressed Lady Revill in a formal letter, asking her wishes with regard to the marking of Louis's grave. The reply leaving him free to act in this matter as he chose, he wrote to Worboys that the grave should remain, for the present, without stone or memorial.

In less than a week – it seemed to him that he had struggled through a month – the goad again drove him westward. He reached the old inn at Norton St. Philip, and under cover of darkness prowled about the precincts of Fallowfield. The next morning, as he strayed with faltering purpose along the high road, an open carriage passed; in it sat Lady Revill with two little girls. Whether she saw him or not he was unable to determine. Perhaps not, for she was leaning back, and had an inattentive air. But this glimpse of her face fevered him. He returned to the inn and wrote a letter, which, after all, he shrank from dispatching.

Shortly before sunset he walked along the path by which, a week ago, he had left Fallowfield. It was too late for an ordinary call at the house; he half purposed delivering his letter to a servant, that Lady Revill might read it and think of it to-night. He passed through the larch plantation, where birds were loud amid the gold-green branches, and on coming within sight of the little chapel lingered wearily. If he meant to approach the house from this point he must wait till gloom had fallen; there was too much risk of encountering some one in the gardens.

He leaned against a trunk.

The sun went down; the birds grew silent. Possessed by unendurable longing he moved forward. But daylight still lingered, and courage to enter the gardens failed him. Pausing by the chapel door, he laid a hand upon the ring, and turned it; the door opened, not without noise, and as he was about to enter a figure rose in the dusk. His heart lept. Lady Revill had been either sitting or kneeling alone, and now she faced the intruder.

He drew back, closed the door, and stepped aside. In two or three minutes he heard the door creak as it again opened. Lady Revill came forth, and stood looking in his direction. Then, with a few quick steps, he advanced towards her.

"Mr. Langley, why are you here?"

"Because I can't live away from you. Because it is so much harder, now, to relinquish the best hope of life than it was years ago."

Question and answer were uttered rapidly, on hurried breath. Gazing steadfastly on the face before him, Langley saw that it was pale and discomposed; the eyes seemed to bear marks of tears.

"Then," she rejoined in the same moment, "I must tell you at once, without choosing phrases, that you are guilty of strange folly."

"That may well be. But the folly has too strong a hold on me. I am sorry to have broken in upon your privacy; but very glad to have met you. Of course I had no idea you were in the chapel."

"You ought not to be here. It's unworthy of you; and if I am to live in fear of being surprised whenever I come out alone—. What more have we to say to each other?"

"If only you will hear me! When one has wasted so many years of life, ever so faint a hope of recovering the past becomes a strong motive."

"Wasted? Why have the years been wasted?" She endeavoured to speak with her usual cold dignity, but her voice had lost its firmness. Langley could not take his eyes from her; pallid, disdainful, with tormented brows, the face had a wonderful beauty in this light of afterglow.

"Why?" he echoed sadly. "Folly, of course. But the natural enough result of what we both remember."

"And whose the blame?" broke from her lips. "Whose the blame?"

"Who is ever to blame for spoilt lives! Fate, I suppose: a convenient word for all the mistakes we live to be ashamed of."

"Convenient for those who can think so lightly of a crime. Your mistake! And what of the other lives that it condemned to unhappiness?"

"Yours, at all events," said Langley, with downcast eyes, "did not suffer from it."

She looked scornfully at him, and answered with bitter irony.

"That thought must be a comfort to you."

"Why not?" His face was suddenly agleam. "What life can have been happier than Lady Revill's?"

"Only your own, perhaps. Oh, is it worth while to waste our sarcasm on each other? You can say nothing that I care to hear. If the best of life is over, so is the worst, thank God! Let us remember that we are man and woman, and respect ourselves."

"It is because I have learnt to respect myself – the strongest, truest desire of my life – that I am here."

"At my cost!" she uttered passionately. "Do I find pleasure in remembering all the misery you brought upon me?"

"Surely you are a little unjust. If your life has been unhappy, are not you in part to blame for it yourself? You don't talk of fate; you account us responsible for what we do."

"With your views, it isn't to be expected you should understand me. What can you know of the revolt against my own feelings – the disgust with life. Oh, how can *you* know what passes in the mind of a girl who loses at once all faith and hope?"

"My views," answered Langley, with gentleness, "allow me to imagine all that. They allow me, also, to compare your acts and mine. It would be easy to flatter you by taking all the blame upon myself. Men generally do so; it helps, they think, to make life possible. They do it 'out of respect for women.' But I can see in it nothing respectful; much the reverse. It is as good as saying that a woman cannot be expected to see facts and to reason upon them. On my side there was wrong-doing; let that be granted. But what of your marriage? Excuse it as you may, was it not worse than what *I* had to avow? You plead outraged feelings, loss of faith and hope, driving you, I suppose, into a sort of cynical worldliness. I, on the other hand, plead my youth and manhood – a far more valid excuse."

She stood motionless, avoiding his eyes.

"And it is idle to pretend," he went on, still quietly, "that you can judge me now as you did then. It is worse than idle to stand before me as an injured woman, austere in her rectitude. Whatever *I* have to regret, *you*, Lady Revill, have yet more."

The dusk thickened. A breeze stirred in the larches. Lady Revill cast a sudden look in the direction of the house, and moved a few steps; then paused, and faced her companion again.

"You came to tell me this?"

"No. To tell you that the love you rejected is stronger now than then. I could not do so whilst I thought that you loved another man."

"You never thought it."

"I could not suppose that Lord Henry Strands spoke falsely."

"Nor did he. I had given him every reason, short of absolute promise, to believe that I would marry him. But what has marriage to do with love?"

"Little enough, I dare say, as a rule. Perhaps I have no right, even now, to speak to you as if you were a free woman?"

"Oh, I am free." She laughed. "Free as ever I was."

"If so, I have more to say. After all, I *can* honestly take upon myself the blame for all that happened. If only I had not been such a pedant in morals! I was absurd, when I thought myself nobly honest. I had no right whatever to make known what I did."

Lady Revill met his eyes, and for a moment reflected.

"You not only had the right," she answered, "but it was your plain duty."

"But think. Your parents did not deal honestly with me – nor with you. You were not told the whole truth. And I might have foreseen that. They wished to guard you from me."

"It would have made no difference."

"Perhaps not – and yet I think it would. You were not a girl of the brainless kind. You condemned me because I seemed to have acted with vulgar unscrupulousness; whereas I had fulfilled every obligation."

"You never offered to marry her."

"Thank heaven, no!" He went on vehemently. "Are you determined to echo the silliest cant? What sort of marriage would that have been? Have we not known of such? You are speaking in defiance of all that life has taught you. I, when I committed that folly of telling your father an irrelevant fact, at all events believed myself to be compelled in honour to do so. But you, with your knowledge of the world, degrade yourself when you repeat mere moral phrases, wholly without application. Neither for the mother's sake, nor for the child's, ought I to have married her: and you know it. It was my plain duty to marry the woman I loved – who let me hope that she loved me in return. I ought to have said not a word of things past and done with."

"But they were not done with."

"Yes; in any sense that could have affected our marriage. Suppose, when you had been my wife for a long time, you had learnt of the poor boy's existence – even as you did. Can you wrong yourself so utterly as to pretend that this would have troubled our happiness? I know you too well. You are not a woman of that kind."

Again she turned, and moved a few paces. Her hands hung clasped before her.

"One thing you have said truly," were her next words, in a low, sad voice. "My parents did not deal honestly with me. They owed me the whole truth. Still, it would have made no difference."

"At the moment, perhaps not. But it would have saved you from that marriage; and in a year or two—"

"You can't understand. We see life so differently."

Langley stepped towards her.

"That is what I don't believe. You hoodwink yourself with the old prejudices, which you have long outgrown, if only you could bring yourself to confess it. Listen, Agnes." She shrank, startled; but he repeated the name, just above his breath. "By your own admission life has satisfied you just as little as it has me. We both see it from much the same point of view; we both look back on a dreary failure. You have lived in slavery to all manner of conventional hopes and fears – playing your part well, of course – but a part of which you were weary from the day you undertook it. You have had social success, honour – and hate the memory of it. I – well, you know the course that I have followed. Not even my flatterer could name it a 'career.' A life of sluggish respectability. Oh, infinitely respectable, I assure you! An immaculate life, by the ordinary standard; and what a waste of golden, irrecoverable time! If you and I had met in the year after your marriage, and in a flood of passion had braved everything – going away together – defying the sleepy world: how much more worthy of ourselves than this honourable ignominy!"

"You forget yourself."

"I have forgotten myself too long. It was Louis who awakened me, taught me how low I had sunk. Did his bright young life never excite the same feeling in you? Was conscience really on your side when you tried to shape him to the respectable pattern?"

She raised her hands, as if in appeal, and let them fall again.

"Since I met you again, I have learnt how much of youth there is still in me. Shall I give up my dearest hope, as I did so many years ago? You too are young; and you have learnt the worthlessness of mere social ambition. Isn't it true? Another upward step was before you; a higher title; but the cost of it was a lie – and you *could* not!"

"Yes; that is true," she answered, softly.

"And the poor boy – hadn't he a part in it?"

She kept silence. Dusk was passing into clouded night; the breeze in the larches sang more loudly.

"You have not told me why you kept him to yourself, and treated him as a child of your own."

"One often acts without reasoned motive."

"But in looking back – in recalling the time when you must have debated with yourself—"

"I did wrong," she uttered impulsively. "Forgive me for that – forgive me, and let us say good-bye."

"No! I said good-bye once, to my sorrow. Agnes, in a new life—"

He tried to take her hand, but she withheld it, and spoke with sudden firmness.

"I shall not marry again. I have made it impossible, and purposely."

"How? You fear the judgment of your world?"

"I fear nothing, but the voice of my own conscience – I can't talk about it; my mind is made up. I shall never marry again. I have said all I can say; now we must part."

"And you will waste your life to the end?" he said, distantly.

Lady Revill flashed a glance at him, and spoke with nervous tremor.

"Waste? Why need my life be wasted? Is there no hope for me apart from your society?"

"If I answer what I think" – an involuntary laugh broke the words – "none! If I didn't believe that you and I were destined for each other, I should not be here. I believed it long years ago. I believed it again, when I talked of you at Athens. And I have believed it more strongly than ever since the grief we have suffered in common. Nothing that you have said destroys my confidence."

"Then words have no meaning."

"You have made marriage impossible – how?"

"Marriage with *you* was long ago made impossible, by your own act."

"Evasion; and you don't believe what you say. Not my act, but the false light in which it was shown to you. I dare to say that you loved me, and I was not as unworthy of you as you were made to think. Let your tongue be as frank as your heart, and say that you wish for the old time back again, with clearer knowledge. And you have it!"

"I must leave you."

"To go and sorrow that the world, or your own false pride, forbids you doing as you would. Presumption, you call it? I dare everything, for your sake as well as my own. I know how strong it is – all I have to overcome. If I had been bolder, then, how different our lives! I ought not to have accepted your refusal. I ought to have spoken with you, face to face, and told you all with my own lips. Then, even if you had still refused me, you would never have married the man you did not love. I have more courage now. You know what might be said of me – a man with just a bachelor's income. Do I care? I know that *you* can have no such thought. You do not doubt for a moment the sincerity of my love. And but for habit – pride—"

"Yes, if it will convince you. Nothing you can ever say will prevail against them."

"Agnes, you are too proud to live on in the old way. You will respect yourself. The foolish hum-drum of such a life as you have led—"

"My life is my own. I have better use for it than to surrender it into another's hands. It is true that I shall live no longer in the old way. I shall have few friends. Mr. Langley, will you be one of them?"

Her voice was soft, but implied no submission. It sounded weary, and Langley, after a moment's silence, offered his hand.

"Will you let me see you again?"

"If you give me your word that it shall be only as a friend. And not soon. Not till you have been to Athens again."

"I can't promise that. Let me see you in a month's time."

Lady Revill turned towards the house, but looked back, and spoke hurriedly.

"You give me your word not to try to see me for a month?"

He promised, and the next moment stood there alone. Through the deep shadow of the trees, he made his way to the meadow path. Before him, in the western sky, glimmered a rift of pale rose, severing storm-cloud. The burning heat of his temples was allayed; then a sudden chill ran over him, and his teeth chattered.

~ *Chapter 13* ~

HE had caught a cold, and spent a sufficiently miserable fortnight in getting rid of it. His spirits were not improved by the arrival of a long letter from Athens, giving him a full account of Louis's illness and death. On the day after receiving it, he sent this letter to Mrs. Tresilian; for it contained mention of her. "If I don't get over this," Louis said, at the moment of the unexpected relapse which rapidly proved fatal, "tell Mrs. Tresilian that to the end I thought of her just as I wrote last."

On recovery, Langley was for two or three days the guest of his friends at Hampstead, and there occurred his next meeting with Mrs. Tresilian. They walked together in the pleasant garden, and conversed with an intimacy like that of long acquaintance. From talk concerning Louis, the lady passed to a kindred subject.

"A week ago I heard from Lady Revill – a very kind and very surprising letter. Perhaps you already know of it?"

"An answer to a letter you wrote—?"

"No. I did write, almost immediately after you came to see me; I couldn't help doing so. The answer to that came quickly – a few lines of very formal politeness, telling me nothing at all. I was the more surprised when I heard again. I could hardly believe what I read. Lady Revill wished to know whether it was in her power to help in the work with which my name was connected."

"A week ago?"

"Ten days, perhaps. What does it mean? A friend had told her something about the Bermondsey settlement, and it interested her greatly. Personally she could do nothing; but if a stranger might be allowed to offer help in the shape of money—. Of course it was worded very nicely, and in the upshot it amounted to this, that our society might draw upon her to any extent! I was really at a loss. Can you explain?"

Langley shook his head, smiling.

"But you, I have no doubt, are the 'friend' she mentioned."

"Lady Revill asked me for some account of what you were doing. I didn't foresee anything of this kind. It was hardly the sort of offer you could accept, I suppose?"

"I thought a great deal about it. We, down yonder, are in no particular want of money; it's personal assistance we need. I wrote at some length, explaining this. I added, however, that there were enterprises in which I took an interest, which wanted as much money as could be got. In a day or two I heard again; just as nice a letter. It's a wretched thing that people misunderstand each other so, just because they are never brought in contact. I thought Lady Revill detested me, and my opinion of her – well, it was not favourable. From poor Louis's talk, I got the idea that she was in many ways an excellent woman, but narrow-minded, and rather arrogant. Her first note confirmed it. But now she writes in the most amiable spirit; with something the very reverse of pride. What does it mean?"

"I can only suppose that Louis's death has touched the better part of her nature."

After a pause, Mrs. Tresilian asked:

"How is Lord Henry Strands likely to regard this change?"

"Impossible to say."

Langley spoke in a tone of indifference, and the subject was dropped.

"Could you dine with me on Thursday, next week?" said the other, presently. "In Connaught Square, I mean, not in East Lane. My brother will be there. I am sure he would like to know you; he's a good scholar, I believe, and has travelled in the East. Nowadays he lives at—" She named a town of the North Midlands. "He goes in for municipal affairs, and sometimes signs his letters to me – 'Paul the Parochial.' He takes a pride in his provincialism, and really I think he's doing a lot of good work. Do you know the town at all?"

"Never was there."

"Paul seems to have unearthed all the local talents," went on Mrs. Tresilian, in her mirthful spirit. "He rails against centralisation, persuades the large people to live at home and be active – and so on. A good deal of Ruskin in it,[29] of course, but he has ideas of his own. Will you come on Thursday?"

"I will, with pleasure."

It was an odd experience when, among the little group of people assembled for dinner at his friend's house, Langley found at least three whose names had long been held by him in contempt or abomination. There was a political woman, from whose presence, a short time ago, he would have incontinently fled; this evening he saw her in a human light, discovered ability in her talk, and was amused by her genial comments on things of the day. A man known for his fierce oratory in connection with "strikes," turned out a thoroughly good fellow, vigorous without venom, and more than tinctured with sober reading. The third personage, an eccentric offshoot of a noble house, showed quite another man at close quarters than as seen through the medium of report. After the society in which, when he saw society at all, his time had chiefly been spent, Langley tasted an invigorating atmosphere. These people, one and all, had a declared object in life, and seemed to pursue it with single-mindedness. But most was he pleased with Mrs. Tresilian's brother; in many respects, as five minutes' talk assured him, a man after his own heart: refined, scholarly, genial. This gentleman began by speaking of Louis Reed, whom he had met only once, but whose qualities he discussed with such sympathetic insight, such generous appreciation and kindly regret, that the listener had much ado to command his feelings.

He found an opportunity of private speech with his hostess, and inquired whether Lady Revill was still in the country. Mrs. Tresilian thought so.

"I should like to meet her," she added, "but I still feel doubtful of my reception if I appeared before her in the flesh. We have again exchanged letters – to the heaping of more coals upon my head. Her deference really shames me. The rascal that is in all of us – in all women, that is to say – laments that I am not a professional organiser of sham charities. What an opportunity lost! You know that I don't talk of this to every one," she added gravely, "I feel sure that her motive is one which you and I are bound to respect."

Not many days had now to elapse before Langley would be released from the promise which forbade him to approach Fallowfield. He lived impatiently, but the gloom was passing from his mind, and hope grew one with resolve. An effort enabled him to interpret the "month" liberally; he waited till the close of the fifth week, then wrote to Lady Revill, and begged permission to see her. His reason for writing before he journeyed into Somerset was a suspicion that Lady Revill would not be found in her country home; it surprised him not at all when her reply came – with only the inevitable delay – from the house in Cornwall Gardens. In friendly phrase, he was invited to call next day.

On entering, he saw with surprise that the hall was stripped of its ornaments, and all but bare. No hour having been mentioned, he had come in the afternoon; but plainly he need not fear the presence of ordinary callers. From somewhere within echoed the sound of hammering. A maid-servant admitted him; proof that the regular establishment had been broken up.

From the drawing-room had vanished all pictures and *bric-à-brac*; only the substantial furniture remained. Langley tried to recognise a good omen, but chill discomfort fell upon him, and Lady Revill's countenance – she stood waiting in the middle of the room – did not support his hope. She smiled, indeed, shook hands with show of cordiality, and began at once to apologise for the disorder about her; but this endeavour to seem cheerfully at ease put no mask upon the pain-worn features.

"I shall be so glad when it's over," she said, with a smile, turning from Langley's gaze. "I hate business of every kind."

"You will have no house in town?"

"I shall never live in London again."

Langley threw aside his hat and gloves, stood for a moment with his hands behind him, then looked steadily at her.

"Somewhere on the Continent – wouldn't that be better?"

"No. Fallowfield will be my home."

"You know why I have come to-day?"

Their eyes met. He saw the quivering strain she put upon herself to reply quietly.

"Much better that you hadn't come. But let it be over as soon as possible."

"Your answer is still the same?"

"As I told you it would be."

The sound of hammering came from above. Langley struggled with the frantic impulse of his nerves.

"What are you going to *do* down there?" he asked, with uncivil abruptness.

"Live very quietly, and – and try to atone for all my sins and follies."

Her voice broke midway, but she forced it to complete the sentence.

"I see. In other words, bury yourself alive. Turn ascetic – torment yourself – find merit in misery. And in defiance of the brain that tells you that this is the greatest sin and folly of all! Well, happily it isn't possible."

"The impossible thing," she answered, in a tone of forbearance, "is to make you understand how much I have suffered, and how greatly I have changed."

Her soft, low accents subdued his violence.

"Dearest, how can you so deceive yourself? You – you – to be cloistered, and imagine that your soul will profit by it! You know it is mere illusion. Do good, if you will; and first of all," he smiled, "give yourself to the man whose supreme need is the need of you."

"You have had my answer."

"Only the answer prompted by a mistaken sense of duty. Your duty is to fulfil yourself – to be all it is in your power to be. Yield yourself to a man's love, and be perfect woman."

He held his hands to her; she drew back, and spoke impetuously.

"You mean the woman who has no will of her own? You have my answer, and must accept it."

He gazed at her, as if for a moment doubting; but saw that in her face which roused him to impassioned tenderness.

"How strange it is, Agnes. We seem so far apart. The long years of utter separation – the meeting at length in cold formality – the bitterness, the reproaches – so much that seems to stand between us; and yet we are everything to each other. If you were the kind of woman who has no will of her own, could I love you as I do? And if I were less conscious of my own purpose, would you listen to me? There is no question of one yielding to the other, save in the moment which overcomes your pride and leaves you free to utter the truth. Those are the old phrases of love-making – they rise to a man's tongue when his blood is hot. We shall never see the world with the same eyes: man and woman never did so, never will; but there is no life for us apart from each other. Our very faults make us born companions. Your need of me is as great as mine of you. We have forgiven all there is to forgive; we know what may be asked, and what may not. No castles in the air; no idealisms of boy and girl; but two lives that have a want, and see but the one hope of satisfying it."

He waited, and saw her lips still harden themselves against him.

"You pretend to read my thoughts, yet you have no understanding of my strongest motive. This is quite enough to prove that we are really far apart, and not only seem to be so."

"Then add one word," said Langley. "Say that you don't love me – say it plainly and honestly – and there's an end."

Her self-command was overborne by a rush of tears.

"Why will you torture me? I am trying so hard to do right. My life is misery, and there is only one way to gain peace of mind. I must do as my conscience bids. It is *you* who deceive yourself. What real love can you feel for a woman whom you can't respect? You have said you don't respect me – and how should you? I have lived so basely. Since my marriage, not a day I can look back upon without shame. I am trying to humble myself; to live in the spirit of the religion which I believe, though I have so long forgotten it. I hated Mrs. Tresilian, because she seemed to rob me of the love I prized so. It was paltry jealousy – of a piece with all the rest of my life. Now I have forced myself to beg for her good will. I will do all I can to help her – in the way she taught Louis to follow. And you, too, I have injured, in my selfishness. Forgive me, if you can. For me there is no happiness – or only in self denial. I have lived through the worst; I have broken with the world which was everything to me – ambitions, pleasures. Don't make it harder for me. I am doing as you bid me – trying to be all it is in my power to be – all the *good*, after so much evil."

Langley had grasped her hand.

"If you can make me believe that your life will really be better apart from me. I wait for that one word. Do you love me, or not?"

She drew away, but he detained her. The trembling body which at any moment his strength could overcome seemed to declare his victory over the soul. Conventions, social and personal, the multiform restraints upon civilised man before the woman he desires, but who will not yield herself, vanished like a tissue in fire. She was falling, but his arm supported her. So slight and weak a tenement of flesh, now that the proud spirit was exorcised. Holding her, heart to heart, he saw the anguished pallor of her face flush into rosy shame, saw the moist eyes dilate, the lips throb – all of her divinely young and beautiful.

"No – no – I cannot—"

"You can and will—"

"I *cannot* marry you! I have said that I should never marry again, said it so solemnly—"

"To some one else, you mean. What of that! It is *force majeure.*"

He laughed exultantly.

"I cannot!"

"Not at once. Time to think and understand and accept your dread fate – why, of course. Time even to repent, Agnes, though not in sackcloth and ashes. You have done ill, and so have I, but it is not to be repaired by asceticism. Break down the walls about you – not add to their height and thickness! Walk in the summer sunlight, dearest, and look to the rising of many a summer sun!"

"What right have I to take the easy path?"

"Health and joy are the true repentance. All sins against the conscience – what are they but sins against the law of healthy life?"

"I have sinned so against others. And to make no atonement in my own suffering—"

"The old false thought. Health and joy – it is what life demands of us.

And then remember. To marry a mere unheraldic mortal, to exchange the style of chivalry for a bourgeois prefix – is not that punishment enough? I almost fear to ask it of you."

She released herself and stood apart, head dropping.

"I have given no promise. A long time must pass—"

Langley smiled.

~ *Chapter 14* ~

ON an October afternoon Langley sat in his old room at Athens, writing. But no books were piled about him, and his countenance had undergone a change since the day when he bent in idle enjoyment over the page of Aristophanes. It was graver, yet not so old; smoother, but more virile. Play of features – a light in the eye, a motion of brow and lips – expressed the thoughts he was penning.

"Once, when we turned together out of the hot, dusty highroad into a little village graveyard shadowed with cypresses – it was near Colonus, by the banks of the Cephisus – Louis read with pleasure the Greek words painted on the wooden crosses: Ἐνθάδε κεῖται³⁰ – classical Greek, looking so strange to him in this modern application. Could it have been done without pedantry, I should have liked to set the words on his marble; to my ear they are better than 'Here lies'; so restful in their antiquity, echoing so softly the music of the old world. But the simplest inscription is the best – the one name by which we called him, and the date of his death. Happily he does not lie among the foolish monstrosities of the Greek cemetery, which I described to you – the skulls and bones, the gilded shirt-studs, and so on. Your wish is respected: on the marble is carved a cross.

"The day has been hot, and in the town intolerably glaring. Soon after sunrise I went to Phaleron and bathed, then lingered about the seashore, thinking – well, of what should I think? You were in your garden, no doubt, among the leaves and flowers of English autumn. I saw you walking there, alone, and hoped that your thoughts were on the shore of Attica.

"Then a midday meal with Worboys. I like the old pedant, and feel for him no little respect. After all, he does what I myself am bent on doing; the business of archæology has taken such strong possession of him that he lives in it with abounding vigour. He has no thought at all for the modern world; to him every interest of to-day – save the doings of excavators – seems vulgar and irrelevant. After all, this is admirable. All the more so that he is utterly devoid of personal ambition; he cares not the least to make a name, and to be respectfully regarded by his fellows. He loves an inscription for its own sake. If he has a personal hope in the matter, I rather think it would take the form of a desire to die in the trenches, and be buried at Colonus along with Ottfried Müller and Charles Lenormant.³¹ But he is too humble to express such a wish.

"Heavens! you should hear him talk of you. The Medici had no such incense of laudatory gratitude as Worboys burns daily upon your altar. He sincerely believes that history can show no grander instance of benevolent and enlightened patronage. He will carve your name on the walls of some temple yet unearthed. He will chant you in the valleys of Peloponnesus, and perhaps in the wildernesses of Asia Minor. Now all this is very fine; it tells of a sound heart, and possibly of a brain far from contemptible. Woman in the flesh he will never love (he speaks tenderly of the Caryatides on the Acropolis), but you he worships. I find it inspiriting to be with him. By the by, I have of course told him nothing. About Louis he shall never know more than he does now.

"The day after to-morrow he goes off with his German friend. They are more than brothers. For my own part, I stay here until I have a letter from you. I am impatient, of course. Whatever you write—"

A knock at the door stayed his hand. He bade enter, and there appeared a boy, who, showing white teeth in a smile, and uttering a few words of Greek, delivered a letter.

Alone again, Langley let the unbroken envelope lie before him. He could read the first post-mark, and he observed the date. When his hand was quite steady, he took a penknife and released the sheet of note-paper. It presented but a few lines. After reading them several times, he put the letter in his pocket, hid away his own unfinished writing, and went out.

A few hours later he dined with Worboys and the archæologist's German comrade. It was a cheerful meal, but Langley chose to listen rather than to talk. Afterwards they sat smoking for a long time; then the English friends walked a short distance together.

"It's uncertain, then, how long you stay?" said Worboys.

"No. I have decided to leave to-morrow. And, by the by, I am going back to be married."

Worboys stood still.

"You amaze me!"

"Surely there are more improbable things?"

"Of course, of course. But – you never hinted—. Will you tell me who it is?"

"Yes. You know her. It is Lady Revill."

Worboys drew a deep breath, and clutched his friend's hand.

"I can't say what I should wish to. This is wonderful and magnificent! Ah, what things have happened since we met in the Kerameikos!"

When Langley was in his room again he returned to the unfinished writing.

"I was interrupted by the arrival of your letter. After reading it, I went out and rambled till dark. The sunset was unspeakably glorious – the last of many such that I have seen at Athens. This morning I wished that you were here; at evening, as I stood on the Areopagus, I was glad to know that I had to travel to find you – in the world of realities.

"As Louis said, this is mere fairyland; to us of the north, an escape for rest amid scenes we hardly believe to be real. The Acropolis, rock and ruins all tawny gold, the work of art inseparable from that of nature, and neither seeming to have bodily existence; the gorgeous purples of Hymettus; that cloud on Pentelikon, with its melting splendours which seemed to veil the abode of gods – what part has all this in our actual life? Who cares to know the modern names of these mountains? Who thinks of the people who dwell among them? Worboys is right; living in the past, he forgets the present altogether. I, whose life is now to begin, must shake off this sorcery of Athens, and remember it only as a delightful dream. Mere fairyland; and our Louis has become part of it – to be remembered by me as calmly, yet as tenderly, as this last sunset.

"Dearest, I finish this letter and post it here. It may possibly reach you at Fallowfield a few hours before I come. I have no word of thanks, no word of love that I can write. But already I am with you. Yes, let the past be past. To you and me, the day that is still granted us."

Notes

~ Chapter 1 ~

1. Pilafi: a hot-tasting dish made from rice and sometimes vegetables, served with meat.
2. The peak of Lycabettus or Lycabettos is one from which a panorama of Athens can be seen; so is that of Hymettus, famous for its honey and its quarries.
3. Temple of Theseus: in his guide book on Greece Baedeker notes that this "so-called" temple, though more archaic, possesses a distinct affinity with the sculptures of the Parthenon. He considers that Theseus may be regarded as the actual founder of Greece.
4. The Piræus is the sea port of Athens, which had a population of about 70,000 at the time Gissing wrote his novel.
5. The Kerameikos or Ceramicus or Potters' Quarter at Athens, a district NW of the Acropolis partly within the city walls. The part outside the walls was used as a burial ground.
6. Pausanias (2nd c. A.D.) was the author of an extant *Description of Hellas*. It is a guide book written for travellers, in which, taking successively the various parts of Greece, he enumerates the objects in them most worthy to be seen: that is statues, pictures, tombs and sanctuaries with their legends, derivations of names, anecdotes and historical digressions. He is lucid about the fantasies of legends.
7. The Cyropædia, that is the education of Cyrus, is a narrative by Xenophon in eight books of the career of Cyrus the Great. It is more concerned with ideals than with reality.
8. *Soles occidere et redire possunt*: Suns may set and rise again. Catullus, *Carmina*.
9. In the Place de la Constitution were situated the large hotels and cafés. On the east side the Place was bounded by the Royal Palace, the space in front of which was laid out with orange trees and oleanders, being embellished with a marble fountain.

~ Chapter 2 ~

10. In Greek mythology Hermes was the son of Zeus and Maia.
11. The codices (singular: codex) were the ancestors of books, and vellum replaced papyrus. In the oldest texts or inscriptions, as Louis Reed correctly observes, following Gissing's notes in his diary, there was no division or space between the words, and little to help the reader in the way of signs or punctuation. A short stroke under the line often indicated the point where there was a pause in the sense or a change of speaker in dramatic texts.

12. The Theseion: the best preserved edifice of the ancient Greek world and an imposing one which owes its singularity, Baedeker says, to its massive construction, to the vigorous vitality of its sculptures, the golden-yellow hue of its marble and to its preservation. The conflicting views about its being or not a temple of Theseus are discussed by Baedeker in his learned volume on Greece. It was the German scholar Ross who first disputed the connection between Theseion and Theseus.

13. The two German words may be translated by prolixity of details and minuteness.

14. Salamis, Marathon, Pentelikon: Salamis is an island, off the Piræus, for a long time a subject of contention between the Megarians and the Athenians. The adjoining sea was the scene of the great naval battle in which the fleet of Xerxes was defeated by the Greeks.—The plain of Marathon is some 22 miles NE of Athens.—Pentelikon is a mountain 3,600 feet high about ten miles from Athens.

15. Thermopylae is the name of a pass successfully defended by Leonidas in the days of the Persian invasion (480 B.C.).

16. Phaleron was the main harbour of Athens before the Persian Wars and the development and fortification of the Piræus. The Long Walls of Athens connected the city with the Piræus and Phaleron. They were begun about 460 B.C.

~ Chapter 4 ~

17. Cephisus, Colonus, Phaleric Bay: The Cephisus is the river which waters the great plain of Attica. It is exhausted by irrigation before it reaches the sea. The other sites mentioned in this paragraph are in the vicinity of Athens.

18. Mount Aigaleos or Ægaleos is met on the road from Athens to Eleusis, the latter town being connected in ancient times with its mysteries celebrated in honour of Demeter, the earth-goddess.

19. Akrokorinthos or Acro-Corinth is a mountain with a fortress at the top, which could be reached on foot or on horseback.

20. Louis casually enumerates places like Ægina, Salamis, Munychia, the Olympus, Tænarum, etc, which had been familiar to Gissing since childhood, and some of which he no longer had to imagine after his journey to Greece in late 1889. They had historical and literary connotations which he recalled with emotion.

~ Chapter 5 ~

21. The statue of Athena Parthenos, 42 ½ feet in height, is the most admired work of Phidias. By Central Museum Gissing means the National Archæological Museum, which contained the national collections of antiquities. It was in the Room of the Athena that Worboys had seen a small copy of the Athena Parthenos. Pheidias or Phidias (born c. 500 B. C.) was one of the greatest Athenian artists. A friend of Pericles, he died in prison, having been accused of theft and impiety.
22. Return to London via Patras and Brindisi was the normal route, which Gissing had followed in December 1889.
23. Landor was one of Gissing's favourite authors. He had in his library a copy of *Imaginary Conversations* in the Camelot Series (Walter Scott, 1886) which contains many marginal pencillings. The present quotation, slightly adapted, from *Pericles and Aspasia*, a collection of imaginary correspondence, is from letter CLXXIII, Aspasia to Pericles, where it reads "sail among the islands of the Ægean."

~ Chapter 6 ~

24. Worboys delights in the enumeration of place names in this paragraph. Gissing did not visit all these sites, but he could see them on the maps and in the text of his Baedeker.
25. Here again Gissing has in mind the route he followed in his journey back from Athens to London. The words pronounced by Langley, *Non cuivis homini contingit adire Corinthum* (it is not everyman's lot to go to Corinth), are from Horace, *Epistles,* I, xvii, line 36. Corinth was viewed as the headquarters of luxury and refinement. Hence the idea that it is not every man's good fortune to be able to see such great cities.
26. Helicon is a mountain in Boeotia, regarded as sacred to the Muses. Mount Parnassos, about 8070 feet high, was the lofty mountain whose summit is associated with the worship of Apollo and the Muses.
27. Corfu, the Corcyra of ancient times, is the largest of the Ionian islands. Gissing mentions it in his diary in December 1889, as well as in *The Private Papers of Henry Ryecroft* (Autumn III). Another mention occurs in *New Grub Street*, ch. 27.

~ *Chapter 11* ~

28. Norton St. Philip is a village between Bath and Frome. The battle of Sedgmoor, the last pitched battle in England, took place in 1685. The Duke of Monmouth (1649-1685) was captured here and subsequently beheaded on Tower Hill. Wellow is another village near Bath.

~ *Chapter 13* ~

29. The allusion is to Ruskin as social critic, thinker and reformer.

~ *Chapter 14* ~

30. The Greek words mean: Here he wished to rest.
31. Ottfried Müller (1797-1840), German scholar, archæologist and historian of ancient art, and Charles Lenormant (1802-1859), French archæologist, Egyptologist and numismatist. His son, François Lenormant, archæologist and numismatist, was the author of *La Grande-Grèce*, a book greatly admired by Gissing.

Bibliography

1. Bibliographical Note

Sleeping Fires was commissioned by T. Fisher Unwin in January 1895, and the manuscript lay completed by 1 March. Composition was facilitated by the fact that part of the background of the narrative was set in Greece, which Gissing had visited in late 1889. On realizing that his handwriting was becoming smaller and smaller he decided to have his manuscript typed by a professional typist. Gissing was given the choice by the publisher of having his novel published either in the Pseudonym Library or in the Autonym Library. He wisely opted for the latter solution, considering that his reputation could not benefit from the publication of a book on the title page of which his name did not appear. The volume came out in two formats – in cloth, the book selling at two shillings, and in paper, copies being priced at one shilling sixpence.

The official date of publication being 7 December 1895, a second English edition or more accurately impression dated 1896 had to be prepared. It was for sale, like the first, in European countries and British Colonies, and available in both formats.

An American edition was published by Appletons in late March 1896 at 75 cents.

Two more English editions are on record: the Fisher Unwin Cabinet Library Edition (1927), which was available in cloth at 3s.6d and in leather at 5s.; the Harvester Press edition (1974) with a prefatory note by Pierre Coustillas, in mauve cloth binding, of which 750 copies were printed.

In 1983, in the wake of John Halperin's book, *Gissing: A Life in Books*, the University of Nebraska Press published a paperback edition of the novel with a yellow and light mauve cover design selling at $4.95.

A Japanese publisher, Hokuseido, did much to promote the book (in the original language) among teachers and readers of English literature at a time when the political authorities of Japan objected to Gissing's pacifism and antimilitarism. Preceded by an introduction by Masanobu Oda, who was to publish a critical study of Gissing in 1933, and by a good portrait of Gissing in the mid-1890s, the successive impressions of the novel under the Hokuseido imprint from 1930 to 1943 were at least four in number.

A sophisticated Japanese translation of the novel, to which was added *By the Ionian Sea*, was also published, by Shubun International, in 1988 in both hardback and paperback. It was the work of the most active Gissing scholar in Japan at the time, namely Shigeru Koike.

The most recent translation of *Sleeping Fires* is the Greek one by Maria Dimitriadou, published in Athens in 2000. The text is preceded and followed by biographical and critical comments. The book also contains illustrations in colour by the translator.

The whereabouts of the manuscript are unknown. Indeed, like the typescript which was based on it, it may well have been destroyed by Gissing.

2. List of Reviews

1895
Scotsman, 16 December, p. 4
Sketch, 25 December, p. 474
Whitehall Review, 28 December, p. 12
Queen, 28 December, p. 1198 (St. Barbe)

1896
Glasgow Herald, 2 January, p. 2
Saturday Review, 11 January, p. 48 [H. G. Wells]
Publishers' Circular, 11 January, p. 53
Black and White, 11 January, p. 52
Lloyd's Weekly Newspaper, 12 January, p. 9
Literary World (London), 17 January, p. 47
Speaker, 18 January, p. 81
Globe, 22 January, p. 3
Athenæum, 25 January, p. 116 [Lewis Sargeant]
Bookman (London), January, p. 130
Daily Telegraph (Australia), 1 February, p. 9
Woman 5 February, p. 7 (Barbara, i.e. Arnold Bennett)
Newcastle Daily Leader, 6 February, p. 6
Pall Mall Gazette, 17 February, p. 4
Academy, 22 February, p. 154 (George Cotterell)
The Times, 22 February, p. 10 [Long]
Graphic, 22 February, p. 224
Chicago Tribune, 23 February, p. 42 (Jeannette L. Gilder)
Bookseller, 6 March, p. 296
Sydney Morning Herald, 7 March, p. 4
Australasian Review of Reviews, 20 March, p. 261
Australasian, 21 March, p. 569
Chicago Times Herald, 28 March, p. 9 (Mary Abbott)
Sun (Melbourne), 3 April, p. 3
New York Times, 5 April, p. 31
Chicago Tribune, 11 April, p. 10
Daily Inter Ocean (Chicago), 11 April, p. 10
Literary World (Boston), 18 April, p. 117
Chicago Journal, 18 April, p. 9
Outlook (New York), 25 April, p. 772
San Francisco Chronicle, 26 April, p. 4
Boston Evening Transcript, 30 April, p. 6 (Kate Woodbridge Michaelis)
Westminster Review, April, p. 472

~ *Bibliography* ~

Bookman (New York), June, p. 367
Godey's Magazine, August, p. 208
Current Literature, August, p. 185

3. Articles and later Comments

Michel Ballard, "*Sleeping Fires* as a Thematic Ramble through Gissing's Devices and Patterns," *Gissing Newsletter*, October 1975, pp. 1-11

Pierre Coustillas, "Review," *Gissing Newsletter*, July 1984, pp. 28-31

— — (editor), Gissing's *Diary*, Hassocks: Sussex, Harvester Press, 1978. The entries for November and December 1889 are largely concerned with the Greek background of *Sleeping Fires*

Selected Reviews

Sleeping Fires – Five First Edition Reviews

Newcastle Daily Leader, 6 February 1896, p. 6

Mr T. Fisher Unwin enjoys what must be considered to be an almost extravagant amount of good fortune. Apparently for the purpose of making his Pseudonym Library famous, new authors of uncommon ability kept cropping up in all directions. "The Autonym Library," consisting of works by authors of already established reputation, did not commence very well, but nearly from the beginning there has been a succession of such good books as prove conclusively that our English authors are very much better masters of the short story than has hitherto been thought to be the case. Mr George Gissing has broken new ground in "Sleeping Fires." He has up to now been the painter of Suburbia. He has told us what sort of lives are lived in Clapham, Brixton, and the Camberwell New Road. There has been abundant cleverness in his work, but little cheerfulness. In "Sleeping Fires" he carries us to Athens, then back to London, then to Athens once more. He has altogether dropped his suburban people for the time being, but he has not dropped any part of his talent in the process. Indeed, scarcely any of his books have been so easy and graceful in style as this. The characters are little more than sketches, of course. The brevity of the book makes that inevitable. But Mr Gissing's manner of sketching character is firm, crisp, decisive, and convincing. "Sleeping Fires" is almost a pleasant book, and that is more than Mr Gissing had led us to expect. Altogether it is a little work that will certainly add to the author's popularity, if not to his reputation, which is already high.

Academy, 22 February 1896, p. 154 (George Cotterell)

In the 'most pellucid air,' and among the joyous gods of Greece, Mr Gissing has thrown off the pessimism and absorption in the more sordid side of life which one has learnt to associate with his name. Throughout this 'Autonym' volume there is a note of hope, of acquiescence in the higher destiny of man and man's power to attain it if he only will; and the end is a triumphant proclamation of the gospel of joy. 'Health and joy,' says

Langley, the hero, 'it is what life demands of us.' He and Agnes Revill have sorrows and shame in their past; and this is the answer he makes to her faithfulness to them, and her shrinking from the happiness that offers itself. The three men who occupy the first half of the book are an admirable play of character—the pedant, out of touch with life already in his middle age; the boy, full of fine enthusiasm and chivalry; and Langley, the half-wearied but still young man of the world, to whom comes all unexpectedly a second youth. As always, Mr Gissing gives every thought its fitting mood, every motive its appropriate act, and every act its inevitable consequences.

Chicago Journal, 18 April 1896, p. 9

George Gissing is among the most prominent of the recent comers on the field of English fiction. He brings to literature rather startling new views on the subject of matrimony, set forth particularly in his novel of last summer, "In the Year of Jubilee." In line with these are further opinions on the subject of man's responsibility for his own misconduct, expanded in his latest romance, "Sleeping Fires," a work of unusual power and interest. Most of the action of the story has taken place before the narrative opens, and the latter is concerned with the dénouement. Langley, the hero of the tale, meets in Greece Louis Reed, a protégé of Lady Revill, Langley's one and only love. Years before she had given him up because of a former liaison of his, of which he had felt it his duty to tell her father. He becomes immediately much attracted to the youth, and when Louis tells him of a disappointment and trouble of his, Langley volunteers to go to England and arrange matters with Lady Revill. Arrived there, he learns from her that Louis is his own child. Close on the heels of this information, which fills him with entire joy, comes news of Louis' illness in Athens, followed soon by his death. Stung with grief and disappointment, he accuses her of having wronged him by having kept him in ignorance of the existence of his child and having separated him from Louis for what might have been so many happy years. She in return says that his early sin cut him off from all rights. It might almost be said that Lady Revill represents the world against Mr Gissing, in the person of Langley. Of course Langley overcomes her scruples and convinces her that he was no worse than she when she made a loveless marriage. The affection which he had thought dead within him springs up again, and after much wooing he finally wins her and the two so long separated are at last united.

Mr Gissing's style is powerful and interesting, his handling of situations masterful, and his point of view original. Not by renunciation and penance, he maintains, can sin be atoned for, but in "health and joy are the true repentance." While not subscribing to his views, one may well admit that the story leaves a vivid and impressive picture on the memory, and is far above the average fiction of today.

Literary World (Boston), 18 April 1896, p. 117

Mr George Gissing is being extravagantly praised and severely criticised. That he is a favourite contributor to the 'Yellow Book' perhaps does not add to his glory in the eyes of sensible readers, and yet no impartial critic can deny to the present vivid and original sketch, which he calls *Sleeping Fires*, unusual power. In the eyes of conservative readers, for a writer to take up a certain side of life relating to the sexes is enough for them to decry him as coarse; to the eyes of readers of the 'Yellow Book' a writer who treats these phases of life is, no matter how unskilfully he wields the pen, certain to be strong and 'virile.' [Here follows a paragraph-length summary of the plot.]

In the drawing of Langley's character the writer shows great skill, and Lady Revill is a woman of a most unusual type. When we consider how short a sketch is *Sleeping Fires*, and yet how strongly differentiated are its four principal characters, we realize that Mr Gissing deserves much, if not all, of the commendation which he has received. We find his work original, artistic, and dramatic. We prophesy for him an increasing popularity, and we think it must be admitted that he handles disagreeable themes with unusual refinement. We should like to see him at work upon themes of a different character.

Boston Evening Transcript, 30 April 1896, p. 6 (Kate Woodbridge Michaelis)

The Ethiopian has changed his skin, the leopard his spots. George Gissing, historian and expounder of the middle classes, has written a book in which we find no one of lower rank than a university man, by choice and not by necessity a tutor, and "Sir" and "Lady" figure largely on his pages!

"Sleeping Fires," announced by the Appletons for February, but unexpectedly delayed until April, has appeared, and the readers of Gissing, those who belong to the division of his admirers – there are two sorts of Gissing readers – have taken it up eagerly, expecting another one of his sermons in the form of novels. The title in itself seemed to promise so much that it was natural to look for something of the same order as "The Emancipated" or "Toilers [Workers] in the Dawn," but as if to show that he is versatile in addition to many other things, he has written for us a book which concerns no evil of the day, which is without a reform problem, and yet is well worth thoughtful reading.

"Sleeping Fires" might almost be called a duet, so closely does the interest centre in Lady Revill and Langley. There are three other characters, and, in a way, the handsome and lovable boy Louis is the motive power of the book, but he only floats across the scene and disappears, while Mrs Tresilian affects us but through her effect on others, and the tutor is just a walking gentleman, brought in now and again for useful purposes and then sent about his business.

But though this clever book treats no topic of the hour, there is a question of vital importance touched upon in its too few pages, and there is a doctrine strongly enunciated. The question is suggested, but not dwelt upon, and readers differ as to the answer Gissing gives – does honesty pay in affairs of the heart? – and I am one of those who believe that he thinks that it does, for the happiness which comes to these two people is of a nobler and more enduring kind, though they have to wait for it some sixteen years, than it would have been had they procured it by lying, in the days of their callow youth.

The great truth proclaimed and dwelt upon is one so robust and healthy that it merits being preached from the house-tops. That joy and happiness are duties, and that by them, repentance can best be shown.

Edmund Langley and Agnes, Lady Revill, have both sinned – the man in the all-too-common way, the woman in committing a loveless marriage; the sins have been against themselves and each other.

These sins are of the past: no tears or anguish can undo them; both sinners recognize this fact, but the knowledge affects them differently, possibly because of the difference of sex. Lady Revill would fain lament the irrevocable past in sorrow and self-abnegation; she considers that she has forfeited the right to be happy, and turns away from the joy within her grasp. Langley, roused from a life of dreamy uselessness by both sorrow and hope, declares that their regret must follow their crimes and be buried out of the sight of men.

"... Time even to repent, Agnes, though not in sackcloth and ashes. You have done ill, and so have I, but it is not to be repaired by asceticism. Break down the walls about you – not add to their height and thickness! Walk in the summer twilight [sunlight], dearest, and look to the rising of many a summer sun."

"What right have I to take the easy path?"

"Health and joy are the true repentance. All sins against the conscience – what are they but sins against the law of healthy life?"

"I have sinned so against others. And to make no atonement in my own suffering –"

"The old false thought. Health and joy – it is what life demands of us…"

Did the book contain nothing of good but this brave and wise gospel, it were well worth the reading, but there are tender and dreamy pictures of modern Greece, seen through the mists from the days of the past, that form fit setting for the figures in the brief drama. "The Acropolis, rock and ruins all tawny gold, the work of art inseparable from that of nature, and neither seeming to have bodily existence; the gorgeous purples of Hymettus; that cloud on Pentelikon, with its melting splendours which seemed to veil the abode of gods" – these are the scenes which Langley leaves to begin his new life of healthy purpose – and to remember the "sorcery of Athens only as a delightful dream."

THREE NOVELLAS

by George Gissing

~ The Paying Guest ~

~ *Chapter 1* ~

IT was Mumford who saw the advertisement and made the suggestion. His wife gave him a startled look.

"But – you don't mean that it's necessary? Have we been extrav—"

"No, no! Nothing of the kind. It just occurred to me that some such arrangement might be pleasant for you. You must feel lonely, now and then, during the day, and as we have plenty of room—"

Emmeline took the matter seriously, but, being a young woman of some discretion, did not voice all her thoughts. The rent was heavy: so was the cost of Clarence's season-ticket. Against this they had set the advantage of the fine air of Sutton, so good for the child and for the mother, both vastly better in health since they quitted London. Moreover, the remoteness of their friends favoured economy; they could easily decline invitations, and need not often issue them. They had a valid excuse for avoiding public entertainments – an expense so often imposed by mere fashion. The house was roomy, the garden delightful. Clarence, good fellow, might be sincere in his wish for her to have companionship; at the same time, this advertisement had probably appealed to him in another way.

"A YOUNG LADY desires to find a home with respectable, well-connected family, in a suburb of London, or not more than 15 miles from Charing Cross. Can give excellent references. Terms not so much a consideration as comfort and pleasant society. No boarding-house. – Address: Louise, Messrs. Higgins & Co., Fenchurch St., E.C."

She read it again and again.

"It wouldn't be nice if people said that we were taking lodgers."

"No fear of that. This is evidently some well-to-do person. It's a very common arrangement nowadays, you know; they are called 'paying guests.' Of course I shouldn't dream of having anyone you didn't thoroughly like the look of."

"Do you think," asked Emmeline doubtfully, "that we should quite *do*! 'Well-connected family'—"

"My dear girl! Surely we have nothing to be ashamed of?"

"Of course not, Clarence. But – and 'pleasant society.' What about that?"

"Your society is pleasant enough, I hope," answered Mumford, gracefully. "And the Fentimans—"

This was the only family with whom they were intimate at Sutton. Nice people; a trifle sober, perhaps, and not in conspicuously flourishing circumstances; but perfectly presentable.

"I'm afraid—" murmured Emmeline, and stopped short. "As you say," she added presently, "this is someone very well off. 'Terms not so much a consideration'—"

"Well, I tell you what – there can be no harm in dropping a note. The kind of note that commits one to nothing, you know. Shall I write it, or will you?"

They concocted it together, and the rough draft was copied by Emmeline. She wrote a very pretty hand, and had no difficulty whatever about punctuation. A careful letter, calculated for the eye of refinement; it supplied only the indispensable details of the writer's position, and left terms for future adjustment.

"It's so easy to explain to people," said Mumford, with an air of satisfaction, when he came back from the post, "that you wanted a companion. As I'm quite sure you do. A friend coming to stay with you for a time – that's how I should put it."

A week passed, and there came no reply. Mumford pretended not to care much, but Emmeline imagined a new anxiety in his look.

"Do be frank with me, dear," she urged one evening. "Are we living too—"

He answered her with entire truthfulness. Ground for serious uneasiness there was none whatever; he could more than make ends meet, and had every reason to hope it would always be so; but it would relieve his mind if the end of the year saw a rather larger surplus. He was now five-and-thirty – getting on in life. A man ought to make provision beyond the mere life-assurance – and so on.

"Shall I look out for other advertisements?" asked Emmeline.

"Oh, dear, no! It was just that particular one that caught my eye."

Next morning arrived a letter, signed "Louise E. Derrick." The writer said she had been waiting to compare and think over some two hundred answers to her advertisement. "It's really too absurd. How can I remember them all? But I liked yours as soon as I read it, and I am writing to you first of all. Will you let me come and see you? I can tell you about myself much better than writing. Would to-morrow do, in the afternoon? Please telegraph yes or no to Coburg Lodge, Emilia Road, Tulse Hill."

To think over this letter Mumford missed his ordinary train. It was not exactly the kind of letter he had expected, and Emmeline shared his doubts. The handwriting seemed just passable; there was no orthographic error; but – refinement? This young person wrote, too, with such singular nonchalance. And she said absolutely nothing about her domestic circumstances. Coburg Lodge, Tulse Hill. A decent enough locality, doubtless; but—

"There's no harm in seeing her," said Emmeline at length. "Send a telegram, Clarence. Do you know, I think she *may* be the right kind of girl. I was thinking of someone awfully grand, and it's rather a relief. After all, you see, you – you are in business—"

"To be sure. And this girl seems to belong to a business family. I only wish she wrote in a more ladylike way."

Emmeline set her house in order, filled the drawing-room with flowers, made the spare bedroom as inviting as possible, and, after luncheon, spent a good deal of time in adorning her person. She was a slight, pretty woman of something less than thirty; with a good, but pale, complexion, hair tending to auburn, sincere eyes. Her little vanities had no roots of ill-nature; she could admire without envy, and loved an orderly domestic life. Her husband's desire to increase his income had rather unsettled her; she exaggerated the importance of to-day's interview, and resolved with nervous energy to bring it to a successful issue, if Miss Derrick should prove a possible companion.

About four o'clock sounded the visitor's ring. From her bedroom window Emmeline had seen Miss Derrick's approach. As the distance from the station was only five minutes' walk, the stranger naturally came on foot. A dark girl, and of tolerably good features; rather dressy; with a carriage corresponding to the tone of her letter – an easy swing; head well up and shoulders squared. "Oh, how I *hope* she isn't vulgar!" said Emmeline to herself. "I don't like the hat – I don't. And that sunshade with the immense handle." From the top of the stairs she heard a clear, unaffected voice: "Mrs. Mumford at home?" Yes, the aspirate *was* sounded – thank goodness!

It surprised her, on entering the room, to find that Miss Derrick looked no less nervous than she was herself. The girl's cheeks were flushed, and she half choked over her "How do you do?"

"I hope you had no difficulty in finding the house. I would have met you at the station if you had mentioned the train. Oh, but – how silly! – I shouldn't have known you."

Miss Derrick laughed, and seemed of a sudden much more at ease.

"Oh, I like you for that!" she exclaimed mirthfully. "It's just the kind of thing I say myself sometimes. And I'm so glad to see that you are – you mustn't be offended – I mean you're not the kind of person to be afraid of." They laughed together. Emmeline could not subdue her delight when she found that the girl really might be accepted as a lady. There were faults of costume undeniably; money had been misspent in several directions; but no glaring vulgarity hurt the eye. And her speech, though not strictly speaking refined, was free from the faults that betray low origin. Then, she seemed good-natured though there was something about her mouth not altogether charming.

"Do you know Sutton at all?" Emmeline inquired.

"Never was here before. But I like the look of it. I like this house, too. I suppose you know a lot of people here, Mrs. Mumford?"

"Well – no. There's only one family we know at all well. Our friends live in London. Of course they often come out here. I don't know whether you are acquainted with any of them. The Kirby Simpsons, of West Kensington; and Mrs. Hollings, of Highgate—"

Miss Derrick cast down her eyes and seemed to reflect. Then she spoke abruptly.

"I don't know any people to speak of. I ought to tell you that my mother has come down with me. She's waiting at the station till I go back; then she'll come and see you. You're surprised? Well, I had better tell you that I'm leaving home because I can't get on with my people. Mother and I have always quarrelled, but it has been worse than ever lately. I must explain that she has married a second time, and Mr. Higgins – I'm glad to say that isn't *my* name – has a daughter of his own by a first marriage; and we can't bear each other – Miss Higgins, I mean. Some day, if I come to live here, I daresay I shall tell you more. Mr. Higgins is rich, and I can't say he's unkind to me; he'll give me as much as I want; but I'm sure he'll be very glad to get me out of the house. I have no money of my own – worse luck! Well, we thought it best for me to come alone, first, and see – just to see, you know – whether we were likely to suit each other. Then mother will come and tell you all she has to say about me. Of course I know what it'll be. They all say I've a horrible temper. I don't think so myself; and I'm sure I don't think I should quarrel with *you*, you look so nice. But I can't get on at home, and it's better for all that we should part. I'm just two-and-twenty – do I look older? I haven't learnt to do anything, and I suppose I shall never need to."

"Do you wish to see *much* society?" inquired Mrs. Mumford, who was thinking rapidly, "or should you prefer a few really nice people? I'm afraid

I don't quite understand yet whether you want society of the pleasure-seeking kind, or—"

She left the alternative vague. Miss Derrick again reflected for a moment before abruptly declaring herself.

"I feel sure that your friends are the kind I want to know. At all events, I should like to try. The great thing is to get away from home and see how things look."

They laughed together. Emmeline, after a little more talk, offered to take her visitor over the house, and Miss Derrick had loud praise for everything she saw.

"What I like about you," she exclaimed of a sudden, as they stood looking from a bedroom window on to the garden, "is that you don't put on any – you know what I mean. People seem to me to be generally either low and ignorant, or so high and mighty there's no getting on with them at all. You're just what I wanted to find. Now I must go and send mother to see you."

Emmeline protested against this awkward proceeding. Why should not both come together and have a cup of tea? If it were desired, Miss Derrick could step into the garden whilst her mother said whatever she wished to say. The girl assented, and in excellent spirits betook herself to the railway station. Emmeline waited something less than a quarter of an hour; then a hansom drove up, and Mrs. Higgins, after a deliberate surveyal of the house front, followed her daughter up the pathway.

The first sight of the portly lady made the situation clearer to Mrs. Mumford. Louise Derrick represented a certain stage of civilisation, a degree of conscious striving for better things; Mrs. Higgins was prosperous and self-satisfied vulgarity. Of a complexion much lighter than the girl's, she still possessed a coarse comeliness, which pointed back to the dairymaid type of damsel. Her features revealed at the same time a kindly nature and an irascible tendency. Monstrously overdressed, and weighted with costly gewgaws, she came forward panting and perspiring, and, before paying any heed to her hostess, closely surveyed the room.

"Mrs. Mumford," said the girl, "this is my mother. Mother, this is Mrs. Mumford. And now, please, let me go somewhere while you have your talk."

"Yes, that'll be best, that'll be best," exclaimed Mrs. Higgins. "Dear, 'ow 'ot it is! Run out into the garden, Louise. Nice little 'ouse, Mrs. Mumford. And Louise seems quite taken with you. She doesn't take to people very easy, either. Of course, you can give satisfactory references?

I like to do things in a business-like way. I understand your 'usband is in the City; shouldn't wonder if he knows some of Mr. 'Iggins's friends. Yes, I will take a cup, if you please. I've just had one at the station, but it's such thirsty weather. And what do you think of Louise? Because I'd very much rather you said plainly if you don't think you could get on."

"But, indeed, I fancy we could, Mrs. Higgins."

"Well, I'm sure I'm very glad *of* it. It isn't everybody can get on with Louise. I dessay she's told you a good deal about me and her stepfather. I don't think she's any reason to complain of the treatment—"

"She said you were both very kind to her," interposed the hostess.

"I'm sure we *try* to be, and Mr. 'Iggins, he doesn't mind what he gives her. A five-pound note, if you'll believe me, is no more than a sixpence to him when he gives her presents. You see, Mrs. Rumford – no, Mumford, isn't it? – I was first married very young – scarcely eighteen, I was; and Mr. Derrick died on our wedding-day, two years after. Then came Mr. 'Iggins. Of course I waited a proper time. And one thing I can say, that no woman was ever 'appier with two 'usbands than I've been. I've two sons growing up, hearty boys as ever you saw. If it wasn't for this trouble with Louise—" She stopped to wipe her face. "I dessay she's told you that Mr. 'Iggins, who was a widower when I met him, has a daughter of his first marriage – her poor mother died at the birth, and she's older than Louise. I don't mind telling *you*, Mrs. Mumford, she's close upon six-and-twenty, and nothing like so good-looking as Louise, neither. Mr. 'Iggins, he's kindness itself; but when it comes to differences between his daughter and *my* daughter, well, it isn't in nature he shouldn't favour his own. There's more be'ind, but I dessay you can guess, and I won't trouble you with things that don't concern you. And that's how it stands, you see."

By a rapid calculation Emmeline discovered, with surprise, that Mrs. Higgins could not be much more than forty years of age. It must have been a life of gross self-indulgence that had made the woman look at least ten years older. This very undesirable parentage naturally affected Emmeline's opinion of Louise, whose faults began to show in a more pronounced light. One thing was clear: but for the fact that Louise aimed at a separation from her relatives, it would be barely possible to think of receiving her. If Mrs. Higgins thought of coming down to Sutton at unexpected moments – no, that was too dreadful.

"Should you wish, Mrs. Higgins, to entrust your daughter to me entirely?"

"My dear Mrs. Rumford, it's very little that *my* wishes has to do with it!

She's made up her mind to leave 'ome, and all I can do is to see she gets with respectable people, which I feel sure you are; and of course I shall have your references."

Emmeline turned pale at the suggestion. She all but decided that the matter must go no further.

"And what might your terms be – inclusive?" Mrs. Higgins proceeded to inquire.

At this moment a servant entered with tea, and Emmeline, sorely flurried, talked rapidly of the advantages of Sutton as a residence. She did not allow her visitor to put in a word till the door closed again. Then, with an air of decision, she announced her terms; they would be three guineas a week. It was half a guinea more than she and Clarence had decided to ask. She expected, she hoped, Mrs. Higgins would look grave. But nothing of the kind; Louise's mother seemed to think the suggestion very reasonable. Thereupon Emmeline added that, of course, the young lady would discharge her own laundress's bill. To this also Mrs. Higgins readily assented.

"A hundred and sixty pounds per annum!" Emmeline kept repeating to herself. And, alas! it looked as if she might have asked much more. The reference difficulty might be minimised by naming her own married sister, who lived at Blackheath, and Clarence's most intimate friend, Mr. Tarling, who held a good position in a City house, and had a most respectable address at West Kensington. But her heart misgave her. She dreaded her husband's return home.

The conversation was prolonged for half-an-hour. Emmeline gave her references, and in return requested the like from Mrs. Higgins. This astonished the good woman. Why, her husband was Messrs. 'Iggins of Fenchurch Street! Oh, a mere formality, Emmeline hastened to add – for Mr. Mumford's satisfaction. So Mrs. Higgins very pompously named two City firms, and negotiations, for the present, were at an end.

Louise, summoned to the drawing-room, looked rather tired of waiting.

"When can you have me, Mrs. Mumford?" she asked. "I've quite made up my mind to come."

"I'm afraid a day or two must pass, Miss Derrick—"

"The references, my dear," began Mrs. Higgins.

"Oh, nonsense! It's all right; anyone can see."

"There you go! Always cutting short the words in my mouth. I can't endure such behaviour, and I wonder what Mrs. Rumford thinks of it. I've given Mrs. Rumford fair warning—"

They wrangled for a few minutes, Emmeline feeling too depressed and anxious to interpose with polite commonplaces. When at length they took their leave, she saw the last of them with a sigh of thanksgiving. It had happened most fortunately that no one called this afternoon.

"Clarence, it's *quite* out of the question." Thus she greeted her husband. "The girl herself I could endure, but oh, her odious mother! – Three guineas a week! I could cry over the thought."

By the first post in the morning came a letter from Louise. She wrote appealingly, touchingly. "I know you couldn't stand my mother, but do please have me. I like Sutton, and I like your house, and I like you. I promise faithfully nobody from home shall ever come to see me, so don't be afraid. Of course if you won't have me, somebody else will; I've got two hundred to choose from, but I'd rather come to you. Do write and say I may come. I'm so sorry I quarrelled with mother before you. I promise never to quarrel with you. I'm very good-tempered when I get what I want." With much more to the same effect.

"We *will* have her," declared Mumford. "Why not, if the old people keep away? – You are quite sure she sounds her *h's*?"

"Oh, quite. She has been to pretty good schools, I think. And I dare say I could persuade her to get other dresses and hats."

"Of course you could. Really, it seems almost a duty to take her – doesn't it?"

So the matter was settled, and Mumford ran off gaily to catch his train.

Three days later Miss Derrick arrived, bringing with her something like half-a-ton of luggage. She bounded up the doorsteps, and, meeting Mrs. Mumford in the hall, kissed her fervently.

"I've got such heaps to tell you! Mr. Higgins has given me twenty pounds to go on with – for myself, I mean; of course he'll pay everything else. How delighted I am to be here! Please pay the cabman; I've got no change."

A few hours before this there had come a letter from Mrs. Higgins; better written and spelt than would have seemed likely.

"Dear Mrs. Mumford," it ran, "L. is coming to-morrow morning, and I hope you won't repent. There's just one thing I meant to have said to you but forgot, so I'll say it now. If it should happen that any gentleman of your acquaintance takes a fancy to L., and if it should come to anything, I'm sure both Mr. H. and me would be *most thankful*, and Mr. H. would behave handsome to her. And what's more, I'm sure he would be only too glad to show *in a handsome way* the thanks he would owe to you and Mr. M. – Very truly yours, Susan H. Higgins."

~ *Chapter 2* ~

"RUNNYMEDE" (so the Mumfords' house was named) stood on its own little plot of ground in one of the tree-shadowed roads which persuade the inhabitants of Sutton that they live in the country. It was of red brick, and double-fronted, with a porch of wood and stucco; bay windows on one side of the entrance, and flat on the other, made a contrast pleasing to the suburban eye. The little front garden had a close fence of unpainted lath, a characteristic of the neighbourhood. At the back of the house lay a long, narrow lawn, bordered with flower-beds, and shaded at the far end by a fine horse-chestnut.

Emmeline talked much of the delightful proximity of the Downs; one would have imagined her taking long walks over the breezy uplands to Banstead or Epsom, or yet further afield. The fact was, she saw no more of the country than if she had lived at Brixton. Her windows looked only upon the surrounding houses and their garden foliage. Occasionally she walked along the asphalte pavement of the Brighton Road – a nursemaids' promenade – as far as the stone which marks twelve miles from Westminster Bridge. Here, indeed, she breathed the air of the hills, but villas on either hand obstructed the view, and brought London much nearer than the measured distance. Like her friends and neighbours, Emmeline enjoyed Sutton because it was a most respectable little portion of the great town, set in a purer atmosphere. The country would have depressed her.

In this respect Miss Derrick proved a congenial companion. Louise made no pretence of rural inclinations, but had a great liking for tree-shadowed asphalte, for the results of elaborate horticulture, for the repose and the quiet of villadom.

"I should like to have a house just like this," she declared, on her first evening at "Runnymede," talking with her host and hostess out in the garden. "It's quite big enough, unless, of course, you have a very large family, which must be rather a bore." She laughed ingenuously. "And one gets to town so easily. What do you pay for your season-ticket, Mr. Mumford? Oh, well! that isn't much. I almost think I shall get one."

"Do you wish to go up very often, then?" asked Emmeline, reflecting on her new responsibilities.

"Oh! not every day, of course. But a season-ticket saves the bother each time, and you have a sort of feeling, you know, that you can be in town whenever you like."

It had not hitherto been the Mumfords' wont to dress for dinner, but this evening they did so, and obviously to Miss Derrick's gratification. She herself appeared in a dress which altogether outshone that of her hostess. Afterwards, in private, she drew Emmeline's attention to this garb, and frankly asked her opinion of it.

"Very nice indeed," murmured the married lady, with a good-natured smile. "Perhaps a little—"

"There, I know what you're going to say. You think it's too showy. Now I want you to tell me just what you think about everything – everything. I shan't be offended. I'm not so silly. You know I've come here to learn all sorts of things. To-morrow you shall go over all my dresses with me, and those you don't like I'll get rid of. I've never had anyone to tell me what's nice and what isn't. I want to be – oh, well, you know what I mean."

"But, my dear," said Emmeline, "there's something I don't quite understand. You say I'm to speak plainly, and so I will. How is it that you haven't made friends long ago with the sort of people you wish to know? It isn't as if you were in poor circumstances."

"How *could* I make friends with nice people when I was ashamed to have them at home? The best I know are quite poor – girls I went to school with. They're much better educated than I am, but they make their own living, and so I can't see very much of them, and I'm not sure they want to see much of *me*. I wish I knew what people think of me; they call me vulgar, I believe – the kind I'm speaking of. Now, do tell me, Mrs. Mumford, *am* I vulgar?"

"My dear Miss Derrick—" Emmeline began in protest, but was at once interrupted.

"Oh! that isn't what I want. You must call me Louise, or Lou, if you like, and just say what you really think. Yes, I see, I am rather vulgar, and what can you expect? Look at mother; and if you saw Mr. Higgins, oh! The mistake I made was to leave school so soon. I got sick of it, and left at sixteen, and of course the idiots at home – I mean the foolish people – let me have my own way. I'm not clever, you know, and I didn't get on well at school. They used to say I could do much better if I liked, and perhaps it was more laziness than stupidity, though I don't care for books – I wish I did. I've had lots of friends, but I never keep them for very long. I don't know whether it's their fault or mine. My oldest friends are Amy Barker and Muriel Featherstone; they were both at the school at Clapham, and now Amy does type-writing in the City, and Muriel is at a photographer's. They're awfully nice girls, and I like them so much; but then, you see, they haven't enough money to live in what *I* call a nice way, and, you know, I should never think of asking them to advise me about my dresses, or anything of that kind. A friend of mine once began to say something and I didn't like it; after that we had nothing to do with each other."

Emmeline could not hide her amusement.

"Well, that's just it," went on the other frankly. "I *have* rather a sharp temper, and I suppose I don't get on well with most people. I used to quarrel dreadfully with some of the girls at school – the uppish sort. And yet all the time I wanted to be friends with them. But, of course, I could never have taken them home."

Mrs. Mumford began to read the girl's character, and to understand how its complexity had shaped her life. She was still uneasy as to the impression this guest would make upon their friends, but on the whole it seemed probable that Louise would conscientiously submit herself to instruction, and do her very best to be "nice." Clarence's opinion was still favourable; he pronounced Miss Derrick "very amusing," and less of a savage than his wife's description had led him to expect.

Having the assistance of two servants and a nurse-girl, Emmeline was not overburdened with domestic work. She soon found it fortunate that her child, a girl of two years old, needed no great share of her attention; for Miss Derrick, though at first she affected an extravagant interest in the baby, very soon had enough of that plaything, and showed a decided preference for Emmeline's society out of sight and hearing of nursery affairs. On the afternoon of the second day they went together to call upon Mrs. Fentiman, who lived at a distance of a quarter of an hour's walk, in a house called "Hazeldene"; a semi-detached house, considerably smaller than "Runnymede," and neither without nor within so pleasant to look upon. Mrs. Fentiman, a tall, hard-featured, but amiable lady, had two young children who occupied most of her time; at present one of them was ailing, and the mother could talk of nothing else but this distressing circumstance. The call lasted only for ten minutes, and Emmeline felt that her companion was disappointed.

"Children are a great trouble," Louise remarked, when they had left the house. "People ought never to marry unless they can keep a lot of servants. Not long ago I was rather fond of somebody, but I wouldn't have him because he had no money. Don't you think I was quite right?"

"I have no doubt you were."

"And now," pursued the girl, poking the ground with her sunshade as she walked, "there's somebody else. And that's one of the things I want to tell you about. He has about three hundred a year. It isn't much, of course; but I suppose Mr. Higgins would give me something. And yet I'm sure it won't come to anything. Let's go home and have a good talk, shall we?"

Mrs. Higgins's letter had caused Emmeline and her husband no little amusement; but at the same time it led them to reflect. Certainly they numbered among their acquaintances one or two marriageable young men who might perchance be attracted by Miss Derrick, especially if they learnt that Mr. Higgins was disposed to "behave handsomely" to his stepdaughter; but the Mumfords had no desire to see Louise speedily married. To the bribe with which the letter ended they could give no serious thought. Having secured their "paying guest," they hoped she would remain with them for a year or two at least. But already Louise had dropped hints such as Emmeline could not fail to understand, and her avowal of serious interest in a lover came rather as an annoyance than a surprise to Mrs. Mumford.

It was a hot afternoon, and they had tea brought out into the garden, under the rustling leaves of the chestnut.

"You don't know anyone else at Sutton except Mrs. Fentiman?" said Louise, as she leaned back in the wicker chair.

"Not intimately. But some of our friends from London will be coming on Sunday. I've asked four people to lunch."

"How jolly! Of course you'll tell me all about them before then. But I want to talk about Mr. Cobb. Please, *two* lumps of sugar. I've known him for about a year and a half. We seem quite old friends, and he writes to me; I don't answer the letters, unless there's something to say. To tell the truth, I don't like him."

"How can that be if you seem old friends?"

"Well, he likes *me*; and there's no harm in that, so long as he understands. I'm sure *you* wouldn't like him. He's a rough, coarse sort of man, and has a dreadful temper."

"Good gracious! What is his position?"

"Oh, he's connected with the what-d'ye-call-it Electric Lighting Company. He travels about a good deal. I shouldn't mind that; it must be rather nice not to have one's husband always at home. Just now I believe he's in Ireland. I shall be having a letter from him very soon, no doubt. He doesn't know I've left home, and it'll make him wild. Yes, that's the kind of man he is. Fearfully jealous, and such a temper! If I married him, I'm quite sure he would beat me some day."

"Oh!" Emmeline exclaimed. "How can you have anything to do with such a man?"

"He's very nice sometimes," answered Louise, thoughtfully.

"But do you really mean that he is 'rough and coarse'?"

"Yes, I do. You couldn't call him a gentleman. I've never seen his people; they live somewhere a long way off; and I shouldn't wonder if they are a horrid lot. His last letter was quite insulting. He said – let me see, what was it? Yes – 'You have neither heart nor brains, and I shall do my best not to waste another thought on you?' What do you think of that?"

"It seems very extraordinary, my dear. How can he write to you in that way if you never gave him any encouragement?"

"Well, but I suppose I have done. We've met on the Common now and then, and – and that kind of thing. I'm afraid you're shocked, Mrs. Mumford. I know it isn't the way that nice people behave, and I'm going to give it up."

"Does your mother know him?"

"Oh, yes! there's no secret about it. Mother rather likes him. Of course he behaves himself when he's at the house. I've a good mind to ask him to call here so that you could see him. Yes, I should like you to see him. You wouldn't mind?"

"Not if you really wish it, Louise. But – I can't help thinking you exaggerate his faults."

"Not a bit. He's a regular brute when he gets angry."

"My dear," Emmeline interposed softly, "that isn't quite a ladylike expression."

"No, it isn't. Thank you, Mrs. Mumford. I meant to say he is horrid – very disagreeable. Then there's something else I want to tell you about. Cissy Higgins – that's Mr. Higgins's daughter, you know – is half engaged to a man called Bowling – an awful idiot—"

"I don't think I would use that word, dear."

"Thank you, Mrs. Mumford. I mean to say he's a regular silly. But he's in a very good position – a partner in Jannaway Brothers of Woolwich, though he isn't thirty yet. Well, now, what do you think? Mr. Bowling doesn't seem to know his own mind, and just lately he's been paying so much attention to *me* that Cissy has got quite frantic about it. This was really and truly the reason why I left home."

"I see," murmured the listener, with a look of genuine interest.

"Yes. They wanted to get me out of the way. There wasn't the slightest fear that I should try to cut Cissy Higgins out; but it was getting very awkward for her, I admit. Now that's the kind of thing that doesn't go on among nice people, isn't it?"

"But what do you mean, Louise, when you say that Miss Higgins and Mr. – Mr. Bowling are *half* engaged?"

"Oh, I mean she has refused him once, just for form's sake; but he knows very well she means to have him. People of your kind don't do that sort of thing, do they?"

"I hardly know," Emmeline replied, colouring a little at certain private reminiscences. "And am I to understand that you wouldn't on any account listen to Mr. Bowling?"

Louise laughed.

"Oh, there's no knowing what I might do to spite Cissy. We hate each other, of course. But I can't fancy myself marrying him. He has a long nose, and talks through it. And he says 'think you' for 'thank you,' and he sings – oh, to hear him sing! I can't bear the man."

The matter of this conversation Emmeline reported to her husband at night, and they agreed in the hope that neither Mr. Cobb nor Mr. Bowling would make an appearance at "Runnymede." Mumford opined that these individuals were "cads." Small wonder, he said, that the girl wished to enter a new social sphere. His wife, on the other hand, had a suspicion that Miss Derrick would not be content to see the last of Mr. Cobb. He, the electrical engineer, or whatever he was, could hardly be such a ruffian as the girl depicted. His words, "You have neither heart nor brains," seemed to indicate anything but a coarse mind.

"But what a bad-tempered lot they are!" Mumford observed. "I suppose people of that sort quarrel and abuse each other merely to pass the time. They seem to be just one degree above the roughs who come to blows and get into the police court. You must really do your best to get the girl out of it; I'm sure she is worthy of better things."

"She is – in one way," answered his wife judicially. "But her education stopped too soon. I doubt if it's possible to change her very much. And – I really should like, after all, to see Mr. Cobb."

Mumford broke into a laugh.

"There you go! The eternal feminine. You'll have her married in six months."

"Don't be vulgar, Clarence. And we've talked enough of Louise for the present."

Miss Derrick's presentiment that a letter from Mr. Cobb would soon reach her was justified the next day; it arrived in the afternoon, readdressed from Tulse Hill. Emmeline observed the eagerness with which this epistle was pounced upon and carried off for private perusal. She saw, too, that in half-an-hour's time Louise left the house – doubtless to post a reply. But, to her surprise, not a word of the matter escaped Miss Derrick during the whole evening.

In her school-days, Louise had learned to "play the piano," but, caring little or nothing for music, she had hardly touched a key for several years. Now the idea possessed her that she must resume her practising, and to-day she had spent hours at the piano, with painful effect upon Mrs. Mumford's nerves. After dinner she offered to play to Mumford, and he, good-natured fellow, stood by her to turn over the leaves. Emmeline, with fancy work in her hands, watched the two. She was not one of the most foolish of her sex, but it relieved her when Clarence moved away.

The next morning Louise was an hour late for breakfast. She came down when Mumford had left the house, and Emmeline saw with surprise that she was dressed for going out.

"Just a cup of coffee, please. I've no appetite this morning, and I want to catch a train for Victoria as soon as possible."

"When will you be back?"

"Oh, I don't quite know. To tea, I think."

The girl had all at once grown reticent, and her lips showed the less amiable possibilities of their contour.

~ *Chapter 3* ~

AT dinner-time she had not returned. It being Saturday, Mumford was back early in the afternoon, and Miss Derrick's absence caused no grief. Emmeline could play with baby in the garden, whilst her husband smoked his pipe and looked on in the old comfortable way. They already felt that domestic life was not quite the same with a stranger to share it. Doubtless they would get used to the new restraints; but Miss Derrick must not expect them to disorganise their meal-times on her account. Promptly at half-past seven they sat down to dine, and had just risen from the table, when Louise appeared.

She was in excellent spirits, without a trace of the morning's ill-humour. No apologies! If she didn't feel quite free to come and go, without putting people out, there would be no comfort in life. A slice of the joint, that was all she wanted, and she would have done in a few minutes.

"I've taken tickets for Toole's Theatre on Monday night. You must both come. You can, can't you?"

Mumford and his wife glanced at each other. Yes, they could go; it was very kind of Miss Derrick; but—

"That's all right, it'll be jolly. The idea struck me in the train, as I was going up; so I took a cab from Victoria and booked the places first thing. Third row from the front, dress circle; the best I could do. Please let me have my dinner alone. Mrs. Mumford, I want to tell you something afterwards."

Clarence went round to see his friend Fentiman, with whom he usually had a chat on Saturday evening. Emmeline was soon joined by the guest in the drawing-room.

"There, you may read that," said Louise, holding out a letter. "It's from Mr. Cobb; came yesterday, but I didn't care to talk about it then. Yes, please read it; I want you to."

Reluctantly, but with curiosity, Emmeline glanced over the sheet. Mr. Cobb wrote in ignorance of Miss Derrick's having left home. It was a plain, formal letter, giving a brief account of his doings in Ireland, and making a request that Louise would meet him, if possible, on Streatham Common, at three o'clock on Saturday afternoon. And he signed himself—"Very sincerely yours."

"I made up my mind at once," said the girl, "that I wouldn't meet him.

That kind of thing will have to stop. I'm not going to think any more of him, and it's better to make him understand it at once – isn't it?"

Emmeline heartily concurred.

"Still," pursued the other, with an air of great satisfaction, "I thought I had better go home for this afternoon. Because when he didn't see me on the Common he was pretty sure to call at the house, and I didn't want mother or Cissy to be talking about me to him before he had heard my own explanation."

"Didn't you answer the letter?" asked Emmeline.

"No. I just sent a line to mother, to let her know I was coming over to-day, so that she might stay at home. Well, and it happened just as I thought. Mr. Cobb came to the house at half-past three. But before that I'd had a terrible row with Cissy. That isn't a nice expression, I know, but it really was one of our worst quarrels. Mr. Bowling hasn't been near since I left, and Cissy is furious. She said such things that I had to tell her very plainly what I thought of her; and she positively foamed at the mouth! 'Now look here,' she said, 'if I find out that he goes to Sutton, you'll see what will happen.' '*What* will happen?' I asked. 'Father will stop your allowance, and you'll have to get on as best you can.' 'Oh, very well,' I said, 'in that case I shall marry Mr. Bowling.' You should have seen her rage! 'You said you wouldn't marry him if he had ten thousand a year!' she screamed. 'I dare say I did; but if I've nothing to live upon – ' 'You can marry your Mr. Cobb, can't you?' And she almost cried; and I should have felt sorry for her if she hadn't made me so angry. 'No,' I said, 'I can't marry Mr. Cobb. And I never dreamt of marrying Mr. Cobb. And—' "

Emmeline interposed.

"Really, Louise, that kind of talk isn't at all ladylike. What a pity you went home."

"Yes, I was sorry for it afterwards. I shan't go again for a long time; I promise you I won't. However, Mr. Cobb came, and I saw him alone. He was astonished when he heard what had been going on; he was astonished at *me*, too – I mean, the way I spoke. I wanted him to understand at once that there was nothing between us; I talked in rather a – you know the sort of way." She raised her chin slightly, and looked down from under her eyelids. "Oh, I assure you I behaved quite nicely. But he got into a rage, as he always does, and began to call me names, and I wouldn't stand it. 'Mr. Cobb,' I said, very severely, 'either you will conduct yourself properly, or you will leave the house.' Then he tried another tone, and said very different things – the kind of thing one likes to hear, you know; but I pretended that I didn't care for it a bit. 'It's all over between us then?' he shouted at last; yes, really shouted, and I'm sure people must have heard. 'All over?' I said. 'But there never *was* anything – nothing serious.' 'Oh, all right. Good-bye, then.' And off he rushed. And I dare say I've seen the last of him – for a time."

"Now do try to live quietly, my dear," said Emmeline. "Go on with your music, and read a little each day—"

"Yes, that's just what I'm going to do, dear Mrs. Mumford. And your friends will be here to-morrow; it'll be so quiet and nice. And on Monday we shall go to the theatre, just for a change. And I'm not going to think of those people. It's all settled. I shall live very quietly indeed."

She banged on the piano till nearly eleven o'clock, and went off to bed with a smile of virtuous contentment.

The guests who arrived on Sunday morning were Mr. and Mrs. Grove, Mr. Bilton, and Mr. Dunnill. Mrs. Grove was Emmeline's elder sister, a merry, talkative, kindly woman. Aware of the circumstances, she at once made friends with Miss Derrick, and greatly pleased that young lady by a skilful blending of "superior" talk with easy homeliness. Mr. Bilton, a stockbroker's clerk, represented the better kind of City young man – athletic, yet intelligent, spirited without vulgarity; a breezy, good-humoured, wholesome fellow. He came down on his bicycle, and would return in the same way. Louise at once made a resolve to learn cycling.

"I wish you lived at Sutton, Mr. Bilton. I should ask you to teach me."

"I'm really very sorry that I don't," replied the young man discreetly.

"Oh, never mind. I'll find somebody."

The fourth arrival, Mr. Dunnill, was older and less affable. He talked chiefly with Mr. Grove, a very quiet, somewhat careworn man; neither of them seemed able to shake off business, but they did not obtrude it on the company in general. The day passed pleasantly, but in Miss Derrick's opinion, rather soberly. Doing her best to fascinate Mr. Bilton, she felt a slight disappointment at her inability to engross his attention, and at the civil friendliness which he thought a sufficient reply to her gay sallies. For so good-looking and well-dressed a man he struck her as singularly reserved. But perhaps he was "engaged"; yes, that must be the explanation. When the guests had left, she put a plain question to Mrs. Mumford.

"I don't *think* he is engaged," answered Emmeline, who on the whole was satisfied with Miss Derrick's demeanour throughout the day.

"Oh! But, of course, he *may* be, without you knowing it. Or is it always made known?"

"There's no rule about it, my dear."

"Well, they're very nice people," said Louise, with a little sigh. "And I like your sister so much. I'm glad she asked me to go and see her. Is Mr. Bilton often at her house? – Don't misunderstand me, Mrs. Mumford. It's only that I *do* like men's society; there's no harm, is there? And people like Mr. Bilton are very different from those I've known; and I want to see more of them, you know."

"There's no harm in saying that to *me*, Louise," replied Mrs. Mumford. "But pray be careful not to seem 'forward.' People think – and say – such disagreeable things."

Miss Derrick was grateful, and again gave an assurance that repose and modesty should be the rule of her life.

At the theatre on Monday evening she exhibited a childlike enjoyment which her companions could not but envy. The freshness of her sensibilities was indeed remarkable, and Emmeline observed with pleasure that her mind seemed to have a very wholesome tone. Louise might commit follies, and be guilty of bad taste to any extent, but nothing in her savoured of depravity.

Tuesday she spent at home, pretending to read a little, and obviously thinking a great deal. On Wednesday morning she proposed of a sudden that Emmeline should go up to town with her on a shopping expedition. They had already turned over her wardrobe, numerous articles whereof were condemned by Mrs. Mumford's taste, and by Louise cheerfully sacrificed; she could not rest till new purchases had been made. So, after early luncheon, they took train to Victoria, Louise insisting that all the expenses should be hers. By five o'clock she had laid out some fifteen pounds, vastly to her satisfaction. They took tea at a restaurant, and reached Sutton not long before Mumford's return.

On Friday they went to London again, to call upon Mrs. Grove. Louise promised that this should be her last "outing" for a whole week. She admitted a feeling of restlessness, but after to-day she would overcome it. And that night she apologised formally to Mumford for taking his wife so much from home.

"Please don't think I shall always be running about like this. I feel that I'm settling down. We are going to be very comfortable and quiet."

And, to the surprise of her friends, more than a week went by before she declared that a day in town was absolutely necessary. Mr. Higgins had sent her a fresh supply of money, as there were still a few things she needed to purchase. But this time Emmeline begged her to go alone, and Louise seemed quite satisfied with the arrangement.

Early in the afternoon, as Mrs. Mumford was making ready to go out, the servant announced to her that a gentleman had called to see Miss Derrick; on learning that Miss Derrick was away, he had asked sundry questions, and ended by requesting an interview with Mrs. Mumford. His name was Cobb.

"Show him into the drawing-room," said Emmeline, a trifle agitated. "I will be down in a few moments."

Beset by anxious anticipations, she entered the room, and saw before her a figure not wholly unlike what she had imagined: a wiry, resolute-looking man, with knitted brows, lips close-set, and heavy feet firmly planted on the carpet. He was respectably dressed, but nothing more, and in his large bare hands held a brown hat marked with a grease spot. One would have judged him a skilled mechanic. When he began to speak, his blunt but civil phrases were in keeping with this impression. He had not the tone of an educated man, yet committed no vulgar errors.

"My name is Cobb. I must beg your pardon for troubling you. Perhaps you have heard of me from Miss Derrick?"

"Yes, Mr. Cobb, your name has been mentioned," Emmeline replied nervously. "Will you sit down?"

"Thank you, I will."

He twisted his hat about, and seemed to prepare with difficulty the next remark, which at length burst, rather than fell, from his lips.

"I wanted to see Miss Derrick. I suppose she is still living with you? They told me so."

A terrible man, thought Emmeline, when roused to anger; his words must descend like sledge-hammers. And it would not take much to anger him. For all that, he had by no means a truculent countenance. He was trying to smile, and his features softened agreeably enough. The more closely she observed him, the less grew Emmeline's wonder that Louise felt an interest in the man.

"Miss Derrick is likely to stay with us for some time, I believe. She has only gone to town, to do some shopping."

"I see. When I met her last she talked a good deal about you, Mrs. Mumford, and that's why I thought I would ask to see you. You have a good deal of influence over her."

"Do you think so?" returned Emmeline, not displeased. "I hope I may use it for her good."

"So do I. But – well, it comes to this, Mrs. Mumford. She seemed to hint – though she didn't exactly say so – that you were advising her to have nothing more to do with me. Of course you don't know me, and I've no doubt you do what you think the best for her. I should feel it a kindness if you would just tell me whether you are really persuading her to think no more about me."

It was an alarming challenge. Emmeline's fears returned; she half expected an outbreak of violence. The man was growing very nervous, and his muscles showed the working of strong emotion.

"I have given her no such advice, Mr. Cobb," she answered, with an attempt at calm dignity. "Miss Derrick's private affairs don't at all concern me. In such matters as this she is really quite old enough to judge for herself."

"That's what *I* should have said," remarked Mr. Cobb sturdily. "I hope you'll excuse me; I don't wish to make myself offensive. After what she said to me when we met last, I suppose most men would just let her go her own way. But – but somehow I can't do that. The thing is, I can't trust what she says; I don't believe she knows her own mind. And so long as you tell me that you're not interfering – I mean, that you don't think it right to set her against me—"

"I assure you, nothing of the kind."

There was a brief silence, then Cobb's voice again sounded with blunt emphasis.

"We're neither of us very good-tempered. We've known each other about a year, and we must have quarrelled about fifty times."

"Do you think, then," ventured the hostess, "that it would ever be possible for you to live peacefully together?"

"Yes, I do," was the robust answer. "It would be a fight for the upper hand, but I know who'd get it, and after that things would be all right."

Emmeline could not restrain a laugh, and her visitor joined in it with a heartiness which spoke in his favour.

"I promise you, Mr. Cobb, that I will do nothing whatever against your interests."

"That's very kind of you, and it's all I wanted to know."

He stood up. Emmeline, still doubtful how to behave, asked him if he would call on another day, when Miss Derrick might be at home.

"It's only by chance I was able to get here this afternoon," he replied. "I haven't much time to go running about after her, and that's where I'm at a disadvantage. I don't know whether there's anyone else, and I'm not asking you to tell me, if you know. Of course I have to take my chance; but so long as you don't speak against me – and she thinks a great deal of your advice —"

"I'm very glad to be assured of that. All I shall do, Mr. Cobb, is to keep before her mind the duty of behaving straightforwardly."

"That's the thing! Nobody can ask more than that."

Emmeline hesitated, but could not dismiss him without shaking hands. That he did not offer to do so until invited, though he betrayed no sense of social inferiority, seemed another point in his favour.

~ *Chapter 4* ~

NOT half an hour after Cobb's departure Louise returned. Emmeline was surprised to see her back so soon; they met near the railway station as Mrs. Mumford was on her way to a shop in High Street.

"Isn't it good of me! If I had stayed longer I should have gone home to quarrel with Cissy; but I struggled against the temptation. Going to the grocer's? Oh, do let me go with you, and see how you do that kind of thing. I never gave an order at the grocer's in my life – no, indeed I never did. Mother and Cissy have always looked after that. And I want to learn about housekeeping; you promised to teach me."

Emmeline made no mention of Mr. Cobb's call until they reached the house.

"He came here!" Louise exclaimed, reddening. "What impudence! I shall at once write and tell him that his behaviour is outrageous. Am I to be hunted like this?"

Her wrath seemed genuine enough; but she was vehemently eager to learn all that had passed. Emmeline made a truthful report.

"You're quite sure that was all? Oh, his impertinence! Well, and now that you've seen him, don't you understand how – how impossible it is?"

"I shall say nothing more about it, Louise. It isn't my business to—"

The girl's face threatened a tempest. As Emmeline was moving away, she rudely obstructed her.

"I insist on you telling me what you think. It was abominable of him to come when I wasn't at home; and I don't think you ought to have seen him. You've no right to keep your thoughts to yourself!"

Mrs. Mumford was offended, and showed it.

"I have a perfect right, and I shall do so. Please don't let us quarrel. You may be fond of it, but I am not."

Louise went from the room and remained invisible till just before dinner, when she came down with a grave and rather haughty countenance. To Mumford's remarks she replied with curt formality; he, prepared for this state of things, began conversing cheerfully with his wife, and Miss Derrick kept silence. After dinner, she passed out into the garden.

"It won't do," said Mumford. "The house is upset. I'm afraid we shall have to get rid of her."

"If she can't behave herself, I'm afraid we must. It's my fault. I ought to have known that it would never do."

At half-past ten, Louise was still sitting out of doors in the dark. Emmeline, wishing to lock up for the night, went to summon her troublesome guest.

"Hadn't you better come in?"

"Yes. But I think you are very unkind, Mrs. Mumford."

"Miss Derrick, I really can't do anything but leave you alone when you are in such an unpleasant humour."

"But that's just what you *oughtn't* to do. When I'm left alone I sulk, and that's bad for all of us. If you would just get angry and give me what I deserve, it would be all over very soon."

"You are always talking about 'nice' people. Nice people don't have scenes of that kind."

"No, I suppose not. And I'm very sorry, and if you'll let me beg your pardon – . There, and we might have made it up hours ago. I won't ask you to tell me what you think of Mr. Cobb. I've written him the kind of letter his impudence deserves."

"Very well. We won't talk of it any more. And if you *could* be a little quieter in your manners, Louise—"

"I will, I promise I will! Let me say good-night to Mr. Mumford."

For a day or two there was halcyon weather. On Saturday afternoon Louise hired a carriage and took her friends for a drive into the country; at her special request the child accompanied them. Nothing could have been more delightful. She had quite made up her mind to have a house, some day, at Sutton. She hoped the Mumfords would "always" live there, that they might perpetually enjoy each other's society. What were the rents? she inquired. Well, to begin with, she would be content with one of the smaller houses; a modest, semi-detached little place, like those at the far end of Cedar Road. They were perfectly respectable – were they not? How this change in her station was to come about Louise offered no hint, and did not seem to think of the matter.

Then restlessness again came upon her. One day she all but declared her disappointment that the Mumfords saw so few people. Emmeline, repeating this to her husband, avowed a certain compunction.

"I almost feel that I deliberately misled her. You know, Clarence, in our first conversation I mentioned the Kirby Simpsons and Mrs. Hollings, and I feel sure she remembers. It wouldn't be nice to be taking her money on false pretences, would it?"

"Oh, don't trouble. It's quite certain she has someone in mind whom she means to marry before long."

"I can't help thinking that. But I don't know who it can be. She had a letter this morning in a man's writing, and didn't speak of it. It wasn't Mr. Cobb."

Louise, next day, put a point-blank question.

"Didn't you say that you knew some people at West Kensington?"

"Oh, yes," answered Emmeline, carelessly. "The Kirby Simpsons. They're away from home."

"I'm sorry for that. Isn't there anyone else we could go and see, or ask over here?"

"I think it very likely Mr. Bilton will come down in a few days."

Louise received Mr. Bilton's name with moderate interest. But she dropped the subject, and seemed to reconcile herself to domestic pleasures.

It was on the evening of this day that Emmeline received a letter which gave her much annoyance. Her sister, Mrs. Grove, wrote thus:

"How news does get about! And what ridiculous forms it takes! Here is Mrs. Powell writing to me from Birmingham, and she says she has heard that you have taken in the daughter of some wealthy *parvenu*, for a consideration, to train her in the ways of decent society! Just the kind of thing Mrs. Powell would delight in talking about – she is so very malicious. Where she got her information I can't imagine. She doesn't give the slightest hint. 'They tell me' – I copy her words – 'that the girl is all but a savage, and does and says the most awful things. I quite admire Mrs. Mumford's courage. I've heard of people doing this kind of thing, and I always wondered how they got on with their friends.' Of course I have written to contradict this rubbish. But it's very annoying, I'm sure."

Mumford was angry. The source of these fables must be either Bilton or Dunnill, yet he had not thought either of them the kind of men to make mischief. Who else knew anything of the affair? Searching her memory, Emmeline recalled a person unknown to her, a married lady, who had dropped in at Mrs. Grove's when she and Louise were there.

"I didn't like her – a supercilious sort of person. And she talked a great deal of her acquaintance with important people. It's far more likely to have come from her than from either of those men. I shall write and tell Molly so."

They began to feel uncomfortable, and seriously thought of getting rid of the burden so imprudently undertaken. Louise, the next day, wanted to take Emmeline to town, and showed dissatisfaction when she had to go unaccompanied. She stayed till late in the evening, and came back with a gay account of her calls upon two or three old friends – the girls of whom she had spoken to Mrs. Mumford. One of them, Miss Featherstone, she had taken to dine with her at a restaurant, and afterwards they had spent an hour or two at Miss Featherstone's lodgings.

"I didn't go near Tulse Hill, and if you knew how I am wondering what is going on there! Not a line from anyone. I shall write to mother to-morrow."

Emmeline produced a letter which had arrived for Miss Derrick.

"Why didn't you give it me before?" Louise exclaimed, impatiently.

"My dear, you had so much to tell me. I waited for the first pause."

"That isn't from home," said the girl, after a glance at the envelope. "It's nothing."

After saying good-night, she called to Emmeline from her bedroom door. Entering the room, Mrs. Mumford saw the open letter in Louise's hand, and read in her face a desire of confession.

"I want to tell you something. Don't be in a hurry; just a few minutes. This letter is from Mr. Bowling. Yes, and I've had one from him before, and I was obliged to answer it."

"Do you mean they are love-letters?"

"Yes, I'm afraid they are. And it's so stupid, and I'm so vexed. I don't want to have anything to do with him, as I told you long ago." Louise often used expressions which to a stranger would have implied that her intimacy with Mrs. Mumford was of years' standing. "He wrote for the first time last week. Such a silly letter! I wish you would read it. Well, he said that it was all over between him and Cissy, and that he cared only for me, and always had, and always would – you know how men write. He said he considered himself quite free. Cissy had refused him, and wasn't that enough? Now that I was away from home, he could write to me, and wouldn't I let him see me? Of course I wrote that I didn't *want* to see him, and I thought he was behaving very badly – though I don't really think so, because it's all that idiot Cissy's fault. Didn't I do quite right?"

"I think so."

"Very well. And now he's writing again, you see; oh, such a lot of rubbish! I can hear him saying it all through his nose. Do tell me what I ought to do next."

"You must either pay no attention to the letter, or reply so that he can't possibly misunderstand you."

"Call him names, you mean?"

"My dear Louise!"

"But that's the only way with such men. I suppose you never were bothered with them. I think I'd better not write at all."

Emmeline approved this course, and soon left Miss Derrick to her reflections.

The next day Louise carried out her resolve to write for information regarding the progress of things at Coburg Lodge. She had not long to wait for a reply, and it was of so startling a nature that she ran at once to Mrs. Mumford, whom she found in the nursery.

"Do please come down. Here's something I must tell you about. What do you think mother says? I've to go back home again at once."

"What's the reason?" Emmeline inquired, knowing not whether to be glad or sorry.

"I'll read it to you: – 'Dear Lou,' she says, 'you've made a great deal of trouble, and I hope you're satisfied. Things are all upside down, and I've never seen dada' – that's Mr. Higgins, of course – 'I've never seen dada in such a bad temper, not since first I knew him. Mr. B.' – that's Mr. Bowling, you know – 'has told him plain that he doesn't think any more of Cissy, and that nothing mustn't be expected of him.' – Oh what sweet letters mother does write! – 'That was when dada went and asked him about his intentions, as he couldn't help doing, because Cissy is fretting so. It's all over, and of course you're the cause of it; and, though I can't blame you as much as the others do, I think you *are* to blame. And Cissy said she must go to the seaside to get over it, and she went off yesterday to Margate to your Aunt Annie's boarding-house, and there she says she shall stay as long as she doesn't feel quite well, and dada has to pay two guineas a week for her. So he says at once, "Now Loo'll have to come back. I'm not going to pay for the both of them boarding out," he says. And he means it. He has told me to write to you at once, and you're to come as soon as you can, and he won't be responsible to Mrs. Mumford for more than another week's payment.' – There! But I shan't go, for all that. The idea! I left home just to please them, and now I'm to go back just when it suits their convenience. Certainly not."

"But what will you do, Louise," asked Mrs. Mumford, "if Mr. Higgins is quite determined?"

"Do? Oh! I shall settle it easy enough. I shall write at once to the old man and tell him I'm getting on so nicely in every way that I couldn't dream of leaving you. It's all nonsense, you'll see."

Emmeline and her husband held a council that night, and resolved that, whatever the issue of Louise's appeal to her stepfather, this was a very good opportunity for getting rid of their guest. They would wait till Louise made known the upshot of her negotiations. It seemed probable that Mr.

Higgins would spare them the unpleasantness of telling Miss Derrick she must leave. If not, that disagreeable necessity must be faced.

"I had rather cut down expenses all round," said Emmeline, "than have our home upset in this way. It isn't like home at all. Louise is a whirlwind, and the longer she stays, the worse it'll be."

"Yes, it won't do at all," Mumford assented. "By the bye, I met Bilton to-day, and he asked after Miss Derrick. I didn't like his look or his tone at all. I feel quite sure there's a joke going round at our expense. Confound it!"

"Never mind. It'll be over in a day or two, and it'll be a lesson to you, Clarence, won't it?"

"I quite admit that the idea was mine," her husband replied, rather irritably. "But it wasn't I who accepted the girl as a suitable person."

"And certainly it wasn't *me!*" rejoined Emmeline. "You will please to remember that I said again and again—"

"Oh, hang it, Emmy! We made a blunder, both of us, and don't let us make it worse by wrangling about it. There you are; people of that class bring infection into the house. If she stayed here a twelvemonth, we should have got to throwing things at each other."

The answer to Louise's letter of remonstrance came in the form of Mrs. Higgins herself. Shortly before luncheon that lady drove up to "Runnymede" in a cab, and her daughter, who had just returned from a walk, was startled to hear of the arrival.

"You've got to come home with me, Lou," Mrs. Higgins began, as she wiped her perspiring face. "I've promised to have you back by this afternoon. Dada's right down angry; you wouldn't know him. He blames everything on to you, and you'd better just come home quiet."

"I shall do nothing of the kind," answered Louise, her temper rising.

Mrs. Higgins glared at her and began to rail; the voice was painfully audible to Emmeline, who just then passed through the hall. Miss Derrick gave as good as she received; a battle raged for some minutes, differing from many a former conflict only in the moderation of pitch and vocabulary due to their being in a stranger's house.

"Then you won't come?" cried the mother at length. "I've had my journey for nothing, have I? Then just go and fetch Mrs. What's-her-name. She must hear what I've got to say."

"Mrs. Mumford isn't at home," answered Louise, with bold mendacity. "And a very good thing too. I should be sorry for her to see you in the state you're in."

"I'm in no more of a state than you are, Louise! And just you listen to this. Not one farthing more will you have from 'ome – not one farthing! And you may think yourself lucky if you still *'ave* a 'ome. For all I know, you'll have to earn your own living, and I'd like to hear how you mean to do it. As soon as I get back I shall write to Mrs. What's-her-name and tell her that nothing will be paid for you after the week that's due and the week that's for notice. Now just take heed of what you're doing, Lou. It may have more serious results than you think for."

"I've thought all I'm going to think," replied the girl. "I shall stay here as long as I like, and be indebted neither to you nor to stepfather."

Mrs. Mumford breathed a sigh of thankfulness that she was not called upon to take part in this scene. It was bad enough that the servant engaged in laying lunch could hear distinctly Mrs. Higgins's coarse and violent onslaught. When the front door at length closed she rejoiced, but with trembling; for the words that fell upon her ear from the hall announced too plainly that Louise was determined to stay.

~ *Chapter 5* ~

MISS Derrick had gone back into the drawing-room, and, to Emmeline's surprise, remained there. This retirement was ominous; the girl must be taking some resolve. Emmeline, on her part, braced her courage for the step on which she had decided. Luncheon awaited them, but it would be much better to arrive at an understanding before they sat down to the meal. She entered the room and found Louise leaning on the back of a chair.

"I dare say you heard the row," Miss Derrick remarked coldly. "I'm very sorry, but nothing of that kind shall happen again."

Her countenance was disturbed, she seemed to be putting a restraint upon herself, and only with great effort to subdue her voice.

"What are you going to do?" asked Emmeline, in a friendly tone, but, as it were, from a distance.

"I am going to ask you to do me a great kindness, Mrs. Mumford."

There was no reply. The girl paused a moment, then resumed impulsively.

"Mr. Higgins says that if I don't come home, he won't let me have any more money. They're going to write and tell you that they won't be responsible after this for my board and lodging. Of course I shall not go home; I shouldn't dream of it; I'd rather earn my living as – as a scullery maid. I want to ask you, Mrs. Mumford, whether you will let me stay on, and trust me to pay what I owe you. It won't be for very long, and I promise you I *will* pay, every penny."

The natural impulse of Emmeline's disposition was to reply with hospitable kindliness; she found it very difficult to maintain her purpose; it shamed her to behave like the ordinary landlady, to appear actuated by mean motives. But the domestic strain was growing intolerable, and she felt sure that Clarence would be exasperated if her weakness prolonged it.

"Now do let me advise you, Louise," she answered gently. "Are you acting wisely? Wouldn't it be very much better to go home?"

Louise lost all her self-control. Flushed with anger, her eyes glaring, she broke into vehement exclamations.

"You want to get rid of me! Very well, I'll go this moment. I was going to tell you something; but you don't care what becomes of me. I'll send for my luggage; you shan't be troubled with it long. And you'll be paid all that's owing. I didn't think you were one of that kind. I'll go this minute."

"Just as you please," said Emmeline, "Your temper is really so very—"

"Oh, I know. It's always my temper, and nobody else is ever to blame. I wouldn't stay another night in the house, if I had to sleep on the Downs!"

She flung out of the room and flew upstairs. Emmeline, angered by this unwarrantable treatment, determined to hold aloof, and let the girl do as she would. Miss Derrick was of full age, and quite capable of taking care of herself, or at all events ought to be. Perhaps this was the only possible issue of the difficulties in which they had all become involved; neither Louise nor her parents could be dealt with in the rational, peaceful way preferred by well-conditioned people. To get her out of the house was the main point; if she chose to depart in a whirlwind, that was her own affair. All but certainly she would go home, to-morrow if not to-day.

In less than a quarter of an hour her step sounded on the stairs – would she turn into the dining-room, where Emmeline now sat at table? No; straight through the hall, and out at the front door, which closed, however, quite softly behind her. That she did not slam it seemed wonderful to Emmeline. The girl was not wholly a savage.

Presently Mrs. Mumford went up to inspect the forsaken chamber. Louise had packed all her things: of course she must have tumbled them recklessly into the trunks. Drawers were left open, as if to exhibit their emptiness, but in other respects the room looked tidy enough. Neatness and order came by no means naturally to Miss Derrick, and Emmeline did not know what pains the girl had taken, ever since her arrival, to live in conformity with the habits of a "nice" household.

Louise, meanwhile, had gone to the railway station, intending to take a ticket for Victoria. But half an hour must elapse before the arrival of a train, and she walked about in an irresolute mood. For one thing, she felt hungry; at Sutton her appetite had been keen, and meal-times were always welcome. She entered the refreshment room, and with inward murmurs made a repast which reminded her of the excellent luncheon she might now have been enjoying. All the time, she pondered her situation. Ultimately, instead of booking for Victoria, she procured a ticket for Epsom Downs, and had not long to wait for the train.

It was a hot day at the end of June. Wafts of breezy coolness passed now and then over the high open country, but did not suffice to combat the sun's steady glare. After walking half a mile or so, absorbed in thought, Louise suffered so much that she looked about for shadow. Before her was the towering ugliness of the Grand Stand; this she had seen and admired when driving past it with her friends; it did not now attract her. In another direction the Downs were edged with trees, and that way she turned. All but overcome with heat and weariness, she at length found a shaded spot where her solitude seemed secure. And, after seating herself, the first thing she did was to have a good cry.

Then for an hour she sat thinking, and as she thought her face gradually emerged from gloom – the better, truer face which so often allowed itself to be disguised at the prompting of an evil spirit; her softening lips all but smiled, as if at an amusing suggestion, and her eyes, in their reverie, seemed to behold a pleasant promise. Unconsciously she plucked and tasted the sweet stems of grass that grew about her. At length, the sun's movements having robbed her of shadow, she rose, looked at her watch, and glanced around for another retreat. Hard by was a little wood, delightfully grassy and cool, fenced about with railings she could easily have climbed; but a notice-board, severely admonishing trespassers, forbade the attempt. With a petulant remark to herself on the selfishness of "those people," she sauntered past.

Along this edge of the Downs stands a picturesque row of pine-trees, stunted, battered, and twisted through many a winter by the upland gales. Louise noticed them, only to think for a moment what ugly trees they were. Before her, east, west, and north, lay the wooded landscape, soft of hue beneath the summer sky, spreading its tranquil beauty far away to the mists of the horizon. In vivacious company she would have called it, and perhaps have thought it, a charming view; alone, she had no eye for such things – an indifference characteristic of her mind, and not at all dependent upon its mood. Presently another patch of shade invited her to repose again, and again she meditated for an hour or more.

The sun had grown less ardent, and a breeze, no longer fitful, made walking pleasant. The sight of holiday-making school-children, who, in their ribboned hats and white pinafores, were having tea not far away, suggested to Louise that she also would like such refreshment. Doubtless it might be procured at the inn yonder, near the racecourse, and thither she began to move. Her thoughts were more at rest; she had made her plan for the evening; all that had to be done was to kill time for another hour or so. Walking lightly over the turf, she noticed the chalk marks significant of golf, and wondered how the game was played. Without difficulty she obtained her cup of tea, loitered over it as long as possible, strayed yet awhile about the Downs, and towards half-past six made for the railway station.

She travelled no further than Sutton, and there lingered in the waiting room till the arrival of a certain train from London Bridge. As the train came in she took up a position near the exit. Among the people who had alighted, her eye soon perceived Clarence Mumford. She stepped up to him and drew his attention.

"Oh! have you come by the same train?" he asked, shaking hands with her.

"No. I've been waiting here because I wanted to see you, Mr. Mumford. Will you spare me a minute or two?"

"Here? In the station?"

"Please – if you don't mind."

Astonished, Mumford drew aside with her to a quiet part of the long platform. Louise, keeping a very grave countenance, told him rapidly all that had befallen since his departure from home in the morning.

"I behaved horridly, and I was sorry for it as soon as I had left the house. After all Mrs. Mumford's kindness to me, and yours, I don't know how I could be so horrid. But the quarrel with mother had upset me so, and I felt so miserable when Mrs. Mumford seemed to want to get rid of me. I feel sure she didn't really want to send me away: she was only advising me, as she thought, for my good. But I can't, and won't, go home. And I've been waiting all the afternoon to see you. No; not here. I went to Epsom Downs and walked about, and then came back just in time. And – do you think I might go back? I don't mean now, at once, but this evening, after you've had dinner. I really don't know where to go for the night, and it's such a stupid position to be in, isn't it?"

With perfect naïveté, or with perfect simulation of it, she looked him in the face, and it was Mumford who had to avert his eyes. The young man felt very uncomfortable.

"Oh! I'm quite sure Emmy will be glad to let you come for the night, Miss Derrick—"

"Yes, but – Mr. Mumford, I want to stay longer – a few weeks longer. Do you think Mrs. Mumford would forgive me? I have made up my mind what to do, and I ought to have told her. I should have, if I hadn't lost my temper."

"Well," replied the other, in grave embarrassment, but feeling that he had no alternative, "let us go to the house—"

"Oh! I couldn't. I shouldn't like anyone to know that I spoke to you about it. It wouldn't be nice, would it? I thought if I came later, after dinner. And perhaps you could talk to Mrs. Mumford, and – and prepare her. I mean, perhaps you wouldn't mind saying you were sorry I had gone so suddenly. And then perhaps Mrs. Mumford – she's so kind – would say that she was sorry too. And then I might come into the garden and find you both sitting there—"

Mumford, despite his most uneasy frame of mind, betrayed a passing amusement. He looked into the girl's face and saw its prettiness flush with pretty confusion, and this did not tend to restore his tranquillity.

"What shall you do in the meantime?"

"Oh! go into the town and have something to eat, and then walk about."

"You must be dreadfully tired already."

"Just a little; but I don't mind. It serves me right. I shall be so grateful to you, Mr. Mumford. If you won't let me come, I suppose I must go to London and ask one of my friends to take me in."

"I will arrange it. Come about half-past eight. We shall be in the garden by then."

Avoiding her look, he moved away and ran up the stairs. But from the exit of the station he walked slowly, in part to calm himself, to assume his ordinary appearance, and in part to think over the comedy he was going to play.

Emmeline met him at the door, herself too much flurried to notice anything peculiar in her husband's aspect. She repeated the story with which he was already acquainted.

"And really, after all, I am so glad!" was her conclusion. "I didn't think she had really gone; all the afternoon I've been expecting to see her back again. But she won't come now, and it is a good thing to have done with the wretched business. I only hope she will tell the truth to her people. She might say that we turned her out of the house. But I don't think so; in spite of all her faults, she never seemed deceitful or malicious."

Mumford was strongly tempted to reveal what had happened at the station, but he saw danger alike in disclosure and in reticence.

When there enters the slightest possibility of jealousy, a man can never be sure that his wife will act as a rational being. He feared to tell the simple truth lest Emmeline should not believe his innocence of previous plotting with Miss Derrick, or at all events should be irritated by the circumstances into refusing Louise a lodging for the night. And with no less apprehension he decided at length to keep the secret, which might so easily become known hereafter, and would then have such disagreeable consequences.

"Well, let us have dinner, Emmy; I'm hungry. Yes, it's a good thing she has gone; but I wish it hadn't happened in that way. What a spitfire she is!"

"I never, never saw the like. And if you had heard Mrs. Higgins! Oh, what dreadful people! Clarence, hear me register a vow—"

"It was my fault, dear. I'm awfully sorry I got you in for such horrors. It was wholly and entirely my fault."

By due insistence on this, Mumford of course put his wife into an excellent humour, and, after they had dined, she returned to her regret that the girl should have gone so suddenly. Clarence, declaring that he would allow himself a cigar, instead of the usual pipe, to celebrate the restoration of domestic peace, soon led Emmeline into the garden.

"Heavens! how hot it has been. Eighty-five in our office at noon – eighty-five! Fellows are discarding waistcoats and wearing what they call a cummerbund – silk sash round the waist. I think I must follow the fashion. How should I look, do you think?"

"You don't really mind that we lose the money?" Emmeline asked presently.

"Pooh! We shall do well enough. – Who's that?"

Someone was entering the garden by the side path. And in a moment there remained no doubt who the person was. Louise came forward, her head bent, her features eloquent of fatigue and distress.

"Mrs. Mumford – I couldn't – without asking you to forgive me—"

Her voice broke with a sob. She stood in a humble attitude, and Emmeline, though pierced with vexation, had no choice but to hold out a welcoming hand.

"Have you come all the way back from London just to say this?"

"I haven't been to London. I've walked about – all day – and oh, I'm so tired and miserable! Will you let me stay, just for to-night? I shall be so grateful."

"Of course you may stay, Miss Derrick. It was very far from my wish to see you go off at a moment's notice. But I really couldn't stop you."

Mumford had stepped aside, out of hearing. He forgot his private embarrassment in speculation as to the young woman's character. That she was acting distress and penitence he could hardly believe; indeed, there was no necessity to accuse her of dishonest behaviour. The trivial concealment between him and her amounted to nothing, did not alter the facts of the situation. But what could be at the root of her seemingly so foolish existence? Emmeline held to the view that she was in love with the man Cobb, though perhaps unwilling to admit it, even in her own silly mind. It might be so, and, *if* so, it made her more interesting; for one was tempted to think that Louise had not the power of loving at all. Yet, for his own part, he couldn't help liking her; the eyes that had looked into his at the station haunted him a little, and would not let him think of her contemptuously. But what a woman to make one's wife! Unless – unless—

Louise had gone into the house. Emmeline approached her husband.

"There! I foresaw it. Isn't it vexing?"

"Never mind, dear. She'll go to morrow, or the day after."

"I wish I could be sure of that."

~ *Chapter 6* ~

LOUISE did not appear again that evening. Thoroughly tired, she unpacked her trunks, sat awhile by the open window, listening to a piano in a neighbouring house, and then jumped into bed. From ten o'clock to eight next morning she slept soundly.

At breakfast her behaviour was marked with excessive decorum. To the ordinary civilities of her host and hostess she replied softly, modestly, in the manner of a very young and timid girl; save when addressed, she kept silence, and sat with head inclined; a virginal freshness breathed about her; she ate very little, and that without her usual gusto, but rather as if performing a dainty ceremony. Her eyes never moved in Mumford's direction.

The threatened letter from Mrs. Higgins had arrived; Emmeline and her husband read it before their guest came down. If Louise continued to reside with them, they entertained her with a full knowledge that no payment must be expected from Coburg Lodge. Emmeline awaited the disclosure of her guest's project, which had more than once been alluded to yesterday; she could not dream of permitting Louise to stay for more than a day or two, whatever the suggestion offered. This morning she had again heard from her sister, Mrs. Grove, who was strongly of opinion that Miss Derrick should be sent back to her native sphere.

"I shall always feel," she said to her husband, "that we have behaved badly. I was guilty of false pretences. Fortunately, we have the excuse of her unbearable temper. But for that, I should feel dreadfully ashamed of myself."

Very soon after Mumford's departure, Louise begged for a few minutes' private talk.

"Every time I come into this drawing-room, Mrs. Mumford, I think how pretty it is. What pains you must have taken in furnishing it! I never saw such nice curtains anywhere else. And that little screen – I *am* so fond of that screen!"

"It was a wedding present from an old friend," Emmeline replied, complacently regarding the object, which shone with embroidery of many colours.

"Will you help me when *I* furnish *my* drawing-room?" Louise asked sweetly. And she added, with a direct look, "I don't think it will be very long."

"Indeed?"

"I am going to marry Mr. Bowling."

Emmeline could no longer feel astonishment at anything her guest said or did. The tone, the air, with which Louise made this declaration affected her with a sense of something quite unforeseen; but, at the same time, she asked herself why she had not foreseen it. Was not this the obvious answer to the riddle? All along, Louise had wished to marry Mr. Bowling. She might or might not have consciously helped to bring about the rupture between Mr. Bowling and Miss Higgins; she might, or might not, have felt genuinely reluctant to take advantage of her half-sister's defeat. But a struggle had been going on in the girl's conscience, at all events. Yes, this explained everything. And, on the whole, it seemed to speak in Louise's favour. Her ridicule of Mr. Bowling's person and character became, in this new light, a proof of desire to resist her inclinations. She had only yielded when it was certain that Miss Higgins's former lover had quite thrown off his old allegiance, and when no good could be done by self-sacrifice.

"When did you make up your mind to this, Louise?"

"Yesterday, after our horrid quarrel. No, *you* didn't quarrel; it was all my abominable temper. This morning I'm going to answer Mr. Bowling's last letter, and I shall tell him – what I've told you. He'll be delighted!"

"Then you have really wished for this from the first?"

Louise plucked at the fringe on the arm of her chair, and replied at length with maidenly frankness.

"I always thought it would be a good marriage for me. But I never – do believe me – I never tried to cut Cissy out. The truth is I thought a good deal of the other – of Mr. Cobb. But I knew that I *couldn't* marry him. It would be dreadful; we should quarrel frightfully, and he would kill me – I feel sure he would, he's so violent in his temper. But Mr. Bowling is very nice; he couldn't get angry if he tried. And he has a much better position than Mr. Cobb."

Emmeline began to waver in her conviction and to feel a natural annoyance.

"And you think," she said coldly, "that your marriage will take place soon?"

"That's what I want to speak about, dear Mrs. Mumford. Did you hear from my mother this morning? Then you see what my position is. I am homeless. If I leave you, I don't know where I shall go. When Mr. Higgins knows I'm going to marry Mr. Bowling he won't have me in the house, even if I wanted to go back. Cissy will be furious: she'll come back from

Margate just to keep up her father's anger against me. If you could let me stay here just a short time, Mrs. Mumford; just a few weeks I should *so* like to be married from your house."

The listener trembled with irritation, and before she could command her voice Louise added eagerly:

"Of course, when we're married, Mr. Bowling will pay all my debts."

"You are quite mistaken," said Emmeline distantly, "if you think that the money matter has anything to do with – with my unreadiness to agree—"

"Oh, I didn't think it – not for a moment. I'm a trouble to you; I know I am. But I'll be so quiet, dear Mrs. Mumford. You shall hardly know I'm in the house. If once it's all settled I shall *never* be out of temper. Do, please, let me stay! I like you so much, and how wretched it would be if I had to be married from a lodging-house."

"I'm afraid, Louise – I'm really afraid—"

"Of my temper?" the girl interrupted. "If ever I say an angry word you shall turn me out that very moment. Dear Mrs. Mumford! Oh! *what* shall I do if you won't be kind to me? What will become of me? I have no home, and everybody hates me."

Tears streamed down her face; she lay back, overcome with misery. Emmeline was distracted. She felt herself powerless to act as common-sense dictated, yet desired more than ever to rid herself of every shadow of responsibility for the girl's proceedings. The idea of this marriage taking place at "Runnymede" made her blood run cold. No, no; *that* was absolutely out of the question. But equally impossible did it seem to speak with brutal decision. Once more she must temporise, and hope for courage on another day.

"I can't – I really can't give you a definite answer till I have spoken with Mr. Mumford."

"Oh! I am sure he will do me this kindness," sobbed Louise.

A slight emphasis on the "he" touched Mrs. Mumford unpleasantly. She rose, and began to pick out some overblown flowers from a vase on the table near her. Presently Louise became silent. Before either of them spoke again a postman's knock sounded at the house-door, and Emmeline went to see what letter had been delivered. It was for Miss Derrick; the handwriting, as Emmeline knew, that of Mr. Cobb.

"Oh, bother!" Louise murmured, as she took the letter from Mrs. Mumford's hand. "Well, I'm a trouble to everybody, and I don't know how it'll all end. I daresay I shan't live very long."

"Don't talk nonsense, Louise."

"Should you like me to go at once, Mrs. Mumford?" the girl asked, with a submissive sigh.

"No, no. Let us think over it for a day or two. Perhaps you haven't quite made up your mind, after all."

To this, oddly enough, Louise gave no reply. She lingered by the window, nervously bending and rolling her letter, which she did not seem to think of opening. After a glance or two of discreet curiosity, Mrs. Mumford left the room. Daily duties called for attention, and she was not at all inclined to talk further with Louise. The girl, as soon as she found herself alone, broke Mr. Cobb's envelope, which contained four sides of bold handwriting – not a long letter, but, as usual, vigorously worded.

"Dear Miss Derrick," he wrote, "I haven't been in a hurry to reply to your last, as it seemed to me that you were in one of your touchy moods when you sent it. It wasn't my fault that I called at the house when you were away. I happened to have business at Croydon unexpectedly, and ran over to Sutton just on the chance of seeing you. And I have no objection to tell you all I said to your friend there. I am not in the habit of saying things behind people's backs that I don't wish them to hear. All I did was to ask out plainly whether Mrs. M. was trying to persuade you to have nothing to do with me. She said she wasn't, and that she didn't wish to interfere one way or another. I told her that I could ask no more than that. She seemed to me a sensible sort of woman, and I don't suppose you'll get much harm from her, though I daresay she thinks more about dress and amusements, and so on, than is good for her or anyone else. You say at the end of your letter that I'm to let you know when I think of coming again, and if you mean by that that you would be glad to see me, I can only say, thank you. I don't mean to give you up yet, and I don't believe you want me to, say what you will. I don't spy after you; you're mistaken in that. But I'm pretty much always thinking about you, and I wish you were nearer to me. I may have to go to Bristol in a week or two, and perhaps I shall be there for a month or more, so I must see you before then. Will you tell me what day would suit you, after seven? If you don't want me to come to the house, then meet me where you like. And there's only one more thing I have to say – you must deal honestly with me. I can wait, but I won't be deceived."

Louise pondered for a long time, turning now to this part of the letter, now to that. And the lines of her face, though they made no approach to smiling, indicated agreeable thoughts. Tears had left just sufficient trace to give her meditations a semblance of unwonted seriousness.

About midday she went up to her room and wrote letters. The first was to Miss Cissy Higgins:— "Dear Ciss, – I dare say you would like to know that Mr. B. has proposed to me. If you have any objection, please let me know it by return. – Affectionately yours, L. E. DERRICK." This she addressed to Margate, and stamped with a little thump of the fist. Her next sheet of paper was devoted to Mr. Bowling, and the letter, though brief, cost her some thought. "Dear Mr. Bowling, – Your last is so very nice and kind that I feel I ought to answer it without delay, but I cannot answer in the way you wish. I must have a long, long time to think over such a very important question. I don't blame you in the least for your behaviour to someone we know of; and I think, after all that happened, you were quite free. It is quite true that she did not behave straightforwardly, and I am very sorry to have to say it. I shall not be going home again: I have quite made up my mind about that. I am afraid I must not let you come here to call upon me. I have a particular reason for it. To tell you the truth, my friend Mrs. Mumford is *very* particular, and rather fussy, and has a rather trying temper. So please do not come just yet. I am quite well, and enjoying myself in a *very* quiet way. – I remain, sincerely yours, LOUISE E. DERRICK." Finally she penned a reply to Mr. Cobb, and this, after a glance at a railway time-table, gave her no trouble at all. "Dear Mr. Cobb," she scribbled, "if you really *must* see me before you go away to Bristol, or wherever it is, you had better meet me on Saturday at Streatham Station, which is about halfway between me and you. I shall come by the train from Sutton, which reaches Streatham at 8.6. – Yours truly, L. E. D."

To-day was Thursday. When Saturday came the state of things at "Runnymede" had undergone no change whatever; Emmeline still waited for a moment of courage, and Mumford, though he did not relish the prospect, began to think it more than probable that Miss Derrick would hold her ground until her actual marriage with Mr. Bowling. Whether that unknown person would discharge the debt his betrothed was incurring seemed an altogether uncertain matter. Louise, in the meantime, kept quiet as a mouse – so strangely quiet, indeed, that Emmeline's prophetic soul dreaded some impending disturbance, worse than any they had yet suffered.

At luncheon, Louise made known that she would have to leave in the middle of dinner to catch a train. No explanation was offered or asked, but Emmeline, it being Saturday, said she would put the dinner-hour earlier, to suit her friend's convenience. Louise smiled pleasantly, and said how very kind it was of Mrs. Mumford.

She had no difficulty in reaching Streatham by the time appointed. Unfortunately, it was a cloudy evening, and a spattering of rain fell from time to time.

"I suppose you'll be afraid to walk to the Common," said Mr. Cobb, who stood waiting at the exit from the station, and showed more satisfaction in his countenance when Louise appeared than he evinced in words.

"Oh, I don't care," she answered. "It won't rain much, and I've brought my umbrella, and I've nothing on that will take any harm."

She had, indeed, dressed herself in her least demonstrative costume. Cobb wore the usual garb of his leisure hours, which was better than that in which he had called the other day at "Runnymede." For some minutes they walked towards Streatham Common without interchange of a word, and with no glance at each other. Then the man coughed, and said bluntly that he was glad Louise had come.

"Well, I wanted to see you," was her answer.

"What about?"

"I don't think I shall be able to stay with the Mumfords. They're very nice people, but they're not exactly my sort, and we don't get on very well. Where had I better go?"

"Go? Why home, of course. The best place for you."

Cobb was prepared for a hot retort, but it did not come. After a moment's reflection, Louise said quietly:

"I can't go home. I've quarrelled with them too badly. You haven't seen mother lately? Then I must tell you how things are."

She did so, with no concealment save of the correspondence with Mr. Bowling, and the not unimportant statements concerning him which she had made to Mrs. Mumford. In talking with Cobb, Louise seemed to drop a degree or so in social status; her language was much less careful than when she conversed with the Mumfords, and even her voice struck a note of less refinement. Decidedly she was more herself, if that could be said of one who very rarely made conscious disguise of her characteristics.

"Better stay where you are, then, for the present," said Cobb, when he had listened attentively. "I dare say you can get along well enough with the people, if you try."

"That's all very well; but what about paying them? I shall owe three guineas for every week I stop."

"It's a great deal, and they ought to feed you very well for it," replied the other, smiling rather sourly.

"Don't be vulgar. I suppose you think I ought to live on a few shillings a week."

"Lots of people have to. But there's no reason why *you* should. But look here: why should you be quarrelling with your people now about that fellow Bowling? You don't see him anywhere, do you?"

He flashed a glance at her, and Louise answered with a defiant motion of the head.

"No, I don't. But they put the blame on me, all the same. I shouldn't wonder if they think I'm trying to get him."

She opened her umbrella, for heavy drops had begun to fall; they pattered on Cobb's hard felt hat, and Louise tried to shelter him as well as herself.

"Never mind me," he said. "And here, let me hold that thing over you. If you just put your arm in mine, it'll be easier. That's the way. Take two steps to my one; that's it."

Again they were silent for a few moments. They had reached the Common, and Cobb struck along a path most likely to be unfrequented. No wind was blowing; the rain fell in steady spots that could all but be counted, and the air grew dark.

"Well, I can only propose one thing," sounded the masculine voice. "You can get out of it by marrying me."

Louise gave a little laugh, rather timid than scornful.

"Yes, I suppose I can. But it's an awkward way. It would be rather like using a sledge-hammer to crack a nut."

"It'll come sooner or later," asserted Cobb, with genial confidence.

"That's what I don't like about you." Louise withdrew her arm petulantly. "You always speak as if I couldn't help myself. Don't you suppose I have any choice?"

"Plenty, no doubt," was the grim answer.

"Whenever we begin to quarrel it's your fault," pursued Miss Derrick, with unaccustomed moderation of tone. "I never knew a man who behaved like you do. You seem to think the way to make anyone like you is to bully them. We should have got on very much better if you had tried to be pleasant."

"I don't think we've got along badly, all things considered," Cobb replied, as if after weighing a doubt. "We'd a good deal rather be together than apart, it seems to me; or else, why do we keep meeting? And I don't want to bully anybody – least of all, you. It's a way I have of talking, I suppose. You must judge a man by his actions and his meaning, not by the tone of his voice. You know very well what a great deal I think of you. Of course I don't like it when you begin to speak as if you were only playing with me; nobody would."

"I'm serious enough," said Louise, trying to hold the umbrella over her companion, and only succeeding in directing moisture down the back of his neck. "And it's partly through you that I've got into such difficulties."

"How do you make that out?"

"If it wasn't for you, I should very likely marry Mr. Bowling."

"Oh, he's asked you, has he?" cried Cobb, staring at her. "Why didn't you tell me that before? – Don't let me stand in your way. I dare say he's just the kind of man for you. At all events, he's like you in not knowing his own mind."

"Go on! Go on!" Louise exclaimed carelessly. "There's plenty of time. Say all you've got to say."

From the gloom of the eastward sky came a rattling of thunder, like quick pistol-shots. Cobb checked his steps.

"We mustn't go any further. You're getting wet, and the rain isn't likely to stop."

"I shall not go back," Louise answered, "until something has been settled." And she stood before him, her eyes cast down, whilst Cobb looked at the darkening sky. "I want to know what's going to become of me. The Mumfords won't keep me much longer, and I don't wish to stay where I'm not wanted."

"Let us walk down the hill."

A flash of lightning made Louise start, and the thunder rattled again. But only light drops were falling. The girl stood her ground.

"I want to know what I am to do. If you can't help me, say so, and let me go my own way."

"Of course I can help you. That is, if you'll be honest with me. I want to know, first of all, whether you've been encouraging that man Bowling."

"No, I haven't."

"Very well, I believe you. And now I'll make you a fair offer. Marry me as soon as I can make the arrangements, and I'll pay all you owe, and see that you are in comfortable lodgings until I've time to get a house. It could be done before I go to Bristol, and then, of course, you could go with me."

"You speak," said Louise, after a short silence, "just as if you were making an agreement with a servant."

"That's all nonsense, and you know it. I've told you how I think, often enough, in letters, and I'm not good at saying it. Look here, I don't think it's very wise to stand out in the middle of the Common in a thunderstorm. Let us walk on, and I think I would put down your umbrella."

"It wouldn't trouble you much if I were struck with lightning."

"All right, take it so. I shan't trouble to contradict."

Louise followed his advice, and they began to walk quickly down the slope towards Streatham. Neither spoke until they were in the high road again. A strong wind was driving the rain-clouds to other regions and the thunder had ceased; there came a grey twilight; rows of lamps made a shimmering upon the wet ways.

"What sort of a house would you take?" Louise asked suddenly.

"Oh, a decent enough house. What kind do you want?"

"Something like the Mumfords'. It needn't be quite so large," she added quickly; "but a house with a garden, in a nice road, and in a respectable part."

"That would suit me well enough," answered Cobb cheerfully. "You seem to think I want to drag you down, but you're very much mistaken. I'm doing pretty well, and likely, as far as I can see, to do better. I don't grudge you money; far from it. All I want to know is, that you'll marry me for my own sake."

He dropped his voice, not to express tenderness, but because other people were near. Upon Louise, however, it had a pleasing effect, and she smiled.

"Very well," she made answer, in the same subdued tone. "Then let us settle it in that way."

They talked amicably for the rest of the time that they spent together. It was nearly an hour, and never before had they succeeded in conversing so long without a quarrel. Louise became light-hearted and mirthful; her companion, though less abandoned to the mood of the moment, wore a hopeful countenance. Through all his roughness, Cobb was distinguished by a personal delicacy which no doubt had impressed Louise, say what she might of pretended fears. At parting, he merely shook hands with her, as always.

~ *Chapter 7* ~

GLAD of a free evening, Emmeline, after dinner, walked round to Mrs. Fentiman's. Louise had put a restraint upon the wonted friendly intercourse between the Mumfords and their only familiar acquaintances at Sutton. Mrs. Fentiman liked to talk of purely domestic matters, and in a stranger's presence she was never at ease. Coming alone, and when the children were all safe in bed, Emmeline had a warm welcome. For the first time she spoke of her troublesome guest without reserve. This chat would have been restful and enjoyable but for a most unfortunate remark that fell from the elder lady, a perfectly innocent mention of something her husband had told her, but, secretly, so disturbing Mrs. Mumford that, after hearing it, she got away as soon as possible, and walked quickly home with dark countenance.

It was ten o'clock; Louise had not yet returned, but might do so any moment. Wishing to be sure of privacy in a conversation with her husband, Emmeline summoned him from his book to the bedroom.

"Well, what has happened now?" exclaimed Mumford. "If this kind of thing goes on much longer I shall feel inclined to take a lodging in town."

"I have heard something very strange. I can hardly believe it; there must have been a mistake."

"What is it? Really, one's nerves—"

"Is it true that, on Thursday evening, you and Miss Derrick were seen talking together at the station? Thursday: the day she went off and came back again after dinner."

Mumford would gladly have got out of this scrape at any expense of mendacity, but he saw at once how useless such an attempt would prove. Exasperated by the result of his indiscretion, and resenting, as all men do, the undignified necessity of defending himself, he flew into a rage. Yes, it *was* true, and what next? The girl had waylaid him, begged him to intercede for her with his wife. Of course it would have been better to come home and reveal the matter; he didn't do so because it seemed to put him in a silly position. For Heaven's sake, let the whole absurd business be forgotten and done with!

Emmeline, though not sufficiently enlightened to be above small jealousies, would have been ashamed to declare her feeling with the energy of unsophisticated female nature. She replied coldly and loftily that the matter, of course, *was* done with; that it interested her no more; but that she could not help regretting an instance of secretiveness such as she had never before discovered in her husband. Surely he had put himself in a much sillier position, as things turned out, than if he had followed the dictates of honour.

"The upshot of it is this," cried Mumford: "Miss Derrick has to leave the house, and, if necessary, I shall tell her so myself."

Again Emmeline was cold and lofty. There was no necessity whatever for any further communication between Clarence and Miss Derrick. Let the affair be left entirely in her hands. Indeed, she must very specially request that Clarence would have nothing more to do with Miss Derrick's business. Whereupon Mumford took offence. Did Emmeline wish to imply that there had been anything improper in his behaviour beyond the paltry indiscretion to which he had confessed? No; Emmeline was thankful to say that she did not harbour base suspicions. Then, rejoined Mumford, let this be the last word of a difference as hateful to him as to her. And he left the room.

His wife did not linger more than a minute behind him, and she sat in the drawing-room to await Miss Derrick's return; Mumford kept apart in what was called the library. To her credit, Emmeline tried hard to believe that she had learnt the whole truth; her mind, as she had justly declared, was not prone to ignoble imaginings; but acquitting her husband by no means involved an equal charity towards Louise. Hitherto uncertain in her judgment, she had now the relief of an assurance that Miss Derrick was not at all a proper person to entertain as a guest, on whatever terms. The incident of the railway station proved her to be utterly lacking in self-respect, in feminine modesty, even if her behaviour merited no darker description. Emmeline could now face with confidence the scene from which she had shrunk; not only was it a duty to insist upon Miss Derrick's departure, it would be a positive pleasure.

Louise very soon entered; she came into the room with her brightest look, and cried gaily:

"Oh, I hope I haven't kept you waiting for me. Are you alone?"

"No. I have been out."

"Had you the storm here? I'm not going to keep you talking; you look tired."

"I am rather," said Emmeline, with reserve. She had no intention of allowing Louise to suspect the real cause of what she was about to say – that would have seemed to her undignified; but she could not speak quite naturally. "Still, I should be glad if you would sit down for a minute."

The girl took a chair and began to draw off her gloves. She understood what was coming; it appeared in Emmeline's face.

"Something to say to me, Mrs. Mumford?"

"I hope you won't think me unkind. I feel obliged to ask you when you will be able to make new arrangements."

"You would like me to go soon?" said Louise, inspecting her finger-nails, and speaking without irritation.

"I am sorry to say that I think it better you should leave us. Forgive this plain speaking, Miss Derrick. It's always best to be perfectly straightforward, isn't it?"

Whether she felt the force of this innuendo or not, Louise took it in good part. As if the idea had only just struck her, she looked up cheerfully.

"You're quite right, Mrs. Mumford. I'm sure you've been very kind to me, and I've had a very pleasant time here, but it wouldn't do for me to stay longer. May I wait over to-morrow, just till Wednesday morning, to have an answer to a letter?"

"Certainly, if it is quite understood that there will be no delay beyond that. There are circumstances – private matters – I don't feel quite able to explain. But I must be sure that you will have left us by Wednesday afternoon."

"You may be sure of it. I will write a line and post it to-night, for it to go as soon as possible."

Therewith Louise stood up and, smiling, withdrew. Emmeline was both relieved and surprised; she had not thought it possible for the girl to conduct herself at such a juncture with such perfect propriety. An outbreak of ill-temper, perhaps of insolence, had seemed more than likely; at best she looked for tears and entreaties. Well, it was over, and by Wednesday the house would be restored to its ancient calm. Ancient, indeed! One could not believe that so short a time had passed since Miss Derrick first entered the portals. Only one more day.

"Oh, blindness to the future, kindly given, That each may fill the circle marked by Heaven." At school, Emmeline had learnt and recited these lines; but it was long since they had recurred to her memory.

In ten minutes Louise had written her letter. She went out, returned, and looked in at the drawing-room, with a pleasant smile. "Good-night, Mrs. Mumford." "Good-night, Miss Derrick." For the grace of the thing, Emmeline would have liked to say "Louise," but could not bring her lips to utter the name.

About a year ago there had been a little misunderstanding between Mr. and Mrs. Mumford, which lasted for some twenty-four hours, during which they had nothing to say to each other. To-night they found themselves in a similar situation, and remembered that last difference, and wondered, both of them, at the harmony of their married life. It was in truth wonderful enough; twelve months without a shadow of ill-feeling between them. The reflection compelled Mumford to speak when his head was on the pillow.

"Emmy, we're making fools of ourselves. Just tell me what you have done."

"I can't see how *I* am guilty of foolishness," was the clear-cut reply.

"Then why are you angry with me?"

"I don't like deceit."

"Hanged if I don't dislike it just as much. When is that girl going?"

Emmeline made known the understanding at which she had arrived, and her husband breathed an exclamation of profound thankfulness. But peace was not perfectly restored.

In another room, Louise lay communing with her thoughts, which were not at all disagreeable. She had written to Cobb, telling him what had happened, and asking him to let her know by Wednesday morning what she was to do. She could not go home; he must not bid her do so; but she would take a lodging wherever he liked. The position seemed romantic and enjoyable. Not till after her actual marriage should the people at home know what had become of her. She was marrying with utter disregard of all her dearest ambitions; all the same, she had rather be the wife of Cobb than of anyone else. Her stepfather might recover his old kindness and generosity as soon as he knew she no longer stood in Cissy's way, and that she had never seriously thought of marrying Mr. Bowling. Had she not thought of it? The question did not enter her own mind, and she would have been quite incapable of passing a satisfactory cross-examination on the subject.

Mrs. Mumford, foreseeing the difficulty of spending the next day at home, told her husband in the morning that she would have early luncheon and go to see Mrs. Grove.

"And I should like you to fetch me from there, after business, please."

"I will," answered Clarence readily. He mentally added a hope that his wife did not mean to supervise him henceforth and for ever. If so, their troubles were only beginning.

At breakfast, Louise continued to be discretion itself. She talked of her departure on the morrow as though it had long been a settled thing, and was quite unconnected with disagreeable circumstances. Only midway in the morning did Mrs. Mumford, who had been busy with her child, speak of the early luncheon and her journey to town. She hoped Miss Derrick would not mind being left alone.

"Oh, don't speak of it," answered Louise. "I've lots to do. You'll give my kind regards to Mrs. Grove?"

So they ate together at midday, rather silently, but with faces composed. And Emmeline, after a last look into the nursery, hastened away to catch her train. She had no misgivings; during her absence, all would be well as ever.

Louise passed the time without difficulty, and at seven o'clock made an excellent dinner. This evening no reply could be expected from Cobb, as he was not likely to have received her letter of last night till his return home from business. Still, there might be something from someone; she always looked eagerly for the postman.

The weather was gloomy. Not long after eight the housemaid brought in a lighted lamp, and set it, as usual, upon the little black four-legged table in the drawing-room. And in the same moment the knocker of the front door sounded a vigorous rat-tat-tat, a visitor's summons.

~ *Chapter 8* ~

"IT may be someone calling upon me," said Louise to the servant. "Let me know the name before you show anyone in."

"Of course, miss," replied the domestic, with pert familiarity, and took her time in arranging the shade of the lamp. When she returned from the door it was to announce, smilingly, that Mr. Cobb wished to see Miss Derrick.

"Please to show him in."

Louise stood in an attitude of joyous excitement, her eyes sparkling. But at the first glance she perceived that her lover's mood was by no means correspondingly gay. Cobb stalked forward and kept a stern gaze upon her, but said nothing.

"Well? You got my letter, I suppose?"

"What letter?"

He had not been home since breakfast-time, so Louise's appeal to him for advice lay waiting his arrival. Impatiently, she described the course of events. As soon as she had finished, Cobb threw his hat aside and addressed her harshly.

"I want to know what you mean by writing to your sister that you are going to marry Bowling. I saw your mother this morning, and that's what she told me. It must have been only a day or two ago that you said that. Just explain, if you please. I'm about sick of this kind of thing, and I'll have the truth out of you."

His anger had never taken such a form as this; for the first time Louise did in truth feel afraid of him. She shrank away, her heart throbbed, and her tongue refused its office.

"Say what you mean by it!" Cobb repeated, in a voice that was all the more alarming because he kept it low.

"Did you write that to your sister?"

"Yes – but I never meant it – it was just to make her angry—"

"You expect me to believe that? And, if it's true, doesn't it make you out a nice sort of girl? But I don't believe it. You've been thinking of him in that way all along; and you've been writing to him, or meeting him, since you came here. What sort of behaviour do you call this?"

Louise was recovering self-possession; the irritability of her own temper began to support her courage.

"What if I have? I'd never given *you* any promise till last night, had I? I was free to marry anyone I liked, wasn't I? What do *you* mean by coming here and going on like this? I've told you the truth about that letter, and I've always told you the truth about everything. If you don't like it, say so and go."

Cobb was impressed by the energy of her defence. He looked her straight in the eyes, and paused a moment; then spoke less violently.

"You haven't told me the *whole* truth. I want to know when you saw Bowling last."

"I haven't seen him since I left home."

"When did you write to him last?"

"The same day I wrote to Cissy. And I shall answer no more questions."

"Of course not. But that's quite enough. You've been playing a double game; if you haven't told lies, you've acted them. What sort of a wife would you make? How could I ever believe a word you said? I shall have no more to do with you."

He turned away, and, in the violence of the movement, knocked over a little toy chair, one of those perfectly useless, and no less ugly, impediments which stand about the floor of a well-furnished drawing-room. Too angry to stoop and set the object on its legs again, he strode towards the door. Louise followed him.

"You are going?" she asked, in a struggling voice.

Cobb paid no attention, and all but reached the door. She laid a hand upon him.

"You are going?"

The touch and the voice checked him. Again he turned abruptly and seized the hand that rested upon his arm.

"Why are you stopping me? What do you want with me? I'm to help you out of the fix you've got into, is that it? I'm to find you a lodging, and take no end of trouble, and then in a week's time get a letter to say that you want nothing more to do with me."

Louise was pale with anger and fear, and as many other emotions as her little heart and brain could well hold. She did not look her best – far from it, but the man saw something in her eyes which threw a fresh spell upon him. Still grasping her one hand, he caught her by the other arm, held her as far off as he could, and glared passionately as he spoke.

"What do you want?"

"You know – I've told you the truth—"

His grasp hurt her; she tried to release herself, and moved backwards. For a moment Cobb left her free; she moved backward again, her eyes drawing him on. She felt her power, and could not be content with thus much exercise of it.

"You may go if you like. But you understand, if you do—"

Cobb, inflamed with desire and jealousy, made an effort to recapture her. Louise sprang away from him; but immediately behind her lay the foolish little chair which he had kicked over, and just beyond *that* stood the scarcely less foolish little table which supported the heavy lamp, with its bowl of coloured glass and its spreading yellow shade. She tottered back, fell with all her weight against the table, and brought the lamp crashing to the floor. A shriek of terror from Louise, from her lover a shout of alarm, blended with the sound of breaking glass. In an instant a great flame shot up half way to the ceiling. The lamp-shade was ablaze; the much-embroidered screen, Mrs. Mumford's wedding present, forthwith caught fire from a burning tongue that ran along the carpet; and Louise's dress, well sprinkled with paraffin, aided the conflagration. Cobb, of course, saw only the danger to the girl. He seized the woollen hearthrug and tried to wrap it about her; but with screams of pain and frantic struggles, Louise did her best to thwart his purpose.

The window was open, and now a servant, rushing in to see what the uproar meant, gave the blaze every benefit of draught.

"Bring water!" roared Cobb, who had just succeeded in extinguishing Louise's dress, and was carrying her, still despite her struggles, out of the room. "Here, one of you take Miss Derrick to the next house. Bring water, you!"

All three servants were scampering and screeching about the hall. Cobb caught hold of one of them and all but twisted her arm out of its socket. At his fierce command, the woman supported Louise into the garden, and thence, after a minute or two of faintness on the sufferer's part, led her to the gate of the neighbouring house. The people who lived there chanced to be taking the air on their front lawn. Without delay, Louise was conveyed beneath the roof, and her host, a man of energy, sped towards the fire to be of what assistance he could.

The lamp-shade, the screen, the little table and the diminutive chair blazed gallantly, and with such a volleying of poisonous fumes that Cobb could scarce hold his ground to do battle. Louise out of the way, he at once became cool and resourceful. Before a flame could reach the window he had rent down the flimsy curtains and flung them outside. Bellowing for the water which was so long in coming, he used the hearthrug to some purpose on the outskirts of the bonfire, but had to keep falling back for fresh air. Then appeared a pail and a can, which he emptied effectively, and next moment sounded the voice of the gentleman from next door.

"Have you a garden hose? Set it on to the tap, and bring it in here."

The hose was brought into play, and in no great time the last flame had flickered out amid a deluge. When all danger was at an end, one of the servants, the nurse-girl, uttered a sudden shriek; it merely signified that she had now thought for the first time of the little child asleep upstairs. Aided by the housemaid, she rushed to the nursery, snatched her charge from bed, and carried the unhappy youngster into the breezes of the night, where he screamed at the top of his gamut.

Cobb, when he no longer feared that the house would be burnt down, hurried to inquire after Louise. She lay on a couch, wrapped in a dressing-gown; for the side and one sleeve of her dress had been burnt away. Her moaning never ceased; there was a fire-mark on the lower part of her face, and she stared with eyes of terror and anguish at whoever approached her. Already a doctor had been sent for, and Cobb, reporting that all was safe at "Runnymede," wished to remove her at once to her own bedroom, and the strangers were eager to assist.

"What will the Mumfords say?" Louise asked of a sudden, trying to raise herself.

"Leave all that to me," Cobb replied reassuringly. "I'll make it all right; don't trouble yourself."

The nervous shock had made her powerless; they carried her in a chair back to "Runnymede," and upstairs to her bedroom. Scarcely was this done when Mr. and Mrs. Mumford, after a leisurely walk from the station, approached their garden gate. The sight of a little crowd of people in the quiet road, the smell of burning, loud voices of excited servants, caused them to run forward in alarm. Emmeline, frenzied by the certainty that her own house was on fire, began to cry aloud for her child, and Mumford rushed like a madman through the garden.

"It's all right," said a man who stood in the doorway. "You Mr. Mumford? It's all right. There's been a fire, but we've got it out."

Emmeline learnt at the same moment that her child had suffered no harm, but she would not pause until she saw the little one and held him in her embrace. Meanwhile, Cobb and Mumford talked in the devastated drawing-room, which was illumined with candles.

"It's a bad job, Mr. Mumford. My name is Cobb: I daresay you've heard of me. I came to see Miss Derrick, and I was clumsy enough to knock the lamp over."

"Knock the lamp over! How could you do that? Were you drunk?"

"No, but you may well ask the question. I stumbled over something – a little chair, I think – and fell against the table with the lamp on it."

"Where's Miss Derrick?"

"Upstairs. She got rather badly burnt, I'm afraid. We've sent for a doctor."

"And here I am," spoke a voice behind them. "Sorry to see this, Mr. Mumford."

The two went upstairs together, and on the first landing encountered Emmeline, sobbing and wailing hysterically with the child in her arms. Her husband spoke soothingly.

"Don't, don't, Emmy. Here's Dr. Billings come to see Miss Derrick. She's the only one that has been hurt. Go down, there's a good girl, and send somebody to help in Miss Derrick's room; you can't be any use yourself just now."

"But how did it happen? Oh, *how* did it happen?"

"I'll come and tell you all about it. Better put the boy to bed again, hadn't you?"

When she had recovered her senses Emmeline took this advice, and, leaving the nurse by the child's cot, went down to survey the ruin of her property. It was a sorry sight. Where she had left a reception-room such as any suburban lady in moderate circumstances might be proud of, she now beheld a mere mass of unrecognisable furniture, heaped on what had once been a carpet, amid dripping walls and under a grimed ceiling.

"Oh! Oh!" She all but sank before the horror of the spectacle. Then, in a voice of fierce conviction, "She did it! *She* did it! It was because I told her to leave. I *know* she did it on purpose!"

Mumford closed the door of the room, shutting out Cobb and the cook and the housemaid. He repeated the story Cobb had told him, and quietly urged the improbability of his wife's explanation. Miss Derrick, he pointed out, was lying prostrate from severe burns; the fire must have been accidental, but the accident, to be sure, was extraordinary enough. Thereupon Mrs. Mumford's wrath turned against Cobb. What business had such a man – a low-class savage – in *her* drawing-room? He must have come knowing that she and her husband were away for the evening.

"You can question him, if you like," said Mumford. "He's out there."

Emmeline opened the door, and at once heard a cry of pain from upstairs. Mumford, also hearing it, and seeing Cobb's misery-stricken face by the light of the hall lamp, whispered to his wife:

"Hadn't you better go up, dear? Dr. Billings may think it strange."

It was much wiser to urge this consideration than to make a direct plea for mercy. Emmeline did not care to have it reported that selfish distress made her indifferent to the sufferings of a friend staying in her house. But she could not pass Cobb without addressing him severely.

"So *you* are the cause of this!"

"I am, Mrs. Mumford, and I can only say that I'll do my best to make good the damage to your house."

"Make good! I fancy you have strange ideas of the value of the property destroyed."

Insolence was no characteristic of Mrs. Mumford. But calamity had put her beside herself; she spoke, not in her own person, but as a woman whose carpets, curtains and bric-à-brac have ignominiously perished.

"I'll make it good," Cobb repeated humbly, "however long it takes me. And don't be angry with that poor girl, Mrs. Mumford. It wasn't her fault, not in any way. She didn't know I was coming; she hadn't asked me to come. I'm entirely to blame."

"You mean to say you knocked over the table by accident?"

"I did indeed. And I wish I'd been burnt myself instead of her."

He had suffered, by the way, no inconsiderable scorching, to which his hands would testify for many a week; but of this he was still hardly aware. Emmeline, with a glance of uttermost scorn, left him, and ascended to the room where the doctor was busy. Free to behave as he thought fit, Mumford beckoned Cobb to follow him into the front garden, where they conversed with masculine calm.

"I shall put up at Sutton for the night," said Cobb, "and perhaps you'll let me call the first thing in the morning to ask how she gets on."

"Of course. We'll see the doctor when he comes down. But I wish I could understand how you managed to throw the lamp down."

"The truth is," Cobb replied, "we were quarrelling. I'd heard something about her that made me wild, and I came and behaved like a fool. I feel just now as if I could go and cut my throat, that's the fact. If anything happens to her, I believe I shall. I might as well, in any case; she'll never look at me again."

"Oh, don't take such a dark view of it."

The doctor came out, on his way to fetch certain requirements, and the two men walked with him to his house in the next road. They learned that Louise was not dangerously injured; her recovery would be merely a matter of time and care. Cobb gave a description of the fire, and his hearers marvelled that the results were no worse.

"You must have some burns too?" said the doctor, whose curiosity was piqued by everything he saw and heard of the strange occurrence. "I thought so; those hands must be attended to."

Meanwhile, Emmeline sat by the bedside and listened to the hysterical lamentation in which Louise gave her own – the true – account of the catastrophe. It was all her fault, and upon her let all the blame fall. She would humble herself to Mr. Higgins and get him to pay for the furniture destroyed. If Mrs. Mumford would but forgive her! And so on, as her poor body agonised, and the blood grew feverish in her veins.

~ *Chapter 9* ~

"ACCEPT IT? Certainly. Why should we bear the loss if he's able to make it good? He seems to be very well off for an unmarried man."

"Yes," replied Mumford, "but he's just going to marry, and it seems – Well, after all, you know, he didn't really cause the damage. I should have felt much less scruple if Higgins had offered to pay—"

"He *did* cause the damage," asseverated Emmeline. "It was his gross or violent behaviour. If we had been insured it wouldn't matter so much. And pray let this be a warning, and insure at once. However you look at it, he ought to pay."

Emmeline's temper had suffered much since she made the acquaintance of Miss Derrick. Aforetime, she could discuss difference of opinion; now a hint of diversity drove her at once to the female weapon – angry and iterative assertion. Her native delicacy, also, seemed to have degenerated. Mumford could only hold his tongue and trust that this would be but a temporary obscurement of his wife's amiable virtues.

Cobb had written from Bristol, a week after the accident, formally requesting a statement of the pecuniary loss which the Mumfords had suffered; he was resolved to repay them, and would do so, if possible, as soon as he knew the sum. Mumford felt a trifle ashamed to make the necessary declaration; at the outside, even with expenses of painting and papering, their actual damage could not be estimated at more than fifty pounds, and even Emmeline did not wish to save appearances by making an excessive demand. The one costly object in the room – the piano – was practically uninjured, and sundry other pieces of furniture could easily be restored; for Cobb and his companion, as amateur firemen, had by no means gone recklessly to work. By candle-light, when the floor was still a swamp, things looked more desperate than they proved to be on subsequent investigation; and it is wonderful at how little outlay, in our glistening times, a villa drawing-room may be fashionably equipped. So Mumford wrote to his correspondent that only a few "articles" had absolutely perished; that it was not his wish to make any demand at all; but that, if Mr. Cobb insisted on offering restitution, why, a matter of fifty pounds, etc. etc. And in a few days this sum arrived, in the form of a draft upon respectable bankers.

Of course the house was in grievous disorder. Upholsterers' workmen would have been bad enough, but much worse was the establishment of

Mrs. Higgins by her daughter's bedside, which naturally involved her presence as a guest at table, and the endurance of her conversation whenever she chose to come downstairs. Mumford urged his wife to take her summer holiday – to go away with the child until all was put right again – a phrase which included the removal of Miss Derrick to her own home; but of this Emmeline would not hear. How could she enjoy an hour of mental quietude when, for all she knew, Mrs. Higgins and the patient might be throwing lamps at each other? And her jealousy was still active, though she did not allow it to betray itself in words. Clarence seemed to her quite needlessly anxious in his inquiries concerning Miss Derrick's condition. Until that young lady had disappeared from "Runnymede" for ever, Emmeline would keep matronly watch and ward.

Mrs. Higgins declared at least a score of times every day that she could *not* understand how this dreadful affair had come to pass. The most complete explanation from her daughter availed nothing; she deemed the event an insoluble mystery, and, in familiar talk with Mrs. Mumford, breathed singular charges against Louise's lover. "She's shielding him, my dear. I've no doubt of it. I never had a very good opinion of him, but now she shall never marry him with *my* consent." To this kind of remark Emmeline at length deigned no reply. She grew to detest Mrs. Higgins, and escaped her society by every possible manoeuvre.

"Oh, how pleasant it is," she explained bitterly to her husband, "to think that everybody in the road is talking about us with contempt! Of course the servants have spread nice stories. And the Wilkinsons" – these were the people next door – "look upon us as hardly respectable. Even Mrs. Fentiman said yesterday that she really could not conceive how I came to take that girl into the house. I acknowledged that I must have been crazy."

"Whilst we're thoroughly upset," replied Mumford, with irritation at this purposeless talk, "hadn't we better leave the house and go to live as far away as possible?"

"Indeed, I very much wish we could. I don't think I shall ever be happy again at Sutton."

And Clarence went off muttering to himself about the absurdity and the selfishness of women.

For a week or ten days Louise lay very ill; then her vigorous constitution began to assert itself. It helped her greatly towards convalescence when she found that the scorches on her face would not leave a permanent blemish. Mrs. Mumford came into the room once a day and sat for a few minutes, neither of them desiring longer communion, but they managed to exchange inquiries and remarks with a show of friendliness. When the fifty pounds came from Cobb, Emmeline made no mention of it. The next day, however, Mrs. Higgins being absent when Emmeline looked in, Louise said with an air of satisfaction:

"So he has paid the money! I'm very glad of that."

"Mr. Cobb insisted on paying," Mrs. Mumford answered with reserve. "We could not hurt his feelings by refusing."

"Well, that's all right, isn't it? You won't think so badly of us now? Of course you wish you'd never set eyes on me, Mrs. Mumford; but that's only natural: in your place I'm sure I should feel the same. Still, now the money's paid, you won't always think unkindly of me, will you?"

The girl lay propped on pillows; her pale face, with its healing scars, bore witness to what she had undergone, and one of her arms was completely swathed in bandages. Emmeline did not soften towards her, but the frank speech, the rather pathetic little smile, in decency demanded a suave response.

"I shall wish you every happiness, Louise."

"Thank you. We shall be married as soon as ever I'm well, but I'm sure I don't know where. Mother hates his very name, and does her best to set me against him; but I just let her talk. We're beginning to quarrel a little – did you hear us this morning? I try to keep down my voice, and I shan't be here much longer, you know. I shall go home at first; my stepfather has written a kind letter, and of course he's glad to know I shall marry Mr. Cobb. But I don't think the wedding will be there. It wouldn't be nice to go to church in a rage, as I'm sure I should with mother and Cissy looking on."

This might, or might not, signify a revival of the wish to be married from "Runnymede." Emmeline quickly passed to another subject.

Mrs. Higgins was paying a visit to Coburg Lodge, where, during the days of confusion, the master of the house had been left at his servants' mercy. On her return, late in the evening, she entered flurried and perspiring, and asked the servant who admitted her where Mrs. Mumford was.

"With master, in the library, 'm."

"Tell her I wish to speak to her at once."

Emmeline came forth, and a lamp was lighted in the dining-room, for the drawing-room had not yet been restored to a habitable condition. Silent, and wondering in gloomy resignation what new annoyance was prepared for her, Emmeline sat with eyes averted, whilst the stout woman mopped her face and talked disconnectedly of the hardships of travelling in such weather as this; when at length she reached her point, Mrs. Higgins became lucid and emphatic.

"I've heard things as have made me that angry I can hardly bear myself. Would you believe that people are trying to take away my daughter's character? It's Cissy 'Iggins's doing: I'm sure of it, though I haven't brought it 'ome to her yet. I dropped in to see some friends of ours – I shouldn't wonder if you know the name; it's Mrs. Jolliffe, a niece of Mr. Baxter – Baxter, Lukin and Co., you know. And she told me in confidence what people are saying – as how Louise was to marry Mr. Bowling, but he broke it off when he found *the sort of people she was living with*, here at Sutton – and a great many more things as I shouldn't like to tell you. Now what do you think of—"

Emmeline, her eyes flashing, broke in angrily:

"I think nothing at all about it, Mrs. Higgins, and I had very much rather not hear the talk of such people."

"I don't wonder it aggravates you, Mrs. Mumford. Did anyone ever hear such a scandal! I'm sure nobody that knows you could say a word against your respectability, and, as I told Mrs. Jolliffe, she's quite at liberty to call here to-morrow or the next day—"

"Not to see *me*, I hope," said Emmeline. "I must refuse—"

"Now just let me tell you what I've thought," pursued the stout lady, hardly aware of this interruption. "This'll have to be set right, both for Lou's sake and for yours, and to satisfy us all. They're making a mystery, d'you see, of Lou leaving 'ome and going off to live with strangers; and Cissy's been doing her best to make people think there's something wrong – the spiteful creature! And there's only one way of setting it right. As soon as Lou can be dressed and got down, and when the drawing-room's finished, I want her to ask all our friends here to five o'clock tea, just to let them see with their own eyes—"

"Mrs. Higgins!"

"Of course there'll be no expense for *you*, Mrs. Mumford – not a farthing. I'll provide everything, and all I ask of you is just to sit in your own drawing-room—"

"Mrs. Higgins, be so kind as to listen to me. This is quite impossible. I can't dream of allowing any such thing."

The other glared in astonishment, which tended to wrath.

"But can't you see, Mrs. Mumford, that it's for your *own* good as well as ours? Do you want people to be using your name—"

"What can it matter to me how *such* people think or speak of me?" cried Emmeline, trembling with exasperation.

"Such people! I don't think you know who you're talking about, Mrs. Mumford. You'll let me tell you that my friends are as respectable as yours—"

"I shall not argue about it," said Emmeline, standing up. "You will please to remember that already I've had a great deal of trouble and annoyance, and what you propose would be quite intolerable. Once for all, I can't dream of such a thing."

"Then all I can say is, Mrs. Mumford" – the speaker rose with heavy dignity – "that you're not behaving in a very ladylike way. I'm not a quarrelsome person, as you well know, and I don't say nasty things if I can help it. But there's one thing I *must* say and *will* say, and that is, that when we first came here you gave a very different account of yourself to what it's turned out. You told me and my daughter distinctly that you had a great deal of the very best society, and that was what Lou came here *for*, and you knew it, and you can't deny that you did. And I should like to know how much society she's seen all the time she's been here – that's the question I ask you. I don't believe she's seen more than three or four people altogether. They may have been respectable enough, and I'm not the one to say they weren't, but I *do* say it isn't what we was led to expect, and that you can't deny, Mrs. Mumford."

She paused for breath. Emmeline had moved towards the door, and stood struggling with the feminine rage which impelled her to undignified altercation. To withdraw in silence would be like a shamed confession of the charge brought against her, and she suffered not a little from her consciousness of the modicum of truth therein.

"It was a most unfortunate thing, Mrs. Higgins," burst from her lips, "that I ever consented to receive your daughter, knowing as I did that she wasn't our social equal."

"Wasn't *what*?" exclaimed the other, as though the suggestion startled her by its novelty. "You think yourself superior to us? You did us a favour—"

Whilst Mrs. Higgins was uttering these words the door opened, and there entered a figure which startled her into silence. It was that of Louise, in a dressing-gown and slippers, with a shawl wrapped about the upper part of her body.

"I heard you quarrelling," she began. (Her bedroom was immediately above, and at this silent hour the voices of the angry ladies had been quite audible to her as she lay in bed.) "What *is* it all about? It's too bad of you, mother—"

"The idea, Louise, of coming down like that!" cried her parent indignantly. "How did you know Mr. Mumford wasn't here? For shame! Go up again this moment."

"I don't see any harm if Mr. Mumford had been here," replied the girl calmly.

"I'm sure it's most unwise of you to leave your bed," began Emmeline, with anxious thought for Louise's health, due probably to her dread of having the girl in the house for an indefinite period.

"Oh, I've wrapped up. I feel shaky, that's all, and I shall have to sit down." She did so, on the nearest chair, with a little laugh at her strange feebleness.

"Now please *don't* quarrel, you two. Mrs. Mumford, don't mind anything that mother says."

Thereupon Louise's mother burst into a vehement exposition of the reasons of discord, beginning with the calumnious stories she had heard at Mrs. Jolliffe's, and ending with the outrageous arrogance of Mrs. Mumford's latest remark. Louise listened with a smile.

"Now look here, mother," she said, when silence came for a moment, "you can't expect Mrs. Mumford to have a lot of strangers coming to the house just on my account. She's sick and tired of us all, and wants to see our backs as soon as ever she can. I don't say it to offend you, Mrs. Mumford, but you know it's true. And I tell you what it is: To-morrow morning I'm going back home. Yes, I am. You can't stay here, mother, after this, and I'm not going to have anyone new to wait on me. I shall go home in a cab, straight from this house to the other, and I'm quite sure I shan't take any harm."

"You won't do it till the doctor's given you leave," said Mrs. Higgins with concern.

"He'll be here at ten in the morning, and I know he will give me leave. So there's an end of it. And you can go to bed and sleep in peace, Mrs. Mumford."

It was not at all unamiably said. But for Mrs. Higgins's presence, Emmeline would have responded with a certain kindness. Still smarting under the stout lady's accusations, which continued to sound in sniffs and snorts, she answered as austerely as possible.

"I must leave you to judge, Miss Derrick, how soon you feel able to go. I don't wish you to do anything imprudent. But it will be much better if

Mrs. Higgins regards me as a stranger during the rest of her stay here. Any communication she wishes to make to me must be made through a servant."

Having thus delivered herself, Emmeline quitted the room. From the library, of which the door was left ajar, she heard Louise and her mother pass upstairs, both silent. Mumford, too well aware that yet another disturbance had come upon his unhappy household, affected to read, and it was only when the door of Louise's room had closed that Emmeline spoke to him.

"Mrs. Higgins will breakfast by herself to-morrow," she said severely. "She may perhaps go before lunch; but in any case we shall not sit down at table with her again."

"All right," Mumford replied, studiously refraining from any hint of curiosity.

So, next morning, their breakfast was served in the library. Mrs. Higgins came down at the usual hour, found the dining-room at her disposal, and ate with customary appetite, alone. Had Emmeline's experience lain among the more vigorously vulgar of her sex she would have marvelled at Mrs. Higgins's silence and general self-restraint during these last hours. Louise's mother might, without transgressing the probabilities of the situation, have made this a memorable morning indeed. She confined herself to a rather frequent ringing of the bedroom bell. Her requests of the servants became orders, such as she would have given in a hotel or lodging-house, but no distinctly offensive word escaped her. And this was almost entirely due to Louise's influence for the girl impressed upon her mother that "to make a row" would be the sure and certain way of proving that Mrs. Mumford was justified in claiming social superiority over her guests.

The doctor, easily perceiving how matters stood, made no difficulty about the patient's removal in a closed carriage, and, with exercise of all obvious precautions, she might travel as soon as she liked. Anticipating this, Mrs. Higgins had already packed all the luggage, and Louise, as well as it could be managed, had been clad for the journey.

"I suppose you'll go and order the cab yourself?" she said to her mother, when they were alone again.

"Yes, I must, on account of making a bargain about the charge. A nice expense you've been to us, Louise. That man ought to pay every penny."

"I'll tell him you say so, and no doubt he will."

They wrangled about this whilst Mrs. Higgins was dressing to go out.

As soon as her mother had left the house Louise stole downstairs and to the door of the drawing-room, which was half open. Emmeline, her back turned, stood before the fireplace, as if considering some new plan of decoration; she did not hear the girl's light step. Whitewashers and paperhangers had done their work; a new carpet was laid down; but pictures had still to be restored to their places, and the furniture stood all together in the middle of the room. Not till Louise had entered did her hostess look round.

"Mrs. Mumford, I want to say good-bye."

"Oh, yes," Emmeline answered civilly, but without a smile. "Good-bye, Miss Derrick."

And she stepped forward to shake hands.

"Don't be afraid," said the girl, looking into her face good-humouredly. "You shall never see me again unless you wish to."

"I'm sure I wish you all happiness," was the embarrassed reply. "And – I shall be glad to hear of your marriage."

"I'll write to you about it. But you won't talk – unkindly about me when I've gone – you and Mr. Mumford?"

"No, no; indeed we shall not."

Louise tried to say something else, but without success. She pressed Emmeline's hand, turned quickly, and disappeared. In half-an-hour's time arrived the vehicle Mrs. Higgins had engaged; without delay mother and daughter left the house, and were driven off. Mrs. Mumford kept a strict retirement. When the two had gone she learnt from the housemaid that their luggage would be removed later in the day.

A fortnight passed, and the Mumfords once more lived in enjoyment of tranquillity, though Emmeline could not quite recover her old self. They never spoke of the dread experiences through which they had gone. Mumford's holiday time approached, and they were making arrangements for a visit to the seaside, when one morning a carrier's cart delivered a large package, unexpected and of unknown contents. Emmeline stripped off the matting, and found – a drawing-room screen, not unlike that which she had lost in the fire. Of course it came from Louise, and, though she professed herself very much annoyed, Mrs. Mumford had no choice but to acknowledge it in a civil little note addressed to Coburg Lodge.

They were away from home for three weeks. On returning, Emmeline found a letter which had arrived for her the day before; it was from Louise, and announced her marriage. "Dear Mrs. Mumford, – I know you'll be glad to hear it's all over. It was to have been at the end of October, when our house was ready for us. We have taken a very nice one at Holloway. But of course something happened, and mother and Cissy and I quarrelled so dreadfully that I went off and took a lodging. And then Tom said that we must be married at once; and so we were, without any fuss at all, and I think it was ever so much better, though some girls would not care to go in their plain dress and without friends or anything. After it was over, Tom and I had just a little disagreement about something, but of course he gave way, and I don't think we shall get on together at all badly. My stepfather has been very nice, and is paying for all the furniture, and has promised me a lot of things. Of course he is delighted to see me out of the house, just as you were. You see that I write from Broadstairs, where we are spending our honeymoon. Please remember me to Mr. Mumford, and believe me, very sincerely yours, Louise E. Cobb."

Enclosed was a wedding-card. "Mr. and Mrs. Thomas Cobb," in gilt lettering, occupied the middle, and across the right-hand upper corner ran "Louise E. Derrick," an arrow transfixing the maiden surname.

Bibliography

1. Bibliographical Note

The Paying Guest was commissioned by Max Pemberton on behalf of Cassells on 28 March 1895 and Gissing promised the publishers to let them have his manuscript in the autumn. In early July he chose the title. Composition, despite interruptions, only took him about a fortnight from 2 to 16 July and Gissing obviously enjoyed writing this satirical novella. The publishers were greatly pleased with what they called his first comedy in their dithyrambic announcements, but Gissing's embarrassment was reflected in his correspondence. He had patiently constructed a public image of himself as a serious novelist and he consequently jibbed at the commercial efforts which attempted to show his work in a new light. This private reaction notwithstanding, the story, as is attested by the number of binding variants, was a good seller, and it was indeed a very clever satire of a new pretentious mode of life characteristic of the mid-1890s.

Perhaps because the story was later viewed essentially as a period piece somehow overtaken by the evolution of public taste in England as the outbreak of the Boer War was approaching, Cassells did not reprint the book. Besides the firm was at no time noted for its fiction list. So that *The Paying Guest* did not enjoy a second life in England until 1982 when the Harvester Press published a critical edition edited by Ian Fletcher of this entertaining piece of fiction (750 copies).

In America *The Paying Guest* enjoyed a first career under the Dodd, Mead imprint in 1895 in various garbs, a success which encouraged the firm to publish *Charles Dickens, a Critical Study* some two years later. In 1969 AMS included the title in their programme of Gissing reprints. In this photographic reprint the original type was considerably enlarged.

Although two French translations are in the editor's collection (one of them by Gabrielle Fleury) there is no record of publication, but two editions in the original language were published in Japan and in Italy. The former, a Kinseido publication, first appeared in 1953. It was reprinted some fifteen times until the 1970s. The Italian edition, with an introduction and notes by Francesco Badolato, was issued by Edizioni Canova of Treviso in 1973.

2. List of Reviews

1896

Daily News, 10 January, p. 6
Scotsman, 13 January, p. 3
Glasgow Herald, 16 January, p. 7
Weekly Sun, 19 January, p. 2

~ *Bibliography* ~

Daily Chronicle, 21 January, p. 3
Star, 21 January, p. 1
Globe, 22 January, p. 3
Public Opinion, 24 January, p. 112
Athenæum, 25 January, p. 116 [Lewis Sargeant]
New York Times, 25 January, p. 10
Chicago Evening Post, 25 January, p. 5
Sketch, 29 January, p. 44 (O. O., i.e. W. Robertson Nicoll)
New Age, 30 January, p. 286
Philadelphia Record, 31 January, p. 6
To-Day, 1 February, p. 409
Black and White, 1 February, p. 150
Publishers" Circular, 1 February, p. 130
San Francisco Chronicle, 2 February, p. 8
Bookseller, 7 February, p. 124
Chicago Tribune, 8 February, p. 14
Birmingham Daily Post, 24 February, p. 7
Boston Evening Transcript, 28 February, p. 6
Academy, 29 February, p. 173 (Percy Addleshaw)
Illustrated London News, 7 March, p. 302
Book Buyer, March, pp. 88-9
Hearth and Home, 2 April, p. 799 (Paper Knife)
Saturday Review, 18 April, pp. 405-6 [H. G. Wells]
Overland Monthly, April, p. 468
The Times, 29 May, p. 13
The Times Weekly Edition, 5 June, p. 405
Bookman (New York), June, p. 367

3. Articles and later Comments

C. J. Francis, 'The Paying Guest,' *Gissing Newsletter*, April 1977, pp. 1-8
Ian Fletcher, Introduction to the Harvester edition of *The Paying Guest* (1982)
Pierre Coustillas, 'The Paying Guest and the Praise it Won in 1896,' *Gissing Journal*,
    October 1996, pp. 20-23

Selected Reviews

The Paying Guest — Five First Edition Reviews

Daily News, 10 January 1896, p. 6

Mr George Gissing is the English Balzac of middle-class suburban life. The tragedy of its respectability, its genteel inanities, its dullness and vulgarities is depicted with convincing and unexaggerated truthfulness. The stamp of sincerity is on all that Mr Gissing writes. His last story, *The Paying Guest*, the new volume of Messrs Cassell's Pocket Library, contains in a minute compass many of his finest qualities. It is a faithful record of what is, after all, not much worth recording; its worth comes in that it is all so finely observed, so admirably well executed. The scene is a genteel suburban residence in Sutton. A young, not too well off, couple sufficiently refined are tempted to take 'a paying guest.' Louise Derrick, the guest in question, is the fatherless daughter of a grossly vulgar and violent-tempered mother, who has lately married again a rich City man. Between Louise and her stepsister there is no love lost. Miss Derrick herself has been fairly educated, she is lawless, self-willed. She has no distinction or delicacy of perceptions, but she is good-natured, has a certain rough sense of justice, and she recognises and is impressed by the superior manners and culture of her host and hostess. She takes a liking to them and to her new surroundings. The irruption of this young woman into the well-ordered domestic household is as that of the familiar bull in a china shop, and the consequences are as disastrous. Her unromantic love affairs are presented with touches of quiet humour that help somewhat to relieve the sombre sordidness of an ignoble comedy. Mr Thomas Cobb, the successful suitor, with his brutality of plain speech, his commonness and sturdy honesty, is not attractive, yet he interests us. Almost every figure in the book interests, only because it is so alive. Mr Gissing's style is admirable. There is not a bungling touch throughout marring the clearness of his execution.

Chicago Evening Post, 25 January 1896, p. 5

One of the brightest stories of the season is told by George Gissing when he sets down circumstantially the facts that led to the small domestic tempest which swept the erstwhile peaceful household presided over by the eminently respectable people, Mr and Mrs Mumford. 'The Paying Guest' is deliciously natural throughout, and fairly sparkling with irresistibly humorous situations. The heroine is constructed on the most original lines, and possesses a bewildering wealth of faults, with not one of the virtues which seem indigenous to the numerous sisterhood of heroines. Louise is certainly trying, but there is a dash and frankness about her which quite makes up for her ignorance and amusing defiance of many sacred and revered rules of social etiquette. And George Gissing is consistent (a rare quality in a novelist), and stands by his heroine loyally, positively refusing to allow that young lady to emerge from the last chapter beautifully metamorphosed regarding her faults – a proceeding which he would have accomplished had he yielded to the accepted proprieties of novel writing. Louise starts out with a volcanic temper and impossible manners and marvel of romances! she keeps these characteristics intact to the very end of the story. The trouble, which proves so vastly entertaining to read about, started with the Mumfords' desire to enhance their rather limited income by welcoming to their hearth and home a young woman who, through fault quite evenly distributed, cannot live at home. She pays handsomely and there is a tacit understanding that her hostess is to launch her into society, in a modest way. But the girl is really impossible, and the "unmerciful disaster" which follows for ever in her wake has an alarming way of including others, which proves death to the domestic peace and happiness of the Mumford household. She is continually having ill-bred "rows" with her kith and kin, and such is the power of a bad example she actually contaminates the high-bred and sweet soul of Mrs Mumford, to such an extent that she too evinces a degraded inclination to "have it out" herself with all those who cross her path. But how to get rid of "the paying guest" is a momentous question, and not until everybody concerned becomes entangled in the pettiest kind of squabbles does the way out of the difficulty appear. Mr Gissing's manner of telling a story is irreproachable; he elaborates just enough and no more, while he temperately refrains from exaggeration, no matter what the provocation may be. Much of the charm of his work lies in his delightful attitude toward his characters. He artfully conceals his personality, and recounts in the simplest manner possible what befell them, and never does Mr Gissing intrude his views and his personality. His name is on the title page, to be sure, but after that he disappears from the scene and leaves his characters to live, move and have their being according to their own sweet will.

Bookseller, 7 February 1896, p. 124

We have here a few pages from the history of a middle-class family in a London suburb which may well have been drawn from the life, of which Mr Gissing's artistic treatment has made the sketch almost, if not quite, a real work of art. Many persons will no doubt agree with Mr and Mrs Mumford that the introduction of a boarder into a quiet home, even if she pays three guineas a week, is often a costly arrangement, and though, in the present instance, the crisis is not very serious, when Miss Derrick leaves, everyone is, we think, much more comfortable. The *dramatis personæ*, if we may use such a formidable term, are sketched with manifold ability, and altogether the little volume will prove one of the best of the Publishers' Pocket Library to which it is the latest addition.

Boston Evening Transcript, 28 February 1896, p. 6

Each one of Gissing's books that has come into our hands of late supports the first-formed judgment. He sustains his individuality in every page – a unique individuality, insomuch as it is shorn of many of the features that are commonly found in the writings of so-called realists. Gissing is a prince in this school, yet his stories are singularly free of the baldness of utterance – the oftentimes brutal prodding we receive from others in his realm. For example, in "The Paying Guest," published lately – a little story, most unpretentious, and simply written – there is but one character worth studying; there is but one event in the entire pages that approaches towards the thrilling, yet it is never once stupid. Strange and most novel is the style of Gissing, as shown in this work. One is half-inclined to laugh on finishing the story and murmur: "How simple!" at the same time wondering why the impression is so strong, indelible and lasting. But it is there. The imprints of Louise Derrick's complex nature are forever fixed in our minds. We understand this unheroic-like heroine as did none of the nearer, conventional, undersized figures about her; we understand her as does only Gissing himself; and why? Not because the author has dissected her make-up, bit by bit – we should have lost patience during such an operation, and have learned to hate her heartily, as did those about her, with their narrow visions, apparently seeing the bad outweigh the good; only Cobb, the blunt, the shrewd, the finally successful lover, saw the meaning of her vagaries, and he but dimly. Gissing has, by the magic handling of simplest words, by a wonderful penetration and pellucid style – a very cathode ray of literature – pierced and made transparent one of the most fascinating as well as difficult types of every-day life.

Saturday Review, 18 April 1896, pp. 405-6 [H. G. Wells]

Here is Mr Gissing at his best, dealing with the middle-class material he knows so intimately, and in a form neither too brief for the development of character nor too lengthy for the subtle expression of his subtle insight to grow tedious. The paying guest is a young person, 'not quite the lady,' who has quarrelled with her stepfather and half-sister at home; and the genteel entertainers are the Mumfords of Sutton. They are thoroughly nice people are the Mumfords, and they know the Kirby Simpsons of West Kensington and Mrs Hollings of Highgate; and, indeed, quite a lot of good people. Then there are the Fentimans – 'nice people; a trifle sober, perhaps, and not in conspicuously flourishing circumstances; but perfectly presentable.' The Mumfords live at Sutton, 'the remoteness of their friends favoured economy; they could easily decline invitations, and need not often issue them. They had a valid excuse for avoiding public entertainments – an expense so often imposed by mere fashion.' What a delightful analysis of the entire genteel spirit that last phrase implies! And they kept three servants to minister to their dignity, although entertainments were beyond their means. In the remote future, when Mr Gissing's apotheosis is accomplished, learned commentators will shake their heads over the text, well nigh incapable, in those more rational times, of understanding how these people with their one child could have been so extravagantly impecunious. Yet we, in this less happy age, know how true it is. In and about London there must be tens of thousands of Mumfords, living their stiff, little, isolated, pretentious, and exceedingly costly lives, without any more social relations with the people about them than if they were cave-dwellers, jealous, secluded, incapable of understanding the slightest departure from their own ritual, in all essentials savages still – save for a certain freedom from material brutality. Mrs Mumford's great dread was that this paying guest of hers would presently drop an aspirate; but that horror at least was spared her. But the story of the addition of the human Miss Derrick to the establishment, her reception, her troubles, and her ignominious departure, must be read to be believed. The grotesque incapacity of everyone concerned to realise for a moment her mental and moral superiority to the Mumfords is, perhaps, the finest thing in an exceedingly entertaining little volume. Why, one may ask, is it so much more entertaining than the larger novels of Mr Gissing? Mr Gissing has hitherto been the ablest, as Mr George Moore is perhaps the most prominent, exponent of what we may perhaps term the 'colourless' theory of fiction. Let your characters tell their own story, make no comment, write a novel as you would write a play. So we are robbed of the personality of the author, in order that we may get an enhanced impression of reality, and a novel merely extends the preview of the police-court reporter to the details of everyday life. The analogous theory in painting would, of course, rank a passable cyclorama above one of Raphael's cartoons. Yet so widely is this view accepted that the mere fact of a digression condemns a novel to many a respectable young critic. It is an antiquated device, say these stripling moderns, worthy only of the rude untutored minds of Sterne or Thackeray. By way of contrast and reaction, we have the new heresy of Mr Le Gallienne, who we conceive demands personality, a strutting obtrusive personality, as the sole test of literary value. Certainly the peculiar delight of this delightful little book is not in the truth of the portraiture – does not every advertising photographer exhibit your Mrs Mumford and her guest with equal fidelity at every railway station? – nor in the plausible quick sequences of events, but in the numerous faint flashes of ironical comment in the phrasing that Mr Gissing has allowed himself. We congratulate Mr Gissing unreservedly on this breaking with an entirely misleading, because entirely one-sided, view of the methods of fiction. Thus liberated, his possibilities widen. Mr Gissing has an enviable past as a novelist; a steady conquest of reviewers to his credit. He has shown beyond all denial an amazing gift of restraint, a studious avoidance of perceptible wit, humour, or pathos that appealed irresistibly to their sympathies. Now if he will let himself go, which he may do with impunity, and laugh and talk and point with his finger and cough to hide a tear, and generally assert his humanity, he may even at last conquer the reading public.